LARGE PRINT

The Chosen

**Center Point
Large Print**

**This Large Print Book carries the
Seal of Approval of N.A.V.H.**

The Chosen

SHARON SALA

CENTER POINT PUBLISHING
THORNDIKE, MAINE

This Center Point Large Print edition
is published in the year 2006 by arrangement with
Harlequin Enterprises, Ltd.

The text of this Large Print edition is unabridged. In other
aspects, this book may vary from the original edition. Printed in
Thailand. Set in 16-point Times New Roman type.

ISBN 1-58547-720-6

Library of Congress Cataloging-in-Publication Data

Sala, Sharon.
   The chosen / Sharon Sala.--Center Point large print ed.
      p. cm.
   ISBN 1-58547-720-6 (lib. bdg. : alk. paper)
      1. Large type books. I. Title.

PS3569.A4565C46 2006
813'.54--dc22

                                                    2005024951

Dedication

During the writing of this book, it seemed difficult for me to focus on fiction, even though the story was one I wanted to tell.

The reason for my distraction was that we were at war, and at the writing of this dedication are still at war, with no end in sight.

It seemed a bit shallow to be dwelling on my deadlines when there were families who had loved ones in the midst of fighting, and others who were having to bury fallen loved ones who'd died in the line of fire.

The dedications in my books have always meant a lot to me. I don't just dash off a casual couple of thoughts and call it done.

And while this is such a small thing to do for our men and women in the military who are sacrificing so much, it is the only thing I can do for them, besides remembering them in my prayers.

So, for every man and woman who wears a military uniform of the United States of America, and for every soldier who has perished in the line of fire, and for every family who's sacrificed the ultimate, and for those who still fight, I honor you and pray for you, and I dedicate this book in your names.

Prologue

"I'm dying. They won't say it, but I hear it in their voices. They look at my chart and then look away. Please, oh please, don't let me die!"

Jay Carpenter's panic was as silent as his voice. The last thing he remembered was slapping one of his girls for holding back money on him. He'd been running more than a dozen girls for over six years, and no matter how careful he was in picking them, there was always one who had to mess things up.

He remembered the impact of his palm against her face, and then he'd felt a sharp pain behind his right ear. After that, everything started spinning around him. He vaguely remembered the girls screaming and someone shouting, "Call 911!" And then everything had gone black.

All he knew now was that he was in a hospital, where he'd had surgery to remove a brain tumor, and that he had a fever that wouldn't abate and an overwhelming sense of despair.

Alice Presley was in her eighteenth year of nursing, and during that time, thousands of patients had come under her care. She considered herself an old hand at the job and often claimed that she'd seen it all. But that was before the patient in bed 315B was admitted.

She kept a wary eye on him as she bathed him, even though he was unconscious again. She'd looked at his chart often enough to know the history.

His name was Jay Carpenter—a fortysomething pimp who had passed out in his apartment and suffered a seizure.

He had been admitted with hallucinations.

The initial diagnosis of drug overdose had been dropped after the discovery of a tumor involving his pituitary gland and part of his brain.

Surgery had been performed, but unsuccessfully. Only part of the tumor had been removed.

He had a continuing fever, and kept lapsing in and out of a coma.

The only difference between this man and the countless others she'd ministered to was the fact that when he was conscious, he scared her.

His eyes were so dark they appeared to be black, and there was an odd smell about him that no amount of bathing seemed to change. It was a smell that she associated with the morgue, and if she didn't know better, she would think he was already dead.

Just as the thought moved through her mind, he coded. Without a second of hesitation, she hit an alarm bell and then began performing CPR.

Nurses rushed in with a crash cart, followed by a pair of doctors who'd been on the floor making rounds. Each knew the other's purpose and skillfully went through the motions of recovery, even though their initial efforts seemed futile.

● ● ●

"No, no, no! Not yet! Not like this!"

Jay Carpenter took his last breath at the same time that his soul left his body. It wasn't anything like what he'd expected. There was no struggle to breathe, only a cessation of pain. For a brief moment, he was above his body and looking down, and then a force unlike anything he'd ever known began pulling at him—or whatever it was that he'd become. The gravity of his earthbound body was missing, and the only thing he could liken it to was the lack of control he'd once felt on the downhill slide of a giant roller coaster. Light surrounded him, bathing him in a warmth and love unlike anything he'd ever known. It was everything he'd ever wanted as a child and lacked as an adult—a love and acceptance he'd never believed existed. It was perfect, so perfect, but then something began to go wrong. The light that had warmed him began to retract. The implication didn't sink in until the joy in his heart was replaced by an overwhelming sense of hopelessness.

The air began to vibrate with a multitude of voices wailing in chaotic abandon. The sound pierced his being, paining him in a way that stabbing knives would have pained his earthly flesh. What was left of that warmth and love had dissipated, replaced with every earthly fear he'd ever had—and in a quantity beyond imagination. Panic was followed by a horrifying realization.

This wasn't heaven.

It was hell.

He began to scream, but the sound was lost in the wail of the countless souls already inhabiting the space. It was too late for regret. It was too late to ask God for forgiveness. It was too late—too horribly late—for everything.

Burning lakes of fire rose up before him. The stench of sulfur was without and within as evil surrounded him. Just at the point of complete absorption, something happened. Only seconds from extinction, the same feeling of motion he'd had earlier was back, only this time he was being pulled up instead of down.

"Praise God!" he cried. *"I'm going to heaven after all."*

Then a loud, hideous roar came at him from below, and although no words were ever spoken, still he heard the devil's vow.

"You'll never go to heaven. You're already mine!"

"I've got a pulse!"

Jay thought he screamed, even as he was being sucked back into his body. He wanted to shout, to laugh and cry, to thank the doctors and nurses for bringing him back to life, but words were still beyond him.

It was days before he was cognizant enough to speak coherently. By that time, he had come to a definite sense of purpose and set his mind upon a twisted and daunting task. What he'd seen of hell had worked deep into his being. He knew it was inevitable that he would die again. It came to all men in good time, but to assure himself that his second journey would not be a repeat of the first, he had come up with what he considered a foolproof road to heaven.

After a disconcerting discussion with his surgeon, in which he'd learned they'd been unable to remove all of the tumor and he was living on borrowed time, his dedication to his plan became even firmer. He couldn't bear to think about having to spend eternity away from that warm, comforting light of love. The more he thought about it, the more convinced he became that something drastic must be done. Within hours of being released from the hospital, he began his first step toward what he believed would be perfect redemption.

One

Nine months later

January DeLena was one of Washington, D.C.'s most well-known journalists. On 9-11, she'd been on-site and broadcasting only minutes after the plane had flown into the Pentagon. Then the world had watched as she'd abandoned her microphone and begun helping survivors who'd come running out of the building. By the time she'd remembered what she'd been sent there to do, she was covered in soot and blood, and had cursed and cried on air. Normally, that would have gotten her fired, but not that day. That day she'd only voiced what the nation had been feeling. By the end of the week, everyone knew the name of the pretty television journalist who'd called Osama Bin Laden a bad name.

Over time, it became apparent that January DeLena wasn't just a pretty face. When it came to getting a story, she was tenacious, which was why on this night she was on the streets of the red-light district at one-thirty in the morning, mingling with the homeless, instead of sleeping in her own bed.

For months, she'd been hearing a rumor about a man who called himself the Sinner and who claimed to have had a near-death experience. Now she'd heard he was moving among the homeless and the lawless, preaching his own version of eternity. In most cases, this would have been just a story about another religious zealot. However, this story had a unique twist, and unique was the key to January's success.

It had become fashionable to speak of near-death experiences. Many had written books on the subject, usually claiming that they hadn't wanted to come back, and that they'd felt a great sense of peace in death. But this man had a different story to tell, and one that had tweaked her curiosity. According to the gossip on the street, this man had literally been to hell and back, and lived to tell the tale.

Now January huddled beneath the awning of a sec-ondhand store as wind blew rain against the backs of her legs. She didn't mind so much getting wet, but the stench emanating from the woman with her was overpowering, and getting wet only added to the odor. She turned her back to the wind and tried not to breathe too deeply as she spoke to the woman beside her.

"So, Marjorie, you say you've seen the Sinner yourself?"

Marjorie Culver's fingers curled a little tighter around the push bar on her shopping cart. It had been a long time since anyone had taken notice of her, and the attention made her feel a little disoriented and vulnerable. Still, she felt no threat from this woman and finally nodded.

"Yep . . . I saw him two, maybe three days ago. He was beneath an overpass near the Potomac, passing out coupons for a free fish sandwich from Captain Hook's. He had a whole basket of 'em. Someone said they were probably fakes, but I took one anyway, and they took it at the drive-through when I gave 'em my order."

Then she laughed, as if struck by the humor of going through a drive-through on foot.

"Was he preaching?" January asked.

Marjorie shrugged. "I guess you could call it that."

"What do you mean?" January pressed.

"Well, he was holding a Bible and all, but what he was saying sounded pretty radical. I don't think he was quoting any scriptures." She shrugged again. "It didn't really matter, though. No one was paying him any mind. They just wanted the coupon for the free sandwich."

January nodded. She certainly understood. There had been days in her youth when she might have done just about anything for something to eat. Thank God those times were far behind her.

"Do you know where he lives?" January asked.

Marjorie frowned. "Nowhere and everywhere, I guess. I wasn't sure, but I got the impression that he was one of us."

"You mean homeless?"

Marjorie glared. "For some, it's a choice, you know."

January backed off on her intensity. "I'm not demeaning your existence, Marjorie. I was only asking as a means of locating him so I can talk to him myself."

Marjorie frowned and shoved her cart a little closer to the door she was leaning against. The stuff in her cart was all she owned, although she'd long since forgotten what all was in there.

"Yeah, well . . . I can't help you any on that. I'm not into addresses myself."

January sighed. She hadn't meant to, but she'd obviously insulted the woman. "All right then," she said, and gave Marjorie's arm a quick squeeze. "Thank you so much for talking to me, Marjorie." Then she slipped a hundred dollars worth of twenties into Marjorie's hand. "Get yourself a room tonight and treat yourself to something good to eat."

Marjorie was taken aback by the money and for a moment thought about being insulted all over again, but then a quick gust of wind blew rain down her neck. She took the bills and stuffed them into one of her countless pockets.

"Yeah . . . I'll do that," she said, then added, "See you on the TV."

"Absolutely," January said, wondering when Marjorie ever got to watch TV, and made a dash toward her car, which was parked less than half a block away.

Once inside, she locked the doors and breathed a quick sigh of relief that she had a home to go to and a car to get her there. When she turned the key, the sound of the engine starting echoed the jump of her heartbeat. As she turned on the windshield wipers, a tall thin man wearing dirty white pants and a shirt that hung loose to his knees stepped out of the alley in front of her. His clothes were sopping wet. His long hair was equally soaked, and plastered to his face and neck, as was the beard hiding most of his face. There was a brief moment of connection as their gazes met. When he began to smile, she hit the headlights, flipping them on bright. It was his signal to move, which he did, but without shifting his gaze.

The expression in the man's eyes made January shudder. The degradation of the place and its people hit her like a slap in the face, and for the first time in her life made her doubt the wisdom of following this story.

Then she gathered her wits and reminded herself of how far she'd come from the poor little Latino girl from Juarez, Mexico, to the woman she was today. She'd worked long and hard to gain credibility, and apologized for nothing. With renewed vigor, she slammed the car into gear and stomped on the accelerator. Tires squealed as rubber burned. All she needed was a hot bath and a good night's sleep, and she would be fine.

Less than a mile from her apartment, a police cruiser came racing past her, running with lights and siren. Up ahead, she could see what appeared to be at least a half-dozen more police cars and almost as many emergency vehicles.

Immediately, her heartbeat accelerated as her instinct for the story rose. But she reminded herself she was not on duty, and as she drove past, saw the news crew from her station.

Kevin Wojak was standing near an ambulance with a mike in his hand, speaking directly into a camera as rain peppered his face. She smirked. All he had to do was take a few steps to the left and he would have been standing under a canopy, but that would have diluted the dramatic effect he was obviously going for.

Wojak considered January competition.

January considered Wojak a pain in the ass.

Despite her reluctance to watch Wojak working the camera, she was forced to stop as an ambulance pulled away from the scene. When it raced past her, she said a quick prayer for the occupants, then waited for traffic to clear.

As she waited, a tall, dark-haired man suddenly stepped out from between two parked police cars and walked in front of her vehicle, momentarily spotlighting himself in her headlights, much as the bearded man on skid row had done earlier. But her reaction to this man was far different. She knew him intimately, had made love to him in her bed, on the living room floor, in her shower, and once in her walk-in closet—but only in her dreams. Benjamin North, one of D.C.'s finest homicide detectives, didn't know it, but he haunted her sleep, taunting her with his heavy-lidded stare and slow, sexy smile.

In reality, they'd done little more than trade jibes at various crime scenes—his springing from disgust at the arrival of the media and hers from what she considered unfair disrespect. Except for one night over a year ago.

With the windshield wipers swishing back and forth in January's line of vision, she thought back to the disaster that had brought them together.

It had been snowing for hours, which was frustrating for the crime scene investigators, because the snow had covered up whatever clues might have been left behind that might help them find out who had killed Mandy Green.

She hadn't taken up much space in the world, and what space she had had been what nobody else wanted. Now she was dead—raped and strangled, although the coroner couldn't say which had come first. What was newsworthy about the murder of this particular hooker was that, according to the ID Mandy Green had in the purse beneath her arm, she was only twelve years old.

Benjamin North had been assigned to the case. What he hadn't known until his arrival at the scene was that the victim was a child. Granted, the child was wearing a faux fur coat and knee-high white boots, but that was all.

When he lifted the blanket to look at the body, he stilled, too shocked to let go, too numb to look away. Her baby lips were smeared with a dark red lipstick; her wide, sightless eyes were a clear, pure green. Her hair was red and curly and wet from the snow in which she was lying. But it was her pale, childlike body that knocked him for a loop. She had buds where her breasts were meant to be, and a small thatch of pubic hair that had just begun to grow. One leg was lying at an awkward angle, and her right arm had been flung over her head, as if the attacker had shoved it out of the way to do his deed.

"Jesus," Benjamin whispered, and then dropped the blanket and turned away.

His hands were shaking and his stomach was rolling. He could handle anything but kids. They got to him every time. He lifted his head and took a deep breath, hoping the blast of cold air would clear the horror from his mind. As he did, he noticed that a news crew was already here.

"Damn vultures," he muttered, as his control shattered.

He strode past crime scene investigators, street cops and a waiting ambulance, ready to do battle. He rounded the bumper with a fight on his mind and found no one to fight.

The camera crew was nowhere to be seen. He turned abruptly, expecting to see them across the parking lot, getting film of the victim. The only people he could see were the crew from CSI and a couple of patrol cops.

It wasn't until he started to walk away that he heard someone on the other side of the hedge, crying. He walked around it, then froze.

He knew who she was. Everyone knew January DeLena. But he'd never seen her like this.

"Lady, you're not supposed to be here," he said gruffly.

January flinched. She hadn't heard him walk up, and she wasn't in a mood to talk. She raised her head and then swiped at the tears on her face before turning around.

Oh perfect. It's North. I don't need any more grief right now.

She meant to argue, to state her rights to get the facts of a story—her usual freedom of speech and press argument. But when she opened her mouth, her sorrow betrayed her.

"Did you see her?" she cried. "She's only a child."

A huge, hiccuping sob came out between an inhale and an exhale as she threw her arms up in the air and then hit the trunk of a tree with the flat of her hand. "Where is God when things like this happen?" She spun angrily, her face streaked with fresh tears. "You're the detective. You tell me!" she cried. "Where is God now?"

Ben was stunned by her rage. It was like looking at a mirror image of what he was feeling. When she turned on him, he acted without thinking. He grabbed both her arms at the wrists and pushed her against the tree she'd just hit.

"Stop it," he said. "You don't want to hit me. You could get arrested for assaulting an officer."

She looked up at him, but saw nothing but a blur through her tears.

"Why don't they get her out of the snow? It's fucking freezing, and they've let her lie in the snow like a piece of trash."

Ben felt her pain. Without thinking, he pulled her into his arms. She fought him, pushing and moaning and trying to get free. He dodged blows and turned a deaf ear to her curses as she wailed at everything from God to the lowest lizard, and still he held her. And when she wore herself out from the grief and the rage, he took out his handkerchief and wiped the tears from her face—and then kissed her.

It wasn't anything planned, and if he'd had his head on straight, it wasn't anything he would ever have done. But he was as appalled by the waste of the brief

20

life as she was and it seemed natural to give comfort to another grieving soul.

Too stunned by the taste of him on her lips, she didn't move. But when reality began to click in and she knew this wasn't part of some dream, she slid her arms around his neck and wholeheartedly kissed him back.

She had a vague memory of unbuttoning his coat and sliding her hands beneath his sweater to the warmth of his skin before they both gasped and then stepped back.

There was a long moment of silence in which they stared at each other in disbelief. Then, without saying a word, January picked up her tote bag and disappeared.

By the time Ben came to his senses and walked out from behind the hedge, the news van was driving away.

"That did not happen," he muttered, and then headed back toward the crime scene to finish his job.

Someone honked a horn.

January reacted with a jerk as she was thrust back into the here and now. Her fingers tightened around the steering wheel as Ben passed beyond the glare of her headlights. Still she watched him, eyeing his rain-slicked hair and the weary set of his shoulders, and wondered where he'd been when he'd gotten the call to come out. Had he been wrapped in some sweet woman's arms, or had he been sleeping alone? Even though she watched him until he disappeared into the shadows, there were no answers to satisfy her curiosity.

Finally the traffic cleared and she was able to get home. As she pulled into the parking lot at her apartment building, she saw that all the spaces in front of the place were taken. That meant driving behind the building, which she hated. The security lights were few and far between, and the parking was allocated between a half-dozen Dumpsters. When she circled the place and realized the only vacant spot was right beside an over-flowing trash bin, she stifled a curse.

She parked and got out, her nose wrinkling in disgust from the odor. Ignoring the rain that persistently fell, she sidestepped some garbage that had fallen out onto the concrete, then made a run for the back door.

As she ran, it occurred to her that the parking lot in this upscale neighborhood didn't smell all that different from the area of the city Marjorie Culver called home. But that was where the similarities ended.

Letting herself in with a passkey, January breathed a sigh of relief as the security door locked firmly behind her.

The hallway was wide and well-lit, and led directly to the elevators in the front lobby. The faint scent of pizza emanating from someone's apartment reminded her that she'd skipped dinner, and made her wish she'd had the foresight to pick up some takeout on the way home.

Still, when she finally let herself into her home, food was the last thing on her mind. She locked the door and then began undressing as she walked through the rooms, leaving a trail of sodden clothes on her way to the bathroom. Despite the mild June weather, the rain had chilled her all the way through. The warm jets of water from the shower felt like liquid silk on her skin. She stayed until the chill was gone from her body, then got out and dried quickly. By then, her limbs were starting to shake. She crawled into bed, remembered to set the alarm, and pulled the covers up around her shoulders as her head hit the pillow. Within seconds, she was asleep.

Benjamin North was a fifteen-year veteran of the D.C. police force. He'd seen his share of blood and gore, and had become callous to most of it. But there were times, like tonight, when he wished to hell and back that he'd stayed in Montana on the family ranch, like his father had wanted. Tonight, he would rather be facing a mountain lion barehanded than have to tell the parents of the young woman who'd been found dead on the side of the highway that she'd been beaten to death before being set on fire. And the only reason they knew this for a fact was that the boy who'd been with her was still alive—barely—to tell the tale.

He glanced back at the scene of the crime one more time, giving away none of the emotions he was feeling as the crime scene investigators began packing up their things. The coroner had come and gone, taking what was left of Molly O'Hara with him. The ambulance that had sped off earlier was racing against time to get Molly's boyfriend into surgery before he bled out on the rain-soaked thoroughfare.

Ben shuddered, then angrily shoved his fingers through his hair, combing the wet strands back from his face as he glanced around for Rick Meeks, his partner. Meeks was still interrogating two passersby, who'd been the ones to call 911. When Rick looked up, Ben waved him over. Moments later, Rick made a quick dash through the rain to their car.

"What's up?" he asked.

"We've got an ID on the dead girl," Ben said. "The boy's parents have been notified and are en route to the hospital where he's being taken."

"Does she have any next of kin?" Rick asked.

Ben nodded. "Mother and father about thirty minutes from here. We have the go-see."

His partner grimaced. "Damn, I hate this part of the job."

Ben nodded in agreement. "I do, too, so let's get this over with."

They got in the car without speaking. Ben rechecked the name and address the injured boy had given him, then made a U-turn in the street. It was two forty-five in the morning, and he still had to break a mother's heart before he could go home.

Jay Carpenter braked for a red light. Out of habit, he glanced up into the rearview mirror, checking the traffic behind him. Between the rain and the time of night, the streets were almost deserted. His gaze slid from the view through his back window to the reflection of himself in the mirror. His appearance was completely different from the way he'd looked after being released from the hospital. His resurrection had changed his focus in life. He neither looked nor behaved the same way he had before.

The Off Duty sign on his yellow cab was lit up, but it didn't stop two hookers on the opposite corner of the intersection from hailing him. Their clothes were plastered to their bodies and the overabundant makeup they were wearing was running down their faces like wet paint. Even though he was bone-tired and wanting nothing but a warm bed, when the light turned green, he drove through the intersection and then pulled to the curb and picked them up.

His nose wrinkled as they piled in the back seat. Despite the makeup and clothes they were wearing, they couldn't have been more than twenty. One of them had a black eye. He could tell because part of the makeup she'd put on to hide the bruising had washed off in the rain. The other one was shaking—obviously in need of a fix—and they both smelled like stale cigarettes and sex.

"Thanks a bunch," Black-eye said.

"Yeah, thanks," Druggie echoed.

"God bless you," Jay said.

They both seemed startled that his accent was so obviously American. His long ponytail and full beard gave him a foreign appearance.

"Yeah, sure, thanks," Black-eye said, then rolled her

eyes at her friend and stifled a giggle.

"Where to?" Jay asked.

Druggie gave him an address. Jay pulled away from the curb without turning on the meter. Both girls noticed it and then shrugged.

Jay saw the byplay but chose to ignore it.

"Do you know Jesus?" he asked.

Black-eye looked as if he'd just spat in her face, but Druggie laughed aloud.

"Yeah, I think I gave him a blow job last week."

Black-eye frowned.

"Shut up, Dee-Dee. That isn't funny."

Druggie, who he now knew as Dee-Dee, shrugged and lit up a cigarette.

"Oh, screw you, Phyl. Don't get uptight with me," Dee-Dee said.

Phyl unconsciously stroked the purple-and-black bruise beneath her eye, then turned and stared out the window without answering.

Jay wondered what she was thinking and then wondered how they'd come to this place in their life. He felt sad for them, remembering his own downfall and how fortunate he was that he'd been given a second chance to rectify his sins.

He stopped for another red light, although there wasn't another car in sight.

"Come on, mister. We're beat," Dee-Dee said. "No one's coming. Drive through."

"The laws of God weren't made to be broken," he said softly.

Dee-Dee snorted. "God didn't have anything to do with traffic lights."

"God is everywhere," Jay answered.

"Crap, mister. What are you . . . some Jesus freak?"

"I've been to hell. I don't want to go back," he said.

"Yeah, well, we live in hell, so step on the gas and get me there fast. I've had enough of your shit."

"I'll pray for you," Jay said a few minutes later, as he pulled up to the curb of the address they'd given him, and stopped. "Go with God," Jay added.

"Whatever," Dee-Dee said, and slid out of the back seat.

But the girl with the black eye wasn't as callous.

"Thanks a lot," she said, then added, "Dee-Dee didn't mean anything by what she said. She's just had a hard time in life."

Jay eyed the purple-hued bruise on her face.

"Go home," he said.

"We're already there," Phyl said.

"No. Not here. Go back where you came from."

This time, she was the one who laughed in his face.

"So my mother's old man can fuck me for free again? I don't think so. At least out here I get paid."

She slammed the door and dashed through the rain into the apartment building.

Jay sat for a moment, listening to the rain hitting the windshield. As he sat, pain suddenly struck behind his right eye. It was so sharp and so unexpected that he grabbed his face in reflex, as if it had been dealt a blow. He doubled over the steering wheel, wondering if he would draw another breath. Slowly, slowly, the pain subsided and he was able to look up. When he did, his sight was blurred, and for a moment he feared he was going blind; then he realized it was only rain obliterating the view.

He was struck with an overwhelming sadness. So it had begun. The doctors had warned him it would. Panic hit him like a fist to the gut. He had hoped for more time. He wasn't ready.

Then he reminded himself that he wasn't the one in charge. So what if he wasn't ready? That didn't mean he couldn't get that way fast. Satisfied that it wasn't too late, he put the car in gear and slowly drove away.

Even after he got home to his one-room apartment, he felt a sense of urgency. Memories of the symptoms of his previous illness began pushing at the back of his mind. So far these symptoms weren't as severe, but he felt off-kilter. What if he didn't live long enough to offset the sins of his previous lifestyle? He'd been preaching and trying to do good to his fellow man, but now he felt it wasn't going to be enough. The panic that ensued left him weak and shaking. He didn't want to go to hell.

"God help me. What do I do?"

The answer came as a thought, soundless, quiet, but affirming.

Live as I *lived.*

Two

January was getting ready for a live on-the-spot interview with a man who, only an hour earlier, had rescued a woman and child from the Potomac River. She glanced at her watch. In less than three minutes, they would be live on the air, but the hero of the moment was still throwing up, due to what he called an unfortunate side effect of stress.

"January, two minutes and counting," Hank, the cameraman, said.

She glanced at the backside of the man puking in the bushes, and rolled her eyes.

"How are we doing?" she asked.

The man shuddered, then turned around.

"I'm sorry, Miss DeLena. This will pass, I promise you."

"We're on the air in two minutes. Is there anything I can get you that might help settle your stomach?"

He shrugged, then wiped a shaky hand across his face.

"Sometimes something salty helps."

January grinned, tossed her microphone to Hank and raced to the news van for her purse. Moments later she was back, carrying a pack of salted nuts. She tore into the pack and shook a couple into the man's hands.

"I don't know if I'd be eating anything just yet if I

were you, so why don't you just suck the salt off of them and then spit them out?" she suggested.

"Yeah, right," he said, and shakily popped the nuts into his mouth.

To January's relief, the salt began to work. By the time they went on air, the hero of the moment was standing steady beside her, recounting the events. As soon as the interview was over, January thanked the man and followed Hank to the van.

"Good job, January," Hank said.

"Thanks, Hank, same to you."

"Hell of a thing he did, jumping into the river like that."

"Yes, and not once, but twice. First the child, then the mother."

Hank nodded. "Yeah, and he says he can't swim."

January slid into the seat and dropped her bag onto the floor.

"Fear does strange things to people," he stated.

January leaned back in the seat as her thoughts slid elsewhere.

"And sometimes fear makes people do strange things," she muttered. "Let's go, okay?"

"Yeah, sure," Hank said.

It was just after three in the afternoon, and the first time Ben and Rick had a chance to eat some lunch. They'd stopped at a little place called Jerry's Java, but not for the coffee. The coffee sucked, but the burgers were good.

Rick pointed to the television mounted on the wall above the diner counter.

"Hey, North, get a load of this."

Ben was reaching for the salt when he looked up. His gaze landed on the woman's face hogging most of the screen, and for a moment, he forgot to breathe.

There was a tiny bead of sweat at the corner of her right eyebrow. When the camera pulled back, revealing the slender curve of her neck, and the red jacket and scarf she was wearing, his jaw went slack. Ketchup ran out of the bun he was holding, then down through his fingers onto his plate as he exhaled with a sigh.

It was January DeLena with one of her famous on-the-spot interviews—nothing he hadn't seen a dozen times before. Only that didn't change the sudden ache in his gut. He wanted her. As much as he had the first time he'd kissed her, and as much as he did every night when he went to bed. There was no denying the lust. But that was all it was—lust. No way would a self-respecting cop get mixed up with a news hog. Too many cases had been screwed up because the media had released information before it was time. Their "the public has a right to know" claims were a pain in the butt to a hard-working cop trying to crack a case, and she was no exception, although, to be fair, he couldn't remember any specific time when she'd per-sonally screwed up a case of his. Still, she was a jour-nalist, which made her part of the problem.

He glanced around the diner, hoping that no one else

31

had seen him gawking like a lovesick teenager. Satisfied that everyone was too busy eating to pay any attention to him, he forgot the salt and took another bite of his burger before allowing himself a second glance.

Damn, she looked hot. Her eyes were the color of dark chocolate, and that mouth of hers was enough to make a man lose his mind. Her lips were full and pouting, her mouth just wide enough to allow a man a most indecent sexual fantasy.

He groaned.

Rick glanced at him. "You okay?"

"Yeah, just bit the inside of my mouth," Ben said. It was a lie, but it was better than admitting the truth.

Rick nodded, then pointed to the French fries on Ben's plate.

"You gonna eat all those?"

"Yes," Ben said, without taking his eyes from the screen.

Rick shrugged, gave the fries a last longing look, then waved down the waitress behind the counter and ordered a piece of pie.

When January's interview was over, the show cut back to the news anchor. At that point Ben lost interest and settled down to finish his food before Rick ate it off his plate. But the news bulletins weren't over. Rick pointed to the TV again, this time laughing.

"Check out the nutcase."

Ben glanced back up at the screen. It showed a man in some sort of costume. From what he could tell, he appeared to be one of those religious zealots. What was funny, though, was that he was preaching on the steps of the IRS building.

"What's with the robe and sandals?" Ben asked.

"Who knows?" Rick muttered, then signaled the waitress, who was hurrying past them with a carafe of fresh coffee. "Hey, honey, put some ice cream on that pie of mine, will you?"

"Yeah, sure. Give me a sec," she said, and hurried away.

Ben spied Jerry, the owner of Jerry's Java, and pointed to the television.

"Jerry, would you turn up the volume?" he asked.

Jerry picked up a remote from behind the counter and aimed it at the television.

". . . seemed bent on casting out the money changers." The news anchor turned to his co-anchor and grinned. "I'm certainly not advocating this kind of behavior, but I have to admit that every April 15, I get the same feeling."

"Sounds like the man needs to see a shrink," Rick said.

"Don't we all?" Ben muttered, and dug into his fries.

January was at her desk working on a story for the ten-o'clock news when her phone rang. She answered it absently, still focused on ending the sentence she'd been typing, but her attention shifted when her caller spoke.

"I've been told that you're looking for me."

January's fingers froze on the keyboard. She glanced up and then around, checking to make sure someone wasn't playing a joke. Everything seemed on the up and up.

"Who is this?" she asked.

"Just a sinner trying to right his wrongs."

January's heart skipped a beat. Sinner? Was this the man who called himself the Sinner? The man who claimed he'd been to hell?

"Are you the preacher who calls himself the Sinner?"

"I'm not a preacher, and everyone is a sinner. It's what we do to rectify our sins that matters."

"Did you really have a near-death experience?" January asked.

"No."

Excitement fizzled. "So you didn't have a near—"

"It wasn't *near* death. It *was* death, and it was hell," he said.

Excitement resurrected, she said, "Oh! Would you consider—"

"Why are you looking for me?" he asked.

"That's what I've been trying to say. I want to interview you."

"Why?"

"Well . . . because it would be—"

"A good story?"

Her excitement shifted to her voice. "Yes, but also one that would be meaningful. Think of the people who might change their ways because of what you experienced . . . what you saw. So, what do you say?"

"No."

January frowned. "Why not?"

"Jesus didn't present himself to the world in that manner, so neither will I."

January sighed. "Are you one of those WWJD people?"

"I'm not familiar with that term. What does WWJD mean?"

January picked up a pen. "It means What Would Jesus Do? The letters WWJD have become synonymous with a certain group of young people who advocate abstinence from drugs, sex and all sorts of sinful behaviors."

There was a long moment of silence, then January heard a tremor in his voice.

"If I'd belonged to something like that, maybe I wouldn't be in the place I am today."

"Then reconsider," January begged. "I can make you famous. Think of all the good you could do . . . the number of people you could reach with your message. What do you say?"

"I say that's *your* agenda, Miss DeLena, not *mine*. My agenda is already in place and moving forward."

January's interest shifted. "Agenda? What agenda might that be?"

"My agenda is your story," the man said.

January's fingers tightened on the receiver.

"Then tell me what it is! What is your agenda? What are you talking about?"

"He told me . . . live as I lived. So I am."

"Who told you?"

"Jesus Christ, my lord and savior."

The line went dead in her ear. January slammed the phone down in disgust, then pulled her notebook from the back of the desk drawer. She wanted to get down every word he'd said before she forgot them. Her hands were shaking as she wrote. She didn't know what he was talking about, but she was determined to find out.

She finished her story and turned it in just under deadline. As soon as she could, she headed out of the studio and back to the streets. There was a story in this, she could feel it.

One week later

In a city full of lawmakers, it stood to reason that there would also be a part of the city allotted to law-*breakers*. In the old days, it had been called the red-light district; now, some just considered it a good place to get lost.

It was there, on a street corner, that a tall, bearded man who called himself Brother John stood on a milk crate and held audience to a small crowd. Even though he was being heckled constantly, his message became no less fervent. His clothing was a mishmash of Hindi and African, but his Cajun accent, red hair and beard, and light-colored eyes marked him as a man with Louisiana roots.

"It's not too late to know the Lord," he promised. "Any day now, He'll be coming back! Do you want to be left behind? Listen to me, now. Jesus is coming. Jesus is coming!"

"By land or by sea?" someone yelled.

The heckler didn't faze him. He just raised his voice a little louder.

Jay was transfixed by the preacher on the street corner. As a convert to the Lord, he'd been watching this man for several months now, knowing that when it became necessary, Brother John would play a vital part in helping Jay get to glory. It was all so perfect— as if God Himself was guiding Jay's every move.

When Brother John raised his voice, Jay moved closer, drawn by the passion in his voice and the look in his eyes. It was fervor. He knew it well. It burned within him, too.

When Jay was so close that he could see blue veins bulging on the backs of the man's hands, he lifted his head, his nostrils flaring.

Brother John's gaze settled on Jay, and as it did, the preacher stuttered, suddenly racked by the same kind of fear that had dogged his steps through four years in Vietnam. Then he shook off the thought as being foolish, and focused his attention on the man standing at his feet.

"Welcome, brother," John said.

Jay started to smile.

Brother John's belly knotted. He knew as well as he

knew his own name that he was in the presence of evil.

"Who are you?" he whispered.

Jay Carpenter held out his hand. "I'm the man you've been waiting for."

Rick Meeks had already commented that it was a piss-poor night for working a homicide. Ben hadn't argued, although he was of the opinion that it was the victim who should have had the right to complain. A dead man was a dead man, but the added indignity of being beheaded seemed, to Ben, a large case of overkill.

He squatted down beside Fran Morrow, waiting for her to bag whatever it was she had picked off the forehead of the victim. She was pushing sixty, a tad on the skinny side and cranky as hell, but she was one of the best crime scene investigators in the city.

"Hey, Fran, how long you think he's been dead?"

"Ever since someone lopped off his head," she snapped.

Ben tried another angle. "And when do you think that might have happened?"

"If I was guessing, which you know damn well I don't do, I'd say maybe two or three hours."

He made a couple of notes in his notebook. "Anything you can tell me about the murder weapon?"

"It was sharp."

Ben shifted, then stood abruptly. "Come on, Fran. I don't like being out here any more than you do, but I need something to work with."

She motioned toward one of the other investigators as she got up.

"Bag him up," she ordered, then turned toward Ben. "I'll send you a complete report as soon as I know more."

"Thanks," he said, and headed back to the perimeter, where his partner was interviewing a witness. Just then a news van pulled up.

"The vultures have arrived," he muttered, then cursed beneath his breath when he realized it was January DeLena who was getting out of the van. "Son of a bitch."

Meeks looked up. "What?"

"News crew's here."

"Your turn to head 'em off. I'm taking a statement."

Ben eyed the wino who'd found the body. He was still crying. Ben couldn't blame him. But the longer he stood here, the closer that woman was going to get. He hadn't seen her up close or talked to her since that night behind the hedge, and he wasn't looking forward to it now. He set his jaw and turned around just as January slipped beneath the crime scene tape and headed toward him.

He quickly grabbed her elbow, escorting her back to the perimeter as he sent the cameraman back to the van with a warning look.

"Come on, Miss DeLena, you're not allowed in here and you know it."

The words January meant to say were rolling around

in her head, but when she'd seen Benjamin North walking toward her, they hadn't come out in the proper sequence. Then, when he'd taken her by the arm, she'd lost her train of thought.

"The public allows . . . I mean, it's a job for . . . Shit."

Almost immediately, she felt a flush spreading across her face, and hoped to goodness it was too dark where they were standing for Detective Yummy to see.

January's discomfort became a source of amusement for Ben. It was the first time he'd seen Miss Hot-To-Trot at a loss for words, and he couldn't let it go.

He grinned.

January glared.

"Since when is murder funny?" she snapped.

"Did I say it was? Did I say anything to you except to indicate—once again, I might add—that you're trespassing?"

January sighed. "Come on, North. You know me. I don't give up details until you give me the go-ahead."

"And I don't make deals with the media. Please get back."

January stood her ground with an intensity that surprised him.

"Is it true?" she asked.

"Is what true?" he countered.

"The victim . . . was he really beheaded?"

Ben flinched. Damn. Someone on the scene was feeding info to the media. They had to be, or she wouldn't have gotten here this fast with that kind of information.

"Who told you that?" he asked.

"Never mind. Just answer me. Is that the truth?"

"It's none of your business," he snapped.

"Do you know his name?"

"Not yet."

January shifted from one foot to the other. She had to know, even though she feared the truth. Finally she blurted out another question, and this time she got Ben's attention.

"Is the victim the same guy who preaches hell and damnation on the street corners?"

Ben grabbed her by the arm and pulled her toward a streetlight.

"I don't know, but if he is, what does that mean to you?"

She shrugged. "Maybe nothing."

"Would you recognize his face if you saw him?"

"Yes."

Ben turned and waved at Fran Morrow.

"Hey, Fran . . . hold up a minute, will you? We might have an ID on the victim."

Fran frowned at January, then glared at Ben.

"She won't know a hill of beans. She just wants a scoop on the others."

"No cameras. I promise," January said.

Fran stopped the men who were moving the body into the van and then unzipped the upper portion of the bag.

41

The head rolled a bit to the right, then tilted back toward the left before it came to rest.

January swallowed the bile that rose up her throat and peered in.

"It's him," she said, and then covered her face with her hands. "Dear God, it's him."

"Him, who?" Ben asked, as Fran zipped the bag and proceeded to load up her cargo.

"He calls . . . called himself Brother John," she said.

"And how do you know him?" Ben asked.

January dropped her hands and looked away.

"January! Look at me," he demanded, but she was staring down, as if she'd taken a sudden interest in his shoes.

Ben took her by the shoulders, gently but firmly.

Startled by the unexpected contact, she pulled out of his grasp.

"Get your hands off me," she muttered.

"Fine," Ben said, and jammed his hands into his pockets. "But you invited yourself into my investigation, so you can answer the questions. How do you know him?"

"I work the streets a lot. You know that," she said.

"Somehow I can't picture you listening to sermons on street corners."

She looked up at him. "Why, Detective, I didn't know that you pictured me at all."

This time it was Ben's face that turned red.

"Listen to me, lady. This isn't a game. What do you know about that man that I don't?"

She sighed, her shoulders slumping. "He called himself Brother John. He's from somewhere in Louisiana, and he's a Vietnam vet. That's all I know about him."

There was a slight inflection to the word *him* that led Ben to believe she might know something else indirectly related to the case.

"What aren't you telling me?" he asked.

January hesitated. What she knew was mostly a bunch of suppositions and guesses, and she was too much of a professional to put her reputation on the line with a story she couldn't prove.

"That's all I know about him. Really." Then she added, "But I think there's something else going on down in that place. There's a man down there who calls himself the Sinner, and there's gossip on the street that he's doing some really weird things."

"Homeless people do weird things. My next-door neighbor does weird things. The world is full of weirdos, and Jesus freaks are everywhere."

"Fine. You asked. I told you. Now if you're not going to give me anything else, I've got a story to turn in."

"You don't have anything," Ben said.

"I have enough. Chopping a man's head off is news, whether you like it or not."

She turned abruptly and ran toward the van.

Ben watched her go.

Whether Ben liked it or not, January DeLena's information about their victim being a Vietnam vet was paramount in helping them with identification and locating his next of kin. By ten o'clock the next morning, he'd learned the man's name was Jean Louis Baptiste. He had one daughter, a woman named Laurette Bennet, who lived near New Orleans. She'd cried all the way through their conversation, then thanked him for the call before she hung up.

Ben followed suit by laying the receiver back on the cradle. Then he opened his desk drawer, took out a bottle of aspirin and shook three out into his hand. He'd awakened with a headache, and it wasn't getting any better. He would have liked to blame it on January DeLena's unexpected visit to the crime scene last night, but that wouldn't have been fair. There were plenty of reasons why his head would be hurting, the strongest of which came from the phone call he'd just made. He hated notifying next of kin, and so far this week, he was two for two.

He popped the pills into his mouth, then started to wash them down with the last of his coffee, only to realize the cup was empty. The aspirin were already beginning to melt on his tongue, so he bit the bullet and crunched them between his teeth like candy. The sour, bitter taste sent him straight to the water cooler. He drank until the taste was washed out of his mouth and wished the bitter part of his job would disappear as easily.

The church was small and in a less than desirable part of the city, but the doors were never locked, which was the reason Jay Carpenter had chosen it. He lay prostrate in the aisle near the altar, flat on his belly with his arms outstretched, parallel to his shoulders, in much the same manner as Jesus had been nailed to the cross. He didn't hear God from down there, but it made him feel righteous.

He wore a white shirt—oversize and untucked—while the pale gray fabric of his loose, wide-legged pants was soft and creaseless. His long, dark hair fell forward, completely covering his face.

He was praying aloud, trying to block out the memory of Brother John's screams, although it was no use. He could still smell the coppery scent of Brother John's blood, although he'd washed himself judiciously. He had tried to explain to the man what a special and integral part of Jay's journey he had become, but Brother John had not been impressed. It bothered Jay that there had been resistance, although he was certain he was doing what God meant him to do.

A door banged in another part of the building as Jay continued to wrestle with his demons; then he heard footsteps.

The priest.

It was bound to be the priest.

He didn't want to talk to anyone. There was nothing to be said that he didn't already know. A siren wailed somewhere outside the building, fading as the vehicle moved away, but the sound triggered an old pain behind his right eye, followed by a muscle tic near the corner of his mouth.

He knew what was wrong. The tumor was growing again. The knowledge was frightening. Instinct told him to go back to the doctors, but he knew if he did, they would keep him. He would die there, just as he'd done before, and he wasn't ready to die. Not yet. He needed to be certain that everything possible had been done to cancel out the sins of his past before he succumbed to the inevitable. And he knew how to do it. After all, he'd heard the words from God Himself.

Live as I *live.*

That was what he'd heard. That was what he was determined to do, and after tonight, he was one step closer to glory. When the approaching footsteps were just outside the door of the sanctuary, Jay got up swiftly and left.

He went out onto the streets with more purpose. It was time to gather his disciples around him, and he knew who the first one would be.

After filing her story on the murdered man in the park, January had gone straight home to a hot soaking bath. She'd stayed in the water until it turned cool, but it hadn't been enough to wash away the memories of what she'd seen that night. Hours later, she was still awake and going through her notes, trying to come to terms with the unfolding drama.

She'd been in the business long enough to know that there were all kinds of oddball, off-the-wall fanatics who followed voices only they could hear, and who still remained harmless to everyone but themselves.

But as much as she would have liked to believe that the man called the Sinner was one of them, she didn't buy it.

She'd spread her notes out on the dining room table, from the earliest incidents she'd learned of to the latest, the beheading of Brother John. No matter how many times she tried to tell herself it was only coincidence that tied them together, she failed.

It was close to daybreak when she gathered up the papers and slipped them back into a file. Her hands were shaking and her eyes red-rimmed from exhaustion and lack of sleep. Today was her day off. Usually she spent it running personal errands and shopping for food she rarely had time to eat, but not today. Today she was going to crawl into bed, pull the covers up over her head, and pray for a long and dreamless sleep.

A short while later she was in bed. The curtains were drawn and the phone unplugged, but as weary as she was, she couldn't get past a feeling of impending doom.

Three

Jay's first attempt at bringing in disciples had been promising. He already knew a man named Simon Peters from a shelter where he sometimes ate. It had been almost too easy to sway the man to his way of thinking.

Simon Peters was a man with no purpose. Following a street preacher and passing out bookmarks with Bible verses had been a way to make the day go quicker. And when the preacher brought two more into the fold, it was like having a party.

A big black man named Andy, who the preacher called Andrew, and Andy's friend, Jim, who the preacher called James, became Simon Peters's companions. They rode with the preacher to different destinations in his old yellow cab, dined on hamburgers and hot dogs, and bowed their heads in unison when he broke out in prayer. For a while it was great, and then, as it comes to all things, the honeymoon ended.

They were standing beneath an awning as the rain poured down beyond. Water splattered the hems of their pants and chilled them all the way to the bone. The three men wanted nothing more than to go down to the Sisters of Mercy shelter, get a bowl of soup and maybe play checkers. They had a good time with the preacher, all right, and he fed them real good. But there were times when they didn't feel all that sociable, and for Simon Peters, today was one of those days.

And, because he had balked, so had Andy and Jim.

Jay was incredulous. He had the day all planned, and to have all three of his disciples turn mutinous had been an ultimate betrayal.

"What do you mean, you don't want to come? We have this all planned. We're driving into Virginia to—"

Simon Peters pointed to the rain.

"Look, preacher, it's cold and wet, and frankly, I don't give a damn about lost souls today. I don't feel like being all that friendly. I'll catch up with you tomorrow, maybe. But today, I just want to go get me a bowl of soup." He shivered slightly. "I feel like I might be coming down with something."

Jay glared, but there was nothing he could do about it. He could hardly force three grown men to come with him when they were determined to refuse.

"Fine," he muttered. "And after all I've done for you."

Jim felt guilty, but he wasn't going to go without the others. "Look, preacher. We'll go tomorrow for sure, okay? Just come by tomorrow and we'll be here waiting."

Jay turned, strode back to his cab and got in. He felt thwarted and betrayed, and wanted to scream. But as he sat, he began to think—and as he thought, he began to plan.

He would fix them. They didn't know it, and obviously didn't understand, but they couldn't walk away from him like this. He needed them to help him get to heaven.

Two weeks later

The pain behind Jay's eye was a throbbing annoyance as he loaded the last of his suitcases into the

49

trunk of his cab. He glanced longingly at his old apartment building, then reminded himself what lay ahead. After one last look, he got in the cab and drove away. His apartment had not amounted to much, but it was definitely more comfortable than the place where he was going now. However, it was time to join his growing band of disciples. The Lord hadn't separated Himself from His men. Jay could do no less.

Almost two weeks ago he'd found an old warehouse on the outskirts of the city that had been abandoned for years. The area around it was nothing but a wasteland of junk, metal and old rubber tires. It was an obscure graveyard of outdated machinery and abandoned vehicles, and he'd watched it for days before assuring himself that it was of no consequence to anyone.

Then he'd rented an arc welder and done a little renovating in some of the rooms that had once served as offices. The skill was a leftover from his high school days in shop class, and he would never have imagined using it again. Still, life had a way of presenting a series of surprises, and this had been one of them.

Now that he was done with the changes he'd needed to make, it was time for him to join his companions, who had moved in a week ago. The old warehouse was three stories high and had not been used in years. He called it the catacombs, because of the rabbit warren of offices on the ground floor.

Besides the offices, there was an enormous blast furnace the size of the largest office, plus piles of abandoned scrap metal and stacks of wooden pallets.

Since Jay's future did not include increasing his earthly wealth, doing without electricity and running water in the building had been inevitable. Instead, he'd invested his small savings into some camping gear, chosen the largest office cubicle for himself and unpacked his gear for the day when he would be living in the warehouse. He had made his daily trek to visit the three disciples already in residence, bringing them food, reading aloud from the Bible and praying with them. It was a little disappointing that their adjustment period was taking so long. He ached for the day when they would all live in loving unity together. It was his hope that living beside them would seal the bond. It was why he'd decided to move in with them.

It was a couple of hours before dark as he pulled his cab into the warehouse. He manually tugged down the big overhead door, locking it from the inside, then carried his suitcases into his new residence and lit a Coleman lantern, taking comfort from the small circle of light. Rats scurried into corners as he set up his cot, adding a small pillow and a sleeping bag to serve as bedclothes. Frowning, he pulled a half-dozen rat traps from a bag, then baited and set them in various places near the walls. He unpacked a portable toilet and situated it behind a stack of wooden pallets, then pounded a nail into the wall and hung a fresh roll of toilet paper from the spike.

Smiling now at the room's homey transformation, he unpacked a small propane stove, quickly assembled it, then put a pan of water on to boil before sorting through an assortment of dehydrated foods and boil-in-a-bag meals. He chose a beef and gravy packet and then dropped it into the simmering pan of water. As he waited for it to heat, he took out a coffeepot, poured a small amount of bottled water into it and set it on the second burner to heat. Once the water was steaming, he stirred in some instant coffee, poured it into a cup, then leaned back and took a careful sip, savoring the warm, nutty taste of hazelnut cream. He glanced at the stove, then poked a finger at the boil-in-a-bag meal, testing it for doneness. Judging it as needing a couple more minutes, he picked up a sack containing canned meat and crackers, some bottles of water and some fruit, turned off the flame under the burner and started out the door. Then he stopped, retraced his steps, retrieved a covered pail and set out again.

His footsteps echoed on the concrete floor as he moved toward the rooms at the other end of the building. Daylight was drawing to a close, but there was still enough light coming in from the small windows above the catwalk for him to see. He sidestepped the dusty wooden pallets and broken packing crates scattered about, wincing slightly at the sight of rats scurrying back into the shadows as he passed.

About halfway down the length of the building, a flock of pigeons in the rafters took flight. At that point, he began hearing voices. The sound filled his heart. It was his faithful disciples awaiting his return.

He shifted the sack of food to the crook of his arm and hastened his steps. When he reached the first door, he unlocked it.

The odor of excrement met him head-on as he stepped into the room, followed by a string of curses from the tall, angry man chained to the opposite wall.

It was Simon Peters, and he was sporting a week-old beard and the clothes he'd been abducted in. There were running sores around his wrists where the iron shackles rubbed. The pain only added to his anger.

"There you are, you bloody bastard. I'm near to dying of thirst here, never mind the fact that my belly has started chewing on my backbone, and that chamber pot you call a bathroom is past running over."

Jay inhaled slowly, giving himself a mental countdown to calm his displeasure with Simon. The man was a whiner.

"Good evening, my dear Simon, I trust—"

"I'm not your dear anything, you crazy son of a bitch. Let me go."

"Now, Simon, we've already had this conversation. You know that's not possible. You wouldn't stay with me willingly, and there is so much work we have yet to do."

"Work? Work! What kind of work am I going to be doing chained in this shit-hole?"

Jay sighed. "Simon, Simon . . . You know it's your own fault. If you had a better attitude and had given me reason to trust you, you would be out on the streets right now, preaching God's word."

Simon Peters's features ran the gamut of expressions. It was as if he didn't know whether to laugh or cry. His own fault? Attitude? Trust? This man who called himself the Sinner was delusional.

"You're right," Simon said. "Sinner, I beg your forgiveness."

Jay beamed and raised his hand over Simon Peters's head, then closed his own eyes as he began a prayer.

"Father, forgive this man for his shortcomings, and give him the wisdom and knowledge to follow me all the way to glory."

Simon's anger wilted as frustration and fear took its place.

"Oh God," Simon begged. "I don't want to go to glory, I just want out."

Jay frowned. "Soon, my son. Soon." Then he took out a can of Vienna sausages, a small packet of crackers and an orange, and set them on a nearby table, along with a fresh bottle of water.

"Don't forget to bless the food before you eat," he said.

"I can't reach the table," Simon said, as tears began to run down his cheeks.

Jay pushed the table within reach of the chained man, glanced at the overfull portable toilet and sighed. He opened the lid on the bucket, shook a liberal dusting of quicklime onto the contents from the pail he carried, then made the sign of the cross before backing out of the room. He shut and locked the door before moving to the next.

This time, when he walked inside, he was met with total silence. This was the last disciple he'd gathered, and he'd instantly shut down. Jay had chained him to the wall like all the others, and he was lying on the floor, curled into a fetal position. The food from the last time Jay had visited was right where he'd left it, minus the bits that had obviously been eaten by rats. Jay moved closer, suddenly afraid that he'd find him dead.

"Matthew . . . my son . . . are you ill?"

Matthew Farmer shifted closer to the wall and folded his arms over his head. He was covered in excrement and soaked in urine, and there were raw patches on his scalp, as if he'd pulled out his own hair in clumps.

Jay frowned. "Matthew . . . speak to me."

Silence.

"Pray with me, Matthew. . . . Let Our Father in heaven heal your woes."

"Matthew Farmer—Airman First Class—799442013. Matthew Farmer—Airman First Class—799442013. Matthew—"

"Shut up!" Jay shouted, then regretted his outburst when the chained man urinated on himself, then began to cry.

"Don't hurt me . . . please don't hurt me."

Jay sighed.

"I have no intention of hurting you, but you're going to have to buck up and do your part."

"Let me go . . . let me go. . . . Matthew Farmer—Airman First Class—799442013 . . . Matthew—"

Jay stood, kicked the uneaten food aside and left some fresh food and water where Matthew could reach it. Since Matthew had not been using the portable potty, there was no need to open his little plastic bucket. He could hardly put quicklime onto the man's skin and clothing, so he said a rapid prayer and left him to his suffering. It was Jay's opinion that what was between each man and God was a personal thing that no one should disturb. Obviously Matthew Farmer was in emotional pain. He just didn't know how to alleviate it and still follow his own path.

It had to be said that Jay was losing faith in choosing this particular disciple. The man obviously had some prior issues with the military and didn't understand the importance of his place in the Sinner's journey. But what was done was done, although Jay could still hear Matthew repeating his name, rank and serial number as he shut and locked the door.

For a moment he stood looking up at the ceiling and the skeletal frame of iron and steel, then down toward the row of doors running the length of the building. There were fifteen of them, although Jay had need of only the twelve, besides one for himself.

With a couple of disciples left to visit and eight others yet to bring to the fold, he was feeling a bit overwhelmed. He knew he was doing what God had commanded him to do, but his confidence in his ability to make this work was beginning to wane. He took a deep breath and shifted his load to one arm as he rubbed at his temple, trying to ease the internal pain with external touch.

It didn't work, nor had he expected it to.

He consoled himself with the fact that he still had Andrew and James. Andrew was turning out to be his rock. Jay unlocked the third door and walked inside. With only one small window, high up the wall and covered in years of grime, this room was the darkest of the lot. For a moment the place seemed empty, but as his eyes began to adjust, he saw movement in the shadows.

"Andrew . . . my beloved Andrew. How have you been?"

The big black man moved into the half-light. He was bald and bare from the waist up. He had tied his T-shirt around his head like a turban and wore his shoes on his hands, leaving his feet bare.

When he saw Jay, his lips parted in a clownlike grin. A droplet of spittle slid from the corner of his lip down onto his chin as he pointed at the sack Jay was holding.

"Andy's hungry."

Jay sighed. He hadn't realized the full extent of Andrew's mental incapacity when he'd joined the disciples, but he'd put his trust in God that his choices would be blessed, and had to believe there was a place for Andrew somewhere in the mixture.

"I brought you some food and water," Jay said.

As he set the food out on a table, he noticed that the

port-a-potty had been spilled and was lying on its side. Rats crawled in and out of it like ants at a picnic. Jay fought an urge to retch as he righted the pot with the toe of his shoe, then sprinkled quicklime all over it, both inside and out.

"Daddy . . ."

Jay looked up. He'd told Andrew to call him brother, but Andrew had gotten the message somewhat screwed up and persisted in saying "Daddy" instead.

"Andy's thirsty."

Without thinking, Jay handed him a fresh bottle of water. Anxious now to get back to his own room, to his supper and a bed, he unloaded the canned meat and crackers onto the table, left an orange, as well, then bolted from the room. He could hear Andy muttering and laughing as he tore into the food.

With one last disciple to visit and feed, Jay went into James's room, almost as an afterthought.

At first, he thought James was just asleep, and then realized he was watching his every move.

"James, I've come with food."

"Let me out."

Jay frowned.

"You know that's not possible. You had your chance but chose to abandon me. I've explained how important it is for all of my men to stay with me, so you're just going to have to endure."

"I'm not one of your men," James cried.

Jay dumped the last of the meat, crackers and water near the man, then rolled an orange toward him, as

58

well. He sprinkled some quicklime in the toilet, then said a brief prayer.

"Fuck you," James said.

Jay frowned.

"You should not speak so disrespectfully in the presence of the Lord."

James stared in disbelief.

"What? You think you're God?"

"No, no, of course not," Jay said. "I'm speaking in the general sense."

"Go to hell," James muttered.

"Don't say that!" Jay cried. "Don't you ever say that."

Then he stomped out, slamming the door behind him as he went. He stopped outside the door, then turned and leaned forward, momentarily resting his forehead against the surface.

Outside, a sudden clap of thunder rattled the roof, followed by a bright shaft of lightning. A torrent of sound began to fill the old building as wind picked up outside. It blew into broken windows with a high, whistling sound, racing through an unseen corridor, only to be sucked out through other openings like an invisible vacuum. The whistle turned into a moan and then a roar.

Jay glanced nervously over his shoulder, half expecting to see demons emerging from the shadows as he hurried toward his own room. The sound of his footsteps was muffled by the storm overhead. Something raced across Jay's path, darting into the shadows to his right. He resisted the urge to run. He had nothing to fear—not even the Devil himself—not as long as he was living a true and righteous life.

Saturday night had come none too soon for Ben. It was his first weekend off in more than a month, and while he had no special plans, the fact that he could go to sleep tonight knowing an alarm wasn't going to go off in his ear the next morning gave him a good feeling.

He'd given some serious thought to calling one of his female acquaintances—maybe share a meal and see where it went from there—but when he went through the names in his little black book, he drew a blank. The women were fine. He was the one who was getting picky.

Every time he thought of making love to a woman, a certain pushy female journalist kept coming to mind. He kept remembering the softness of her mouth, the scent of her perfume and the perfect fit of their bodies, wondering if she held her breath when she came or if she screamed.

He cursed himself for letting his mind go where his body had no business being. But it had rattled him enough that he opted to spend the weekend on his own, which was why he was in this little nondescript restaurant, eating dinner all alone.

His steak was cooked just right, and his fries were perfect—thick and just a little bit greasy. He was chewing a bite of steak and buttering a warm dinner roll when January DeLena walked into the place.

She was wearing a short black dress with a neckline that plunged close to her navel, and a hemline that barely covered her thighs. Her hair was loose and brushing her shoulders, and her long, shapely legs looked even longer with the three-inch heels she was wearing. He knew he was gawking, but he couldn't find the gumption to quit. She was looking around the room, obviously planning to meet someone for dinner, and all he could do was envy the lucky bastard who'd gotten to her before he had.

He was staring and couldn't seem to stop, but when she turned unexpectedly and caught him watching, he inhaled sharply. To his disgust, the half-chewed bite of steak he'd been eating was sucked right down his throat, where it lodged. At that point his knife slipped just enough that he buttered his thumb instead of the bread, then dropped the knife and knocked over his glass of Coca-Cola as he was reaching for his napkin so he could try to cough up the steak that was stuck.

He didn't see her look of shock as his face turned a dark, ruddy hue, nor did he see her racing toward him, because he was busy trying not to choke to death.

Suddenly January was at his table. He would have said hello, but he couldn't draw enough air to speak. Before he knew what was happening, she grabbed him from behind, yanked him up from the chair and began performing the Heimlich maneuver. To his complete humiliation, the chunk of steak popped out of his mouth and onto the table. He groaned, then inhaled deeply, grateful for the air that began filling his lungs.

People from surrounding tables who'd witnessed January's lifesaving technique soon recognized her and began to clap. The manager appeared, panicked that one of their customers had nearly perished at the table, swept the offending piece of meat up into a napkin and gave it to a passing waiter, had the spilled cola cleaned up and put a fresh tablecloth down before returning Ben's food to the proper place. During the cleanup, he offered January a complimentary meal for being the heroine of the hour.

"Oh . . . that's not necessary," she said, batting absurdly long eyelashes at both the manager and Ben. "I'm meeting someone here for dinner, but thank you anyway."

The manager thanked her one last time and left her alone with Ben. Before he could say anything, a couple from a nearby table came rushing over and asked January for her autograph. That started a small rush of diners who followed suit. January looked at him, smiled an apology for interrupting his meal, and proceeded to sign her name to everything from dinner napkins to a waiter's tie.

Ben was nodding and smiling and wishing her to perdition. If she hadn't come into the restaurant looking like a million-dollar hooker, he wouldn't have choked. And if he hadn't choked, there would have been no need for her to play the heroine. He wanted to tell everyone that he hadn't been in any danger and that she was a royal show-off, but that would have made him appear an unappreciative asshole. And the last thing he wanted was to draw any more attention and end up the lead story on the late-night news.

"Can this be over now?" he muttered, as January signed a final autograph.

She glanced at Ben, realized he was fairly pissed, and quickly brought an end to the show.

"Of course," she said, and waved as the last of the people moved away. "Are you sure you're all right?" she asked.

He eyed the plunging neckline, measured it against his thundering heartbeat, and wasn't sure what to say without getting his face slapped.

"Uh . . . yeah. And thanks."

"No problem," she said, then glanced at her watch before giving the room another quick scan.

"So . . . who's the lucky man?" Ben asked, then wished he'd kept his mouth shut.

Referring to her date as lucky meant he envied the man, and letting January DeLena see him weak and wanting couldn't be good.

"He's late," she said. "Do you mind if I sit with you until he shows?"

"Uh . . . yes. I mean, no, I don't mind."

She slid into the empty chair at his table and then pointed at his food.

"That looks good." Before he could comment, she'd swiped a French fry, dragged it through a pile of ketchup and took a big bite. "Umm, good. I'm starved."

Ben frowned. He didn't share his food. Ever. But there was something about watching that French fry sliding into her mouth, and those perfect white teeth biting into it, that tied a knot in his belly.

"How do you eat your steak?" she asked.

"With my teeth."

She blinked once, slightly surprised at his wit, and then laughed out loud.

The truth was, Ben hadn't been making a joke, he'd been trying to shut her down. But now that she thought he was witty, he decided to play it for all it was worth next time an opportunity arose.

"No, seriously," January asked. "How do you like it?"

"Medium rare."

Her eyes widened as the smile on her face spread.

"Me, too. How neat is that?"

He sighed, resisted the urge to pull his plate out of reach of her hands, and offered her a bite of steak.

"Oh, no, I couldn't," she said, then waved down a passing waiter. "I'll have a margarita and a slice of cheesecake."

The waiter hurried away to turn in the order, leaving Ben to figure out what was going on in her head.

"I thought you said you were starving," he said.

"Umm, I am," she said, and pointed to his fries. "Do you mind?"

She took another without waiting for an answer, ran it through the ketchup and this time shoved the whole fry in her mouth.

Ben groaned.

She frowned. "Are you all right? I mean . . . I didn't hurt you or anything, did I?"

"No. I'm fine . . . and by the way, thank you again for saving my life."

"I don't know as I did all that, but it is scary not being able to breathe, isn't it?"

He started to argue, then figured honesty would get him further than his pride.

"Yes, it was scary. Are you sure you don't want to order something else besides a drink and dessert?"

She smiled. "Nope. If I'm going to be stood up, then I'm not going home hungry, and since I'm choosing, I'm choosing my favorites."

He grinned. "Good thinking," he said, and pretended he didn't see her picking French fries off his plate as he went on eating his steak.

"So, North . . . are you a native of D.C.?" January asked.

"No. Montana."

January was surprised enough to quit filching French fries. She eyed his broad shoulders, remembered his long legs and slim hips, and tried to picture him in boots and Levi's instead of slacks and a suit coat. She also remembered what his mouth felt like on her lips, and that he'd had tears in his eyes for the little dead girl someone had turned into a hooker.

Ben felt slightly uncomfortable under her studied gaze but was afraid to ask what she was thinking.

"Where in Montana?" she finally asked.

"Outside of a little town called Hastings. My parents

have a ranch. They raise cattle."

"Brothers and sisters?"

"Three sisters."

Her eyebrows arched. "Oooh, only son. Didn't follow in Daddy's footsteps. How did that go down?"

Ben frowned but didn't answer. He'd noticed an unattached man giving the room the once-over. As much as he hated to do it, he was guessing her date had arrived. He pointed.

"By any chance is that your date?"

January looked over her shoulder, rolled her eyes, then turned to Ben.

"Yes. Excuse me a minute. I'll be right back."

"But, aren't you going to—?"

He didn't have time to finish his question; she was already gone. He watched her weaving her way through the maze of tables, saw the expression on the man's face go from late to lust and knew just how the sorry sucker felt. At least the guy was one up on Ben. He didn't have anything in his mouth to choke on except his excuse for being late.

Then, when he saw January turn her face away from the kiss the man meant to plant on her lips, he didn't bother to stifle a grin. It appeared to Ben that January wasn't a woman who liked waiting.

He saw her waving her arm, and the man shrugging and talking. Obviously he didn't talk fast enough, because January suddenly held up one hand in a motion that meant she'd heard enough; then she pivoted sharply and headed back toward Ben's table.

66

Ben stood. January flopped back down into the chair she'd just vacated and folded her arms across her chest.

"Oh, for goodness sake, sit down and finish your food," she muttered.

Ben glared. He'd been trying to do that for some time now, but she wasn't making it easy.

"Thank you so much for permission to eat," he muttered.

January sighed, then reached across the table and laid her hand on his arm.

"I'm sorry. I was just ticked. I hate people who are late. Even more, I hate myself for finally saying yes to a date with that creep only to have him pull this. I should have heeded my own warning signal and kept telling him no."

Before Ben could comment, the waiter returned with her cheesecake and drink.

"Will there be anything else, Miss DeLena?" he asked.

"No, thank you," she said, then picked up her fork and took a quick bite of the cheesecake, closing her eyes in ecstasy as she savored the flavor melting on her tongue.

Ben glanced down at what was left of his steak and indicated that the waiter could remove his plate.

"May I bring a dessert menu?" the waiter asked.

Ben eyed the look on January's face.

"I'll have what she's having . . . but with coffee."

The waiter nodded and left, while Ben kept

watching January's face. She couldn't have been any more turned on if she'd been having an orgasm.

"You're really into sweets, aren't you?" he asked.

"Ummm," she moaned, then took another bite of the dessert. "So good," she said, as the cheesecake slid past her tongue, then down her throat.

Ben cleared his throat. "I'll bet you are."

January's eyes came open. "What did you say?"

Shit. He'd been made.

Somehow, he managed to keep a straight face. "I said . . . I'll skip the bar, meaning, I'm driving, so I won't be drinking."

She frowned. His gaze never wavered. His mouth didn't twitch. Finally she decided she'd simply misunderstood.

"Yes, well, that's a good idea," she muttered, and then toasted him with her drink before taking a quick sip. "I came by cab, and the margarita is delicious, too. It's too bad you can't—"

"Oh, I can," Ben mumbled. "I just know better."

Her frown deepened. "Are we talking about two different things here?"

The waiter came back, saving Ben from having to answer. He quickly dug into his dessert, skillfully shifting her focus by asking her why she'd decided to become a reporter.

"For the same reason you became a cop."

"Oh, so now you know why I chose police work?" Ben asked.

"Do you like what you do?" she countered.

"Most days," Ben admitted.

"You're good at it," she said.

Ben didn't bother to hide his surprise.

"And you know that because . . . ?"

"Did you get Brother John's real identity?" January asked.

Ben reeled from the change of subject, so fast that he answered before he thought.

"Yes."

She nodded. "That's good. I'm glad I was able to help."

"I'm not talking about this," Ben said.

January smirked. "Well . . . actually, you already are, but don't worry. I'm not going to quote you or anything horrible like that."

The cheesecake in Ben's stomach did a quick one-eighty. For a moment he was afraid it might come back up.

"Can I ask you one last thing?" she murmured.

"Maybe," he said, ever cautious when it came to the media.

"Did he have any next of kin?"

"Who?"

She rolled her eyes.

"Brother John . . . the man who was murdered."

"Yes, actually, he did."

She nodded. "That's good. I think it would be sad to die without someone left behind to grieve. What was his name . . . his real name?"

"Jesus, lady. Don't you have someplace else to be?"

Her expression fell.

The moment he said it, Ben wished he could have taken it back, but it was too late.

"Look, Miss DeLena . . . January . . . I didn't mean that like it sounded. But damn it, you make me nervous, okay?"

She thought about that for a moment, took another drink of her margarita, then picked up her purse.

"You make me nervous, too, Benjamin North. One of these days we'll have to figure out a way to calm ourselves down, won't we?"

With that, she dug a handful of bills out of her purse and tossed them on the table.

He knew he was going to regret this, but it was no longer a secret. Next of kin had been notified. It was a matter of public record.

"His name was Jean Louis Baptiste."

January's face went pale. She sat for a moment, then got up from the table and left the restaurant without looking back.

Ben was in over his head. He was so busy watching the sway of her hips beneath that tiny black dress that he never noticed she'd been afraid.

Four

Daylight was still at least an hour away when January woke up. She glanced at the clock, groaned,

70

turned her pillow over to the cool side and tried to go back to sleep, but it was no use. Her mind had gone into gear the moment her eyes were open. She would never have believed that being stood up on a date would wind up being the best night of her life.

Benjamin North liked her, she was sure of it. He just didn't know it yet. It was unfortunate that their first off-work moment together had been spent with her dislodging a hunk of steak from his throat. Things like that tended to put men on the defensive. Traditionally, they were the ones who liked to do the rescuing.

A faint ding sounded from the kitchen, signaling that her coffeemaker had come on. She sat up on the side of the bed and then leaned forward, resting her elbows on her knees as she noticed a tear in the lace on her nightgown. That was the story of her life. It appeared perfect, like the polish on her toenails, but there was always a little flaw just waiting to surface.

She glanced at the clock again, then looked out the window. The sky was clear, and she was too wide-awake to stay in bed. It wasn't often that she found time for a workout. Maybe a good run through the neighborhood would get the day off to a good start and reset her mental focus.

Before she could talk herself out of it, she pulled her hair up into a ponytail, dressed in jogging clothes, put on her favorite sneakers, and headed for the kitchen and the freshly brewing coffee. She drank it in front of the kitchen window, gauging the new light of day and the weather with a practiced eye, then pocketed sunglasses and her house key, and out the door she went.

Even at this time of the morning, traffic was brisk. She paused at the curb, waiting for a chance to cross, then, when the break came, jogged across the street. Once there, she did a few warm-up exercises. The sun was up now, just high enough above the horizon to be right in her eyes as she turned east. She put on the sunglasses, patted her pocket to make sure her house key was still there and took off.

The air was brisk with a bit of breeze. It ruffled the tiny wisps of January's hair around her temples and cooled the quick sheen of perspiration on her forehead as she ran. The jolt of her feet on the pavement matched the rhythm of her heartbeat, making her feel one with the world. She ran through the neighborhood, aiming for the small park up ahead. When she hit the footpath that wound beneath the trees, she kicked up her pace.

It was good to get away from the traffic and sidewalks, and get under the trees. If she squinted her eyes just right and focused on the limbs shading the running path, she could almost believe she was at her grandmother's home in Houston, Texas. Within moments, she'd let her mind wander back to a kinder, gentler time, remembering the gingerbread cookies her *abuela* made and going fishing with her daddy.

Lost in thought, she'd circled the running path twice before she became aware of passing time. She hadn't brought her watch but knew it must be time to head for home. She was at the point of turning back when a man walked out from between some bushes onto the footpath only feet in front of her.

"Look—"

It was all she had time to say before they collided. They went down in a tangle of arms and legs. January winced as her elbow scraped the ground, but the man's shoulder cushioned her forehead, preventing her from further injury. Embarrassed, she rolled off him and jumped up. He followed her up, touching her shoulders to steady her, then picking at leaves and grass on her clothes.

"I'm really sorry," he said. "It's my fault. I wasn't paying attention to where I was walking. I didn't realize there was a jogging path here. Are you all right?"

January was hurting, but not badly. She touched a finger to the scrape on her elbow. It stung but was hardly life-threatening. Shakily, she brushed the loose hair away from her face and retightened her ponytail.

"Yes . . . I think so," she said, for the first time getting a good look at the man.

He was tall and thin. His hair was long and pulled back at the nape of his neck into a ponytail. If it had been the seventies, he would have passed for a flower child. But it wasn't the seventies, and if she'd had to put a name to his appearance, except for his accent, she would have guessed he was from the Middle East. His shirt and pants were of the same soft white fabric, and the cut of the clothes was such that they moved with the motion of his body. His smile was somewhat hidden by his beard, but when her gaze moved from his beard to his eyes, she froze. She'd seen him before—but where?

The air stilled. January felt as if she was standing outside her own body, watching this moment take place. She could hear her own heartbeat loud in her ears, as well as the sharp chatter of a squirrel in a nearby tree. His eyes were so dark they appeared to be black. There were no visible signs of pupils or expression, just the feeling that there was nothing within.

No soul.

The thought came and went so quickly that it startled her. She took a defensive step backward and then wrapped her arms around herself as if a cold wind had just blown past.

As she watched, the man's smile widened.

"I know you," he said softly. "You're that television reporter. You're January DeLena, aren't you?"

"Yes. Yes, I am, and I'm going to be late for work."

"Of course," the man said, and then closed his eyes, lifted his hands palms upward toward heaven and began speaking in a loud, sonorous voice. "Bless this woman, Father, for she does good in Your name. Amen."

Granted, the man was an odd one. Even so, his prayer should not have been upsetting, but for some reason she couldn't name, it was. By the time he finished and opened his eyes, she was already backing up.

"You're afraid," he said softly.

"No, no, I'm not," January said, but it was a lie, and she hated that he knew it. "I really have to go."

She turned abruptly and began to run—out of the park, through the neighborhood, back to her apartment—and never looked back.

It didn't bother her that he'd recognized her. That happened to her all the time. But she'd seen him before; she just couldn't remember where, and that *did* bother her.

She was in the shower, and had just washed her hair and was lifting her face to the spray, when a flash of memory struck.

The night she'd been down in the old part of town talking to that homeless woman—what was her name? Oh yes . . . Marjorie. There had been a man who'd crossed in front of her car in the rain. That was who the guy in the park reminded her of. But he surely wasn't the same one. That would be more than coincidence.

The weird thing about the man in the park was that he'd prayed for her, and she'd been looking for a street preacher. The one who called himself Sinner. And Sinner knew she was looking, because he'd called her and told her to leave him alone.

She turned off the shower, grabbed a towel and stepped out onto the bath mat.

Was it possible? Could the man from the rain and the man in the park be one and the same? And if they were, was he the Sinner? If he was the Sinner, then she felt decidedly uncomfortable. It was too much like being stalked.

Finally she convinced herself that that was too big a coincidence to be true, that there were dozens of homeless men who were street preachers, and she dressed for work, forcibly putting the man out of her mind.

Jay stayed outside her building until she left for work. She didn't see him, of course, because she wasn't looking for him. He'd become skilled at blending into the background. However, it cost money to feed his disciples and it was going to cost even more when they were all in the fold, so it was time for him to get to work, too.

Confident that his plan was progressing as intended, he walked back to the park to get his cab and, like January, began his day.

Bart Scofield was late for work. The alarm hadn't gone off. The coffeepot quit before even an inch of coffee had run into the bottom of the pot. He'd spilled jam on his only clean shirt, and when he'd gone out to get in the car, it wouldn't start. Frustrated and angry, he called a cab, then sat outside on the front porch to wait.

He was on his cell phone when the cab arrived. He opened the door without looking at the cab driver, tossed his briefcase into the back seat and followed it inside. Once seated, he focused on the driver and frowned.

Another foreigner. Didn't citizens of the United States drive cabs anymore?

"Where to?" the driver asked.

Bart's frown lessened as he gave the address. The accent sounded American. Then he remembered the call he'd been on and put the phone back to his ear.

"Sorry . . . my cab just arrived," he said, then grimaced and laughed. "Don't ask. It's already been one hell of a day and I haven't even gotten to work yet." He paused, listening to the caller on the other end of the line, then opened his briefcase and dug through some papers. "Yes . . . I have it right here. It's going to be a go for the Carson project. The figures are right on." He chuckled. "Yes, yes, I agree. I'll be opting for that corner office with my name on the door."

He disconnected, slipped the phone into his briefcase and then leaned back. There was a fast-food restaurant up ahead. Remembering the coffee he'd missed, he leaned forward and spoke to the driver.

"Hey, buddy . . . pull into the drive-through at McDonald's. I want some coffee."

"Yes, sir," the driver said, and turned on the blinkers before easing off the street into the parking lot. "What do you want?" he asked, as he stopped at the intercom.

"Coffee . . . and a Danish," Bart said, and tossed some bills into the front seat.

A short time later they were back on the street. Bart was sipping coffee between bites of his sweet roll when his cell phone rang again. Juggling the coffee and roll, he opened the briefcase and, once again, grabbed the phone.

"This is Bart. Yes . . . I know I'm late, but I'm less than ten minutes from the office. No . . . I didn't over-sleep. The car wouldn't start. I had to take a cab. Yes . . . I have the figures. See you in a few."

He disconnected again, dropped the phone back into his briefcase and took another bite of the roll. At that point, he glanced toward the rearview mirror and real-ized the driver was staring at him.

"Please pay attention to the traffic," Bart said shortly.

The driver's gaze slid from Bart's face to the traffic. In the mirror, Bart could see him smiling.

This fare was the third one of the morning for Jay. He'd had no idea when he'd picked the man up that he was going to be special. But the moment he'd heard him identify himself as Bart, he knew. The Lord was helping him fulfill his mission. Bartholomew. One of the chosen twelve.

He glanced into the rearview mirror again, making sure his fare was otherwise occupied, then pressed the button on the armrest, automatically locking all the doors.

The click was minute, the sound lost in the sur-rounding noise of traffic and horns. As he pulled up to a red light, he reached behind him and shut and locked the small door in the clear, Plexiglas panel that sepa-rated the front seat from the back.

Scofield was occupied with wiping the sticky

residue from the sweet roll off his fingers as Jay pressed a button beneath the dash. A small amount of ether was released from a tiny plastic tube hidden in the seat behind Bart's head.

Within seconds, Bart's eyes were rolling back in his head. By the time the light changed, he was slumped over in the seat. Jay went through the intersection, then backtracked and drove toward the warehouse district. Within the hour, Bart Scofield had a new place of residence and Jay had another disciple.

He knew, though, that unlike the others he'd picked up, Scofield was a man who would be missed. Which was why, when he didn't show up at the office and his co-workers began calling his cell phone, he couldn't answer, because the phone was now at the bottom of the Potomac.

By the time noon came and went, and because he was the mayor's best friend, a missing person's report had gone out and detectives were tracing Bart Scofield's movements that morning. All they knew for sure was that he'd taken a cab from home to work. They had his address and were checking all the cab companies to see which one had picked up a fare at Scofield's home. It wasn't until they came up with a company that had sent a cab to Scofield's address, only to find that he was already gone when they arrived, that they began to believe something more was going on.

They were now looking for an outlaw cab.

Their driver was a loner—driving a personally owned car without working under the auspices of a local company. They called them outlaw cabs because they often stole other drivers' fares.

Sometimes they worked their own business by being available on the streets during rush hour. At other times, they scammed fares from company cars during slow times by having a scanner that picked up calls going out to other drivers. All the driver had to do was show up at the address ahead of the company cab, steal the fare and collect the money. With this being the case, it was going to prove far more difficult to discover who had picked up Bart Scofield. And they had to find out who had picked him up, because once the report of the missing man had gone to the D.C. police, the media quickly descended. Because Bart Scofield wasn't a nobody. He was the mayor's golfing buddy and best friend.

January was at her desk when she saw Kevin Wojak doing a live, on-the-spot piece from Bart Scofield's place of business. She stopped what she was doing to listen.

". . . talked to him last. At the time, he stated he was in a cab and only minutes away from work. But Bart Scofield never reached his destination. It's been six hours now, and no word. Authorities fear the worst. At this point, no ransom demand has been made, but—"

January reached for a pen and paper, and wrote down Scofield's name. A man gone missing. There was nothing to indicate this had anything to do with the story she was following, although more and more street people were claiming that some of them were missing and had been for weeks. She would have bet a month's salary that no one had reported those people missing. Very few of the street people would willingly go to the law for anything.

Another man gone missing could be just a coincidence, but she wasn't going to blow it off until she checked it out. She needed to go back to the streets—see if she could find some help in putting names to the others. There might be a connection, there might not, but her reporter's instincts said there was. She just needed to find it.

She was still fiddling with her pen, drawing doodles on the paper around Scofield's name, when the phone rang at her desk. She answered absently, her mind still on the abduction.

"DeLena."

"Hey, it's me, Ben."

Her heart skipped a beat.

"I swear, Officer, I didn't do it," January said.

He laughed in spite of himself. The real January DeLena was nothing like he'd imagined.

"Actually, that's not true," Ben said. "You *are* guilty."

January lowered her voice and slid into a fake Hollywood version of a gangster's moll.

"Okay, copper, you got me. So what is it I'm supposed to have done?"

He was still smiling. "I tried to remember if I'd thanked you the other night, and so, on the off chance that I hadn't, I'm thanking you now."

"Thank me? For what?"

"I know I'm not your favorite person, but I'm real fond of living, so I'm thanking you for saving me when I was choking."

"Oh . . . well, sure, although I think you already did. Thank me, I mean. Anyone would have done the same. I'm just happy it all turned out all right. I would have hated it to progress to artificial respiration without a little participation from you."

Ben laughed out loud. She'd caught him off guard again.

"Yeah, well, if it's another kiss you want, I always pay my debts. Consider yourself warned."

January's toes curled inside her shoes. She wished she had some measure of control when it came to Ben North, but she didn't. It was her opinion that facing one's weaknesses ultimately made one a better person. If this was true, then she was a good candidate for sainthood.

"I'll hold you to that," she said, and then quickly changed the subject before she got in over her head and made a complete fool of herself. "Say . . . I don't suppose you've made any inroads into solving the murder of Jean Baptiste?"

Ben frowned. "You know I'm not going to talk about that."

She sighed. "It never hurts to try."

He grinned, then was glad she couldn't see him. Knowing January, she would view that as knuckling under.

"At any rate, I owe you one," he said softly.

The rumble of his voice sent a shiver up her spine. "And I won't let you forget it, either."

"I never thought for a minute that you would."

"Okay . . . um, it was good to talk to you," January said.

Ben started to say more, then saw his partner approaching and shut the conversation down quick before Rick found out who he was talking to.

"You, too," he stated, then added, "Be careful out there."

"Same to you," January said, and sighed when she heard him disconnect.

Bart Scofield woke up in total confusion. He had no idea where he was or how he'd gotten there. The last thing he remembered, he'd been on his way to the office. His head was reeling, and his thoughts were fuzzy. He rolled from his side to his back and had started to stand up when he realized his movements were hindered. But by what?

It wasn't until he raised his hands that he began to panic. Iron bracelets encircled his wrists. Attached to the bracelets were two lengths of heavy chain, which in turn were attached to iron rings in the wall.

"What the—"

He scrambled to his feet and began yanking at the

chains. The harder he yanked, the more frightened he became.

"Help!" he yelled. "Help! Help! Somebody help!"

To his shock, he began hearing voices—laughing, crying, shouting. The cacophony was too confusing to sort out what they were saying. All he knew was that he wasn't alone.

"Who are you?" he called. "Somebody . . . anybody . . . tell me your names."

There was a brief silence, then a man spoke.

"My name is Simon . . . Simon Peters. What month is this?"

"Late July," Bart said.

"Dear Lord," he said. "It's been almost a month."

"Hello," another voice said.

"Who are you?" Bart called.

"My name is Andrew Warren Williams, but Mother calls me Andy."

Bart frowned. The man sounded simple. What the hell was going on here that could explain this madness?

"Who is that?" he yelled. "Who's crying? Come on, man . . . talk to us. What's your name?"

"James, but everyone calls me Jim. Andy is my friend."

"Who else is here?" Bart called out.

"Matthew Farmer . . . Airman First Class . . . 799442013."

"Don't bother him," Simon said. "He's having a tough time here." Then his voice broke, and he, too, began to cry. "Hell, we're all having a tough time."

"Who did this?" Bart asked.

"The cabbie. It was the cab driver," Simon said.

Bart frowned, trying to recall the man's face, but all he could remember was a long ponytail and a beard.

"But why?" Bart called out.

"He calls us his disciples," Simon said. "He thinks he's Jesus."

"What's going to happen to us?" Bart asked.

"Matthew Farmer . . . Airman First Class . . . 799442013. Matthew Farmer . . . Airman First Class . . . 799442013."

The hair on the back of Bart's neck stood on end as he listened to the captive repeating his name, rank and serial number. Obviously the man had once been a POW. What irony that he'd come back to the States, only to be subjected to what must, for him, amount to a living nightmare.

Bart didn't want to think about what was going to happen. He kept telling himself that people would surely be looking for them, and that they would surely be found before long. Then he remembered Simon's remark. He'd been here almost a month. Why hadn't they been found? Bart was religious about watching local and national news, and not once had he heard a mention of any missing men.

Slowly he turned, for the first time surveying his surroundings. The portable commode was obvious, as was a small table. He moved toward the only door in the room but was stopped by the chains at least six feet from the exit. There was a tiny window mounted up near the sixteen-foot-high ceiling, but it was so grime encrusted that only minimal light came in.

When Bart heard a rustling sound behind the commode, he flinched, then watched in horror as a large rat ambled out from behind the pot. Bart could see its nose twitching as it tested the air for scents, and wondered how in the name of God he was going to get out of this place alive. At the same time, it occurred to him that he might die in here. His stomach turned, and his knees went weak.

As the rat moved toward him, he backed up against the wall. One of the prisoners was whimpering. It took a bit for him to realize it was himself that he heard.

Finally the rat disappeared through the space under the door. Bart leaned against the wall, then slid all the way down to the floor. His head was throbbing, his heart pounding so hard he couldn't hear himself screaming.

But he was.

And the others heard.

Simon Peters cursed and turned his face to the wall, while in the room next to him, Matthew Farmer put his hands over his ears and began hammering his head against the floor.

James rolled into a fetal position and began to wail.

Andy didn't bother to join the manic chorus. Minutes before, he'd managed to catch one of the rats that infested the building, and now he was clutching it in both hands. As the other men screamed and cried, he grabbed the rat's neck and squeezed, harder and harder, until blood started coming out of the rat's nose and ears. When the eyeballs suddenly popped, he laughed aloud and threw it across the room.

Jay circled the block to his warehouse twice before he pulled around to the back and drove in. Even then, he sat in the cab without getting out, watching the opening in the rearview mirror, as well as scanning the large open space of the warehouse floor. Nothing had changed. Same stacks of wooden pallets. Same forlorn feeling of failure. Satisfied that all was as it should be, he opened the car door. But his sense of security quickly disappeared when he heard the racket coming from the other end of the building. He jumped out of the cab and started running, tracking the loudest wails to the room where his newest disciple, Bart, now resided.

Without taking the usual precautions, he unlocked the door with shaking hands and dashed inside. Bart Scofield's business suit was covered in blood. His nose was dripping blood, as were several cuts on his forehead. His wrists were bracelets of blood, with spreading bruises just visible beneath the once white shirt cuffs.

"Bartholomew . . . what's happened? What's wrong?"

Bart Scofield was past pain and out of his mind when he turned on the cab driver. Still running on the adrenaline of panic, he whipped one of the chains up in the air and then brought it down and around Jay's neck.

Jay managed one panicked squawk before he went down. It was instinct that made him grab at the chain with both hands, and it was the only thing that saved him from a broken neck. He felt a finger bone snap as the chain tightened, but it was that pain that saved his life. Without thought of what would happen when he let go of the chain, he bolted to his feet and dived headfirst at his latest disciple.

Scofield slipped on the puddle of urine in which he'd been standing and lost his hold on Jay as he went down. He landed flat on his back. His head snapped backward, hitting the floor with a sickening thud. After that, he didn't move.

Jay rolled off him, then sat up.

"Bartholomew . . . are you all right?"

Bart wasn't talking.

Jay nudged Bart's shoulder. When the man didn't respond, he moved a little closer and felt for a pulse. The only thing he felt was the trembling of his own hands.

"No," Jay muttered, then got up on his hands and knees and tried again, to no avail.

He slid his hand beneath Bart's head, testing for a wound. At first he felt nothing; then something odd caught his attention and he thrust his fingers through the man's hair to the scalp, then beyond. Shocked, he yanked his hand back. It came away covered in blood and brain matter. Bart Scofield's skull was smashed.

Jay scooted backward like a crab, then scrambled to his feet. This wasn't supposed to happen. He rocked back on his heels, folded his arms across his chest, and began to sway back and forth. A moan slid from between his lips; then he let out a wail.

What did this mean?

Was God angry with him?

Had He taken Bartholomew because Jay had done something bad?

The niggling pain he'd been dealing with all day exploded into a full-blown blast at the back of his neck. He leaned forward until his forehead touched the floor. The scent of urine and blood and desecration filled his nostrils. He opened his mouth to pray and was only slightly surprised when he screamed instead.

He screamed until his throat burned and his voice was gone—until the shock and rage within him were spent. Only then did he allow himself to look at Bartholomew again. Jay's shoulders slumped. It wasn't a bad dream. It was true. The man was dead.

He covered his face with his hands as his mind ran the gamut of panic. What to do now? Only hours earlier it had seemed so simple—adding another disciple to the fold.

He dropped his hands in his lap and closed his eyes. "Lord, You know I never meant for this to happen. You know I would never step off the path You trod. Help me, Lord. Tell me what to do."

Jay sat for what felt like hours. Finally it was the cries from the others that brought him back to his senses. His face was expressionless as he took a key from his pocket and removed the chains from Bart Scofield's wrists. Jay's hands were steady as he grabbed Scofield by the feet and dragged him out of the room.

Simon's pleas for mercy rolled off his conscience. Matthew's repetitive name, rank and serial number didn't bother him tonight. Not even the unusual silence from Andy's and James's rooms caused him concern.

He'd come to the conclusion that this man had been sent by the devil to test him, and because of that, Jay was talking himself into a righteous indignation. How dare this Bartholomew try to pass himself off as a disciple? As worthy?

He was sweating by the time he got to the cab. He popped the trunk, dumped Scofield's body inside and shut the lid. The shouts and screams coming from the rooms behind him distracted him enough that he remembered they hadn't had food or water all day. He took a large sack from the back seat of the cab and retraced his steps.

Simon Peters was hysterical when he entered.

"What happened?" he screamed. "What did you do?"

"There was a traitor in our midst. I dealt with him," Jay said, then set two cans of potted meat, a tube of crackers, an apple and two bottles of water on the table.

As if it was nothing out of the ordinary, he stood there, calmly blessing the food for Simon to eat.

"Have you been reading your Bible?" he asked.

"Let me go," Simon begged.

Jay frowned. "Read the book of John. We will discuss it tomorrow."

"Jesus Christ," Simon sobbed. "You are one crazy motherfucker. Let me go. I swear I won't tell. Just let me go!"

"You do not take the Lord's name in vain!" Jay shouted, swept the food he'd put on the table back into the sack and strode out of the room, leaving Simon with a bottle of water for sustenance.

He was still angry when he entered Matthew's room. It displeased him to see the man coiled in upon himself and lying in his own filth. It appeared as if he was still pulling out his own hair. Jay stifled a curse. For two cents, he would take a hammer to this loser's head and dump him, just like he was going to dump Bartholomew.

Then he sighed. That was the devil whispering in his ear, trying to make him commit a sin. But that wasn't going to happen; he was on the Lord's path. The ache at the back of his neck was making him sick to his stomach. He set out Matthew's food and strode out of the room. By the time he got to Andy's room, his hands were shaking. He entered quickly, checking the whereabouts of the big man. He saw him in the corner, naked and playing with his own erection.

Jay stared at it for what seemed like forever, before he remembered he was the father and Andrew was the son.

"Andrew! Andrew! Stop that this instant!" he

demanded. "It's a sin to do that . . . and what have you done with your clothes?"

Andy was locked into the pleasure of what he was doing and paid no attention to Jay.

When he started to moan, Jay slammed some food down on the table and left.

James wouldn't even look at him as Jay left the food and water. Jay started to bless the man and his food, then stomped out in disgust.

Jay ran all the way back to the cab. His neck was already bruising, and his broken finger was throbbing. But he had to clean his house before he could rest this night.

He opened the overhead door and quickly drove away.

Five

Bart Scofield's body was discovered at daybreak in a Dumpster behind a Chinese restaurant by two men from the city sanitation department. Bart would never have imagined such an ignominious end, to be found lying on top of half-eaten egg rolls and discarded cellophane noodles. But there he was, blessedly past pain, leaving the mystery of his disappearance and murder to those who knew it best.

In another part of town, January stood in a patch of

moonlight, an ivory goddess waiting for her own mythological god to claim her. Ben watched her, speechless at the sight. Then she was suddenly lying beneath him with her legs wrapped around his waist and her fingernails digging into the muscles in his back as he drove himself deep into her heat.

Her breath was warm and shaky near his ear, and she was begging him for things he'd never done to another woman before.

He rocked back on his knees, then lifted her to him. They rejoined with her sitting up, impaled by his erection.

She locked her hands behind his neck and leaned back just enough to shift the pressure point. As she did, she groaned.

Ben wasn't sure, but he thought there was a possibility that he might die from the pleasure.

"Ben, oh, Benjamin . . . love me."

"I already do," he whispered.

"Then show me how much," she begged.

He grabbed her by the waist and—

The phone rang. It was a rude awakening from the most crucial dream he'd ever had in his life. Angry and frustrated by the loss of a climax, even though it would have been a solitary one, he reluctantly answered.

"Hello?"

It was Don Borger, his captain.

"We got a fresh one in the alley behind the China Wok. Meeks is on his way to pick you up. Work this one close. I'm getting a lot of flak on it."

"How come? Who is it?"

"Bart Scofield, the mayor's best friend and one of the golden boys of Media Marketing, Inc."

"We're on it," Ben said.

"Keep me informed," Borger said.

"Yes, sir," Ben said, and hung up.

He dressed without paying much attention to details, then poured himself a cup of coffee to go.

Meeks honked at him from the street. It was his signal that his day had begun.

Considering the place where the body had been dumped, it was difficult for the crime scene investigators to decide what was evidence and what was pure garbage. They couldn't ignore the bit of spring roll in Bart Scofield's ear any more than they could overlook the obvious bondage marks on his wrists. At first glance, the only two things they were sure of were that Scofield was dead and the Dumpster was not the scene of the crime.

Fran Morrow, from the crime lab, was in the Dumpster when Rick and Ben arrived on the scene. Not only was she masked and gloved, but she had pulled a pair of dark green coveralls on over her clothes and traded her regular street shoes for calf-high rubber boots.

"Hey, Fran, what can you tell me?" Meeks asked, as he sauntered up to the Dumpster.

"Americans waste their food," she muttered, then bagged and sealed a man's loafer that was covered with cold fried rice.

Scofield's body had already been photographed and pulled out of the garbage. Ben looked at it, then looked away. Rigor had set in, giving the frozen limbs an obscene appearance. He was about to ask Fran some questions when he caught a glimpse of something shiny from the corner of his eye. He turned, then looked up just in time to catch a bystander leaning over the third-floor fire escape filming with a video camera.

"Hey! You!" he yelled, pointing to the man. "Get down here and bring that camera with you when you come."

The man straightened up, gave Ben the finger and ducked back into the window on the third-floor landing.

"Son of a bitch," Ben muttered, then turned toward the uniformed officers standing by. "Did you see him?" he asked.

"Yeah."

"Go get him and get that camera."

One started up the fire escape, another moved toward the back of the building on the run, while a third ran out of the alley toward the front of the building.

"Damn vultures," Fran muttered, as she pulled down her mask and climbed out. "It's not enough that when it's time for our life to be over, we have no control of how it ends. We have human vultures feeding off our indignities."

"We'll get him," Ben said.

She shrugged. "I hope you're right. It doesn't matter to Scofield, but it will to his family."

"We need a starting place," Ben said. "Have you got one for us?"

Fran had already stepped out of her boots and was peeling off her coveralls. She looked up, grimaced, then reached toward Ben.

"Yeah, I need out of these damn things," she said. "Give me a hand."

Ben curled his nose from the smell coming off her clothes as he braced her while she took off the coveralls.

"Thanks," Fran said, as she rolled them up and stuffed them in a bag. "My cleaners have refused to do any more of my laundry. Can you believe that?"

Ben laughed.

Fran grinned.

"Now we talk," she said.

"Got a silver bullet for us?" Rick asked.

She shrugged. "Make what you will of it. You always do. And, as always, I'll know more when all the tests have been run. Having said that, there were a couple of things that were unusual."

"Like what?" Ben asked.

"Scofield more than likely died from blunt force trauma to the back of the head, but he hasn't been dead more than five or six hours."

Ben picked up on the inference right away.

"But he's been missing for almost twenty-four. That means—"

"He was manacled," Fran said. "And, from what I can see, most of the minor wounds on his body are self-inflicted."

"You're kidding."

"I don't kid."

"Are you sure?" Ben asked.

"No, and I won't be until I run the tests. Until then, that's all I have to say."

"Where do we go with this?" Rick asked.

"That's your problem, not mine," Fran said, then pointed to the other investigators. "You done?"

They nodded.

She eyed the detectives. "Anything else?" she asked.

"Just remember me when you finish your reports," Rick added.

She nodded. "We're out of here."

As they drove off in one direction, the beat cops were coming back with the would-be paparazzi and his camera.

"Hey, North, we got your Peeping Tom and his third eye."

One of the officers handed the camera to Ben.

"What do you want to do with him?" another asked.

"I'm not sure," Ben said. "Stick around a minute, will you? He might need a ride down to the station."

The man was short and dumpy, wearing a pair of pants two sizes too small and a T-shirt that barely covered his hairy belly. His tennis shoes were mismatched, and there was a dirty New York Yankees ball cap covering what appeared to be a nearly bald head.

Ben stared the man down, then eyed the camera.

"Where did you steal it?" he asked.

"I didn't steal nothin', and you ain't got no right to—"

Ben pointed to the badge clipped to his belt.

"This gives me the right to do a lot of things, including confiscating your camera. This is a crime scene, mister. You don't get to violate it. Period."

The man's shoulders slumped.

"What's your name?" Ben asked.

"Morey Arnold."

"So, Morey Arnold. What the hell did you think you were doing?"

He shrugged. "Trying to make a few bucks, that's all."

"Tell me something, Morey. Do you live up there?"

He pointed to the third floor.

"Yeah. So what?"

"So were you home last night?"

"Part of it," Morey said.

Ben's smile quit.

"Which part?"

"I guess I come in around midnight."

Ben looked at his watch and calculated the time between when Fran said the victim had died and when he would have been dumped. It was just after 8:00 a.m. The vic hadn't been dead more than five or six hours, which meant that he would have died after midnight. He hadn't died here, so it would have taken

98

time to load up the body from wherever Scofield had died, and dump him here. There was a possibility that this little scuzzbucket could be their only witness.

"Did you go right to sleep?"

Morey frowned, then sneered. "No, I had a woman with me. I got a piece of tail. She left. I ordered up a pizza. There's some left. Want a piece?"

"What I want is to know if you saw or heard anything out here early this morning that might pertain to this crime?"

"Can I have my camera back?"

"Is it hot?"

Morey cursed, then spat.

"Early this morning, did you hear anything in the alley that was out of the ordinary?" Ben repeated.

"What time?"

"Around one or two o'clock. Maybe as late as five."

Morey's frown deepened, and he pointed to his surroundings.

"This ain't exactly the Hilton. It's always noisy. You learn not to pay the racket any mind or you'd never get rest. Still, after one, you say?"

There were a few moments of silence, then Morey spoke up. "I heard a car in the alley around four. I know cause I was in the bathroom then. I had to pee from all the beer I'd had with my pizza."

"Did you look out?" Ben asked.

"Yeah, after I heard the lid slam on the Dumpster."

"You heard that?" Rick asked.

"Yeah, but that's nothing new. Someone's always

throwing shit away."

"So what did you see when you looked out?" Rick asked.

"Just a cab."

Ben knew that the last time Scofield had been heard from he'd been in a cab, and this strengthened the possibility that the cab driver had perpetrated the abduction and subsequent murder.

"Did you get a number? What color was it? Did you see the driver?"

"No. Yellow-and-black. No. How about that camera?"

"Give Detective Meeks here your phone number and address. We'll let you know."

"Damn it," Morey muttered. "How am I gonna make my rent if you take—"

"Try a real job," Ben said shortly.

"Look at me!" Morey said. "Who's gonna hire someone looking like this?"

"That's a poor excuse, buddy," Ben said. "There are at least a half-dozen shelters and charities within a twenty block radius around here that would outfit you for nothing. Now get lost before I change my mind and take you downtown."

Morey didn't hesitate. Seconds later, he was gone.

"You know he stole that camera," Rick said.

Ben shrugged. "We're homicide. You want to handle the paperwork it's going to take to fob him off on Theft?"

"No."

"Well, me neither," Ben said. "So let's go see what we can find out about a rogue yellow-and-black cab."

It was January's day off and just after 9:00 a.m. She had just picked up some clothes from the dry cleaners when she heard the news on the radio about a body in a Dumpster. She didn't think much about it until she returned home from her errands.

The portable television in her kitchen was on, and she was only half listening to the local news as she put away the groceries she'd bought. But her attention changed when she heard a news report identifying the body as that of the man who'd gone missing yesterday. Bart Scofield's status had gone from missing person to homicide.

Even though she didn't know him, she was saddened to learn that he had been murdered. It also reminded her that he couldn't possibly be connected to the rumors she'd been hearing about missing homeless men. To her knowledge, none of them had returned, alive or dead.

She finished her chores, then sat down to balance her checkbook, but soon found she couldn't concentrate. She kept thinking about those missing men and the gossip about a street preacher who'd been to hell and returned to tell the tale. Without referring to the copious notes she'd been keeping about him, she couldn't remember when she'd begun tying the two things together.

She was staring off into space, the checkbook forgotten, when her phone rang. The call was of no consequence, but it refocused her plans for the day. As soon as the conversation was finished, she changed her clothes, got her purse and a notepad, and headed out the door. She was determined to get a new lead on the Sinner or chuck the story idea altogether.

The Sisters of Mercy Shelter for the Indigent and Homeless never closed its doors to the needy. It kept the nuns on their toes, trying to make do with never quite enough food or beds to go around. Still, it didn't stop them from doing God's work. From time to time, Mother Mary Theresa pulled double duty by not only being in charge of the distribution of charity benefits, but also taking her turn at serving in the food line.

January knew Mother Mary Theresa personally, having volunteered to help serve Thanksgiving meals to the homeless for the past three years. Mother Mary T., as the street people called her, knew more about what went on in the streets than any local drug dealer, and was less likely to give the wayward a break. She didn't believe in excuses and prayed for the souls of the lost only because it was her duty. She was a little woman with a mighty presence and held the respect of all who knew her.

So when January appeared at the homeless shelter to find Mother Mary T. going through a truckload of donated items, she knew that if she wanted answers, she would have to work through the questions.

Mother Mary Theresa was holding a lamp base, giving the wiring a critical look, when January walked up.

"Hello, Mother Mary T. Looks like you've hit pay dirt."

The nun frowned as she turned to see who was speaking, but when she recognized January, she greeted her by losing the frown and waving toward the back of the truck.

"Yes, and I could use some help. Get yourself up here with me. We can talk while we work."

"Now why did I know you were going to say something like that?" January asked, as she climbed inside.

Mother Mary T. snorted lightly. "I expect that's because you've heard it before." She handed January a lamp shade. "See if this fits that lamp over there, and what's on your mind?"

January took the shade to the other side of the truck and began unscrewing the finial as the tiny nun picked up a huge stack of bedclothes and tossed them out to a helper who was standing on the street below.

"You know what makes me tired?" Mother Mary T. asked.

"What?" January replied, as she screwed the shade to the lamp base.

"People that donate dirty things to the poor . . . as if they're not good enough to warrant a wash and tumble dry before giving the stuff away. Just look at those sheets. Dirty. Stained. Some of them in rags. If it was me, I'd be ashamed." Then she sighed. "However, it is my lot in life to make sure God's lambs are not shamed. Therefore, my fellow sisters and I will be washing away other people's filth before dispensing these very generous gifts."

January grinned. "You know, Mother Mary T., you're one of the few people I know who can be truly sarcastic with a straight face."

The little nun sighed. "It wasn't very godly of me, was it?"

January lost the smile.

"On the contrary. You're one of the most godly people I know."

Mother Mary T. fidgeted at the unexpected praise, then took the lamp out of January's hands and pointed to a couple of broken-down recliners.

"Have a seat, girl. I've a mind to take a breather, and I don't want to be looking up at you while we talk."

January sat, and Mother Mary Theresa sat next to her.

"So what's on your mind? I know you well enough to know this isn't a social visit."

January leaned forward with her elbows resting on her knees. Subconsciously, she lowered her voice, unwilling for anyone else to hear what she was going to say.

"Have you ever heard of a street preacher who calls himself the Sinner?"

Mother Mary T. frowned. "Sinner. Hmm, yes, that sounds familiar, but I've never met him. Why?"

January hesitated, then spoke.

"During the past few months, I've been hearing talk that some men—men from the shelters and the streets—have disappeared. Have you heard anything like that?"

The little nun crossed herself before speaking and, like January, lowered her voice.

"I hear all manner of things," she said. "Most of it the devil's work." Then she added, "But, to answer your question, yes. Some of the regulars here at the shelter talk about people having gone missing. Why?"

"I have a theory that may or may not tie it all together."

"Tie what together, girl?"

"The preacher and the missing men."

Mother Mary T. threw up her hands. "Saints above, January. You can't possibly take any of that seriously? The homeless are already missing when they come here from somewhere else. Often, they leave as anonymously as they came. Besides that, none of them are in good health. I can't bear to think of how many die alone in sewers and abandoned buildings and are never found."

"I know, but—"

"But nothing. If you want to do a story on something, focus on the fact that we're short of money. We need donations for the upcoming winter. Coats, blankets, food . . . you name it."

January sighed. "I will. I promise I will, but humor me on this, will you?"

"You promise you'll do it in advance of the cold weather?"

"Yes, ma'am," January said.

"Well, that's that, then. Exactly what do you want to know?"

"Names. I need names," January said.

The aging nun frowned. "Of those who've gone missing recently?"

January nodded.

Mother Mary T. leaned back in her recliner, folded her hands in her lap and then closed her eyes, as if she was about to take a nap. January knew better. This was her thinking mode.

"Let's see," the nun muttered. "A month or so ago, Delroy . . ." She opened her eyes and pointed to January. "You remember him—the big man with no legs, scoots around on a couple of modified skateboards."

"Yes . . . yes, I do," January agreed.

Satisfied, Mother Mary T. continued. "Anyway . . . Delroy came to the center in a terrible mood. Said someone had stolen his best friend. I didn't think much of it at the time, but then I remembered a similar complaint a month or so before that. Red Susie, the black girl with a patch on her eye, claimed that her friend had disappeared. She was blaming alien abduction. You can see why I don't pay much attention to their rambling."

"Were there more?" January asked, taking notes as they talked.

Mother Mary T. frowned. "It seems there was one

other person I heard some of them talking about, but I can't recall the— Oh! Wait! I remember. It was the fellow who won't sleep inside. No matter what kind of weather, he won't go indoors. They say he was a POW in Vietnam and that enclosed spaces make him crazy."

"Their names, Mother Mary T. Do you know their names?"

Her forehead furrowed as she began to count them off on her fingers.

"Delroy's friend is Simon. I don't know his last name. None of them have last names, you know. And as far as that goes, I have no way of knowing if the names they go by are their true given names, either."

"It doesn't matter," January said. "Simon, you said. Do you know the others?"

"Hmm, I think Red Susie called her friend Andy, and she mentioned something about Andy's friend Jim.

"Andrew? James?"

Mother Mary shrugged. "She never used those names, but I suppose that's right."

"And the vet? Did he have a name?"

"They called him Crazy Matt. I thought that was harsh, but he answered to it, just the same."

January wrote down the name, then, beside it, the formal version. Matthew.

She glanced down the list, and as she did, the hair rose on the back of her neck.

Simon

Andrew

Matthew

James

She remembered the man who'd gone missing and then turned up dead.

Bart. Bartholomew.

If this was a coincidence, it was pushing the boundaries. The names of five of Christ's disciples from the Bible.

"Did Delroy or Red Susie ever mention the street preacher?"

"Not that I know of," Mother Mary T. said.

January frowned, her shoulders slumping.

"Have they said anything—anything at all—about where they saw their friends last? Maybe who they were with? Something like that?"

Mother Mary rolled her eyes. "Well, remember, Red Susie blamed the aliens." Then she chuckled. "Only these aliens, I believe, were driving cabs."

January stifled a gasp as Mother Mary T. suddenly frowned.

"Now that's strange," she said. "I never put that together before."

"Put what together?" January asked.

"If I remember correctly, Delroy also said something about Simon getting into a cab. He was angry because they drove off without waiting for him."

January looked down at the list of names. Was this the connection? But how did this tie into the Sinner? Frustrated, she leaned back in the old recliner, and dropped her notebook and pen back into her purse.

Maybe there wasn't a connection. Maybe she was trying to make a story out of coincidences.

She sighed.

She knew better. It was the first rule of thumb for reporting. Stick to the facts. Don't twist them to make them fit something else.

"Is there anything else, dear?" Mother Mary T. asked.

January sighed.

"No, I guess not."

"Was this of any help to you?"

"Yes. Thank you so much for your time."

"You're welcome, dear. However, if there's nothing else I can help you with, I need to get back to work."

"Okay, sure," January said, as she got up. She stepped down from the truck, then straightened her clothes.

"Goodbye, January. Don't be a stranger," the little nun called.

"Okay," January said, waving as she walked away.

Six

The phone was ringing as January walked in the door. She dropped her purse on the hall table and then moved toward the kitchen, intent on letting the answering machine pick up. The machine kicked on, and her message began to play. It wasn't until she heard the caller's voice that she stopped. A chill of foreboding made her slow to react, but as the man continued to talk, she moved to answer.

As soon as Carpenter heard January's cheery greeting and invitation to leave a message, he leaned back against the inside of the phone booth and closed his eyes. It was the answering machine. He needed a warm body, not a machine. He cursed before he could stop himself, then silently begged God's forgiveness.

The pain in his head was worse than it had ever been. The stress and grief from what had happened to Scofield were weighing heavily on his conscience. He wanted to believe that he'd read the signs wrong, that just because a man named Bart had gotten into his cab didn't mean he was "the one" God meant for him to claim. But what if he was wrong? What if he'd just damned himself to an eternity in hell because he'd killed one of God's disciples?

A sudden pain went from one eye to the other. It was so sharp and unexpected that he screamed. At that point, his ears began to ring, as if someone had hit him hard at the back of the head. The air inside the booth was hot, accentuating the odor of stale cigarettes and unwashed bodies that lingered there, but he had to pull himself together. When the prerequisite beep sounded, signaling for the caller to begin speaking, he took a deep breath and made himself concentrate.

"January DeLena. Always on the prowl for that story, even though I asked you to leave me alone.

Don't deny that you're still looking for me, because I saw you today. I heard you. You and that nun. Why won't you leave me alone? I have things to do that don't concern you."

January grabbed the receiver.

"Hello? Hello?"

Tears were streaming down Jay Carpenter's face. The pain in his ears was so severe that, at first, he didn't hear her answering.

"Hello? Are you there?" January repeated.

Jay shuddered, then closed his eyes, making himself focus.

"Leave me alone."

"Tell me about the missing men," she demanded.

He flinched. How could she know? He made himself calm. She didn't know anything. She couldn't possibly. For whatever reason, she was just guessing.

"I don't know what you're talking about," he said.

January *was* guessing, but she wasn't going to pass up this opportunity to push a few buttons just to see what popped up.

"Matthew, Simon, James, Andrew and Bart. Those are their names, aren't they? What did you do with them, and what was wrong with Bart? Why did you kill him?"

"He was the wrong one," Carpenter muttered, unaware that he'd just given himself away.

January gasped. She had not expected that.

"What do you mean, the wrong one? Are you admitting that you abducted, then killed, Bart Scofield?

Why? Why did you do it, and where are those other men?"

Carpenter shook his head like a dog shedding water, but it didn't stop the pain, and the buzzing in his ears became worse.

"I didn't say that." He slid to the floor of the phone booth as his legs gave way.

"Yes, you did," January said. "Why was Bart Scofield wrong?

"I don't know what you're talking about," Carpenter said, and wondered if that was himself he heard whining. "I called to tell you to stop looking for me. You're messing everything up."

January could tell something was wrong with the man. His voice was shaking, his words slurring.

"Messing up what? What are you doing?"

"Saving myself," Carpenter said. "Why can't you understand? I'm walking in His shoes."

"Whose shoes?"

"His," Carpenter yelled, then began rocking where he sat, unaware that with every backward sway of his body, he was bumping the back of his head against the wall of the booth. "I have to. I have to. I can't go back. Not there. Never there again."

"Go where?" January asked.

"Hell. Don't you understand? I can't go back."

"I don't want to talk about hell. I want you to tell me where the other men are. Did you kill them like you killed Scofield?"

"Shut up!" Carpenter shouted. "Stop saying that!

You don't know what you're talking about."

"Then tell me," January begged. "Tell me."

Someone knocked on the door of the phone booth. Carpenter squinted his eyes and looked up. A couple of young black women were staring down at him from outside. He struggled to his feet.

"Just stop it. I'm warning you," he mumbled, then hung up the phone and pushed his way out.

As he bumped into one of the women, he grabbed his head.

"Hey, mister, are you all right?" she asked.

Carpenter was holding on to his head with both hands, as if it would fall off his neck if he turned it loose.

"God is with me," he said, and staggered toward his cab.

"That's good to know," the other girl muttered. "I been wondering where the hell He went."

"Hush your mouth, girl. That's blasphemy," her friend said.

"Don't you be throwing words at me that you can't even spell," the first girl responded.

It was the last thing Carpenter heard before he got in the cab and drove away.

January was shaking when she hung up the phone. She had no idea what the man who'd just called her looked like. Was he the same one she'd seen in the rain, then in the park? She didn't know and couldn't prove it. She didn't even know for sure if he was the man who called himself the Sinner. Even though he'd unintentionally admitted knowing of Bart Scofield's death, he hadn't said enough to incriminate himself.

Still, she couldn't ignore what had just happened. But what should she do? Tell the police? What could she tell them?

Almost immediately, she thought of Ben North. Maybe she could talk to him in an unofficial capacity. He would know whether there was anything valid in the two phone calls.

Yes. She had to do that much.

She reached for the phone, then realized she didn't know Ben's number, home or cell. After looking for him in the phone book with no success, she realized that her only option was to call the department and have them relay a message, which she hated to do. In her job, staying objective was imperative. Having a personal relationship with a cop, no matter how vague, could put both of them in a precarious position. Still, she couldn't sit on the little bit of information she had about a murder investigation. Before she could talk herself out of the impulse, she picked up the phone.

It was five minutes after one in the afternoon before Ben and Rick had a chance to stop for lunch. Ben was all for grabbing something at a drive-through before following up on a lead regarding the Scofield murder. Some cab company had reported an outlaw cab had picked up one of their fares. But Rick didn't want to eat in the car.

"Where to, then?" Ben asked, as they sat at an intersection, waiting for the light to turn green.

Rick leaned across the steering wheel, pointing to a Chinese restaurant across the way.

Ben's stomach rolled.

"You've got to be kidding," he muttered.

"What? Why not?" Rick asked.

"I've already seen all the Chinese food I care to look at on Scofield's body. I have no intention of eating any."

Rick shrugged. "Oh yeah. That. Well, we can—"

"The light's green," Ben said.

Rick straightened up and accelerated through the intersection. "How about pizza?" he asked.

"Sure, why not?" Ben countered.

A few minutes later they were sitting in a booth, studying the menu, when Ben's cell phone rang. He glanced at the number.

"It's the precinct," he said.

"So answer it," Rick said. "Maybe you won the lottery and they're trying to find you."

Ben grinned. "You order the pizza while I find out what's up."

He got up from his seat and walked out of the dining area into a hallway leading to the bathrooms as he answered.

"This is North."

"Detective North, you have a request to call a Miss

115

DeLena as soon as possible."

Ben frowned. "Concerning what?"

"The caller didn't say, sir."

"Yeah, okay," Ben muttered. "Just a second while I get a pen." He fumbled with his notebook and pen a moment before he spoke. "What's the number?"

The number was relayed. The call ended.

A large metal something hit the floor in the kitchen beyond the double doors where he was standing. Someone yelled. Someone else cursed and slammed a door.

He could smell tomato paste and baking bread.

Some kid was poking quarters in a pinball machine at the end of the hall. Ben thought it was an odd place to put a game. What did the establishment think the patrons would do? Play a little pinball while waiting for their turn to pee?

He stared at the number he'd written down, then at the phone he was holding. What was January up to now? What possible reason could there be for him to call her as soon as possible?

"Are you waiting to go?"

Startled by the question, he turned around.

"I'm sorry. Were you speaking to me?" he asked.

The man pointed to the door to the men's room.

"Is it locked or something? Are you waiting?"

"Oh. No. Sorry, go right ahead," Ben said, and stepped back.

The man moved past.

Ben absently noted the shower of dandruff flakes on

the man's shoulders, then moved toward the exit. Standing here like a fool wasn't getting him anywhere. All he had to do was dial a number, for God's sake. So he did.

January was peeling an apple when the phone rang. She saw the caller ID, dropped the apple and knife into the sink, and grabbed the phone on the second ring.

"Hello . . . Ben, thank you for calling me so promptly."

Ben was a bit taken aback that she knew it was him, wondered if she was psychic as well as sexy, then remembered caller ID.

"Yeah, well, no problem. What's up? The message sounded serious. Is it?"

"I think so."

The slight hesitation in her voice made her sound breathless, which threw his mind into thinking about how he could make her lose her breath—and quite possibly her mind. Then he reminded himself that he was on duty.

"What's it about?"

"Bart Scofield's murder."

The smile slid off his face.

"What the hell do you know about that?"

"It's a little complicated. I'm off today. Could you come by?"

"Give me your address," he said. "Rick and I will come over.

"Rick? Who's Rick?"

"My partner, Rick Meeks."

January hesitated. She didn't want to announce her theories to the world without something to back them up, and that had yet to surface.

"Uh . . . I was wondering if we could talk about this first without involving anyone else, just in case I'm making a big deal out of nothing."

He frowned. "This isn't a fishing expedition to try and get information out of me for some story, is it?"

There was an immediate shift of anger in her voice.

"You know something, North? I'm not always about the damn story, and I'm no masochist, either. I suspect I'm already the butt of countless jokes at your precinct, and don't bother denying it. I don't need more grief from a bunch of doughnut butts. You can come by yourself, or not at all."

"Doughnut butts?"

The line went dead in his ear.

"Doughnut butts?"

Before he thought, he ran a hand across his own belly. It was still flat and firm enough to brag about, should the need arise.

"Doughnut butts."

He started to grin. By the time he got back to the booth and the meal, he was chuckling. He didn't know what was going to happen between them, but whatever it was, it damn sure wouldn't be boring.

"Who was that?" Meeks asked, as Ben reached for a piece of pizza and put it on his plate.

Ben started to make something up, then changed his mind. Just because he'd promised to leave his partner behind that didn't mean he was going to lie to him.

"None other than Miss January DeLena herself," Ben said, shaking a liberal serving of red pepper flakes over the slice.

Rick eyed the flakes, knowing the heat the pepper would add, and then grinned at Ben.

"Looking for a little action, is she?"

Ben set the bottle of pepper flakes down with a thump. The look on his face served as further punctuation.

"Shut up, Meeks. Just for once, shut up."

Meeks shrugged, but he maintained a smirk, which Ben also resented.

"She called, saying she might have some info on the Scofield murder."

Meeks's smirk stopped as he let his slice of pizza drop back onto the plate.

"Holy Moses, what are we waiting for?"

"She wants to talk to me alone."

Meeks frowned. "I hope you told her—"

"I said I would."

Meeks's frown deepened. "What's that all about? Since when do we let civilians pull shit like that?"

"Look," Ben said. "She thinks what she knows might amount to nothing, and she doesn't trust the department not to make her out to be some big joke. She doesn't trust us not to screw up her reputation."

Meeks leaned back, eyeing Ben curiously.

"But she trusts you?"

Ben shrugged. "Little to none, but I guess it's enough. It can't hurt anything, and you'll know everything I know as soon as the interview is over."

"Whatever," Meeks said. "But I'm registering a complaint."

"Duly noted," Ben said. "Now pass the Parmesan. I'm not going anywhere until I finish my pizza."

It was almost three in the afternoon when Ben pulled into the parking lot of January's apartment building. He got out with somewhat of an attitude—a "How dare you demand my presence under your terms?" set to his jaw. But by the time he was ringing her doorbell, his belly was in knots. When he heard her footsteps on the other side of the door, he jammed his hands into his pockets and thrust his chin forward. He wasn't going to let her get under his skin again.

Then she answered the door.

"Thanks for coming," January said, as she stepped back and motioned for Ben to come in.

She was barefoot, and wearing something loose and just sheer enough to hint at what lay beneath. The dress was the color of crushed raspberries, and he wanted nothing more than to taste the smile on her lips to see if she was as sweet as she looked.

"Well . . . are you going to stand out there all day?" she asked.

I probably should. But he didn't voice the thought. Instead, he nodded and walked in.

He followed her from the small foyer into the living room.

"Sit anywhere," she said.

He chose the largest easy chair.

There was a satisfied look on her face as she plopped down in one opposite.

"I knew you'd pick that one," she said.

"I better not be here because you've suddenly decided you're psychic," Ben drawled.

January laughed. The sound wrapped around Ben's heart and gave it a gentle squeeze, as if to remind him that she was already an irresistible force.

"Oh, definitely the contrary, although I have to admit that in my job, it could sure come in handy," she said.

Ben began to relax.

"Okay . . . but we can both agree on the fact that you're very astute. Yes?"

She grimaced. "I used to think so, but lately I've begun to doubt myself."

He leaned forward, resting his elbows on his knees.

"Talk to me, January. Tell me why I'm here."

Her shoulders slumped, and for a moment Ben saw weakness and what appeared to be fear in her eyes, but it was gone as quickly as it had appeared.

"Promise you'll hear me out before you make any judgments?"

"I promise," he said.

She nodded, then folded her hands in her lap.

"I'm not sure where to start."

"Start where stories always start. At the beginning."

She grinned wryly. "Well, it was not a dark and stormy night, however . . ." The smile disappeared. "You've heard of near-death experiences, right?"

"Yes, but what—"

"You promised to hear me out first, remember?"

"Sorry. Please continue."

"Near-death experiences have always intrigued me, so I try to follow up when I hear about one. That's what started me down this path. Last Thanksgiving I was down at the Sisters of Mercy shelter, helping serve dinner to the homeless when I heard two men talking about this street preacher who called himself the Sinner. They said he was claiming that he'd died while in a hospital, then was resurrected, only his story had a different twist. That's when I started looking for him."

"What made his story different from all the others?"

"He claimed that when he died, he didn't experience any bright light or tunnel to glory. He said he'd gone to hell."

Ben straightened abruptly.

"Are you serious?"

"Yes, but I don't know if he is. I've been trying to find him for months now, but with no result. Until recently."

"You've found him?"

"No. I think he's found me."

The expression of interest on Ben's face turned hard.

"Have you been threatened?"

"Not exactly . . . Well, sort of, but not seriously."

"Damn it, January, either he did or he didn't. Which is it?"

She looked up, then away, staring past the dining room table to a point outside the window.

Ben could see the reflection of a vase of flowers on the table behind him in January's eyes. Mesmerized by the sight, he wasn't really listening when she finally answered.

"The first time he called me, I was at work. He said he heard I'd been looking for him. He told me to stop."

Breath caught in the back of Ben's throat. He'd never considered the thought that what she did could put her in danger.

"Did he threaten you?"

"Not really. I asked him if it was true that his near-death experience had taken him to hell."

"He didn't agree with you, did he?"

"He never came out and admitted it that time. What he did say was that I needed to leave him alone so he could do what he needed to do."

"And that was . . . ?"

"It was all very esoteric, but he kept saying something about 'walking in his shoes,' or 'living as he lived,' words to that effect."

"Walking in whose shoes?" Ben asked.

January glanced up, gauging the expression on Ben's face as she answered.

"I think he was referring to Jesus Christ."

"Look, January. I hate to poke a hole in your story, but there have been hundreds of crazies on the street who think they're Jesus. Besides that, what does any of this have to do with Bart Scofield's kidnapping and murder?"

"I'm getting to that, and you're the one who told me to start at the beginning, so I did. Now shut up and let me finish. After that, feel free to see yourself to the door."

Ben regretted his outburst, but it was too late to take it back.

"Sorry," he muttered.

She rolled her eyes but resisted the urge to give him another dig.

"Anyway, as to Bart Scofield . . . I think the street preacher, the man who calls himself the Sinner . . . I think he did it."

Ben held up his hands, then stood.

"Okay. Wait. How in hell do you get from a near-death experience in hell to kidnapping and murder? No wonder you didn't want anyone else to hear this."

January shot to her feet and shoved a finger into Ben's chest.

"He called me again today. He was pissed off because I'd been down to the Sisters of Mercy shelter asking about some missing men."

Ben's eyes bugged. "There's more? Missing men, I mean?"

January sighed, then threw her hands into the air.

"Oh Lord, haven't I mentioned them before?"

"No."

"Okay . . . well, here's the deal. Street people have been going missing. In each case, the last time they were seen was getting into a cab, and the homeless don't take cabs. Understand?"

Ben's eyes narrowed. Now she had his attention. Scofield had last been heard from in a cab.

January didn't wait for him to answer.

"I went to see Mother Mary Theresa. She belongs to the Sisters of Mercy and runs the shelter where I volunteer. I asked her if she'd heard about the missing men. Long story short, she had. When I heard about Scofield going missing, I wondered if he was a victim of the Sinner, too, although he was anything but homeless. Then Scofield turned up dead, and I dropped the notion that the Sinner was involved. You see, none of the other men have turned up dead . . . at least, I don't think they have, although it's careless of me to assume that, because they could be lying in some morgue now, unidentified."

Ben sat back down. He was so damn confused that it didn't bear thinking about.

Then January added, "What I've been trying to get said is . . . the same man, whoever he is, called me today. Again he told me to leave him alone, and this time he wasn't only angry, he seemed ill, or in pain. I asked him point-blank if he had anything to do with the missing men. He sort of went off his rocker. I asked him if he had taken Bart Scofield, too, and do you know what he said?"

"I don't even know what *you've* been saying," Ben muttered.

January glared.

"He said that Scofield had been the wrong one."

Suddenly she had Ben's attention.

"What?"

"The wrong one. He said Scofield had been the wrong one. I asked him if he'd taken the other men. He told me to leave him alone, that I was messing everything up.

"I kept asking him why he was doing it and he said he couldn't go back. I asked him back to what, and he said hell. He said he was walking in his shoes so he wouldn't go back to hell."

"Okay, so you got a phone call from a nutcase who said a murdered man was a mistake, which is certainly suspicious. However, if you don't know who this Sinner is or what he looks like, then how are we to find him and interrogate him?"

"Well, that's your job. Mine is news. I felt it was my duty to tell you about the phone calls."

"Do you really believe he's responsible for all this?"

January hesitated, then nodded.

"Yes."

"Why? Nothing you've said, except for that bit about the cab and Scofield being the wrong one— which, by the way, could be interpreted a couple of different ways—ties a street preacher to a kidnapping and murder."

"Would it change your mind to know that the names

of at least four other missing men are Simon, Matthew, Andrew and James?"

"I don't see what you're—"

January ticked the names off again, adding one other bit of her theory to the pot.

"If you knew that a man who was trying to recreate the life of Jesus Christ had begun kidnapping men with the names of Simon, Matthew, Andrew and James, and one named Bart—Bartholomew—whom he called the wrong one . . . what would you think?"

Ben felt the blood draining from his face.

"The disciples . . . Christ's disciples. But why?" he asked.

"Remember how he said he was 'walking in his shoes'? What if he was being literal? What if he thinks that recreating Jesus's world and walking the same path that Jesus walked—in *His* shoes—will keep him out of hell? He kept saying he couldn't go back to hell."

Ben got up and paced toward the window, then stopped and paced back to where January was sitting.

"How much of this can we prove?"

"None of it."

Ben stared at her as if he hadn't heard her correctly, but her expression never wavered.

"You're serious, aren't you?"

"Yes."

"Okay, now I know why you didn't want to make this an official statement, but you did give us somewhere to start, and that can be made known. We can

127

say that you got an anonymous call from a man who said that Scofield's murder was . . . a mistake. That's close enough. Officially, we won't mention the possibility of a connection between the other missing men and Bart Scofield, but trust me, I won't forget it."

January felt a huge sense of relief. Finally someone besides herself was in on the theory.

"There are a few other weird things that the Sinner is reported to have done."

"Like what?" Ben asked.

"Several months ago, there was a lot of talk about a street preacher passing out coupons for a free fish sandwich at Captain Hook's Fish and Chips to everyone who stopped to listen."

"I don't get it," Ben said.

"It's a stretch, but think of Christ feeding the multitudes with the baskets of fish and the loaves of bread. Fish sandwich. Fish and bread."

Ben's gut knotted.

"You're really on to something, aren't you?"

January nodded. "Yes, I think so."

Before he thought, he moved closer to her, then took her by the shoulders.

"Be careful. If you're right about the connections, then you've got to remember that this man who calls himself the Sinner is also a murderer. And he knows who you are. Probably *where* you are. I don't want to get a call one night and find out that you've become one of his victims."

His grip was firm on her shoulders. The expression

on his face was dead serious. But it was the look in his eyes that made a believer out of her. January sighed. She'd been waiting on this moment ever since the first time.

"You're going to kiss me again, aren't you?"

"Yes."

"Finally," she said, and slid her arms around his neck.

Seven

Subconsciously, Ben had known getting involved with January DeLena could be dangerous, but he hadn't known it might be lethal. The moment their lips met, he lost his sense of self. She consumed him with nothing but the kiss—tender, even timid, and yet filled with such passion.

For January, the kiss sealed her fate. She didn't know how she was going to survive the rest of her life without this man, but she couldn't let herself believe this kiss was anything more than the inevitable outcome of their ongoing sparring. Ben didn't know, and she didn't have the guts to tell him, that she'd been in lust ever since the day she'd first seen him. Then the kiss had changed everything. With very little effort, her lust could so easily turn to love.

Ben was the first to pull away, and he did so with a groan.

"This probably shouldn't have happened," he said softly, as he cupped her face and traced the shape of her lower lip with his thumbs.

January's knees went weak. "But it did."

A crooked grin replaced the concerned expression on his face.

"Did it ever," he said, then remembered why he'd come. "I'm going to follow up on everything you told me."

She nodded. "I expected you to."

"I can't promise anything," he added.

She lifted her chin in a defensive manner. "I didn't ask for promises."

Ben's eyes darkened.

"No, you didn't, did you?" He sighed. "But I want you to promise me something."

"Like what?" January asked.

"Be careful. It's not good that some nut has fixated on you."

January frowned. "Other than asking me to leave him alone, he's never threatened me."

"Yes, but if you're right about him, then we know he's capable of murder."

January's heart skipped a beat.

"I never . . . I mean, I didn't think of—" She backed up a step. "Yes, of course you're right. I'll be more cautious."

Ben hated this. He'd put fear on her face, but for her sake, she had to be wary.

"I'm sorry. I didn't mean to frighten you, it's just

that when you're dealing with the mentally unbalanced, there's no predicting what might happen."

"I'll be careful, and . . . thanks for coming by."

Ben had just been dismissed. After the kiss they'd shared, it wasn't the way he wanted to leave her, but she was holding the door open for him to exit.

"If you have any further contact with your caller, let me—"

"I will," January said, then looked away.

Ben started to reach for her, wanting to regain the connection they'd just shared, then changed his mind. For professional reasons, he needed to maintain some distance.

"Good afternoon," he said.

January glanced back at him, then nodded.

"You, too."

He moved out of the foyer and into the hall outside her door. He turned around for a last word, only to have the door closed in his face.

"Well, hell."

The abruptness of their parting was as unexpected as her call had been. He dug in his pocket for the car keys and then started toward the elevator, but the farther he got from her door, the more unsettled he felt. They'd shared something unexpected, but very special, when they'd kissed. Walking away like this felt wrong. He was all the way to the elevator when he suddenly turned around.

January was still in the foyer, reliving every moment

of Ben's visit, when her doorbell rang, startling her from her musings. She glanced through the peephole and saw Ben. She groaned. She'd maintained her composure so well before, but now she was going to have to pretend indifference all over again.

Tentatively, she opened the door. "Did you forget something?"

"Yes."

He kicked the door shut behind him and pinned her against the wall.

"What are—"

He kissed her. Hard. Leaving her with no doubt as to what he'd forgotten or what he wanted.

January moaned against the pressure of his lips, then wrapped her arms around his neck and kissed him back.

Ben shuddered as he swept her up into his arms. "This may be a—"

"Don't talk." She pointed down the hall. "First door on the right."

His eyes narrowed sharply as his nostrils flared. He moved without thought other than to get this woman naked and in bed.

The bedroom door was ajar. He kicked it open and strode in, still carrying January. The bed was to the left of him. He moved toward it. When his knees hit the edge of the mattress, he gently laid her down, then followed her descent.

Without wasted motion, he stretched the full length of himself on top of her just long enough to realize they were a perfect fit, then slid his arms beneath her and rolled until she was the one on top.

January went from captive to captor as they rolled, alleviating the brief moment of panic she'd felt at being so out of control. At that point, she rose up on her elbows and stared down at his face.

His eyes were dark with passion, his lips glistening with moisture from the kiss they'd just shared. She could feel his body changing beneath her, and shuddered with sudden longing to be one with this man.

"You better not regret this later," she muttered.

His voice was low and husky. His arms tightened around her back.

"Same goes for you, lady."

She nodded. "Fine, then."

"Honey, you aren't just fine . . . you're perfect."

Then his eyes darkened even more as he cupped the back of her head and pulled her down.

Her lips were soft, yielding to the demand of his own, yet her touch was urgent—a silent plea for everything he had to give her.

Insanity came quickly, marred by the frustration of too many clothes between them. Before January knew it, Ben was tearing at his own clothes and helping her off with her own at the same time.

His shoes and her sandals.

His jacket and her dress.

His shirt and pants.

Her pink bikini panties.

Everything—until finally there was nothing left to

remove but the wrapper on a condom he'd laid on the end table beside the bed.

Ben was beyond thinking.

The job.

His partner.

The District of Columbia Police Department.

A dead man named Bart Scofield.

They might as well never have existed. At this moment, nothing mattered but January. Even as he was kissing her, he was aware of the silken texture of her skin. When she straddled his thighs and then reached for the condom, every muscle in his body tightened. And when she peeled the condom from the wrapper and fitted it on him, he groaned.

January leaned forward, and as she did, Ben slid his hands around her back and pulled her down, crushing her breasts against his chest and her lips against his.

Body to body, hearts beating in time, they rode the building wave of need until waiting another moment longer to be together was impossible. With one swoop, Ben rolled, taking January with him. Instinctively, she shifted to accommodate the weight of his body, and then stifled a cry when he slid between her legs.

"Have mercy," Ben gasped, when she locked her ankles at the base of his spine.

With one simple stroke, all the emptiness and loneliness of January's life was gone.

"Make love to me, Ben."

"Oh, lady . . . I already am," he said softly, and began to move.

The rhythm of their bodies matched the rhythm of their hearts, keeping time to a song only lovers could hear. Over and over the beat continued, taking them further and further away from reality until, finally, it was January who fell first.

One moment she was lost in the mind-blowing pleasure of their lovemaking; in the next, it was as if she'd been slammed against a wall. The force of her climax made her lose her breath as she swiftly came undone. Before she could gather her senses, Ben cried out. One low, guttural groan that came from deep inside him shattered the silence in the room.

"Lord," Ben whispered, as he buried his face beneath the curve of her chin.

Then, once more, he took her in his arms and rolled, until this time they were lying side by side and face-to-face.

January felt disoriented and weightless. She clung to him in mute desperation, as if she would float away if he suddenly let go. Ben seemed to sense her panic and held her just that little bit tighter.

"January . . . honey, are you all right?"

She shuddered.

"I may never be all right again."

He sighed as he held her, but he knew what she meant. They were forever changed by what had just happened.

"But I'm not sorry," January added, as she combed

her fingers through his hair. "Never sorry."

"Me neither," Ben echoed.

Before they could say more, his cell phone rang.

"Well, hell," he muttered.

January sighed. "Reality surfaces."

He swiped a shaky hand across his face. As he reached for the phone, January rolled away, sat up, then quickly disappeared into the adjoining bathroom.

Ben had a brief glimpse of her shapely backside before the door closed between them. He glanced at the caller ID, recognized his partner's number, then swung his legs over the side of the bed and sat up before answering.

"Hey, Rick, what's up?" he asked.

Meeks frowned. He was still pissed that Ben had gone to the reporter's home alone.

"Where are you?" he asked.

Ben eyed the crumpled sheets and the clothes they'd shed in wild abandon.

"Uh . . . in traffic."

"Good. How far are you from the station?"

"Maybe thirty minutes. Why?"

"The heat's coming down from the mayor's office pretty hard. Captain has called a press conference for five o'clock. He wants everything we know on his desk within the next hour so he can prepare a statement."

"Yeah, okay," Ben said.

"So . . . ?"

"So what?" Ben asked.

136

Rick cursed beneath his breath.

"DeLena . . . did she give you anything valid?"

Ben stifled a groan, thinking about what she'd told him, and then what they'd done. She'd given him more than he'd ever expected. Trouble was, he didn't know what the hell he was going to do about it—or her.

"I'll tell you all about it when I get to the station."

"Yeah, all right," Meeks said. "Later."

"Yeah . . . later," Ben echoed, and reached for his clothes.

At that point January came out of the bathroom wearing a lightweight bathrobe and a smile. It faded slightly as she saw he was already dressing.

"Duty calls," Ben said.

"Of course," she said, and then came around the foot of the bed, took his slacks from the bedpost and handed them to him.

"Thanks," he said.

January shrugged. "No problem," she said softly. "I'll give you a little privacy."

But when she started to walk past him, Ben caught her by the wrist and pulled her to him.

"I don't want privacy, I want you," he growled, and then raked her lips with a hard, almost angry kiss.

January moaned, then kissed him back.

The moment was brief, but it did not lessen the passion that still simmered between them.

"It's not what you're thinking," Ben said. "This isn't some hit-and-run piece of ass . . . not for me it's not.

We might not have meant for this to happen, but by God, it has, and I don't want this to be a one-time thing."

"Me neither," January said.

He smiled. "As much as I regret it, I really have to go."

January nodded. What he'd said had gone a long way to untying the knot in the pit of her stomach.

"I understand," she said, and handed him his shirt.

"I'll call you," he answered, then pulled it on and began to button it.

As he did, he noticed that the third button down from the top was missing, and he seemed to remember yanking at the shirt hard enough earlier to send the button flying. A swift knot of longing came and went in his belly, but there was no time to follow up with a repeat session. He glanced at his watch, then skipped past the missing button and began to tuck his shirt into his slacks.

"Promise?" she asked.

Ben paused. "Promise that I'll call you? Count on it."

"I will."

Ben put on his jacket and then patted his pockets to make sure he wasn't leaving anything behind. But when January followed him through the apartment, then let him out the door, he had a feeling that he was leaving something very important behind—his heart.

January stood in the foyer for a few moments after he was gone, then reached for the dead bolt and gave it a turn. The click of tumblers punctuated his exit.

Meeks was at his desk when Ben got back to the precinct. When he saw Ben, he grabbed his coffee cup and stood up, nodding toward the break room.

Ben followed him there.

"What's up?" he asked.

"You," Meeks said.

Ben frowned. "What are you talking about?"

"Captain knows you were at DeLena's place."

All expression disappeared from Ben's face. He went from anger to guilt.

"And how did he know that? You're the only one I told."

A red flush spread up Rick's neck to his face.

"Captain asked where you were. . . . I told him you were at DeLena's following up a lead. So what? Was it supposed to be a secret?"

Ben didn't answer as he strode out of the break room.

"Hell, you never told me it was a secret," Rick said, as he hurried to catch up.

Ben kept walking, past his desk, past Rick's desk, all the way to the captain's office. He knocked once, then went inside, closing the door in Rick's face.

There was a knot in Rick Meeks's belly as he, too, knocked for permission to enter. When it was given, he entered with his shoulders hunched and his head down.

"Sit," Captain Borger said. He pointed to an empty

chair, then turned his attention back to Ben. "So you were at January DeLena's residence?"

"Yes."

"And you were there because . . . ?"

Ben never raised his voice, but his anger at the situation was evident.

"Just for the record, Captain, I resent the hell out of this formal interrogation. You're both acting as if I did something wrong."

Borger leaned forward. The expression on his face was cold and fixed.

"You can resent any damn thing you please, but meanwhile, I'm fielding crap from the mayor and every one of his minions while we scramble to figure out what the hell happened to Bart Scofield. So if you have any information, I want it."

"I'll tell you what DeLena told me, but it's not going to be anything you can take to the bank."

"What the hell are you talking about?" Borger asked.

Ben glanced at Rick, who was still looking down at the floor, then stared straight into the captain's face.

"I got a call from January DeLena during lunch today, although I suppose you already know that. She said she had some info that might pertain to Scofield's murder, but she wouldn't talk unless I came alone. This pissed off my loyal partner, but it couldn't be helped. I treated the information as I would treat any tip from an informant. I played her game as far as I thought prudent. I went alone."

Borger relaxed. "Look, North, I'm sorry I came down on you so hard. Just tell me what you know."

Ben wasn't as ready to play friendly with the two people who should have believed in him to begin with, so the tone of his voice remained cool.

"I got to Ms. DeLena's home around three. After she started talking, I quickly realized why she didn't want to make a formal statement to the police."

"Probably because she wanted to keep the story for the evening news," Rick muttered.

Ben didn't waste so much as a glance at Rick, but the look on Borger's face shut his partner up.

"So what's the scoop?" Borger asked.

"Ms. DeLena has been working on a story on her own for several months. It has to do with people who have died and then been brought back to life. Near-death experiences, that sort of thing. Anyway, during her research, she heard about some street preacher who calls himself the Sinner, who had a similar experience, only his claim was that he hadn't gone to heaven. He'd been in hell. You can imagine why she was looking for him."

"What does this have to do with Scofield's disappearance?" Borger asked.

"I'm getting to that," Ben said. "One day a few weeks ago, she said this guy called her at work. Told her to quit looking for him, that she was messing everything up. Then she said he called her again today and said the same thing. Only Ms. DeLena said that because of some things she'd learned between the first call and the one she received today, she had reason to believe that this street preacher might have been involved in Scofield's disappearance, so she asked him point-blank if he'd killed Bart Scofield."

"The hell you say!" Borger snapped, and sat straight up in his chair. "Then what?"

"After that, he hedged when she asked him again if he had anything to do with Scofield's death, but he said a real weird thing. He told her that Scofield was 'the wrong one.' After that, he clammed up." Then Ben glanced at Rick. "I was on my way back to fill my partner in on everything when he called to tell me about your news conference. I told him there wasn't anything you'd be able to use for the conference other than that we were following up on some new leads."

"I don't get it," Borger said. "What does she know that even made her think this guy might be responsible for Scofield's murder?"

Ben hesitated. He'd told January he wouldn't divulge any more than he had to, and the way he was feeling now, he wasn't in any mood to break his word.

"I don't know anything more than what I just told you. She doesn't know what the Sinner looks like, so we have no way of finding him to pick him up for questioning. She did say that if he called again, she would definitely let us know."

"We could get a court order and tap her line," Rick said.

"Which one?" Ben snapped. "He called her once at work and once at home. I can guarantee that television

142

station isn't going to go for a phone tap, and neither is DeLena—and we don't have enough to push the judge to issue an order for either place."

"Well, hell," Borger said, then opened a drawer and pulled out a bottle of antacids. He shook a handful into his palm, popped them in his mouth and began to chew.

"Look," Borger said. "Make this a priority. Get out on the streets and find this preacher who calls himself the Sinner, then bring him in for questioning."

"Yes, sir," Ben said, then added, "But not with Meeks."

Rick looked up.

"Now see here," he sputtered. "I didn't—"

Borger interrupted. "Look, North, Meeks didn't—"

"I'm not working with someone I can't trust," Ben said.

"You'll work with whoever I tell you to work with," Borger said.

Ben stood. "No, sir, I won't. So am I fired?"

Borger picked up the antacid bottle and threw it back in the desk, then slammed the drawer shut. He glared at both men.

"I don't need this shit," he yelled.

Ben silently stood his ground.

"Damn it, North, you and Meeks kiss and make up or—"

Ben took off his badge and gun and started to lay them on Borger's desk. When the captain realized how serious Ben was, he threw up his hands in defeat.

"Fine! Get your ass out there on the streets and find me a killer. You'll have no one but yourself to blame when you wind up in trouble with no backup."

"At least I won't have to wonder if it's my partner who's going to betray me." Even as he said it, he wondered how much of his anger was directed at Meeks and how much had to do with his own confused feelings for January DeLena.

Meeks was livid. He jumped to his feet and grabbed Ben's jacket.

"I didn't betray your ass. I just answered the captain's question. You have no right to—"

Ben grabbed Rick's wrist and yanked his hand away.

"Don't add lying to the mix. You were pissed off because I went to question DeLena without you. If it had been anyone else, you wouldn't have thought twice about it."

Rick paled. His shoulders slumped as Ben pushed him aside.

"She's a damn reporter," he muttered.

"If you're so sure that she's playing us, then tell me why she called? She didn't have to tell us anything to make her story."

"We've been partners for nine years," Rick mumbled.

"I know," Ben said quietly. "You're the one who forgot." With that, he walked out of the captain's office without looking back.

"Go home," Borger said to Meeks. "When you come in to work tomorrow, you'll be working with someone else."

"But, Captain, you know I didn't—"

"Take your lumps like a man, Meeks. Bottom line is, your partner doesn't trust you, so you need a new one."

"But, Captain . . ."

"Go home. Have a better attitude when you get in tomorrow. As for what happened here today, it stays between the three of us."

Rick was in shock when he left, wishing he could take back the last five hours of his life and live them over.

Ben was still furious when he got home that evening. He stomped through his town house without purpose, hurt and angry at everything that had transpired. His center of gravity had shifted, and it would take time to come to terms with what had happened in both his professional and personal life.

Today he'd lost a friend as well as a partner—and it was partly his own fault—but he'd gained something, as well. He didn't know where this newfound relationship with January DeLena was going, but he knew he wasn't willing to give it up.

Eight

Carpenter had just dropped off a fare when the pain hit, knotting muscles in a spasm that began at the base of his skull and ran the full length of his jaw and neck. He grabbed at his head as a gut-wrenching moan slid out from between his teeth.

The fare he'd let out was about to close the door when he witnessed Jay's attack.

"Mister . . . Mister, are you all right?"

Jay could hear someone talking, but answering was impossible. His tongue felt thick, and his jaws were locked. He moaned, then choked.

The fare yelled to the passersby, "Call 911! Something's wrong with the cab driver."

Jay grunted, wanting to tell him to shut up, that his voice hurt his head, but the only sounds that came out of his mouth were garbled. He'd had this pain before, but it had always abated quickly. This time it wasn't. This time the symptoms persisted. He couldn't help but fear that this was the end—that he'd failed to recreate heaven on earth before his second passing.

Then, finally, the pain eased. When he looked up, to his dismay, a group of people had gathered around his cab.

Oh no.

If they came and took him away to a hospital, he would die in there before his mission was finished. His words were slurred as he struggled to focus both thoughts and vision.

"Go 'way. Let me be."

"You can't leave like this. You're obviously ill. Let us help," the fare said, reaching through the window and grabbing Jay's arm.

"No help."

Jay yanked his arm away, put the cab in gear and pulled out from the curb without bothering to look behind him. Only the skill of the other drivers on the road kept him from causing a major collision.

Jay careened down the street, weaving between lanes with no regard for lights or cars. By the time the ambulance arrived, he was long gone.

For the rest of the night, every time Jay saw a cop car, he ducked into an alley or took the turn at the next block. The pain in his head had eased to a dull ache. Not for the first time, he longed for the comfort of his old apartment. A hot bath and a clean bed sounded like heaven, instead of the cot and the camping equipment at the warehouse.

But then he thought of Jesus, and the suffering He'd endured before He'd gone to be with His Father in heaven, and told himself to suck it up. He couldn't worry about his own misery. There were disciples yet to gather, others to be fed, and much to be done before he went home to glory.

He turned on the Off Duty sign, dug through his jacket pocket, and pulled out the day's receipts and counted them. Two hundred and forty-seven dollars. It wasn't the best haul he'd ever had, but it would hold him over for the next few days, which he intended to devote to finding the rest of his men. They were out there, just waiting for him to bring them home.

He drove until he came to a supermarket, parked

beneath a broken security light, then ducked his head as he went inside, making sure he dodged the security camera.

The persistent headache he was learning to live with prompted him to hasten his shopping. He bought the usual—canned meats, crackers, bottled water—but tonight, he added bananas as a change of pace. As he was moving toward the checkout lane, he thought of Matthew's deteriorating condition and tossed some basic first-aid items into the cart, as well. Matthew had already pulled out large clumps of his hair, and Jay feared he would get infections in the wounds. It sickened his heart to know how disturbed this Matthew was. If he'd only known, he would have chosen another.

He wouldn't let himself think about Bartholomew. The whole incident had been tragic from beginning to end, and he blamed himself for jumping to conclusions—for assuming that just because a man named Bart had gotten into his cab, he was the one God meant him to choose. From now on, he was gathering his people from the streets, as he'd intended. God had proclaimed, "The meek shall inherit the earth." Jay needed to remember that.

He paid for his groceries, then hurried outside. There was one more stop he wanted to make before he got home. He needed to make sure that God understood Bart's death had been an accident, and the best place for that kind of communication was in a house of the Lord.

Father Patrick had been a priest for thirty-seven years. He prided himself on knowing the names of all the regulars in his congregation. But the man lying prostrate on the floor down in front of the altar was a stranger to him.

He'd been watching him for the better part of ten minutes. During that time, the man had wept, begged, cursed and moaned, and had not uttered one syllable of a word Father Patrick understood. He hesitated to intrude, but the man seemed ill, possibly incapable of moving from where he lay. Because of that, he stepped out of the shadows and moved toward him.

"My son . . . are you ill?" Father Patrick asked.

Jay jumped as if he'd been shot. He rolled over onto his back, his eyes wide and fear-filled. Even after he recognized the man as a priest, he still didn't relax.

"Leave me alone," he muttered, and scrambled to his feet.

"I'm sorry," Father Patrick said. "I didn't intend to intrude. I thought you were in need of assistance."

Jay thoughts were scrambled. He was tired and sick—so sick—but he was afraid to trust. Still, the man *was* a servant of God. Who would better understand?

He glanced up at the priest again, then staggered to a pew and collapsed.

Father Patrick went to him, put an arm around Jay's shoulders, and held him as he would a child.

"Do you need medical assistance?" he asked.

Jay shook his head. "No, not like you mean. I'm dying, Father, and it's okay. I died once before. There's really nothing to it."

Father Patrick's heart went out to the man. His appearance was strange—foreign, even—yet his speech belied his dress.

"So you know the Lord, then?" Father Patrick asked.

Jay grimaced as his eyes filled with tears. His head was pounding again.

"The Lord? Not as I should, and I didn't meet Him first time around, but I'm hoping to up my odds this time."

Father Patrick frowned. "What are you saying, my son?"

"I've never been to heaven, but I have seen hell." In a voice so soft the priest had to lean down to hear it, he added, "And I heard the devil's voice."

Father Patrick flinched. He couldn't imagine what kind of a life this man must have lived to put himself in such a place, and even though he knew his own faith was enough to protect him on this earth, he still felt a sudden presence of evil.

"I'll pray with you, son," Father Patrick.

Jay staggered to his feet.

"Thank you, but I'd rather you prayed *for* me."

Father Patrick sighed as he, too, stood up.

"Of course. What is your name?"

"Just call me the Sinner. He'll know who I am."

With that, Jay walked away.

January was at her desk when her phone rang. She answered it absently, her thoughts still on the piece she was working on for the nightly news.

"Ms. DeLena?"

"Yes?"

"This is Sophia Harlow from Sheltering Arms. Remember we met during this past year's fund-raiser?"

"Yes, of course," January said. "I remember. How can I help you?"

The woman laughed. "That's just like you, and one of the reasons I'm calling. You're such a shining example to us all with your giving nature, and it's my pleasure to tell you that you've been chosen by the board of all three women's shelters in the tri-state area as Woman of the Year."

It was one of the few times in her life when January found herself speechless.

"You're kidding," she said finally.

Sophia laughed again. "No, I'm not. The presentation will be made during our annual fund-raiser, which is the Black and White Ball this coming Saturday. I realize this is late notice, but for some reason, it's tradition. The honoree is never notified before the week of the event, so who am I to thwart convention?"

"I don't know what to say," January said, and stifled the urge to giggle. "I'm honored."

151

"Great! An official notification was overnighted to you today, with all the information about the time and place. It should be at home waiting for you when you get there. Of course you're invited to bring a guest, whether a husband or significant other, or just a friend."

Without prompting, January found her thoughts turning to Ben. . . .

"Yes, well, thank you," she said.

"That's that, then," Sophia said. "We'll see you Saturday night, and again . . . congratulations."

"Thank you," January said. "Thank you so much."

One of the producers walked past her desk just as January disconnected.

"Who put that smile on your face?" she asked.

January giggled. "Just some good news."

"That's great," she said. "So how's the piece coming?"

"Almost ready," she said, called back to reality. "It'll be done within the next ten minutes."

"Great," the producer said, and strode away.

January made herself focus on finishing. When she was done, she hit Send and e-mailed the piece directly to her producer's computer.

With that out of the way, her mind turned to the real issue at hand: who to take to the award ceremony. Only one name appeared: Ben North. He probably wouldn't like it. No man she'd ever known liked the fluff and hustle of formal affairs and wearing a tux. But it was him or no one. She would rather go alone than take a friend or drag out her little black book. The last time she'd done that, she'd been stood up. Still, nothing ventured, nothing gained. The phone calls they had exchanged since making love had been a little awkward. All he could do was say no.

She reached for the phone and started to call him at work, then changed her mind. Instead, she flipped through her Rolodex, got his home phone number and dialed it. The luxury of calling his home was that she would be talking to an answering machine. As soon as it clicked on, she began to speak.

"Ben, it's January. I've just gotten a rather nice call from a charity organization I've worked with in the past, telling me that they're honoring me as Woman of the Year at their annual Black and White Ball on Saturday. They said I could bring a guest. I'm asking you. You have to wear a tux. I'll let you know time and place later. If you're going to weasel out of this invitation, just leave a message on my machine. That way you won't have to hear me wailing."

Smiling to herself, she hung up and started thinking about what to wear. A new gown was definitely in order.

After Jay's visit to the church, his physical condition had improved, which raised his confidence, as well. He'd made several visits to the Sisters of Mercy shelter and had a couple of hot meals. Like many of the others, he ate without looking up or interacting with those around him in any way. And before he left, he meandered into the clothing area, taking whatever they would let him have in the way of extra clothes and blankets. The days were still comfortable, but the nights could get chilly. He wanted to make sure that his disciples would be warm.

Mother Mary Theresa looked across the room at Jay. She'd been watching him recently, curious as to why he took different sizes of men's clothing and asked for more blankets than an individual normally received. Ever since January's last visit to the shelter, Mother Mary T. had been determined to help her own favorite helper get some answers, and this man fit the description of the street preacher she'd been hearing about. If January was right about someone kidnapping people off the streets, she wanted to help stop it. She wouldn't have admitted it, but she was getting something of a kick out of playing sleuth, and she made a promise to herself that she would speak to this man before he left.

Jay kept a low profile while listening to the chatter around him. Tonight he was changing the setup at the warehouse. He'd spent the last few days outfitting what had once been a huge blast furnace so that the disciples could be together. He'd decided the problems he'd been having with the men were coming from the fact that he'd isolated them from each other. In the Bible, he pictured the disciples sleeping, eating and doing their Master's work together. He didn't know what he'd been thinking by keeping them apart.

He smiled to himself as he drank the last of his

coffee. If things went as he planned, he would be adding two more disciples to the fold this very night. As he got up from the table to carry his paper plate and cup to the trash, he caught a glimpse of motion from the corner of his eye. He turned just in time to come face-to-face with an elderly nun.

"Good day," Mother Mary T. said. "It's good to have you here."

Jay nodded, as he reached down to pick up the garbage bag full of clothes and blankets.

But the little nun wasn't satisfied.

"I've seen you here before, haven't I?" she asked.

Jay nodded again and started toward the exit. The elderly nun was right behind him.

"My name is Mother Mary Theresa."

Jay didn't respond as she'd hoped by offering his name—not even a fake one. He just kept on walking.

She wasn't ready to give up easily, however. She stepped quickly, walking just far enough ahead of him so that Jay was forced to stop to keep from stepping on her.

"I've been told you also do God's work."

Jay frowned.

"I have to go now," he said, and tried to step around her. To his dismay, she just moved with him.

"Are you the man who calls himself the Sinner?"

Jay's heartbeat stuttered, but somehow he managed to keep his composure.

"Aren't we all sinners in the eyes of God?" he asked, and then pushed past her and hurried away.

Mother Mary T. was frustrated. She thumped a fist against the side of her leg. Although *Murder, She Wrote* was one of her favorite television oldies, she was definitely no Jessica Fletcher. With a jut to her chin, she followed his exit, only to find he'd gotten himself lost in the crowd outside the building. She was on her way back inside when a cab drove past. She glanced up and, to her surprise, saw the same man behind the wheel.

"Oh Lord," she muttered. "It *is* him. It has to be." She hurried inside to a phone to call January.

It was almost ten o'clock when Ben finally got home. Two hours to midnight, and he was just now going to have dinner. He had Chinese takeout in one hand and a handful of mail tucked under the other arm when he unlocked the door. He tossed his keys on the hall table as he passed, and dumped the mail and food on the kitchen counter before going to change.

A few minutes later he came back into the kitchen wearing a pair of gym shorts and an ancient T-shirt from a Grateful Dead concert. The carpet felt good against his bare feet as he carried his tray of takeout into the living room. He was reaching for the remote when he noticed that the red light on his answering machine was blinking. He took a big bite of egg foo yong and then punched the play button, quickly deleting a message from the cleaners, one from the pharmacy and one from the staff psychiatrist reminding him that he had yet to make his annual visit. With one message left to play, he dug into the cashew chicken with gusto, then nearly choked when he heard January's voice.

At first he smiled as he chewed. He felt an odd burst of pride as she mentioned the award she would be getting, which was quickly followed by a frown when he heard her mention the word "tux." He was already shaking his head when the shaky tone of her voice caught his attention. It was her mention that he could refuse the invitation by leaving a message on her machine that caused a big surge of guilt to replace his male reluctance for folderol.

"Well, hell," he muttered, then swallowed.

He stared at the light switch on the opposite wall, as if some magic sign would appear to tell him what to do. The last time he'd worn a tux had been at least ten years ago, at a friend's wedding. He didn't own one, which meant he was going to have to rent. Something told him that a rental tux at a fancy charity ball would be like wearing a sign on his back that read Lacking in Class.

He poked his chopsticks into the carton of fried rice, speared a tiny shrimp and popped it in his mouth as he ran through a mental list of excuses he could give her for not going. He thought about it all the way through an order of sweet-and-sour chicken, some beef-and-broccoli stir-fry, and two spring rolls slathered with hot mustard and duck sauce. He washed it all down with a bottle of Pepsi, then broke open his fortune cookie.

He read it, then groaned.

You will do something new with the love of your life.

"Well, hell," he said again.

He thought about it for less than two seconds, then reached for the phone book and flipped through the Yellow Pages. There were dozens of shops renting formal wear. He marked the three closest to where he lived, then marked the place in the phone book by leaving it open and turning it upside down.

He dumped the takeout boxes in the garbage and glanced at the time. It was fifteen minutes after midnight. Time enough to have a shower and get a few hours sleep before the alarm went off. Just before he stepped into the shower, he looked into the mirror, combed his fingers through his hair several times and decided he needed a haircut, as well.

It wasn't until later, when he was almost asleep, that it hit him. If he went to that damn ball with January DeLena, he would be expected to dance, and God help him, he'd been born with two left feet. He didn't know what rhythm meant, and he couldn't find the beat if someone was standing beside him and using the drumsticks on his head to mark it.

He sighed in defeat, then rolled over onto his belly and fell asleep, dreaming of dancing with January in front of all the people at the ball while his tuxedo fell apart at the seams.

Jay was almost delirious with excitement. The first four disciples were in their new surroundings. It hadn't been easy, either. Having to put sleeping pills in the water and then wait for them to take effect had been worrisome, but he'd gotten it done. And, during the last six hours, he'd picked up two more disciples.

He pulled into the warehouse and then lowered the door before unloading his last fare of the day—a free ride to a street hustler named James. This would be his second disciple named James, which was as it should be.

This James, who called himself Jimbo, was twenty-seven and a product of the state of Virginia's social services system. He had no family and few friends, and would never be missed. Jay was patting himself on the back for his choices as he pulled Jimbo out of the back of the cab and began dragging him toward the new common room he'd commandeered.

Tonight he was going to have the first Bible study with six of his precious disciples. Simon, Matthew, Andrew, James, John, and, with the newest disciple he was bringing home tonight, a second James. This was what had been missing. Even Matthew, who hadn't communicated directly with him since the day he'd found him, was quiet in the new room. Whether it was the fact that he was no longer alone or that he'd begun to trust Jay, Jay didn't care. Surely the turmoil was at an end, and he was going to devote whatever time it took to bring peace.

Johnny Marino didn't know how he'd wound up chained inside some big metal bin. The last thing he remembered was being in the alley behind Petrowski's Deli, minding his own business and digging through a trash bin for empty pop cans, when a cab had pulled into the alley. He had given the driver a cursory glance, then turned back to his digging, felt a sharp blow to the head, then everything went black. Now he had shackles around his wrists and was chained to a wall between a black man and a man who called himself Jim.

Tom Gerlich was sixty-three years old, but once he had been a promising young college athlete.

Then there was Vietnam.

After that, Tom Gerlich came back a burned-out, drugged-out facsimile of his former self, and he'd never recovered. He'd haunted the back streets and alleys of his native New Jersey without ever finding solace, and then they'd built the Vietnam Memorial in Washington, D.C. His initial visit had been meant only to honor his fallen comrades, but he'd found himself returning almost monthly until, finally, he stayed. For some reason, being close to those names was as close as he would ever come to truly being home.

So he, like countless other homeless vets, became a shadow in D.C., just as he'd been in New Jersey, living without making waves. He'd expected to die the same way—not locked up in this loony bin. He'd already tried to pull free of the wrist chains, cursed the man closest to him, and wondered how long he would be able to stay sane chained to this wall.

He'd recognized the man they called Matthew. He'd seen him on the streets before. Knew he was a vet. Knew he'd been a POW. He felt sorry as hell for the poor bastard. From the looks of him, PTSD had kicked in and led to some bad flashbacks. It made him all the more determined to stay alive—at least long enough to squeeze the life out of the crazy shit who had a thing for collecting losers.

Then the door opened. Everyone turned toward the sound. When they saw the cab driver they began to talk, some begging, some cursing. Then they realized he was dragging in another man, and the room went silent.

It was Tom Gerlich who broke the silence.

"What the fucking hell are you playing at?" he growled.

Jay frowned.

"Cursing is a tool of the devil," he said, and proceeded to fasten wrist and leg chains to his newest victim.

Matthew moaned.

The man named Simon cursed, then started to cry.

The huge black man, who called himself Andy, picked his nose and then wiped it on the wall near his head.

Johnny Marino was still confused as to what was actually happening, and had yet to shake the last of the drugs that had put him out.

The new victim was beginning to come around. His first glimpse of his new abode was looking at the backside of a half-naked black man. In a panic, he tried to get up. That was when he realized that he, like the other men standing against the wall, was chained to it.

"Hey! What's going on here?" he cried, then winced when the sound of his own voice shot a pain through his head that started in one ear and went straight to the other. "Oh! Oh, fuck," he moaned, and sat down on his butt and put his head in his hands.

But Gerlich hadn't survived four years in Vietnam without becoming tough as the old boots he wore. He'd survived a country of jungle crazies. It was going to take more than one kook to take him down.

"The devil, you say? Well, you oughta know," Tom yelled. "From the looks of this place, I'd say you two are on a first name basis."

Jay spun, shocked and angered that anyone could possibly believe that of him.

"Look around you! How could you say such an evil thing? How could you accuse me of such deceit? How could you doubt me? Don't you know? Don't any of you know what you are to me?" Then he moved to the center of the room and lifted his arms upward, as if he was beseeching the heavens. "Lord! Lord! Why have you forsaken me?"

In that moment, a slow knowing came to him. This was his Garden of Gethsemane. Thomas was doing nothing more than what he'd been meant to do, which was doubt. God was testing Jay's faith now by giving him disciples who doubted, just as Jesus had been tested by the devil all those centuries before.

Jay fell to his knees as the chained men stared at him. Even Matthew had stopped rocking in place and locked his gaze on the man in the middle of the room. When Jay suddenly threw himself forward, lying face down in the middle of the floor with his arms out-stretched, Matthew flinched.

But Jay was at peace. Here, with his helpers around him, he felt closer to God than he had since his mission had begun. With his nose pressed against the filthy metal and his twisted mind on heaven, he began to pray.

The men stared at him, aghast. What was coming out of his mouth made no sense. For the first time, those of them who were capable of rational thought began to realize they were the victims not of a psychopath but of a religious zealot—and a crazy one, at that.

Nine

January was late getting home, and too tired to do anything but clean up and go to bed. She was getting out of the shower when she realized her phone had been ringing, obviously for some time. She reached for a towel as the answering machine kicked on. She heard her voice, asking the caller to leave a message, then quickly realized her caller was Ben. Subconsciously, she clutched the towel in front of her as if he could see her, expecting to hear some half-assed excuse for why he couldn't go.

She was wrong.

"Hey, honey, I got your message. Congratulations big-time. That's quite an honor, and I'm touched that you want to share your big night with me. However . . ."

January wilted. "Here it comes," she muttered, and schooled herself not to cry.

". . . you need to know that I don't own a tux, so the one I'll be wearing will be rented. Black, as required, but it won't be custom-fitted, as I'm guessing the other men's will be." Then he chuckled. "And that's the good news. The bad news is that I can't dance worth shit. Just thought you should know. If these two issues are a problem for you, I'll understand. Otherwise, I expect a second call from you telling me when to pick you up."

January grinned, then sat down on the side of the bed and buried her face in the towel as his voice continued to cruise through her senses.

"Another warning. I'm also not getting you some dumb corsage, because the last time I tried that gesture was my junior-senior prom. I picked out a red, six-carnation corsage for my date that was the size of a football. Her dress was a bright canary-yellow, with this giant ruffle around the neck. She looked like Ronald McDonald. The damn thing—the corsage, that is—came apart in the middle of the Watusi. And since

I can't dance, my version of the Watusi looked more like the last throes of a dying crane. She didn't even let me kiss her good-night."

January fell backward onto the bed and laughed until she hurt. Oh, Lord, but she was falling in love with Ben North in a really big way.

"Anyway," Ben said, "call me with the time. You can leave a message on my machine, too. That way, if you decide you can't bear to risk my inadequacies, you won't hear *my* heart breaking with disappointment. Have a good day, honey . . . and congratulations again."

January was beside herself with joy. She was so excited about Ben's acceptance that she didn't notice that there was already a message on the machine. She ended up not hearing the message from Mother Mary Theresa until it was too late to return the call.

The next morning, her alarm failed to go off, making her late for work. It was almost noon before January remembered the call and they connected.

"Mother Mary T., it's me, January."

The little nun set aside the file she'd been working on and leaned back in her chair. The urge to kick back even farther and prop her feet on the desk was strong, but lack of restraint was one of her failings, and she'd been praying to do better.

"It's about time," Mother Mary T. said.

January frowned. The tone of the nun's voice seemed anxious.

"Is something wrong?" January asked.

"I don't know. . . . Maybe, maybe not. Are you still interested in finding that street preacher?"

Now she had all of January's attention. "Do you know where he is?"

"Not exactly."

January's hopes fell. "Then what?" she asked.

"I might know what he looks like."

January's heart skipped a beat. "Are you serious?"

"Nuns don't lie," Mother Mary T. said.

January grinned. "Is that a rule of the order?"

"It's God's rule. So what are we going to do about this?"

"I don't suppose you have a picture you'd like to share?"

"Sorry," Mother Mary T. said. "However, I do have a good memory. Bring one of those police sketch artists down here and you'll have your picture. I can't promise it's the man you're looking for, but if you can find him, you can do your own eliminating."

"Yes! Oh, Mother Mary T., you're fabulous."

The nun grinned. "Yes, well, not exactly fabulous. I don't think nuns can be fabulous, but I'll allow sharp and savvy. Yes. Sharp and savvy. That sounds about right."

January laughed. "Is there a good time for you?" she asked.

"Get here before I leave for chapel."

"And that would be?" January asked.

"Four o'clock."

"We can do tomorrow, if it's better for you," January added.

"Today is perfect. Before four. Be here."

"Yes, ma'am," January mumbled, as she began leafing through her Rolodex for Ben's work number.

The next thing she heard was a dial tone in her ear. She disconnected, got a free line, then made a call to Ben.

Ben was ignoring the pregnant silences and angry stares coming from Rick Meeks. He didn't have time for emotional turmoil and had no intention of feeding it, so when the phone rang, he answered quickly, thankful for the interruption.

"North."

"Hey, North, I need a favor."

He recognized January's voice immediately.

"Hello to you, too," he said.

She grinned. "Sorry. Hello."

"That's better," he said. "So, what's the favor?"

"I need to borrow the department sketch artist."

"Do I get to ask why?"

"It may be nothing. It might be something. But I have a witness who thinks she may have seen the Sinner."

The smile disappeared from Ben's face.

"The man you think may have killed Scofield?"

"Yes."

Rick Meeks had been eavesdropping on the conversation. When he heard what Ben said, he quit all pretense of working and leaned forward, staring intently as Ben continued to talk.

"And the sketch artist is going to draw the man she saw, right?"

"That's the plan."

"I'll fix it up with the captain," he said.

January hesitated. "Just make sure he understands that there are no promises on this. It's just a lead. And if it pans out that this man *is* the street preacher I've been looking for and you guys can find him and pick him up for questioning, then I still get to interview him."

"I'll mention that to the captain, too."

January frowned. "While you're at it, mention the fact that I'm the one who's been helping you guys. Captain what's-his-face doesn't get to start running the show."

"Borger. His name is Borger, and yes, he does get to say what's happening."

"Why?"

Ben sighed. He heard the anger in her voice, but there was nothing he could do about it, nor would he, even if he could.

"Because we're no longer looking for some guy to add something to your story. We're looking for a killer."

"I know, but—"

"No buts. We're trying to solve a murder. It's our sketch artist. Our rules."

"Fine."

"Fine," he echoed. "When do you want him?"

"Now."

"I don't know if I can make that work."

"Figure something out," January said. "It's my witness. My rules."

"I'll call you back in five."

"I'm at work. Call me here."

She hung up before he could say anything more. He dropped the phone back into the cradle and headed for the captain's office. To his disgust, Meeks was right behind him.

At the door, Ben paused before he knocked, and gave Rick a hard stare.

"What the hell are you playing at now?"

"You gotta get over this shit," Rick said. "I didn't mean to piss you off."

"That's a lie," Ben snapped.

Rick's face flushed. "Yeah, well, so it was a stupid move. That doesn't mean you gotta be mad at me forever."

"I'm not mad at you anymore. Just forget it, okay?"

Rick's expression lightened. "Look, North, here's the deal. I know I've been riding your coattails ever since we partnered up. I guess I panicked, thinking you were trying to dump me. I could have stonewalled the captain, so it's a joke on me that I caused what I feared most." Then he held out his hand. "No hard feelings?"

Ben stared, looking long and hard into his old partner's face. He'd known Rick had issues, but he'd never known he was part of them. It put what had happened in a new context.

"Damn it, Meeks, you've got more hangups than a dozen old maids. You're a good detective, but I'm no damned babysitter. If you can manage to get over yourself, we're square."

Meeks grinned self-consciously. "You serious?"

"Just don't make me sorry," Ben said.

"It's a deal, partner," Rick said, and held out his hand again.

Ben shook it. "That's enough of that," he said. "We have a killer to catch, and January's phone call might have given us a new lead."

"Yeah, I heard," Rick said. "Let's go clear it with the captain."

Ben knocked on Borger's door, then entered. Borger looked up, his eyes widening slightly when he saw the two men.

"So have you two kissed and made up?"

"In a manner of speaking," Ben said. "And we need a favor."

"Like what?" Borger asked.

Ben quickly relayed what January had asked for.

Borger reached for the phone.

"DeLena does not get access to the sketch," Borger said. "I don't want to see that face on the evening news and give him a chance to run."

"She knows," Ben said. "However, if we find him and pick him up, she asked for permission to interview him."

"I'm not making any promises," Borger said.

"That's what I told her," Ben said.

Borger nodded. "All right, then. Take Mitchell. I'll clear it for you. Bring me that sketch the minute it's done."

"Thanks, Captain. Will do."

They exited Borger's office.

"I've got to let January know we're coming," Ben said.

"She gonna be there?" Rick asked.

"It's her lead and her witness, Rick. What do you think?"

"I think it's good she's keeping us up to date."

Ben grinned. "Now you're getting the picture."

"Just asking," Rick muttered. "I gotta go take a leak. Wait for me."

Ben picked up the phone and called January back.

"It's a go, honey. Want us to pick you up?"

"No, I'm taking my own car."

"Okay, so where do we meet you?"

"You know that shelter the Sisters of Mercy run?"

"Yes."

"Meet me there and wait for me in the parking lot. I'll take you to the witness from there."

"Still holding on to a little control?"

"Never doubt it," January said. "Oh . . . and by the way, thanks for taking me up on the invitation. It's Saturday night at the Magnolia Country Club. Pick me up at my apartment at seven."

She hung up before he could say anything more,

although it didn't matter. He was going on a date with January DeLena. It was about time, considering they'd already made love.

"I'm ready," Meeks said.

Ben turned, saw that his partner was back, and nodded.

He unlocked the top drawer of his desk, took out his gun and slid it into the shoulder holster under his jacket.

"Then let's go," he said. "I'm driving."

Meeks shrugged. "Fine with me."

January was already in the parking lot when they arrived.

Rick whistled beneath his breath as he eyed her black slacks, red camisole and red jacket.

"Damn, she's one fine-looking woman," he said.

Ben frowned, although he didn't comment. She *was* a fine-looking woman, and she turned him on, big-time. He wasn't sure what he thought about the fact that she was turning on the rest of the male population, as well. Then he sighed. God, he had it bad. Even *he* knew that was a male chauvinist moment.

"Come on," he said, then looked over his shoulder to the man in the back seat.

"Hey, Mitchell, need us to carry anything?"

"No, I've got it," the sketch artist said, and got out carrying a small case.

Ben headed toward January, leaving the other two men to follow at their own speed.

"Hey," he said softly.

"Hey, yourself," she whispered, then turned on her game face. "Thank you for coming, Detective North."

"No, it's we who should be thanking you for sharing your information." The two other men joined them. "I believe you know my partner, Rick Meeks, and this is our sketch artist, Brady Mitchell."

January nodded. "Gentlemen, if you'll follow me. . . ."

She headed for the building with the three men right behind her. On entering, she made an immediate right. Seconds later, she was knocking on the office door and a female voice invited them to enter.

January led the way in, then stood aside as the three men stopped at the desk.

"Gentlemen, this is Mother Mary Theresa, head of the Sisters of Mercy shelter. Mother Mary T., this is Detective North, Detective Meeks, and sketch artist Brady Mitchell."

Religious training in the Catholic Church was nearly always an unforgettable experience. For two of the three men, it brought back feelings of panic. Ben had been raised Methodist. Other than a deep and abiding respect for his elders, he had no childhood memories to overcome. He stepped forward and held out his hand.

"Mother Mary Theresa, let me say in advance how appreciative we are that you've come forward."

The little nun didn't bother to hide a frown.

"I didn't come forward, as you put it, for anyone but January. She's been looking for a certain street preacher. I might have seen him." Then she looked at January as she pointed to the detectives. "What's all this about? I thought we were just going to be working with the artist."

January couldn't lie.

"There's a possibility that the street preacher I'm looking for could also be Bart Scofield's killer."

The nun was aghast. "You didn't tell me the man was dangerous."

"I'm not sure he is," January said. "And we won't know until he's picked up and interrogated. So may we proceed?"

Mother Mary T. glared at January. "We'll talk about this later," she said, then waved toward the men. "Sit. Let's get this over with."

Brady Mitchell opened his case and pulled out a large drawing pad and a couple of charcoal pencils. He shifted his chair behind the desk next to Mother Mary T.

"It will make it easier for us to work if you're watching as I draw," he said.

She agreed readily.

"Now," Brady said, "are we talking about a Caucasian or another ethnicity?"

"Caucasian," the little nun said.

"Shape of his face?"

"Sort of long . . . long and slender. And he had a high forehead and a slightly hooked nose."

Brady nodded as his pencil flew across the paper; then he paused.

174

"His eyes . . . ?"

"Large, very dark and large," she said, then added, "With eyelids that appear sleepy."

"Hooded?" Brady asked.

"I'm sorry?" the nun replied.

"His eyelids . . . did they appear hooded, maybe something like this?" he asked, as he refined his sketch.

"Yes, yes, like that," Mother Mary T. said.

"What about his mouth?" Brady asked.

The nun frowned. "I don't remember it much."

"Why not?" Brady asked.

Mother Mary T. slapped herself on the forehead.

"I'm such a dunce. It was because of his beard and mustache. That's why. And he had long hair. Sort of wavy."

"Like how? Like this . . . ?"

Mother Mary T. looked at the sketch, and then leaned back in shock and stared at a framed picture on the wall across from her desk.

"Like that," she said.

They looked up in unison, then followed the direction of her gaze.

January frowned. "He looked like Jesus Christ?"

Mother Mary T. nodded. "I just never thought about it until I saw Mr. Mitchell's sketch emerging. He even dressed similarly, like some Bedouin from the Sahara."

Rick Meeks snorted none too delicately. "So what you're suggesting is that we need to be looking for

Jesus Christ?" he said.

Ben glared at him.

Rick shrugged "What?"

Ben turned to the nun. "Are there any distinguishing marks that you might have forgotten to mention? Maybe a tattoo . . . a scar somewhere?"

"Nothing that I could see, although with all the clothes he had on, he could have been tattooed from stem to stern and I would never have seen it."

Brady put a few finishing touches to his sketch, then held it up.

"Is this as close as you can get?" he asked.

January gasped.

"What's wrong?" Ben asked.

"I've seen that man," she said.

"Where did you see him?" Ben asked.

The park where I run. And down in skid row. But she hedged her answer. "I can't remember, but I know I've seen him."

"Let me see," Rick said, and pushed his way to the front so he could get a better look. He stared intently at the drawing, then, like January, recognition dawned.

"Hey! I think I've seen him, too!"

"You're kidding, right?" Ben asked.

Rick frowned. "No, I'm not kidding. I've seen that face. On television, maybe."

January stepped back, trying a different perspective.

"That's my milieu," she said. "But I'm almost positive that's not where I saw him."

"If there's nothing else, I need to get back to the convent," Mother Mary T. said.

"Can I give you a ride?" January asked.

"No, I have the van," she stated.

"Thank you for your assistance," Ben said.

"You're welcome. Hope it helps." She straightened her robes, patted the crucifix that hung just above her breasts and took a set of car keys from a drawer.

"After you," she said, waiting until they'd all filed out of the office, then locking the door behind them. "January, my dear, stay in touch," she said, and waved goodbye as she hurried away.

"Now what?" January said.

Ben had the sketch. Rick and Brady were already out of the building and on their way to the car. He was trying to think of something to say that might prolong the moment with her.

"I'll get this back to Captain Borger and go from there."

"You'll keep me posted, won't you?" she asked.

"Yes."

January fidgeted with her purse and car keys, not wanting this conversation to end, but lost as to what else to say. Then it dawned on her.

"So you can't dance, huh?"

Ben grinned wryly. "Not worth a lick."

"I suppose, if you're not busy, you might find time to come over one night before Saturday and we could practice a little."

"Dancing?"

The grin on his face made her blush.

"Yes, dancing," she said. "You don't need to practice anything else."

This time it was Ben who was taken aback. He saw her eyes glitter, then watched her stifle a grin.

"If we weren't standing here in front of God and everybody, I'd kiss that smirk right off your face," he said.

"I do not smirk," she said, then laughed out loud.

"I'll call you," he promised.

"Tomorrow night?"

"Yes, tomorrow night."

"You could come for dinner."

"Are you going to cook?"

January sniffed. "You can't dance. I can't cook. But we *will* eat and we *shall* dance."

"Done," he said, and held out his hand.

January took it, shivering slightly as his fingers slowly closed around hers. Breath caught in the back of her throat when his thumb rotated slowly in the middle of her palm. It was the most seductive handshake she'd ever experienced. Embarrassed by what was running through her mind, January pulled her hand away and folded her arms across her chest.

"See you, then," she mumbled.

"You sure will," he promised, then left to catch up with Meeks and Mitchell.

January watched until they were in the car and driving away before she left the building. Even though Ben was out of sight, she still stumbled.

"Darn that man. He's going to make me crazy," she muttered; then she got in her car and returned to work.

Ten

Rick talked all the way back to the precinct. He couldn't let go of the fact that the drawing of their suspect reminded him of someone he'd either arrested, seen or interviewed.

The sketch artist stayed out of it, choosing to ride quietly in the back seat while Ben listened absently, his thoughts still on January.

"I know it's been recently," Rick said. "It's like trying to remember a name that's on the tip of your tongue. You know what I mean?"

"Yeah," Ben said.

"Maybe he was part of that bunch we pulled in for questioning about that dead drug pusher. Remember the one they pulled out of the Potomac with his shoes on the wrong feet?"

Ben stopped for a red light, then peeled a stick of gum and popped it in his mouth while Rick continued to ramble.

"Hey, Ben, remember that guy? You're the one who noticed the shoes."

"I remember the guy, and I remember the users we hauled in with him, and I don't remember anybody looking like Jesus."

Rick snorted in disgust. "Then where? *Where?*"

"It'll come to you. Ease up. You're trying too hard."

"God, this kind of stuff makes me nuts."

The light turned green.

As they drove through the intersection, Ben quickly realized he would have to take a detour. The next street up was blocked off. From where they were sitting, they could see water shooting a good eight feet up into the air.

Rick groaned. "Oh man, isn't there a street in this city that's not under construction?"

"They aren't fixing a street, they're fixing a water main break."

"Same dang thing," Rick muttered.

"It's no big deal, we'll swing past the IRS building and—"

Rick almost jumped out of the seat.

"That's it! Now I remember where I've seen that face. It was that film clip on the guy who wanted to throw the employees out of the IRS building. Remember? We were eating lunch at Jerry's Java, and they were showing the clip on the TV above the counter. The cops were hauling this religious nut down the steps. They showed a close-up of his face, and it just stuck in my mind, you know? He has to have some kind of arrest record. It should be easy enough to check out."

Ben frowned as he turned the corner. He did remember the incident, but unlike Rick, the man's face hadn't registered. He just remembered thinking the man was probably another street preacher.

The hair on the back of his neck suddenly crawled. Street preacher.

They were looking for a street preacher.

Lord have mercy, could it be that easy? Could they have stumbled onto the answer after all?

"I remember the piece, but I didn't focus on the face. Which station ran it, do you remember?"

Rick shook his head. "No."

"Not a problem," Ben said. "It will be easy enough to check out."

"I'll do it," Rick said.

Ben glanced at Rick and made a quick decision. His old partner was trying to redeem himself. It was time to let him.

"All right," Ben said. "I'll fill in the captain, then check the other departments to see who hauled him in. You make some calls and see if we can get a copy of that clip."

Rick smiled, pleased. "Will do," he said.

A few minutes later they arrived at the precinct. Brady Mitchell went one way, and the two homicide detectives went another.

Rick Meeks wasn't the only one bothered by the sketch Brady Mitchell had made. Ever since January had seen that face, she'd been racked with guilt for not telling the police where she'd seen him. She consoled herself with the fact that it wouldn't change anything about their investigation. Besides, she couldn't swear with complete certainty that it was the same man, although she knew in her heart that it was.

She finished the day in a mode that could only be called "low productivity" and left before anyone called her on it. She picked up some Italian takeout on her way home and arrived back at her apartment a few minutes before 8:00 p.m.

The moment she put her key in the door, the stress of the day began to fade. The click of the tumblers locking her in and the rest of the world out sent what was left of the stress into the shadows. She tossed her keys on the hall table as she made her way through the rooms, leaving her takeout in the kitchen as she moved toward the bedroom.

Within minutes, she'd changed from work clothes into a pair of sweats and an old T-shirt. It felt wonderful to be barefoot as she walked into the kitchen, anticipating the pasta primavera waiting for her on the counter. She dug through the cabinets, looking for the bottle of red wine someone had given her last year on Valentine's Day, then remembered she'd emptied that on Valentine's Day of this year to stifle the blue funk she'd fallen into over the fact that, at the age of thirty-one, she was still without a significant other.

A lack of wine with her meal wasn't enough to ruin the mood she was in. She was humming to herself as she snagged a Pepsi from the refrigerator and a plate from the cabinet. She dumped the pasta onto the plate, popped it into the microwave and gave it a minute to heat. It was just long enough for her to get a glass, drop in some ice and fill it to the brim with soda. She took her first sip from the glass while the fizz was still strong, relishing the tickle of bubbles at the tip of her nose. The microwave dinged, signaling that her food was ready. She laid a fork on the plate, picked up her glass and carried her meal to the living room.

The first bite was as good as she'd expected. She chewed and swallowed before she picked up the television remote. She was, by nature, a channel surfer. Part of it had to do with always checking out the competition, and part of it had to do with being easily bored.

She surfed as she ate—except for the green peas, which she left in a small pile at the edge of her plate.

She was on her way to the kitchen to clean up when the telephone rang. She set her dishes in the sink, then reached for the phone.

"Hello?"

"Hey, honey, it's me."

January was thankful that no one could see the silly grin on her face.

"Ben?"

She heard a slight snort of disgust.

"How many other men call you honey?" he muttered.

She burst out laughing.

The moment she started laughing, Ben knew he'd been had. Somehow it seemed more proper to stay pissed, at least for a few more seconds, but he loved the sound of her laugh.

"Okay, you got me," he said.

"I'm sorry," January said. "I just couldn't resist."

"Have you eaten?" he asked.

"Just finished. You?"

"About to start. I just wanted to catch you up on a couple of things."

"About the sketch?"

"Yes. Rick remembered where he'd seen the man."

"Really? Do we know who he is? Have you found him?"

Ben smiled. There was no doubting January's persistence.

"Yes, really. No, we don't know who he is, and no, we haven't found him—yet. However, there's a plus we didn't count on. He's already in the system."

"You mean he's a criminal?"

"Not in so many words, but he *has* been arrested for disturbing the peace."

"What's his name?" she asked.

"That's a small issue we have yet to solve. The only name he gave the cops was Sinner."

"Oh, Ben, it's him. It has to be him. There can't be two men calling themselves the same thing." January shivered. Finally they were on to something.

"I don't suppose you have any address or next of kin?"

"Nothing like that."

She sighed. "Where had Rick seen him? Had he arrested him? Maybe if we—"

"As it turns out, your Sinner was on the news a

184

while back. They removed him from the steps of the IRS building. Seems he was preaching some stuff about kicking the employees out of the building."

"The employees? What do they have to do with anything?" she asked.

"Who knows?" Ben said.

January frowned. "It has to mean something. Everything else he's done seems to be some crazy attempt to copy the life that Christ lived. So . . . the IRS has to do with money and—oh! That's it! The money changers. Remember in the Bible when Jesus went into the temple and threw out the money changers? It's the same skewed reasoning he's used on everything else he's done."

Ben was amazed at the way her mind worked.

"You know something, lady? That sounds just wacky enough to make sense, at least from this guy's point of view. Money changers? Yeah, that would fit. But it still doesn't explain why he killed Bart Scofield. If he's trying to recreate the life of Jesus, that doesn't fly."

"Think of it this way," January said. "For whatever reason, he believes he has to take each step the Bible says Jesus Christ took. He told me that Scofield was the wrong one. That doesn't mean he won't get himself another Bartholomew. And there's one other thing I didn't tell you, because I have no way of knowing he was involved. Still, it fits."

"What?" Ben asked.

January hesitated. All of this was so far-fetched that

it sounded crazy to say any of it aloud, but there was no denying the facts as she knew them.

"You remember the Vietnam War vet who was beheaded?"

"All too vividly," Ben said.

"You remember his name?"

"Yes, Jean Baptiste, but what does—?"

"Say his name in English," she said.

"What . . . you mean John Baptist? What does . . . oh shit. John the Baptist?"

"Yes," she said.

"I feel sick," Ben muttered.

January knew what he meant. She'd gone through the same disbelief months ago when the pattern had begun to emerge.

"You've got to find him," January said.

"No kidding. But at least now we know where you and Meeks saw him," Ben said.

"Oh . . . no, that's not my memory of him. Not at all. I don't know where I was when that piece aired, but I'm completely unaware of it," January said.

Ben frowned. "Really? Well, let me know if you remember anything. It might be the key to finding him."

Another wave of guilt dug at her conscience. The fact that she'd seen him on the street in the rain and in a park early one morning told them nothing. She wasn't willing to admit he might be stalking her, for fear the police would do something that might send him into hiding. Also, if the cops thought she was in danger, they might limit her freedom to come and go to the point that she couldn't do her job. For now, what little else she knew she would keep to herself.

"Yes, I will let you know if I remember. Oh, another thing. What's your captain going to do with the sketch? Is he going to put it out in the papers?"

"No. We have copies all over the precinct, but we don't want this head case to run. If he gets wind that we're onto him, we might never find him."

"Of course," January said. "I wasn't thinking. I just . . ." She sighed. "I have this really bad feeling that we haven't seen the last of him."

"I know. So I'll see you tomorrow night?"

"Absolutely," January said.

"Do I need to bring music to dance to?"

She grinned. "You listen to music?"

"Just because I can't dance doesn't mean I can't sing."

"You sing?" she asked.

"No."

She laughed again. This time louder. This time longer.

He loved the sound of her laugh, and he wasn't sure, but he might be falling in love with *her,* too.

January woke early to take a morning run through the park before going to work. After all the pasta she'd had last night, she needed at least a two-mile run—maybe longer, if she had the time. She thought about the possibility of running into the Sinner again, then shrugged it off.

She washed her face, brushed her teeth and put her hair up in a ponytail. The weatherman had predicted rain, but from the looks of the sky, she figured she had plenty of time for her workout before the weather changed.

She chose a pair of lightweight sweatpants, a sports bra topped by a sleeveless tee, and her most comfortable pair of running shoes, pocketed her house key and headed out the door.

As always, she paused at the curb, checked the traffic both ways, then crossed the street and started to jog. When she reached the intersection, she turned right. Within a few moments, she was out of sight of her apartment building and on her way to the park.

The sun was just coming up, painting the eastern sky a light shade of pale yellow, trimmed in darker shades of blue. Probably the weather change the weatherman had predicted. She glanced at her wristwatch, timing her run so as not to be late for work, then jogged across one more intersection before she moved into the park.

The air smelled damp. Moisture that had collected on the leaves overnight was dripping onto the sidewalk beneath her feet, making the surface a little bit slick. She adjusted her stride accordingly.

A pair of squirrels scampered from beneath a bench and up the nearest tree, scolding her as she jogged past. A half-dozen pigeons that had been perched on a statue took flight, as well, while a few others continued to feed on day-old popcorn they'd discovered beneath some shrubs.

January saw them, but her thoughts were focused on the upcoming day and, even more importantly, on the date she had that night with Ben North.

She saw a pair of men jogging in the distance, and a policeman on horseback riding parallel to her own route. His presence made her feel safer.

As soon as the thought went through her mind, she felt off-kilter. She hadn't known she was uneasy until the thought of feeling safer surfaced. She reminded herself that it was broad daylight. There was no reason to assume she wasn't safe.

She glanced again at her watch, then continued to follow the path that took her back to her apartment.

Sweat was running down the middle of her back now. The muscles in her legs were burning, and there was a stitch in her side—a reminder that she was definitely out of shape and needed to run more often.

Less than a hundred yards from the exit, a park employee stepped out from behind some trees and almost ran into her. He dropped the hedge clippers he was carrying as he grabbed her to keep her upright.

"Oh, I'm so sorry, miss," he said quickly. "I didn't see you coming. Are you all right?"

January was shaking.

"Yes, I'm fine. I didn't see you, either."

"Well, if you're sure you're okay, I'll be on my way," he said.

"Yes . . . sure . . . I'm okay."

He picked up his clippers and hurried on down the path, leaving in his wake a thought that made the skin at the back of her neck crawl. The Sinner had been watching her. In the park, on the streets, even at the homeless shelter. He'd as much as told her he'd seen her there talking to Mother Mary Theresa.

January turned abruptly, assuring herself that the park worker was moving away, then did a slow three-sixty, making sure there was no one else hiding in the bushes, waiting to grab her when she wasn't looking.

She shoved a shaky hand up to her forehead and smoothed a few straggling hairs away from her face, then took a deep breath. Nothing she could see led her to believe she should be concerned. She began to move toward home, telling herself it was fine. But the longer she walked, the more certain she became that she was being watched. She was less than five minutes from her apartment when she began to run, and she didn't slow down until she'd locked her front door behind her.

She still didn't know whether to keep quiet about what she knew, or tell Ben, as she'd promised. One thing was for sure, when he found out, there was every possibility that he would come to the same conclusion she had.

The street preacher—the Sinner, the man who believed he was Jesus—was stalking her.

But why?

She moved to her bedroom, then stopped in front of the mirror.

Her features were marked by her Latino heritage—something she'd always been proud of. Her dark hair and eyes were almost black, like her father's. But her full lips and straight nose came from her mother, as did her laugh. She'd always been proud of herself for overcoming a lot of obstacles related to her sex and her ethnicity. But right now she was wishing with all there was in her that she was some ordinary Caucasian with blond hair and blue eyes and a name like Susie Smith. Only a few people in the business knew her real name, but if the Sinner was one of them, she was in big trouble.

With an angry jerk, she turned away from the mirror, stripping off her clothes as she went. She showered quickly, dressed for the office and headed for the door. Halfway across the living room, she stopped. Her hands were shaking, her fingers curled into fists. She stood for a few long moments, then turned around and went back into her bedroom and opened her closet. She took down a lock box, got the key from the inside the toe of one of her winter boots, then opened up the box.

The gun inside was a semiautomatic, pewter-gray with a full clip lying beside it. She picked up both, loaded the gun, dropped it into her shoulder purse and put the box back on the shelf. It had been at least a year since she'd fired it, but she hadn't forgotten how. If she had to, she would use it.

The added weight of her purse was a comfort as she left her apartment and started down the stairs. Suddenly she stopped, remembering something a cop had once told her about a murder victim. It had to do with predictability. The cop had told her that if the man hadn't been such a creature of habit, his enemies wouldn't have known how to get to him so easily.

She retraced her steps and rode the elevator down instead. If it meant taking a different way to work each day, she was willing. She would do anything it took to stay alive.

As for telling Ben that she, too, remembered where she'd seen the man, she would think about it today and probably tell him tonight.

Probably.

Jay had been sitting in his cab in the alley behind January's apartment when she'd come running from the park. He'd seen her looking over her shoulder before she'd gone into the building. She acted as if she was afraid. He didn't like the thought of her being afraid. He thought about calling her at work today, just to hear her voice, then changed his mind. His obsession with her seemed out of sequence with what he was trying to accomplish, but he was drawn to her and didn't know why. His second chance for redemption was growing shorter by the day, and he had much to do before he felt ready.

As soon as January was safely inside, Jay pulled out of the alley and drove away. A few blocks later, he turned down a busy street and went to work. There was money to be made and more disciples to bring home to the fold.

Eleven

It began to rain just after sunrise. The sound was deafening on the warehouse roof. Every time it thundered, Matthew grabbed handfuls of his hair and wailed.

Simon Peters sat with his back to the wall as if in a coma. His pants were urine stained, and the smell of feces was so strong within the chamber that men less hardened than these would have been unable to breathe without gagging.

For once, Andy wasn't happy. Not even the act of playing with himself could alleviate his fear. Thunder rattled what windows were left in the outer shell of the warehouse. Even the rats seemed uneasy about the storm and moved about without caution, seeking better shelter than what they had.

Tom Gerlich was holding on to sanity by nothing but willpower. His army surplus clothing had been ragged to start with, but he'd been semi-clean. Now he reeked like a soldier who'd been weeks in the jungle without a bath or a change of clothes. Being chained with these men was too reminiscent of being caged with his fellow soldiers in a Vietnamese prison camp.

The man who called himself Jimbo appeared to be in shock. He kept staring at the others as someone might stare at animals in a zoo. It was almost as if he couldn't believe that he was there.

And then there was John. He hadn't stopped cursing since he'd come to and discovered he was chained to the wall.

Tom watched the door intently, waiting for their captor to come back. He knew the man was crazy, but was hoping he could find a chink in the man's insane reasoning that could give them an edge. If they only knew why they'd been brought here, it might help him find a way to get them out.

It thundered again, this time so loud it made Tom's ears ring. He winced, cursing softly beneath his breath at the panic that swept through him. It had been years since he'd felt this helpless, and he hated it.

Then he looked up.

The cab driver was standing in the doorway.

"Good morning, my children," Jay said.

Tom could see the man's mouth moving, but because of the noise from the storm, couldn't hear whatever he said next.

"Why are we here?" Tom shouted.

Jay ignored him, choosing instead to put small sacks of food and water near each man while taking care not to get too close.

Jim grabbed the sack of food and water, but also hit Jay with a request.

"Hey, man, I don't know what you're playin' at here, but I gotta use the facilities."

Jim could have been mute for all the good it did. The cab driver didn't even look at him.

John Marino was twenty-six years old. He'd been on

194

his own for more than ten years and prided himself on being a survivor, but this was beyond anything he'd ever experienced. He didn't know what was going to happen, but it couldn't be good. The nutcase who'd done this was walking around dressed up in costume. And what was his deal? He wanted them to eat but didn't care if they shit their pants?

"Yeah, so do I," John said.

"We must suffer in small ways to do good in other ways," Jay said.

Tom Gerlich slapped the wall so hard that the furnace vibrated.

"We? *We?* Where the fuck do you get 'we' from? You're not chained up like some animal, sleeping in your own shit, and wondering when someone might decide to show up and kill you."

Jay turned on the man, pointing angrily.

"Again you doubt me, Thomas. And again I tell you that I am about doing my Father's work."

"Your father? Who was he, the Marquis de Sade?"

"You do not belittle the name of God Almighty!" Jay screamed.

Gerlich stared.

"You're serious? You actually believe that you're the Son of God?"

If Jay had had anything to throw, he would have thrown it, straight at his doubting Thomas's face.

"I never said I was His son. I never said that, and you can't make me say it! You're bad. You're bad. Maybe I made a mistake with you like I made a mistake with Bart. Maybe I need to replace you, too!"

Simon stood up and yanked at his chains. "Replace all of us!"

"Yes!" others shouted. "Replace us, too."

Lightning cracked somewhere nearby, followed by one long continuous roll of thunder. It passed, leaving Jay shaking with rage. Before he could speak, a pain so sharp that his head felt sliced in two pierced his right eye. He grabbed at his face as he dropped to his knees.

"Shut up! Shut up!" he screamed. "This is your fault. It's all your fault!"

"Replace me," Tom kept shouting, as he yanked and rattled his chains. "Let me go! Let me go, too!"

Jay staggered to his feet with the heel of his hand pressed hard into his eye.

"I didn't let him go, you stupid bastard! He's dead! He's dead! He was the wrong one! Are you the wrong one, too? Are you, Thomas? Are you the wrong one, too?"

Gerlich shuddered. He'd opened a can of worms that he didn't know how to contain. But before he could say anything, the big black man began to cry.

"Andy's scared," he whimpered, and cupped his hands over his ears. "The sky is loud. I don't like loud."

Jay shuddered as the pain began to subside.

"Neither do I," he said. "Neither do I. Please, you don't understand. I need you. I need all of you to make this work."

Simon Peters had been one of the first to be kidnapped. He had no home, no friends and no money. He, more than anyone there, wanted to understand why he'd been taken.

"Why?" he asked. "Why us? Help us understand."

Jay shoved his hands through his hair, then twisted his fingers in the long locks and pulled. In a sick way, the pain in his scalp alleviated the pain inside his head. He was tired—so tired. Tired of trying to make amends. Tired of trying to make sense of things that were all mixed up in his head.

Finally he straightened, combed his fingers through his hair and beard in an effort to maintain some control, and then lifted his chin. His words rang out in strong, sonorous tones.

"I'm dying."

Simon Peters rattled the chains on his ankles.

"So the fuck what? Are you planning on taking us with you?"

Jay spun, facing Simon angrily. "No. No. The first time I died, I went to hell. I'm trying to make amends. Can't you see? Don't you understand? Why doesn't anybody understand? I'm trying to live like Jesus. I'm trying to live the perfect life."

Simon was dumbfounded. "By kidnapping? By killing?"

Jay started to shout, but the sound came out like a scream. "Why, Lord, why? Why can't they understand?"

He began waving his hands above his head as if he

were batting away flying missiles. Spittle was running from the corner of his mouth, and his eyes wouldn't focus.

Then suddenly he stopped and his body stilled, his hands high above his head. For a few moments he didn't speak; then he turned his palms up to the heavens.

"By living as He lived . . . with His disciples, preaching to the masses. I will be saved. *I will be saved.*"

Tom Gerlich shuddered, then swallowed around a knot in his throat. *Disciples? He's gathering disciples?* Then it hit him. He stared at the other men chained to the inside of the blast furnace and thought about their names. There was his fellow vet, Matthew. And his own name was Thomas, of course. And the others. The horror of what he was thinking was too incredible to be true.

"You." He pointed to Simon. "You're Simon."

"Simon Peters."

Tom groaned in fear and went on reciting the other men's names.

"Andy."

"John."

"James."

"Jimbo—James, too."

His eyes narrowed as he spoke the names aloud, more to himself than to them. "Simon whom He also called Peter, Andrew, John, James, Matthew, a second James, and Thomas." Seven of the twelve disciples.

Then he amended the count. At one time there had been eight. Bart. Bartholomew. Only he'd been the wrong one.

Tom felt sick to his stomach. "Okay, men, there's a lesson in here for all of us. We are well and truly fucked."

It was raining when Ben got to January's apartment. Despite what she'd said, he brought his favorite CD and a dozen brownies from his neighborhood bakery.

He knocked, then sniffed appreciatively as the scent of something warm and spicy wafted out into the hall. Before he could identify the smell, the door opened.

She was wearing gray slacks and a silky blue off-the-shoulders blouse. Her hair was hanging loose around her face and neck, and her arms and feet were bare. Ben stifled a groan.

"You look beautiful," he said softly.

"And hello to you, too," January said. "I hope you brought your appetite. I got carried away with the food."

"I brought Willie Nelson and a dozen brownies. Will that suffice?"

January grinned. "Yes, and oh, yes," she said, then took him by the hand and pulled him inside.

She locked the door as he handed her the brownies, then pulled off his jacket. She started to hang it in the coat closet when he stopped her.

"Wait. Don't forget Willie," he said, and slipped the CD out of the pocket.

199

She hung up the coat and then laid the CD near the stereo, beside some others she'd chosen.

"Something sure smells good," he said.

"The best Mexican food this side of Tijuana," she said.

He didn't bother to hide his surprise and delight.

"Mexican! Lady, you are a witch for sure. It's my favorite food."

January smiled. "Mine, too."

He sniffed again, this time identifying some of the aromas.

"I'm smelling warm tortillas and fajitas. What kind?"

"Beef and chicken. I also have quesadillas, chips and salsa and a pitcher of margaritas."

"You must have cooked all day."

"Tia's Taco Tavern did. I don't cook, remember?"

He grinned. "And I don't dance, so let's eat. At least we know we can do that right."

"You pour us a couple of margaritas while I set out the food. The glasses are chilling in the freezer."

He took a chip and dunked it into the bowl of salsa sitting on the dining table, then popped it into his mouth before he got the glasses from the freezer. With a careful hand, he filled them to within an inch of their salty brims, then carried them to the table.

January had transferred the food from the takeout containers to bowls and platters, and set the table with her favorite yellow stoneware.

Ben eyed the spread, appreciating the ambiance

she'd created. "Honey, you might not cook, but you dish up just fine."

January beamed. "I hope you're hungry," she said.

"For you . . . always."

January's smile slipped. The look in his eyes was hotter than the spicy food on the table. She wasn't sure how to respond.

He grinned, then winked and eased the moment by pulling out her chair.

She sat, shivering slightly as he leaned down and kissed the bare skin behind her ear before sitting across from her.

Without missing a beat, he took another chip and dunked it in the bowl of salsa between them.

"Open wide," he said, and popped it in her mouth.

She rolled her eyes as she chewed.

"Good old Tia," Ben said, and grabbed one for himself.

And so it began. The time went as fast as the food that had been on the table. Before Ben knew it, January was pouring coffee and bringing brownies to the table.

"I'm so full I shouldn't be eating this," she said, as she took a big bite of one of the brownies he'd brought.

"We'll dance it off," Ben said.

"Ah yes, the dance lesson," January said, as she licked the chocolate off her fingers. "I need to put on some shoes."

"You have any combat boots?" Ben asked.

"You can't be that bad," she said.

"Yeah, well, we'll see what you say about that later."

"Are you finished?" she asked, rising.

He wiggled his eyebrows and blasted her with a dark, pretend leer.

"With you . . . never."

This time, she laughed.

"You know something, Detective? You could be dangerous." Then her expression changed. "Speaking of dangerous, have you had any luck finding our man?"

"The street preacher? Unfortunately no. But the whole department is on it. Street cops, vice, homicide . . . they're all carrying pictures. We took Brady Mitchell's sketch and compared it to the man in the film clip. It's the same guy, all right. We made copies of his close-up and distributed it with the sketch, as well. If he's spotted, there will be no mistaking him."

January fidgeted, telling herself that it couldn't matter if they knew she remembered where she'd seen him. If they were looking, they were looking everywhere. Still, she thought she would ask.

"You're covering the parks, right? A lot of the homeless roam the parks, especially during the summer months. It's a lot cooler there, you know."

"It's all covered, trust me."

"Good," she said. "Let's dance."

The sudden change of subject should have been a warning sign, but Ben was too interested in getting

January in his arms to notice.

"As soon as I help you clean up, I'm all yours," he said.

It didn't take long to pack away the leftovers and load the dishwasher, and all the while, January thought about the secret she was keeping. It seemed stupid, even childish. The Sinner was obviously dangerous, but instinct led her to believe that if she told Ben North, he would put a stop to her detective work, and that would impact her own credibility as a journalist.

She couldn't be controlled by her own fear or someone else's rules when it meant getting the story. So she kept quiet, promised herself that she would tell him if things changed and she believed that it would matter, and finished the dishes, then went to put on some shoes.

"Remember those boots," he called, as she disappeared down the hall to her bedroom.

"Have faith," she countered, as she stepped into some flat-heeled shoes and then glanced in the mirror.

The dark-eyed, dark-haired woman looking back at her seemed calm and assured. January knew that was a lie. She was so nervous she was shaking. But it wasn't the dance lessons that were bothering her, it was what would come after. They would make love. She wanted it and, at the same time, she feared it. She didn't want to get hurt, but she wanted Ben North badly enough to take the risks.

"Here I come, ready or not," she called.

Music was already playing. It was honky-tonk. She rolled her eyes.

"You've got to be kidding," she said, as she entered the room.

"What?" Ben asked.

"Black-and-white ball, tuxedos, ball gowns, gold, diamonds, enough hair spray to stop a hurricane, and you want to practice dancing to that?"

"Well . . . I just . . ."

She ejected the CD and pointed to the middle of the room.

"Go stand there, please."

He did as she asked, and when the strains of what he called elevator music filled the room, he grimaced. A tuxedo *and* dancing to this music? He had to be crazy.

Then he looked at the woman coming toward him and sighed. He was crazy all right—falling crazy in love.

She walked into his arms, put one hand in his and her other hand on his shoulder.

"It's a waltz," January said.

When they didn't move, she arched an eyebrow.

"You're the man, which means you're leading, remember?"

Sweat beaded suddenly across Ben's forehead.

"Well, hell," he muttered. "Don't say I didn't warn you. Here goes nothing."

He stepped off with his left foot, ran his knee into her thigh, and caught the edge of the little toe on her right foot with his other shoe. It wasn't a true stomp. He only slid into her. Still, the pressure was strong enough to make January wince.

"Oh God, I'm sorry," he said, then added, "I warned you."

"It's fine. I'm fine. We'll start over, and this time, lead with your right foot. Like this. One, two, three . . . one, two, three . . . one, two, three."

Ben stepped off with his right, slid into the second count with his left and tried to turn her on the third count. He slammed her into the wall. There was a long moment of silence as he gazed at her in horror, waiting for whatever came next.

January looked somewhat startled, then shook her head, as if to reposition her brain.

"No harm done," she said, and stepped back into proper form. "We'll try that again. Remember . . . begin with the right foot and then—"

In two steps he dragged her past the sofa toward the foyer and was working toward a dip when January's fingers dug into his shoulder. Instinct told him he'd done something wrong. Good sense told him he needed to stop and ask what, but he was in dip mode, and it was too late to stop.

"Oh Lord," January muttered, as he bent her over backward. Her hair caught on the coatrack on the way down and dragged it halfway across the hall on the way up. It came free just as Ben realized what had happened, but before he could stop, it came loose and fell onto the floor with a loud thump. The look on his face was somewhere between horrified and mortified.

"I'm sorry. Are you all right?"

January didn't know whether to laugh or cry. Her head hurt where her hair had been pulled, and she could no longer feel the toes of her left foot. However, the look on Ben's face told her that he was the one suffering most.

"I'm fine, and you know what? We're going to try this a different way."

"Gladly," he said.

"First, take off your shoes."

"Yeah . . . right," he said.

"I'm going to change the music."

"It won't get any better," he warned her.

"It has to," she said. "It can't get any worse. Besides, you have rhythm. I can attest to that, because we've made love and it rocked my world. Anyone who's as good in bed as you are has to have rhythm in his feet, as well."

He didn't know whether to be pissed off or proud, but he decided to reserve judgment as he took off his shoes.

In a moment the waltz was gone and the familiar strains of Willie Nelson's whiskey voice filled the room.

"You were always on my mind," Ben said.

January turned around. "Really? Why didn't you ever say anything?" she asked.

"No . . . I mean, yes, you were, but that's not what I meant."

Now January was the one who was embarrassed.

"Look, mister, just what are you playing at?" she snapped.

He pointed to the CD player.

"The song—that's the name of it. 'Always on my mind.'"

January's face turned red. "Oh."

Ben stifled a groan. Now he'd done it. Not only had he physically abused her from head to toe, he'd managed to humiliate her, as well.

"Maybe this wasn't such a good idea," he said. "I'm just no good at—"

"Oh, for Pete's sake, stop talking," she muttered. January kicked off her shoes and walked into his arms. "Hug me," she said.

"Now you're talking," he said. "This I can do."

When his arms slid around her waist and his hands locked, she did the same to him. Then she turned her head, resting her cheek near the place where his heart beat loudest.

"Close your eyes," she said.

"Honey, I'd much rather see you when we—"

"Benjamin, shut up. We're not about to have sex."

"Then what—?"

"Please! Do as I ask."

This time he was the one rolling his eyes.

"This is on your head, or feet, as the case may be," he mumbled.

"Close your damn eyes!"

He shut his eyes.

207

"Now quit thinking about me and just listen to the music."

"Without moving?"

January gritted her teeth. "Yes, without moving."

He stood still.

And heard her breathing.

And felt her palms growing damp against his lower back.

She was shaking, but by God, she was still with him. It wasn't the first time he'd made a mess of dancing with a woman, but it was certainly the first time that one had come back for more.

"Do you hear it?" she asked.

"Yes," he said, and ran his fingers through her hair without knowing what the hell she was talking about.

"Do you feel it?" she asked.

"Lord, yes," he said, and ground his hips against her belly.

January pulled back and thumped his chest with her fist.

"Not that! The music . . . the beat . . . the rhythm. For God's sake, quit thinking about sex."

"It's not my fault you turn me on," he said, and ran his forefinger from her chin to the hollow at the base of her throat.

January blinked. "I do?"

"Yes."

"Well then, good and, uh . . . thank you."

He grinned. "Don't mention it."

January sighed. "Please, can we try this one more

time without you feeling me up quite so much?"

Ben frowned. "This is harder than I thought it would be."

"Anything worth doing is worth doing well," she said.

He put his arms back around her waist, waited until she slid her arms around his, and then closed his eyes.

And Willie Nelson finally pulled him under.

January was swaying where she stood, marking her motion to the rhythm of the song. Ben never knew when he started swaying with her, but before long she'd begun shifting from one foot to the other—moving in place.

He followed suit. It wasn't hard. Just a matter of picking up one foot and putting it back down. He began to realize that the words of the song were forming a pattern, as were the percussion, the melody. Could it be this simple, after all—matching the motion of his body to the motion in the music?

"Ha!" he crowed.

January jumped.

"You scared me half to death. What's wrong?"

"The music has repetitive motion."

The delight in his voice made her smile.

"It's called rhythm."

"I never heard it before."

"Probably because you were too busy thinking about sex."

He laughed, picked her up off her feet and swung her around.

"Could be, but don't blame me. All teenage boys come equipped with the same drive . . . engage, activate, then floor it."

January shook her head in pretend dismay, but the light in her eyes gave away her delight.

"It's probably a good thing we didn't know each other in high school. You would have been one of those boys who continually pissed me off."

"If you were as curvy then as you are now, you would have been right."

"So let's see what happens when we move around a little," January said.

Ben grabbed her.

"Easy," she said. "Arms around my waist, eyes closed, follow the music."

"What about running into things and people? If my eyes are closed, I can guarantee someone's going to suffer."

"We're not moving that much," she said. "Just at first . . . just to get the feel of the music . . . okay?"

"Okay," he said. "You're the boss."

"Ooh, I love it when you talk dirty to me," she said.

He slid his arms around her waist and grinned.

"Close your eyes."

He did.

The song had already ended and another one was beginning. Ben opened his eyes. She saw panic.

"What now?" she asked him.

"The music is different."

"So find the motion in this song, as well. It's in

there. You're a detective, for Pete's sake. Find it."

"Yeah. Right."

He pulled her close again, then closed his eyes. The sway of her body was different, just like the music. It took a few moments for him to adjust his movements to hers, but when he finally did, it was there, just as before. To a man who'd never experienced this, it was magic.

He put one hand at the very base of her spine, letting his fingers ride the curve of her backside, as he slid his other arm beneath her shoulder blades, pressing her as close to him as he could.

"Do you feel it?" January asked.

"You don't want me to answer that question," he said, and buried his nose against the curve of her neck. "God, you smell good."

"Tia's taco sauce. It'll do it every time."

Ben grinned. "You are something, woman. Every time I try to make a pass at you, you make me laugh. You do know that, for a man, that's a dangerous sign."

"Stop talking and move your feet."

"Just a little, right?"

"Right," she said, and then breathed a sigh of relief when she was able to follow without having to dodge his steps.

The song ended. Another began.

And before Benjamin Wade North knew it, he was dancing. It wasn't smooth. He was definitely eons away from becoming a Fred Astaire, but he didn't look like a dying crane, and he wasn't walking on January's feet.

Another half hour passed. Ben managed to get through two rounds of elevator music without making a fool of himself or harming January. Finally she called it quits.

"Is the dance lesson finally over?" he asked.

She nodded as she padded across the floor to turn off the CD player.

"You'll do fine."

"I can do better," he said.

She turned around. He was standing right behind her. This time he was the one who held out his hand. She sighed. The inevitable was here.

"Prove it," she said.

Twelve

They were naked before the last echoes of the music died away. He took her first in the hallway, hard and without warning, and standing up.

January came so fast she screamed. When she could breathe again, she wrapped her arms around his neck and dragged him into her bedroom.

At that point Ben was the one flat on his back and losing his mind. He had brief moments of sanity that lasted long enough to see the glorious abandon on January's face. When he came, it was like flying through an explosion—all heat and out of control. When it was over, there were tears in his eyes and January was in his arms. Lulled as he was by exhaustion and the sounds of a receding storm, sleep came easy.

Jay Carpenter had been furthering his plans. Besides the other disciples yet to find, he needed to make a special place apart from the men for the most important woman in his life. He had a new cot and blankets to set out, as well as a portable toilet he planned to conceal behind a stack of old wooden pallets. It was only right that she be given special consideration, and she would need no chains. A mother's love and devotion toward her son were sacrosanct. He would have liked things to be more elegant for her, but that would not have been in keeping with the truth.

And it was truth that was driving him. The growing sense of urgency came from knowing his time left on earth was short, and there was so much left to do. Every time pain or weariness threatened to overwhelm him, he had but to remember the despair of hell.

With the rain still falling, and the wails and curses of his disciples fading from his consciousness, he got back in his cab and drove into the night. There was a box city under a certain overpass that would be full tonight. It would be a perfect place to preach the word of God as he searched for his missing flock.

Phillip Benton had seen hard times before, but never quite this hard. It had been more then eighteen months since he'd been laid off, and nine since he'd been evicted. His wife had taken their two kids and gone home to the Blue Ridge Mountains in Kentucky months ago. She'd cried all the way to the bus station, begging him to come with them, but he'd insisted he would find other work soon, and when he did, he would send for them again. It hadn't happened.

Back in Kentucky, they'd been poor all their lives, but at least they'd had a house to live in and game in the woods to keep them fed. Here in this city that was the heart of the nation, they'd been out of their element, despite the dreams of bettering their existence. Now Phillip was too broke even to get home. Each day that passed pulled him further away from his family and closer to the edge of extinction.

Tonight, when the thunderstorm had rolled in, he'd taken shelter beneath an overpass along with at least two dozen others in similar condition. Normally they were people who would pass on the street without acknowledging each other's existence. Even now, forced to be together by the presence of the storm, they still weren't doing much talking, and the silence among them was eerie, so when the cab pulled up beneath the overpass, everyone looked. Even those who had drifted off to sleep woke up.

Jay saw their faces. Hope was gone. It lifted his heart to know that he could help. He could give them hope. The word of God was always good medicine for hopelessness.

"Good evening, brothers and sisters," he said, as he got out of the cab.

No one spoke, although a few nodded.

He opened the trunk, took out a stack of blankets and laid them on the ground, then went back to the cab. By the time he got the box of canned food from the trunk, the blankets were gone.

"It isn't much, but it's filling," he said, as he began handing out the small tins of Vienna sausages and potted meats. Then he handed two boxes of crackers to a thin, bedraggled female of an indeterminate age. "Would you help pass out some crackers to go with the meat?" he asked.

Her eyes shifted furtively, as if she expected to have to give him something else for the privilege of holding the food. But when he demanded nothing more than he'd already asked, she began to move among the crowd, handing out crackers as she went.

Once the people began to eat, the mood shifted. Jay had known that it would. A full stomach did wonders for depression. And giving these people something they needed, without expectations of them having to give back, made them more receptive to listening to the words of a stranger. As soon as everyone had been served, he lifted his arms and began to move among them.

"Take, eat and be blessed with the love of God," he said. "For those of you who already believe, you are blessed. For those of you who don't know God, or who doubt His existence, I am here to tell you that He's real."

Someone called out from the back of the crowd,

"Yeah . . . so how do you know? What did He do, send you a Christmas card or something?"

Jay pointed up. "I know He's real because I died. I died and was returned."

There was a long moment of silent disbelief, then curiosity struck.

"What was it like?" someone asked. "What did heaven look like?"

"I don't know," Jay said. "I don't know, because when I died, I did not go to heaven. I went to hell. I felt the heat, smelled the stench of evil and despair, heard the wails of lost souls, and I heard the devil's voice."

There was a collective gasp that rose even above the noise of the rain hammering down upon the ground. Then Jay continued. And he was a sight to behold, standing beneath the overpass with the wind tunneling through, his long hair and beard blowing, his clothing wet and plastered to his skin. The tumor growing in his brain had put suffering on his face. It gave him a gaunt, otherworldly appearance that, in their eyes, strengthened his religious persona.

"When I die again . . . and we will all die someday . . . When I die again, I don't want a return ticket to the same place. That's why I'm out here now, preaching to you about the dangers of disbelief and sin. Will you pray with me? Will you confess your sins before God right now and be born again?"

Several people moved forward, caught up in the emotion of the moment and their fear of following in the street preacher's steps. Life on earth was hard enough. Going to hell when they died would be the ultimate slap in the face.

Jay began to pray, touching each of their heads as they came to him. Then he led them out from beneath the overpass, bathing them in what he called tears from heaven, thereby assuring them a permanent place at the hand of God. It certainly wasn't a biblical truth, but it sounded good. And as the people stepped forward one by one, Jay asked them their name, then baptized them in the name of God. As they continued, a tall, bony man with a long, sad face stepped into Jay's line of vision.

Jay reached for him, murmuring a prayer as he touched his head.

"And your name, my son?" Jay asked.

"Phillip Benton."

Jay's heart skipped a beat. Phillip. God had led him to Phillip. Now all he had to do was lead Phillip to his calling.

He patted Phillip's shoulder after the baptism was done, and pulled him aside.

"Despite the chill of the rain, you feel unusually warm. Are you ill?"

Phillip thought nothing of the question, or of answering. After all, the man was a preacher, and where Phillip came from, that was a high mark to have next to a name.

"Yes, sir, I reckon I am," he said. "Been having myself a bit of a cold."

"So, Phillip, why don't you take advantage of the back seat of my cab? I'll be here a while longer. You could get comfortable out of the cold and rain."

"Oh . . . I reckon I'll—"

"No, no, I insist," Jay said.

Phillip didn't need a second urging. The thought of resting on anything padded was too enticing to resist. He nodded his thanks and headed for the cab as Jay continued his work.

Time passed. The storm had yet to let up, but the food had run out. The people crawled back into their boxes and turned their backs to the rain and the man who'd given them a brief respite from their woes. No one had known Phillip Benton before, so no one missed him as the cab sped away.

Phillip had been asleep when Jay got into the cab. It was simple to put up the window between the front and back seats and hit the button to release the shot of ether. Phillip never roused as it filled his lungs, then dulled his senses. It would be morning before he would know anything, and by then he would be chained to the inside wall of the old blast furnace beside a man who seemed obsessed with pulling out bits of his hair.

Walter Lazarus, retired diamond broker from New York City, had moved to D.C. at his wife's insistence, to be closer to their children. They'd found a marvelous town house only minutes from their son and his family, and less than half hour from their daughter and her family. It was, for the elderly couple, the perfect life.

It lasted six years before Walter got sick.

He hadn't even known he was sick until he passed out on the golf course. By the time the test results had come back from the doctor, he'd begun passing blood. At that point, he didn't need a doctor to tell him he was dying, and for Walter, it was okay. He was eighty-seven years old. He'd lived life to its fullest. His only regret was leaving his beloved Etta behind.

As often happens, cancer waited for no man, and three weeks to the day after his collapse, he was gone.

Etta and her family had wailed and grieved and given him the best send-off they could afford, burying him in the most expensive casket, with enough flowers to cover half a football field.

Etta had gone home to hold court with the dozens of mourners who'd come to pay their respects and now must be fed. It was an odd ritual—this expectation of eating large amounts of food at a time when the thought of a single morsel landing in Etta's stomach threatened to make her ill. Still, Walter would have done the same for her, so she did what she had to do and tried not to think of her beloved husband lying six feet under.

Jay saw the obituary by accident as he was cleaning out his cab. He couldn't believe what he was reading, and yet there it was. Walter Leopold Lazarus, age eighty-seven, husband of Etta, father to a son and daughter, grandfather to six grandchildren, and just buried in Perpetual Care Cemetery. His thoughts began to tumble. Lazarus. It couldn't be a coincidence. When he glanced at the paper and realized that it was three days old, he panicked. Lazarus had been raised from the dead on the third day after he was buried, just as Jesus himself had been raised from the dead three days after his crucifixion. If he was meant to follow through on this, he didn't have any time to waste.

He sat down on the edge of the back seat and read the obituary again and again, until the facts were burned into his brain. Two nights ago he'd brought Phillip into the fold, then yesterday the other Simon. With only two disciples to go, should he go for them first, or return Lazarus to the living?

A sudden breeze ruffled the edges of the paper he was holding. He took it as a sign from God. Quickly, Jay finished cleaning out the cab, got out his map to the city and found the location of Perpetual Care. There were things to be done before dark, at which time Lazarus would be rising.

Ben got the call at 6:04 a.m., saying that a body had been found on a bench in a grove of trees not far from the memorial honoring the nurses who'd served in Vietnam. Because of the location, they had to park in the lot near the Lincoln Memorial, and walk up the commons to where the body had been discovered.

The sight was more than bizarre.

When they got there, they found a very well dressed dead man, sitting upright—wearing an Italian suit and Gucci shoes, and tied to the bench with a length of rope, like a puppet on a string.

Ben saw Fran Morrow, the crime scene investigator, crouched in front of the body, staring upward into the dead man's face.

"Hey, Fran, what can you tell us?" Rick asked.

"He's dead," she drawled, as she continued to stare at the face without moving.

There was something odd about her behavior, and Ben picked up on it. He squatted down beside her without actually touching.

"What do you see?" he asked.

She pointed to the man's face. "I think he's wearing makeup."

Ben shrugged. "So he's a transvestite, maybe?"

"In a dress, yes, but not in that suit," she said.

"So what are you thinking?"

"That this isn't a murder."

Ben frowned. "But he's dead."

"There's no visible wound," she said.

"Maybe it was a heart attack," Rick offered.

"And tied to a bench? Explain that," Ben said.

"I can't," Fran said. "But I'll know more after I get him to the lab."

"Any ID on him?" Ben asked.

"Nothing in the pockets," Fran said, then added, "There is one other thing."

"Like what?" Ben asked.

"I detect the odor of embalming fluid."

Ben stared.

Rick's mouth dropped.

"You saying this guy's already been buried and dug up?"

"I'm not saying anything," Fran said. "I just said I smell embalming fluid."

Rick looked at the body one more time, then turned away and spat, as if the taste in his mouth was suddenly too disgusting to bear.

"Oh, great, ghouls and grave robbers. What's next . . . zombies?"

"Somebody could have lifted him from a funeral parlor," Ben said.

Fran shrugged.

"Can you get us some prints?" Rick asked.

Fran nodded as she stood. "If I were you, I'd just check the obits and funerals for the past . . . oh, I'd say four or five days . . . find out how many men over the age of eighty have been buried, then go check the locations. The open grave site will be your winner. Meanwhile, we're going to take him back to the morgue and give him a nice cool slab to rest on while you go find where he'd been planted. Believe me, he more than needs to go back."

January was downing her last bite of scrambled egg when the phone rang. She grabbed the receiver on her way to the sink with her dirty dishes.

"Hello?"

222

"Ms. DeLena . . . January . . . you didn't do as I asked, did you? Although I suppose I should have expected that. Your curiosity is what makes you a good reporter."

January stifled a gasp. It was the same man who'd called her before. Only this time she was going to be the one doing the talking.

"We've met before, haven't we? In the park. Are you stalking me?"

"No."

"Then leave me alone," January said.

"Now you're starting to get the picture," he said. "It's not pleasant to have someone prying into your private business."

January frowned. He had her there. But she wasn't done.

"Your business ceases to be private when it becomes criminal," she said. "You're killing people, aren't you? What's wrong with you, mister? Trying to live up to that name you gave yourself? Sinner. Not very original."

Jay frowned. She was taunting him. He needed to let it go. Patience was a virtue.

"I want you to understand that I'm still walking in His shoes," he said. "Every step He took, every path He trod, every lesson He taught us. The answers are out there. Look for them and you will understand."

"You talk in riddles, Sinner man. If you want to teach the ignorant, you don't speak in riddles. You make yourself plain."

223

Jay thought about that and decided she could be right. If the constant pain in his right eye would lessen up just a bit, he would be able to think more clearly on his own.

"Yes. I see what you mean," he said.

January was more than a little surprised that he'd acquiesced so easily.

"So what's your name, Sinner? I mean your real name. And what game are you playing?"

"My name is of no importance, and I do not play games. I follow in His steps."

January slapped the cabinet with the flat of her hand. The sound echoed loudly enough that Jay heard it and felt her disdain.

"That's nothing but a repeat of your same old story, buddy. Here's the deal. If you don't have anything concrete to prove to me that you're for real, just quit calling."

Jay had wanted her off his back, but now that she'd offered him the option, he felt panic at losing their connection.

"You don't have to believe me. See the truth. Lazarus has risen."

The line went dead in her ear. January slammed the phone down in disgust and then stood there for a moment, going back over the conversation they'd just had. And that last remark—*Lazarus has risen*. What the hell did that mean?

Lazarus died. Jesus raised him from the dead. January thought of Jean Baptiste and the missing men.

The death of Bart Scofield. What could he mean by "Lazarus has risen"?

Then it hit her. She grabbed the phone and called a friend who worked at a local paper.

"*Washington Post*, Emily speaking."

"Emily, this is January. How are you doing?"

"Great, girlfriend, but never as great as you. What's up?"

"I need a favor."

"What else is new?" Emily said.

"It's not a big one. But I need you to check the obituaries for the past week and tell me if a man named Lazarus has been buried recently."

Emily laughed. "Now what, DeLena? You looking for a miracle?"

"No, but I think someone else is," January said.

"My computer is a dinosaur. It'll take me a few minutes to download the info."

"If you don't mind, I'll wait."

"Yeah, okay. I'm going to put the receiver down. Pretend you hear Elvis singing, 'Are You Lonesome Tonight'? It's what I would play if I was important enough to have music when I put people on hold."

January laughed. She could hear Emily moving around her desk. She heard her muttering to herself as the program stalled; then she heard paper tearing. She didn't have to ask to know that Emily was frustrated. Every time that happened, she broke out the chocolate.

A few minutes later, Emily picked the phone back

up. January could hear her chewing.

"M&Ms or Snickers bar?" she asked.

Emily snorted softly. "What? It's not enough that you're beautiful, smart and slender? Now you've gone all psychic? If you are, I hate you."

"I can hear you chewing. What have you found for me?"

"Only because I refuse to acknowledge the jealous streak in my body, I will share info."

"And that would be . . . ?" January asked.

"You were right. A man named Walter Leopold Lazarus was buried four days ago in Perpetual Care Cemetery. Want the address?"

"Yes, please," January said, and took down the info Emily gave her. "Oh . . . Em, did he have any next of kin?"

"Yes, a wife named Etta. Want her address, too?"

"Yeah, sure," January said, and jotted that down, along with the rest of what Emily had told her.

"Anything else?" her friend asked.

"No, but thanks a bunch. I owe you lunch."

"It's a deal," Emily said. "See you on the tube."

They disconnected. The moment the line was free, January called Ben's cell.

Ben and Rick were almost back to the car when Ben's cell phone rang. He looked at the caller ID and grinned as he answered.

"Good morning, January."

Rick wanted to listen, but he'd already messed

226

things up once by being stupid. He wasn't going to repeat that mistake again.

"I'll just be over there," he said, pointing toward the car.

Ben was too focused on January to do more than nod. "You're at work pretty early," he murmured.

"I'm still at home," she said. "And I just had another phone call from our preacher."

"The hell, you say. Did he threaten you again?" All the humor was gone from Ben's voice.

"Not really. It's something else. I have a really weird question to ask you."

"Like what?"

"By any chance, have you guys found the body of a dead man . . . No, wait, I didn't say that right. Have you—"

Ben interrupted, "Found a dead man who'd already gone through one funeral and was shooting for another?"

January gasped. "You have? Already?"

"Yes. He's on his way to the crime lab as we speak. Now tell me what you know," Ben said.

"His name is Walter Leopold Lazarus," January answered.

"Lazarus . . . as in—"

"Exactly."

"Lord have mercy," Ben said. "How do you know this?"

"Because the preacher, when he called, told me that Lazarus was risen. Knowing the other stunts he's been pulling, I took a guess and called a friend at the *Post*, who checked the obits. It's time to tell your captain everything I know. If I come in, will you be there?"

"Rick and I are still on the scene. Give me thirty minutes."

"See you there," January said.

Thirteen

Ben called the captain from the car and told him they were coming in with some breaking info.

"Make me happy," Borger said. "Tell me it's going to help us catch Bart Scofield's killer."

"And then some," Ben said.

"I'll be here," Borger said, and disconnected.

Ben and Rick arrived ahead of January only because they ran with the lights and sirens all the way to the precinct. While January's reputation with the public was good, it was less than favorable within the police department. Too many of her scoops had been at the expense of department mistakes or the result of someone with a big mouth willing to sell what they knew. Ben bet she would never make it to the captain's office unless he paved the way.

"I'll wait out here for her and bring her in," he said.

"Want me to wait with you?" Rick asked.

"No. Go on in and prep the captain. Maybe he'll be

through cursing by the time we get there."

"Right," Rick said, and hurried inside.

Less than five minutes later, January wheeled into the parking lot. Ben was coming toward her before she got out of the car. He grabbed her elbow as she started to exit, and gave her a quick hug.

"I don't like it that this Sinner feels the need to keep calling you."

"You don't know the half of it," January muttered. "Will your captain hear me out?"

"Yes. He won't like it, but he'll listen."

"I brought all the notes I've been keeping."

"Okay. Let's go."

Ben and January ran the gauntlet of cops, their expressions ranging from curious to disbelieving as they headed for the homicide division. Minutes later, January was standing in Borger's office, Ben and Rick behind her. Borger eyed her without comment, then arched an eyebrow at his detectives.

"I don't know why she's on top of something we're investigating and we're standing around with our thumbs up our butts."

"You'll understand when you hear her out, Captain. Not a one of us would have ever gone down this road in the investigation. We deal in facts, and everything she has is theory."

"I don't have time for some bullshit theory, and you know it. Why are you wasting my time?" Borger snapped.

"You'll see. Just hear her out," Ben said.

"She better have something worth talking about," Borger said.

January glared.

"Well, Captain . . . *she* has plenty to talk about, but if you're reluctant to hear *her* out, *she* will be more than happy to take it to *her* boss. *He* will be all over it like flies on shit."

Borger stifled a grin. DeLena had put him in his place, and rightly so.

"Sorry," he said. "Force of habit. Please, have a seat."

"If you don't mind, I'll stand. I think better when I move."

Having said that, she began to pace.

"I'm going to start at the beginning because if I don't, you're never going to believe me."

"All right, I'll hear you out. But answer me one question first."

"If I can," she said.

"When you're through talking, are we going to have a suspect in the Scofield murder?"

"Yes."

"I'm listening," he said.

"This all started because I wanted to do a documentary on people who claim to have had near-death experiences. Several months ago, someone told me about a street preacher who made such a claim, but there was a twist to his story. He claimed that when he died, he went straight to hell, and that when the doctors resuscitated him, he changed his way of living.

I've been looking for him ever since. At first, no one seemed willing to talk to me. As time passed, the stories continued, but no one seemed to know where he could be found. I was about to think he was just some urban myth when I heard a funky story about some street preacher passing out coupons for free fish sandwiches that could be redeemed at a fast-food place. By the time the owner of the fish place found out what was happening, almost a hundred counterfeit coupons had been passed at three different locations. I chalked it up to a scam and thought nothing more of it."

"What does this have to do with anything?" he asked.

"I'm getting there," January said. "Then a man was beheaded. It was when I learned his name that the notion I've been exploring ever since occurred to me. When homeless men began disappearing and I learned their names I knew I was onto something. It was also around then that Bart Scofield was kidnapped. Then he turned up dead and—"

Borger held up his hand. "Look, Ms. DeLena, this is somewhat interesting, but I still don't know where you're going. Can you condense this journey? I have a meeting in a half hour."

January threw up her hands in disgust.

"Condense it? Sure. Here's the scoop, Captain. You've got a head case who's trying to recreate and live the life of Jesus Christ so that when he dies again—and he claims it will be soon—he'll go to heaven, not hell. If that holds true, then consider this."

231

She began ticking off her clues on her fingers.

"The fish coupons . . . he was feeding the multitudes with loaves of bread and baskets of fish, compliments of the restaurant's generosity, but it was still bread and fish. He's been kidnapping homeless men whose names are the same as Christ's twelve disciples. So far, according to a Mother Mary Theresa who runs a shelter for the Sisters of Mercy, at least Simon Peters, Matthew, Andrew, James and John have gone missing. I'm guessing by now there are others. A man was beheaded in one of the parks. He was homeless, too. His name was Jean Baptiste. Say that in English and you've got John Baptist, or John the Baptist. The nut has been calling me for some time now. He knows I've been looking for him. When I asked him why he killed Bart Scofield, you know what he told me? He told me it was the wrong Bart. Bartholomew was the name of one of the disciples. For whatever reason, your Mr. Scofield was the only man he'd taken who wasn't someone off the streets. I can't pretend to know what's in his head, but I know what he said."

"Is that all?" Borger asked.

"No. The drawing your sketch artist did of the man we think is the Sinner matched a man your people arrested for disturbing the peace some time ago."

"We had him in custody?" Borger asked.

Ben shrugged. "For a few hours."

"And we let him go."

"It was disturbing the peace, Captain. How could anyone have known?"

"What was he doing?" Borger asked.

January opened her notebook and laid it in front of Borger. "He was trying to have the employees of the IRS thrown out of the building." She tapped on the page in front of Borger. "Read it for yourself and do the math. IRS out of the building. Money changers out of the temple. Throw the money changers—the IRS—out of the temple . . . or the IRS building."

"Crap," Borger said. "Is that all?"

"At my last count, he was short a few disciples. Besides calling me, I have reason to believe he may be stalking me. He appeared out of nowhere in the park where I run. I believe he was waiting to confront me. I think he got off on talking to me when, at the time, I didn't know who he was."

At that point Ben cursed aloud. January sighed. She'd known he wouldn't like that. She continued.

"And I understand your detectives were called out this morning to the discovery of a body tied to a bench. It fits into the growing pattern."

"You saying he killed someone else?" Borger asked.

"No. The man was old. He died of natural causes and was buried days ago. Last night I think the preacher, in a manner of speaking, resurrected him."

Rick Meeks slapped his leg.

"Morrow said the body looked funky."

"What the hell are you saying?" Borger asked.

"This morning I had another call from the same man. Basically, he was intent on proving to me that my charges against him were faulty. He told me that

Lazarus had risen. I called Ben, who informed me that the body of an unidentified man had been found tied to a bench. He said that the coroner thought the man had already been embalmed. I called a friend at the paper. Four days ago, a man named Walter Leopold Lazarus was laid to rest in Perpetual Care Cemetery. This morning your detectives found him sitting upright and tied to a bench."

Borger leaned back in his chair, too stunned to comment. January continued.

"So now he's raised Lazarus from the dead. None of this is happening in chronological order as it's laid out in the Bible. It's just happening willy-nilly. Probably whenever the opportunity arises. Who knows? But he's not through. If you remember, a disciple will betray him. So I figure whoever he snatches to pass for Judas Iscariot is going to be hanged. I don't know how this man plans to crucify himself, but I can guarantee he's going to give it one hell of a try. I don't know if the missing men are alive or dead, but I believe with every fiber of my being that the man in your sketch is the one who calls himself the Sinner, and I believe he's not done wreaking havoc in our fair city."

"Jesus Christ," Borger muttered.

"Exactly," January said.

"I want this man found," Borger stated.

"The sketch is out," Ben answered. "We're already doing all we can."

"Maybe . . . maybe not," January said. "I've been

thinking about this for a lot longer than you guys have, and I was wondering . . ."

"Name it!" Borger snapped.

"Get your sketch artist back in here. See if he can do a reverse sketch. . . . You know, one of the man without the long hair and beard, and in regular clothes. Someone might recognize him clean-shaven and without the Middle Eastern clothing."

Borger waved his hand.

Rick Meeks bolted from the room to find Brady Mitchell.

Ben leaned against the door with his arms folded, his gaze fixed on January's face. He didn't know what to make of the fact that she hadn't told him about being confronted by this man. He couldn't help but wonder what else she knew that she hadn't told.

Borger eyed January with renewed respect. "You're one hell of a detective, Ms. DeLena. If you ever decide to quit your present career, you might want to consider law enforcement."

"Thanks, but no thanks," January said. "Too many rules."

Borger grinned. "As I understand, you're quite good at breaking them."

"Just doing my job."

Ben interrupted. "Captain, I think we should keep Ms. DeLena under surveillance until this man is brought in. If he's stalking her . . ."

January turned around, her expression pleading with Ben to understand.

"I'm fine. If you tie me down, I can't do my job."

Now he understood why she hadn't told him. And he remembered her specifically asking if they were going to search the parks for the Sinner, as well. She'd been telling him all she could without having her hands tied in return. He wanted to be angry with her, but he understood. He probably would have done the same thing, in the same circumstances.

Borger frowned. He saw Ben's point, but they didn't have the manpower to chase a television reporter all over the city.

"Let's see where we go with the other sketch. And for God's sake, someone go tell the Lazarus family that they're going to have to bury poor Walter all over again before they hear it on the news."

Ben groaned. "Damn it, Captain, you know how I hate breaking bad news to families."

"Well, it's not like they didn't already know he was dead," Borger said.

"I'll go with you . . . if you want," January offered.

Both Ben and Captain Borger answered with a resounding no.

January grinned. "Can't blame me for trying," she said.

"Maybe not, but I *will* blame you if this shows up anywhere on the news before I say it can," Borger said.

"Oh, you can bet it will be on the news, but not from me, and not with the details I've just described. When someone digs up a body and returns it to the land of the living, someone will tell."

• • •

Jay had to resort to the phone book to find his Thaddeus. The name was so out of the ordinary that his hopes of ever coming across it accidentally were slim to nil, and he needed to complete his circle.

Thad Ormin drove a delivery van for a florist. It had been a simple matter for Jay to pay a call on the florist and ask for a delivery of lilies. It had bothered him some that he'd had to go to the shop to make the order, but without a credit card, he had to pay in cash, and no flowers would be delivered without payment in advance.

He'd waited until the shop was really busy, then walked in and asked the first employee he saw who was already busy. She'd written up the work order while answering the phones, which had been perfect. She'd hardly paid him any attention, and when he'd paid cash and handed her a card that he'd already written, she paper-clipped it to the work order without a glance. With a promise that the flowers would be delivered before 5:00 p.m. that day, Jay left.

He figured he had at least a couple of hours before the order would be worked up and sent out, which gave him enough time to do some shopping. Tonight he wanted to have a prayer with his flock, and keeping them quiet while he prayed meant they needed something in their mouths other than their tongues. Lately their words to him had been so harsh as to have given him doubt. He couldn't afford to doubt himself—not

237

at this late date. So he drove to the nearest super-market for more of the usual—canned meats and crackers and bottles of water. Just for a special treat, he picked up two large bags of grapes. He smiled to himself as he checked out. They would be so excited with the change of diet.

As he was getting in the cab, the dull ache behind his eye, which he'd come to accept, suddenly exploded. The pain was so vicious that Jay fell out of the cab onto his hands and knees. Before he could get up, he vomited.

"Hey, mister, are you all right?" someone asked.

Jay felt hands pulling at him. He tried to fight them off, but they wouldn't turn loose. With every ounce of strength he could muster, he threw himself back into the cab and drove off. It was sheer luck that he didn't hit a pedestrian or another car. By the time he got out of the parking lot, the pain had begun to subside. He could see well enough to avoid a wreck, and by the time he got to a side street and parked, his equilibrium was returning.

He shoved the gearshift into Park, then glanced up into the rearview mirror. For a fraction of a second he saw a face of pure evil smiling at him from the back seat. But when he turned around, there was no one there.

"Oh shit, oh shit," he muttered. "Please, not him . . . not that."

He rode the fear and the pain while his thoughts careened from one mad scenario to the next. Maybe he should walk into a fiery furnace. Maybe a trip to the zoo into the lions' den. Maybe the Potomac. That was it. He could walk on water, then people would see. Then they would know that he was living true, living pure.

He didn't know how long he sat there, but when he became aware of the time, he panicked. If Thad Ormin had already delivered those lilies, he'd just wasted fifty dollars. Unaware that he was cursing, he took off from the curb with tires squealing, and laid down about a foot of rubber. Hardly proper behavior for a man of God.

Thad Ormin was a frustrated actor. He'd spent the first ten years out of high school beating the streets of Hollywood trying to get a break. All he'd gotten was a case of clap and two evictions. After being approached to work a drag queen gig, which he'd seriously considered, he'd packed up and taken the first bus back to Ohio. When the redundance of living in Brookville, population 387, got to him, he struck out again, only this time toward the East Coast. He'd gotten a gig doing regional theater in D.C., but when the play closed, he'd stayed on. Not because he loved the city so much, but because he'd fallen in love. Her name was Millicent, but he called her Millie. She was twelve years his senior, a good twenty pounds overweight, and couldn't balance a checkbook to save her soul. But she had the most infectious laugh, could make biscuits better than anyone he knew and loved life. She'd taught him how to do the same. Now thoughts of being famous rarely ever crossed his mind, and when they did, he chalked them up to the frustration of a past life and reminded himself to enjoy the one he had.

The delivery of lilies was his last one for the day, but in a part of the city he'd never covered. He'd circled a ten-block radius several times before it dawned on him that the address for the delivery was a vacant lot and in a less than desirable part of town.

Disgusted with the clerk for writing down the wrong address, he pulled over to the curb and called the flower shop.

"Grammy's Garden," the clerk said, as she answered the call.

"Delores, it's Thad. I need you to check the address on this arrangement of lilies."

She did so, reading off the address on the work order.

"Shoot," Thad muttered. "That's what's on here, too, but it can't be right. It's a vacant lot. Got a name on the person who paid for the order?"

"No. Says here it was paid for in cash."

"Perfect," Thad said. "I'm coming in. We'll leave the lilies in the cooler tonight. Maybe the guy will call back tomorrow wanting to know why his flowers weren't delivered, and we can get the right address then. Okay?"

"Works for me," she said.

Thad disconnected, tossed his cell phone into the

seat beside him and pulled away from the curb. He was halfway back to the flower shop when Jay showed up at the vacant lot. A part of him knew he was too late, but still he waited, unable to give up on the fact that he'd failed.

When he finally left, it was because his stomach growled, which reminded him that not only had he not eaten anything all day, but neither had the men back at the warehouse. Disheartened by the failure of his plans, he drove away.

Within ten minutes of leaving the vacant lot, Jay drove up on the florist van stopped at the side of the street. The hood was up, and the driver was standing in front of the van, leaning over the engine.

Jay's heart skipped a beat. God was still on his side. What other explanation could there be?

He turned on his right signal, moved across traffic, then pulled to the curb in front of the van. He smoothed his hands down his beard and tucked a stray lock of hair back into his ponytail. There were food spots on the front of his shirt and a small tear near the right knee of his pants. He knew he looked as worn as he felt, but it didn't matter. This was the Lord's work. It was meant to be.

"Hey, mister," he said. "Need some help?"

Thad Ormin looked up, frowned uncomfortably at the man's appearance, then noticed the cab. A godsend.

"I don't know what's wrong with this thing," he said. "I'm not much on mechanics. I called a tow truck. Should be here soon."

"If you don't have to go with the van, I'd be happy to give you a ride home. Free of charge, of course. I'm off duty myself."

Thad thought about it. He didn't have to go with the van. It was too late in the day for anything to be repaired. All they were going to do was haul it into the shop. His car was still at the florist, but he could use a ride to pick it up.

"Yeah, that would be great," he said. "I have to wait until the wrecker comes, though. Then, if you don't mind, I could use a ride back to the florist shop to pick up my car. I'd be happy to pay you."

"No problem," Jay said. "I'll just be waiting in the cab when you're ready."

He went back to the taxi to wait. Just to make sure that all was ready, he did a quick check of the system. The canister of ether was full. The window between the front and back seat locked with ease. It was going to be okay, after all.

Within minutes, the wrecker arrived. Jay watched Thaddeus giving directions to the driver, then hid a smile as the man started toward him.

When Thad started to get in front, Jay waved him to the back.

"That door latch is broken," he said, as Thad slid into the back seat.

"Not a problem," Thad declared. "I really appreciate this."

"No, I'm the one who's thankful," Jay said. "Buckle up."

Before he'd gotten to the corner of the block, he'd locked the doors, locked the windows and punched the button on the ether. If Thad Ormin sensed what was happening, he didn't have time to voice his concerns. He was out cold, and Jay was on the way home.

When Thad wasn't home by eight o'clock, Millie panicked. She'd called the florist shop for two hours but with no luck. At that point she'd called the owner, who was surprised by the news. The last thing she'd known, Thad's final delivery had been a bust. His van had broken down on the way back—near the corner of Broad and Descartes—and it had been towed to the repair shop. She'd assumed Thad had gone home, too, and told Millie as much.

Now Millie was scared. Not once in the years that she and Thad had been together had he not called when he was going to be late. She picked the phone back up and called 911.

"Hello, my name is Millie Ormin. My husband, Thad, is missing."

"How long has he been missing, Mrs. Ormin?" the dispatcher asked.

"He was due home by five-thirty. It's almost nine, and I'm really worried."

The concern she'd first heard in the dispatcher's voice slipped to a casual tone.

"Look, Mrs. Ormin, it hasn't even been four hours. This line is for emergencies, and he's probably just—"

"No!" Millie cried. "He's not *just* anywhere. He's missing. He always calls if he's going to be late, and he didn't. His boss said his van broke down. It was supposed to be towed. We don't know if the wrecker ever got there, or what happened to Thad afterward. His car may still be at the shop, Grammy's Garden. Please, I need someone to check this out."

The dispatcher's tone of voice changed again as she understood the situation. "Do you have the location where the van broke down?" she asked.

"Yes," Millie said, and told the dispatcher what Thad's boss had told her.

The dispatcher frowned. It wasn't the best place in the city to have engine trouble, but she said nothing to the distraught wife.

"I'll have a couple of our guys check it out. They'll give you a call afterward. Okay?"

"Yes, thank you," Millie said. "You have my number?"

"Yes, ma'am, it's on the screen."

"Thank you so much," Millie said. "I'll be waiting for their call."

Smith and Walls were the officers who took the call. They soon found the address where the van had broken down, only to ascertain it was no longer there. This prompted a call to the owner of the florist shop, who gave them the name of the towing service that had been used.

They located the man who'd taken the call. The

driver, known only as Butch, told them that the florist deliveryman had given him the address of the garage where the van was to be taken, then had gotten into a cab, which drove away while he was still hooking up the van.

Smith and Walls found the van parked at the repair shop with a basket of wilting lilies in the back, but no Thad Ormin. After a trip to the florist shop, they discovered a car registered to Thad Ormin still parked in the employee parking lot, which told them the man had never made it back.

What they knew for sure now was that the driver of the van had gotten into a cab and disappeared. They were laughing to themselves that the man was probably knocking back a few at some local bar while his wife called out the troops.

It wasn't until Smith and Walls began making the calls to the cab companies to find out which one had picked Thad up, and came up blank, that Walls suddenly picked up the sketch all the officers were carrying.

"What do you think?" he asked.

Smith shrugged. "He's supposed to be some outlaw cab driver, isn't he?"

Walls nodded. "Yeah, but what are the odds that—"

"Isn't there a number to call at the bottom of the sketch?" Smith asked.

"Yeah, a couple actually."

"Call one of them and tell them what we know."

Walls called dispatch and had them patch him

through to the first number, which was Ben North's extension.

Ben was finishing up the paperwork on the Lazarus case when his phone rang. Thankful for the reprieve, he answered quickly.

"Homicide . . . North."

"Detective North, this is Officer Walls. We might have something for you on your outlaw cab driver."

"Like what?" Ben asked.

"We've got a missing man who was last seen getting into what we think was an outlaw cab."

Ben's attention shifted. "What's the deal?"

"Driver of a florist van calls a wrecker to have delivery van towed in. Takes a cab from the site but doesn't get home. It may not amount to anything, but the man's car is still at the florist shop where he works, and they've been closed for hours. His wife swears he's never late without calling."

"The name . . . what's the missing man's name?" Ben asked.

"Let's see, I've got it here on the call sheet. Uh, Ted . . . no, that's not it. Thad. Thad Ormin."

Ben had been doing a little research of his own. The name didn't automatically ring a bell, but he'd already admitted he wasn't the best religious scholar. He grabbed the Bible he'd brought from home and quickly flipped to the tenth chapter of the Book of Matthew. January had pointed out that the first four verses listed the disciples' names, so he did a quick rundown, looking for Thad or any derivative thereof.

He ran his finger down the list, and when he got to Thaddeus, his stomach knotted.

"Yeah, okay," Ben said. "Can you fax your info here to me at the office? I think you just stumbled onto the latest abduction by our street preacher."

"The hell you say," Walls said, then added, "Happy to help. We'll get this info over to you ASAP."

"Appreciate it," Ben said.

"No problem," Walls said.

Ben disconnected, then sat for a moment with his head in his hands.

He didn't know where to go from here or what to make of what was happening. They needed to find this man who called himself the Sinner and get him off the streets, but how did you catch a shadow? The only people who knew the streets as well or better than the cops were cab drivers, and now they had one who'd gone amok. In a city filled with both federal and local law enforcement, no one seemed able to find him.

Ben picked up the phone and started to call Borger, but as he began to punch in the numbers, he realized he was calling January, instead.

Fourteen

January was asleep. It was the first time in weeks that she'd gotten to bed before midnight, and she was so deeply asleep that when the phone rang, she thought she was dreaming. It wasn't until the answering machine kicked on and she heard her own voice in the other room that she rolled over and picked up the receiver.

"Hello?"

Ben winced. Her voice sounded blurry. He knew he'd awakened her, but he also knew that when she found out why he'd called, she wouldn't care.

"January, it's me."

She sat up, then swung her legs off the mattress as she turned on the lamp beside the bed.

"Ben? What's happened? Is something wrong? What time is it?"

"Yes, it's me, honey, and it's late. Sorry I woke you."

"It's okay," she mumbled.

"We think your preacher snatched another disciple."

Now she was well and truly awake. She reached for the pen and paper that she kept by the phone.

"Talk to me."

"A deliveryman from Grammy's Garden—that's a florist shop—has gone missing. His van broke down. Wrecker picked up the van. Cab picked up the driver. Van made it to the repair shop. Driver never showed up at home. Looks like we've got an outlaw cab and a missing deliveryman."

"His name . . . what's the driver's name?" January asked.

"Thad Ormin."

January exhaled on a soft sigh. "Thaddeus. He's taken himself a Thaddeus."

"That's what I thought, too."

"Oh Lord, Ben. We are *so* not in control. This is bad, really bad."

"I know, honey. I know."

"What are we going to do?" she asked.

"You're not going to do anything," he said. "I'm telling you only because you deserve to know. We're the ones on the hot seat, but thanks to you, considerably further along than we were this time yesterday. Go back to sleep. I'll talk to you tomorrow."

"It's already tomorrow," she said softly. "I'll see you tonight . . . if we're still on for the ball?"

"Absolutely," he said. "I have no intention of wasting all those dance lessons."

For some reason January felt like crying. Instead, she pressed her fingers to her lips to stifle the urge, then managed a smile.

"See you tonight, then," she said.

"Can I bring my toothbrush and jammies, too?"

He made her laugh, as if he'd known she was on the verge of tears.

"Yes, please do," she said. "But you may as well leave the jammies at home."

"Hot damn, woman. The stuff you put in my mind is barely legal."

"Yeah, well, I'm pretty partial to your stuff, too."

Now she'd made *him* laugh.

"Thanks for calling me," she added.

"Sure," he said. "But will you promise me something?"

She hedged by saying, "If I can."

"If he calls you again, let me know."

"Done."

"See you later."

"Yes, later," she said.

When they hung up, she lay back down and buried her face in her pillow.

Ben would have given a lot to have been lying there beside her. Instead, he made a call to the captain, and another to Rick. They made arrangements to meet first thing in the morning at the repair shop. If they were lucky, the preacher might have left some fingerprints on the van. If they weren't, then so be it. But it was a place to start.

Thad Orwin woke up. His head was pounding, his stomach was rolling, and it was pitch-black. He didn't know where he was or how he'd gotten there, but he knew he wasn't home. The last thing he remembered was getting into the back seat of that cab.

It took him a few moments to realize someone was snoring nearby and that the stench was so disgusting he almost gagged. Then he heard another sound—the quiet desperation of near-silent sobs.

"Who's there?" he called.

"Shut the fuck up," someone muttered.

Another voice answered. "Leave him alone. You weren't any different when you first arrived."

Thad gasped. How many people were in here, anyway?

"Please . . . who's there?" he repeated.

One by one, eight of the nine men answered by calling out their own name.

"Simon Peters."

"Andy."

"James."

"Jimbo."

"John."

"Phillip."

"Simon, and Matthew is here, too, but he doesn't talk anymore."

"What's your name?" someone asked.

"Thad. Thad Ormin."

"Thad? There wasn't any . . . ah, my mistake. Yes, I believe there was. Thaddeus. Yes, of course. Welcome, Thaddeus. I'm Tom."

Thad rolled over onto his hands and knees, but it wasn't until he tried to stand up that he realized there were restraints on his wrists.

"What in hell?" he muttered.

Someone—he thought it was Tom—laughed.

"You nailed it on the head. This *is* hell. Make yourself comfortable, Thad. Unless we get ourselves a miracle, we're gonna be here a long time."

Thad panicked. Millie! She would be worried out of her mind.

"Who did this?" he asked.

"The crazy cab driver," Tom said.

Thad groaned. He'd known something was weird about that man. If only he'd paid attention to his instincts.

"But why?" Thad asked.

"He's gathering disciples," Tom said.

"Disciples? What kind of disciples?" Thad demanded.

"The same kind Jesus had."

"Jesus? What does *He* have to do with this madness?"

Tom laughed again, but the sound held its own shade of insanity. "He has everything to do with it, buddy," he said. "Our crazy cab driver claims he's dying, and the best we can tell, he thinks he's Jesus. He's gathering his disciples and whatever else he thinks he has to have to get his sorry ass into heaven."

For a few moments Thad was speechless. Before he could gather his wits, something furry ran across his feet.

He gasped, stifling a scream.

"What?" Tom asked.

"Something ran across my feet. I think it was a rat."

"Yeah, they're everywhere," one of the other men said.

"Oh God, oh God," Thad whispered. "I hate rats."

"You'll get used to them," another said.

"Which one are you?" Thad asked.

"John. John Marino, and rats ain't so bad . . . not when you're real hungry. I've eaten 'em before."

Thad felt sick, but he stifled the urge to puke,

knowing that if he did, he would most likely be sitting in it for some time to come.

January slept until 6:00 a.m., then woke suddenly, as if someone had tapped her on the shoulder. She lay there for a moment, wondering if she'd dreamed the touch, or if instinct had awakened her for a reason. It took her a few seconds to remember Ben's call last night, and when she did, she leaped out of bed, her mind racing, wondering what to do first.

She wanted to interview Mr. Lazarus's widow, but she'd been told to back off, so the woman was off-limits for now. She also needed to talk to Mother Mary Theresa—see if she'd heard about any more men going missing. January had a hair appointment at 2:00 p.m., as well as a manicure and pedicure in preparation for the award she would be receiving that night.

At that point, she gasped. Award! Oh Lord! She needed to write some kind of acceptance speech.

"I need coffee," she muttered, and headed for the kitchen.

She was pouring water in the pot when the phone rang. She answered absently, her mind still focused on the unwritten speech.

"Hello."

"Hello to you, too, Ms. DeLena."

January's fingers curled around the receiver. "Creep."

There was a moment of silence, then a sigh. "You disappoint me," Jay said.

"I wish I could say the same, but you're pretty damn predictable," January said.

Jay frowned. "Defiance is not an attractive trait."

"You kidnapped another man, and you dug up a dead one. You snatched yourself a Thaddeus, didn't you? Was he the last?"

Jay began defending himself. "You blaspheme! I did nothing. Lazarus has risen. It is God's will."

"What have you done with the other men? Are they dead, too?"

"My followers will be spreading God's word."

"The police are going to find you, and when they do, they're going to put you away for life."

Jay laughed.

The sound startled January, then made her angry.

"You think that's funny?" she yelled.

"Decidedly," Jay said, and laughed again. "I'm dying, woman. Don't you remember anything I've told you?"

For the first time since he'd started calling her, she began to realize he was serious about that. That he meant *soon,* not just someday. This was something she hadn't given much credence to. Granted, he'd died once, but she'd mistakenly believed that whatever had been wrong with him had been corrected. However, if he was telling her the truth, that meant he'd had a definite diagnosis. From a doctor. Which meant she'd completely missed a huge clue. They all had. They should have been showing his sketch around to the hospitals, too.

"How do you know you're dying?" January asked. "Who's your doctor? Maybe he was wrong. What if you're not ill at all?"

Jay slapped the inside of the phone booth. "The doctors know what's wrong with me, but they couldn't fix it before, so why bother with them again? Besides, there's nothing to know. One day soon my head will burst open from this pain, and then you'll all be able to see for yourselves."

"See what—a brain black with evil? You know what I think? You claim that when you died before that you went to hell, right?"

"I did. I did go to hell. It was terrible. Don't you see? That's why all of this must be done. I'm walking in His footsteps. I'm living as He lived, so that it won't happen again."

"I'll tell you what *I* see," January said. "I see a man who's out of control. A man who thinks he can buy his way into heaven by committing crimes, which makes you crazy, mister. And you know what else I believe? When you came back from hell, you brought the devil back with you."

"No!" Jay screamed. "You lie! You lie!" It was the last intelligible thing he said as pain exploded.

January could tell he was still talking, but the words no longer made sense. She heard him drop the phone. It banged against something—probably the wall of the phone booth—but he didn't disconnect. She could hear him babbling and crying, but she couldn't feel an ounce of sympathy.

She'd started to hang up when it dawned on her that if there was an open line, the police might be able to trace where he'd been calling from. Without hesitation, she left her phone off the hook and ran for her cell phone.

Ben was coming out of a diner with a cup of coffee in one hand and an apricot Danish in the other. His cell phone rang in the middle of his first bite of sweet roll. He hurried to the curb, set his coffee on the hood of the car, then swallowed and answered.

"North."

"Ben. It's me. He just called me again and—"

"Are you all right? Did he say—"

"Ben! Ben! Shut up and listen to me."

Ben took a deep breath. "I'm listening."

"We were talking, and he freaked out. I think he's probably in some public phone booth. I hear traffic and people and city noise. And he keeps babbling words I can't understand."

"What the hell are you saying?" Ben yelled.

Now it was January who took a breath.

"The line between my phone and the place where he made the call is still open. He didn't hang up, and he's still there. I can hear him in the background."

"Oh, man," Ben muttered. "Look. I've got to call some guys at the phone company. Whatever you do, don't hang up that phone."

"Can you trace the call without being here?"

"I'm about to find out," Ben said. "Don't leave. I'll

call you back on your cell."

January disconnected.

The coffeepot bubbled, then burped, signaling the end of the brewing process.

She turned around, then moved to the cabinet and filled her cup. Out of curiosity, she picked up her phone again and listened. She could still hear him banging around and mumbling. She stood without moving, barely breathing, and listening to the sound of a man going mad.

Ben was in a race against time. The call he'd made to the tech at the phone company had finally yielded an address. January had been right. It was a public phone booth in the middle of downtown, and at this time of the morning, with everyone on their way to work, traffic was going to suck.

They couldn't run with lights and sirens for fear of alerting the perp, so they had to cope with traffic the same as everyone else, although police units closer to the address had already been dispatched.

"You think we're gonna be in time?" Rick asked, as Ben sped through an intersection.

"Your guess is as good as mine, but I sure as hell hope so. This guy's a nut."

"Yeah, they're the worst kind, aren't they?" Rick said. "I mean, you can't predict their behavior or anything. They just go off for no reason."

Ben thought of the man stalking January and tried not to worry. She was as street savvy as they came. He trusted her to be careful.

"How much farther?" Rick asked.

"Twenty blocks, maybe more," Ben muttered.

"The cruisers will get there first. They'll probably have him in custody by the time we arrive."

"God, I hope so," Ben said, and slammed on his brakes to keep from running up the back end of an old Cadillac.

"Damn it," Rick shouted, as he slapped the dash of the car. "That old woman has no business still driving. Look at her! She's going to cause a wreck and get someone killed for sure."

"Maybe, but I don't want to be the one to end her life or ours, so ease off. I'm doing the best I can."

"I know . . . I know . . . but think of the press we're gonna get if we're the ones who get this guy off the street. The mayor will be appreciative. Scofield's family will be thrilled, and the captain will be happy, too. Hell, it could mean a promotion for both of us."

Ben thought of January again. "I don't want a promotion. I just want this bastard stopped," he muttered, then sped past the old woman in the Cadillac the minute the traffic parted.

Jay's face was wet with tears. Snot was running from his nose. He felt the moisture, but he hurt so bad, he just assumed it was blood.

People were staring at him. He saw the shock and then the disgust on their faces, and tried to explain, but the words he was thinking wouldn't come out right.

He heard his own voice, and even he didn't understand what he was saying.

The cab was parked less than half a block away, but when he tried to walk toward it, he staggered toward a couple coming out of a diner, instead. When they saw him, the man grabbed his wife's arm and steered them both clear. Jay was still trying to turn around, but his left leg wouldn't work. He was in the middle of the sidewalk with no control over his own body, and a couple of teenage boys were coming toward him like heat-seeking missiles.

He saw the expressions on their faces changing from disinterested to predatory, and tried to run. It was no use. Twice he staggered, and both times he would have fallen to the sidewalk except for the retaining wall to his right. A strong gust of wind flattened his beard to his chest, and for a moment, he caught a whiff of the stench of his own body. The boys began stalking him, laughing and pointing and holding their noses. They looked barely old enough to drive, but their taunts were as old as time.

"Hey, Franco . . . look at the Jesus freak. He got more beard than Santa Claus. What say we give him a haircut and a shave?"

"No, Juanito, he stink too bad for that. What he need is a bath."

"Yeah, Franco . . . you're right. A bath. What he need is a bath."

Juanito broke into a rap, pointing and dancing as he circled around Jay.

"Stink man, stink man . . . standin' on the street.
Turnin' nose and bellies of the people he meets.
Wash your body.
Wash your feet.
Wash your stinky old ass, you Jesus freak."

Jay pointed at them. He tried to yell, but it came out in a roar, which only intensified their hazing. They laughed and jeered, dodging in and out between his arms as he flailed at them.

An elderly well-dressed woman came out of the same diner that the couple had come from earlier. She was walking toward her car when she saw what was happening.

"You! You boys! Get away from that man! Do you hear me? Get away before I call the police!"

They thumbed their noses at her, but took off in a run. Jay leaned against the retaining wall, shaking so hard he could barely breathe.

"Are you all right?" she asked.

Jay staggered again, then realized it was an elderly woman who'd come to his aid. The pain in his head was beginning to subside, giving him enough focus to at least form words.

"You . . . talking to me?"

"Yes. Those boys were harassing you. Are you all right?"

"Yes . . . Don't know why they were—"

Her nose wrinkled as she interrupted him.

"Well, I do," she said. "When was the last time you

actually looked at yourself? You seem like an intelligent person, so why must you be unkempt? Your style of clothing is your choice, but it's filthy. That's not okay. And for goodness sake, young man, at the least, you need a bath, a haircut and a shave. No one will ever take you seriously if they can't bear to breathe the very air around you."

Jay was so taken aback he had no way to respond. He was still gawking when the woman shook her head at him in disdain, stomped off to her car and drove away.

It wasn't until someone honked a horn in traffic that he came to himself. He didn't know what time it was or how long he'd been standing there, but it made him nervous. He'd been in the same place far too long.

He looked around quickly, reorienting himself in relation to where he'd parked his cab, and hurried toward it. It wasn't until he got inside, started the engine and drove back into traffic that he felt even vaguely safe. Although he had no reason to suspect that the authorities were on to him in any way, it was instinct that sent him down an alley. He took it straight through before he came upon a truck being unloaded.

Forced to take regular streets now, he drove out of the alley and headed south. He'd no sooner exited than a man flagged him down at the corner. He pulled up to the curb. It was just what he needed—a new fare.

"Where to?" he asked, as the man got in.

"Is there an Indian restaurant in the area?" the stranger asked.

"Indian?" Jay asked.

"Yeah, man . . . you know, curry and all the fixings."

"Yes, about eight blocks down and maybe five or six east. Is that too far?"

"No. Make that my destination."

"No problem," Jay said, and pulled back into traffic.

Six blocks over, a couple of police cruisers sped past. Jay didn't see them, and if he had, would never have dreamed they were after him. He'd already forgotten that he'd ever called January DeLena and was unaware that he'd left the receiver off the hook.

He took the money from his latest fare, added it to what he had in the glove box and headed for a secondhand store. He'd already decided that his run-in with the boys and the old woman were signs from God telling him to change his appearance. January DeLena had told him the police were hunting for him. He wasn't sure if they knew what he looked like, but chances were they did. If he was to finish his quest, he needed to avoid detection.

It didn't take him long to go through the secondhand clothing shop and pick out a couple of clean outfits, this time choosing jeans and T-shirts and a pair of sneakers. Then he drove to a cut-rate motel, rented a room and headed for the shower. It was after three in the afternoon when he walked into a barbershop.

A slim, middle-aged man was standing behind the counter. "Good afternoon, sir. How can we help you?"

"I want a shave and a haircut."

The man's eyes narrowed as he eyed the length of hair and beard.

"Are we talking a trim?" he asked.

Jay shook his head. "No. Cut my hair close to the scalp and shave the beard completely off."

The barber grinned. "Wow! We're talking about a makeover here."

"Yes, I suppose we are," Jay said.

"Have a seat and we'll get started," the barber said.

Jay slid into the barber chair, stared at his own face one last time, then closed his eyes.

"Do it," he said.

The barber picked up his clippers.

While Jay was undergoing his transformation, Ben and Rick were trying to salvage what they could from the fact that they'd arrived too late to catch their man. Even though the police cars had beaten them there by almost ten minutes, they had been too late, as well. Their report was disappointing. The phone had been used several times since the Sinner's call, his prints no doubt obliterated, though they were checking anyway.

"We were too late," the cop said. "A couple of teenage girls were coming out of the booth when we got here, and they said they'd had to wait on some hooker to finish. We didn't see anyone acting out of character."

"Damn it," Ben muttered.

"So it's a bust?" the cop asked.

Ben nodded. "Looks like it, but thanks for the backup."

"Maybe next time," the other cop said, and returned to his cruiser.

Ben took out his cell phone to report in. As soon as his call was answered, he started talking.

"Captain Borger, this is North. We missed him at the phone booth. At least two dozen people have used it since he abandoned it, and no one remembers seeing anything out of the ordinary, which means either they saw it and didn't want to get involved, they got here too late to see anything, or our perp wandered off somewhere else to finish his meltdown."

"Well, hell," Borger said.

"Yes, sir," Ben responded.

"In the meantime, we got a DOA at the hospital. Gangbanger. Go see if the family who came in with the victim knows anything."

"Yes, sir. We're on our way."

"Where are we going?" Rick asked as they headed back to the car.

"Hospital. Got a victim that came in DOA. Captain said he might be a gangbanger. Wants us to talk to the family before they disperse."

Rick frowned. "I hate working that kind of shit."

"What—gang related?"

"Yeah. That lifestyle doesn't make a bit of sense to me."

"That's because you had a mother and father who took care of you when you were growing up. Most of these kids are on their own, or have a single parent either working two jobs to get by, or working the streets. Either way, the gang represents a family they don't have."

Rick snorted.

"That's too much psychobabble for me. I say, put them to work. They'll find out what it means to pay their way. Not go out robbing and shooting up everything and everyone they see."

Ben shook his head. "Damn, Meeks, that's cold. Out of curiosity, why did you become a cop?"

"It was the big bucks and the fancy clothes," Meeks muttered, and picked at a spot on his necktie.

Ben grinned.

"Yeah, me, too."

Fifteen

The rest of the afternoon had been more of the same for Ben and Rick. Trying to interview witnesses to the gangbanger's death while consoling a mother who excused herself from the hospital waiting room to get high became the highlight of the day. Ben didn't know who he felt sorrier for—the boy whose life had just come to a violent end, or the mother who was so strung out that she had yet to realize her only child was dead.

Finally Ben called it a day and went home to get

ready for the ball. He'd fussed and fidgeted while laying out his clothes, practiced his dance moves while he shaved, and cursed the tie that came with the tux until, finally, he was ready.

His hair was seal-black and still just a little bit damp, but he looked good. In fact, he was so pleased with his appearance that he did a little sidestep, then a three-sixty turn, grabbed his car keys and started out the door.

Then he remembered the toothbrush he'd promised to bring, and went back after it. January had given him permission to stay over. He wasn't fool enough to pass that up.

It was a little before seven when he pulled into the parking lot of her apartment building. He got out, smoothed his hands along the sides of his hair, then hurried inside.

As he stepped off the elevator, he brushed a speck of lint from the front of his tux. When he got to her door, he took a deep breath, then rang the bell.

January had been ready since six. She was sitting on a kitchen barstool with the hem of her floor-length white gown hiked up to her knees and her feet bare, going over her notes as she waited for Ben.

She knew the men had missed catching the preacher, but felt it was only a matter of time. She kept staring at the sketches that the D.C. Police Department had generated and, in an uncharacteristic show of generosity, faxed to her home. They had the sketch Brady

Mitchell had done with Mother Mary T., a copy of the photograph they'd taken from the film clip in front of the IRS building, as well as the reverse sketch she'd asked Brady Mitchell to do by removing the beard and long hair.

It was strange, but the one bare of facial hair looked even more menacing than the others. His mouth, which was barely discernible in the first, held a cruel twist. And his eyes, which had been all but lost because of the thick, flyaway hair, seemed cold and piercing.

She couldn't help thinking that if she only knew his real name and they could find out something about his past, it would explain the crazy path his mind had taken.

She'd also done enough reading on near-death experiences to know that most doctors adhered to the theory that whatever their patients thought they were experiencing as they died was nothing but the last vestiges of imagination in a brain starving for oxygen. In other words, hallucinations based on a lifetime of religious influence or lack thereof.

Her upbringing had taught her differently, but it was hard to find infallible facts on the process of death, other than the cessation of breath.

As she sat, she fiddled with her pen, debating with herself as to when to broach her ideas regarding a new direction in the investigation. She didn't want to step on any departmental toes, but she needed this preacher caught and put away. It gave her the creeps to think about him spying on her, stalking her every move. If he knew as much about her as she feared, she could very well be one of his targets. It was something she would talk to Ben about before this night was over. She also wanted to bring up the idea of taking the sketches to hospitals. If he'd died on the operating table and then been resuscitated, there was a good chance that some doctor or nurse might recognize him—especially a patient claiming he'd been to hell and come back to tell the tale.

She was going through the Yellow Pages of the phone book, writing down names and addresses of area hospitals, when the doorbell rang. Startled by the sound, she glanced up at the clock, then gasped.

It had to be Ben! And she was still without shoes.

She tossed the pen aside and stifled a giggle. Oh Lord, she needed to get hold of her emotions. A whole evening! She was going to spend a whole evening—and night—with Ben North. As far as she was concerned, she'd already gotten her award.

She hurried to the door and opened it wide, and the smile on her face slid sideways. The man on the threshold was a knockout.

"Oh my," she whispered.

Ben was in shock. She looked better than any movie star he'd ever seen.

"Hot damn," he muttered.

"You look amazing," January said.

"You look like a million bucks," Ben replied, and then kissed the side of her cheek. "And you smell even better. Lord! What is that perfume?"

"I'm not wearing any," she said.

His eyes widened. "You're kidding."

"No."

"Then it must be love."

He cupped her face with his hands, then lightly brushed a kiss across her lips without smudging her makeup.

January blinked. He'd said the *L* word. Oh Lord. Was she supposed to say it back, or would that be overkill? Maybe he was just being flip. If that was it and she said the *L* word back to him, then it would embarrass them both when he had to admit he'd only been teasing.

"Um . . . uh, I . . ."

"You're still barefoot," Ben said, and pointed to her feet.

"Yes."

"Don't you think you should put on some shoes before we go?"

"Go?"

"January?"

"Hmm?"

Ben thrust his hand into an inside pocket of the jacket and pulled out a toothbrush.

"My luggage," he said, and handed it to her.

January looked at the toothbrush and then back up at him.

"No jammies?" she asked.

"No jammies."

"Hot damn," she said, then grinned. "I'll just get my shoes."

"Are you going to make a speech tonight?" he asked.

She stuck her tongue out at him. "I'm getting my shoes now."

He grinned. "You are. You *are* making a speech."

She rolled her eyes as she stepped into her shoes. The three-inch heels were little more than soles and straps, but they were silver and a perfect complement to the white strapless dress.

Ben steadied her as she put them on, then took her in his arms. His hands slid along her bare shoulders and back as he pulled her close.

"Ah, January . . . you are so very beautiful and I'm so proud of you. Thank you for letting me be a part of this night."

January blinked back quick tears. She'd never let a man get under her skin like this. She should have felt threatened. Instead, she felt treasured.

"No . . . I should be thanking you," she said softly, as he helped her on with her wrap. "So, are we ready?"

"As we'll ever be," he said, and offered her his elbow.

She slipped her hand beneath it, and out the door they went.

Jay came out of the motel room carrying a garbage bag. He tossed it into a trash bin next to the office, then strode back to his car. He looked fifteen years younger and considerably cleaner. It had been disconcerting to look at himself in the mirror without the long hair and beard, but after the old woman had been so disgusted by his appearance, he'd come to believe she'd been sent to remind him that one didn't have to look like Jesus to live as He'd lived.

Maybe his disciples would benefit from similar renovation. Maybe a bath and some fresh clothes would give them a different attitude. Problem was, he didn't know how to make that happen without a full-fledged mutiny. Still, today was the first time he'd been this hopeful since he'd embarked on this quest.

He slid into the cab, started the engine and pulled out of the parking lot. It was time to go feed his flock, then maybe pay a visit to Mother. It had been some time since they'd shared food and conversation.

". . . and so ladies and gentlemen, it gives me great pleasure to give you our Woman of the Year, Ms. January DeLena."

All eyes were on Ben as he stood, then pulled January's chair back and helped her to her feet. He gave her a good luck wink and sat back down as she made her way to the podium.

The whole evening had been something of a shock to him. Not only had January known the names of most of the bigwigs at the ball, but they'd known her. Senators, cabinet members, an ex-vice president and his wife—all calling her by name, reminiscing about

271

their last meetings. Ben was coming to realize that January DeLena was far more than a local television personality.

As she reached the podium and turned to face the audience, her gaze automatically moved down the length of the head table to the man she'd come with. He was smiling at her. It was all she needed to see.

"Ladies and gentlemen, when I received the news that I was going to be named Woman of the Year by your wonderful organization, I have to admit I was more than a little bit shocked. It's more common for people in my profession to receive letters of admonition in their files, not accolades."

There was a light round of laughter. Ben grinned as a proud parent might. She was doing great.

"However," she continued, "it didn't take long for my shock to change to elation. I never . . ."

Ben was still thinking about the big shots she knew and didn't realize that he'd tuned out what she was saying until he became aware of a loud round of applause. She was already through, and he hadn't heard half of what she'd said. His regret turned to pride as everyone stood, applauding her again as she was presented with an elaborately engraved silver plaque.

She smiled throughout the media attention. This part of the evening was a cinch for a woman whose life was lived out on camera.

Finally she was able to step away from the podium and walk back to Ben. It was with surprise—and delight—that she realized he'd come more than halfway to meet her.

"Congratulations, honey," he whispered in her ear, then gave her a brief hug before helping seat her again.

Once there, January set her award on the table, wrapped her arms around his neck and gave him a genuine hug.

"I'm so glad you were here," she said.

Explaining how he really felt was beyond him. All he could do was hold her and agree.

"Me, too, honey. Me, too."

He was still holding her hand as the host ended the ceremonies. People got up from their tables and began moving about the banquet room, some visiting as they headed toward the dance floor, others moving toward the head table, where Ben and January were still seated.

Ben noticed a dark-haired man with olive skin and dark eyes making his way toward them through the crowd. The expression on his face was nothing short of predatory. It set Ben's teeth on edge. When he realized the man was coming to speak to January, his hold unconsciously tightened as he helped her up.

"Hey, January, long time no see," the man said.

Ben felt her flinch. When he saw her jaw set, he realized that she not only knew the owner of the voice, she didn't much like him. That was enough for Ben.

Still standing within the shelter of Ben's arms, January stepped down from the dais and reluctantly shook the man's hand.

"Rodrigo. It's been ages." She raked him up and down with a gaze that was just short of rude. "You've certainly changed. I almost didn't know you."

Before Rodrigo Rivera could speak up again, January put her hand on Ben's arm and gave it a pat.

"Ben, darling, this is Rodrigo Rivera. We started in the business at the same time at a television station in Houston."

Rodrigo didn't even bother to acknowledge Ben's presence. His full attention was on January.

"I go by Rod now. Like you, I decided to shorten the mouthful of name we Latinos are often burdened with."

January's frown deepened. "I never considered my name a burden."

"But you still changed it."

"I didn't change it. One of my bosses shortened it, just as you have yours."

"Of course, of course," Rod said. "However, that's of no matter. I came to congratulate you." Then he turned to Ben. "I'm sure your husband is proud of you."

"Oh, he's not my—"

Ben grinned. "Benjamin Wade North. I shortened my name, too, and for the same obvious reasons. Just call me Ben."

Ben could tell that Rod was taken aback by his friendliness. Good. It would sucker him in for "the kill."

274

"Are you in the media business, as well?" Rod asked.

Ben laughed aloud and then winked at January, who was somewhat surprised by Ben's behavior. She'd never seen him so outgoing.

"In a manner of speaking, I suppose you could say that," he said. "I'm a homicide detective with the D.C. Police Department."

Rod Rivera was startled, and it showed as he looked at January.

"A cop?"

"A detective," she corrected. "And we're late." She turned to Ben. "Darling, I believe we're expected to start the ball. Shall we go? I want to stop by the coat check on the way into the ballroom and leave my award with my wrap."

"Sure thing, honey," Ben said, then picked up the plaque and offered her his arm. "Ron, it was nice meeting you."

Rivera frowned. "Rod. My name is Rod."

"Oh. Yeah. Sorry," Ben said, and led January away.

January smiled and nodded as they made their way through the crowd of people.

"You know something, Detective? You are just full of surprises."

Ben winked at her, then grinned.

"I'm sure I don't know what you're talking about."

" 'Ron,' " she said, and then laughed aloud. "That really fried him."

"Yeah, I figured as much," Ben admitted.

"I appreciate the backup, but it wasn't really necessary," she said. "I can still handle the odd creep now and then."

"Oh, I know, honey, but you don't understand. I had to."

She frowned. "Had to? Why?"

"It's this thing we guys do when we sense a threat to our territory."

She grinned. "Sort of like dogs peeing on fire hydrants?"

He laughed aloud. "Sort of."

"So exactly what territory did poor old Rodrigo walk into without permission?"

"You," Ben said. "He had his chance with you, and, unless I've completely lost my detecting skills, whatever happened between you two is obviously over. I was just showing him where the boundaries are now."

January stifled a smirk as she watched Ben hand her award over to the coat check girl with a strong admonition to guard it with her life, then pocketed the second claim ticket as he led her into the ballroom.

The band was tuning up, the music slightly off-key.

Ben's eyes twinkled. "This dancing bit might not be as bad as I feared."

"Why do you say that?" January asked.

"Because that music fits the way I dance."

She poked his arm in a teasing manner.

"You're so full of yourself, Benjamin Wade North."

He grinned, then paused. "Hey, that reminds me. You know my real name. So what was that Rivera guy talking about? Is your name something other than January?"

"No. That's my real first name. The rest of it is a mouthful, which we'll save for later. Hear the music? That's our cue."

Ben sighed, then took her by the elbow.

"Shall we dance?"

"Yes, please," she said, and let him lead her onto the dance floor.

On Saturday night the Sisters of Mercy always served soup and sandwiches at the shelter. Tonight it was tomato soup and cheese sandwiches. And because a half-dozen bakeries in the D.C. area had donated doughnuts and sweet rolls that hadn't sold that day, the shelter was also serving dessert.

The addition of dessert to the menu had given a festive air to the big dining hall. One man had eaten, then abandoned his seat for the next man to come along, but had stayed on to entertain. He'd taken up temporary residence in the far corner of the room and was playing music on a borrowed guitar. Every now and then he would serenade the diners, if he happened to remember the words to a song.

A young nun who'd only recently said her final vows was moving among the tables, doing a little skip step to the music as she served them extra water and coffee. Her joy spilled over to the diners, who would laugh uproariously each time she did her little skip, dip and turn.

Jay had come in without notice, sat down and eaten his food without looking up. It wasn't until he finished that he allowed himself to survey the room. The singer was off-key but obviously well-intentioned. He saw faces that were familiar and many that were not. It wasn't until he looked toward the front door that he saw her, greeting the latecomers with a smile and a touch. Just watching her dealing out her brand of concern and compassion made him feel warm inside. He hungered for the warmth she exuded. Then, at the thought of hunger, he remembered his flock and knew they were counting on him for their daily ration of food and water.

"Hey, buddy, you gonna eat that?"

Jay glanced at the man to his right, then down at his plate and the bit of crust and cheese he'd left. He pushed it sideways without comment, ignoring the desperation with which the man took the scraps and stuffed them in his mouth. It wasn't good manners to discuss the degree of hunger with which the indigent lived. However, waste was frowned upon, and it was perfectly acceptable for him to ask for what Jay intended to leave.

Jay stood up and moved toward the door, but the closer he got to the elderly nun at the exit, the more his heartbeat accelerated. She was such a huge part of his journey, and she didn't even know it.

"Good evening," Mother Mary Theresa said, as Jay walked past her. "God bless you," she added.

"God bless you, too . . . Mother," Jay said, and kept

moving without looking back.

He got in the cab and drove straight to the warehouse. He did a quick check of the room he'd prepared for Mother, then took the sack of food and headed for the old blast furnace.

Matthew was whispering. It was the first words any of the others had heard him utter other than his name, rank and serial number. They couldn't understand what he was saying, but they could hear the murmurs and see his lips moving.

Thad was the newest, which explained the level of his defiance. He'd been shouting and cursing for so long that what was left of his voice kept breaking, although his spirit had not.

Tom kept quiet, but considered himself the man with the plan. He'd made up his mind last night that he would not let this beat him. His body might be in chains, but his mind was not. He hadn't lived through Vietnam without mental scars and grudges. He'd come home alive only to be cursed and spat at, derided as a baby killer and for his participation in an unpopular war. He'd been a target in 'Nam, and again in the U.S.A., but he would be damned before he was going to stand for being a victim again. After learning of Bartholomew's fate, he had no intention of winding up like him.

Simon Peters had been there the longest. He was past believing he would live through this, and was so sick of the stench of his own body that he'd literally

279

torn off his clothes rather than sleep in them again. He'd tossed them into the middle of the floor, and if wishing could make it happen, they would already have burst into flames.

The other Simon was a tall, bald man with a severe addiction to alcohol. He been suffering withdrawal and dementia for days, and believed at this moment that he was covered in fire ants, which were devouring his body. His intermittent screams were getting on everyone's nerves.

Phillip Benton had curled up into a ball, refusing to accept his reality.

The two Jameses had obviously known and hated each other from the streets. If Jay had known, he might not have shackled them so close together. As it was, the only thing they could do to each other was spit. The fronts of their shirts were spattered with sputum, as were their faces.

John Marino had always considered himself a tough guy. He'd gotten by on his own for years, scavenging for recyclable material for extra money and doing the dishwashing gig in three different restaurants on three different shifts. The fact that his jobs were surely over and his tiny apartment rented to someone else was more frightening to him than being chained to the wall. He needed routine to accept the rest of his existence, and right now he didn't have it. He cried constantly, unashamed of his tears.

Andy was still naked, as he had been for weeks. It allowed him easier access to his penis, which he continued to play with. He was either in a constant state of erection or asleep, physically exhausted or relaxed from the resulting climaxes. What might have first appeared licentious to the other men was now viewed as pitiful. It was obvious that Andy's mental capacity was less than it should have been, but in a way they envied him for the ability to get lost in his mind rather than having to face the reality of this place.

Jay had a large lantern that put out, as the advertisement promised, a million candles of light; a sack full of meat; fruit and bread; bottles of water, his Bible. The pain in his head and neck had been less today than it had been in months, and he wanted to pray, to thank God for the reprieve as he fed his followers.

He was also curious as to how they would receive his new appearance. For that reason, he turned the lantern on just as he entered the old furnace, and set it in the floor.

Tom was the first to notice that the man who came in was not their captor. He began talking and laughing at the same time.

"Thank God!" he cried, and held out his hands. "Help us, man! You've got to get help. Call the cops. Call 911. We need bolt cutters and medics."

The other men added their cries to the chaos until the sound swelled and roared inside the old furnace, ripping through Jay's head and triggering the lurking pain into an explosion. He reeled from the shock, unprepared for a complete mutiny.

He grabbed his head and started to scream.

The momentary elation Tom had felt at being rescued was gone in an instant. The man had been unfamiliar, but this behavior was not. It seemed that their captor had experienced an extreme makeover. It was their loss that it hadn't gone to his head, as well.

"Christ Almighty," Tom said, then sank to the floor and covered his eyes.

The elation the men had experienced was doused between one breath and the next. A mutual groan of disbelief was followed by a few moments of silence, then sobs. It didn't matter who was weeping. Internally, they'd all experienced death—the death of hope.

Jay tried to focus on his Bible. The words would soothe him. They always had before; surely they would do so again. But despite the powerful lantern, it was too dark to read from it, and there was too much pain in his head for him to remember what he'd memorized.

He took the sack of food and water and threw it against the wall as hard as he could. The loaf of bread flattened on impact, while the cans of meat and bottles of water rolled out and got lost in the shadows.

"Suffer and die, all of you!" Jay screamed, and staggered out the door. He made his way into the little room he called home, and fell onto his cot. He could hear the muted shouts from the men, but right now he didn't care. Instead, he rolled up into a ball, covered his head with his hands and fell asleep, praying to die.

Sixteen

It was four in the morning when Ben woke up to find January curled up against him. At first he thought he was dreaming; then she sighed and turned to face him. When he felt the faint stirring of her breath against his arm, he smiled. He wasn't dreaming, he was in heaven.

Even in the dark, he could see that she was as beautiful asleep as she was awake. Her hair looked like spilled ink against the white bedding, and the nightgown hanging on the bedpost only reminded him of the perfection of the body beneath the covers.

Her eyelashes were fluttering. For some reason, the reality of that touched him. She was dreaming. He hoped it was a good one. God knew she'd given him enough pleasure that he should have a lifetime of good dreams.

As he lay watching her sleep, he began to realize how right this felt—waking up with her in his arms. It seemed impossible that he had ever resented her and wanted nothing to do with her. If he had his way now, he would never spend another night without her.

Finally he closed his eyes and tried to go back to sleep, but just as he began to drift, his belly growled. Once more he tried to get easy, but that hollow feeling in the pit of his stomach signaled its need with another growl.

He sighed.

If he were home, he would be up digging through the refrigerator or channel surfing. He knew January wouldn't mind if he raided her fridge, but he didn't want to wake her. Still, he was familiar enough with his own patterns to know that if he didn't eat, this was the end of his sleep.

Carefully, he slid his arm out from under her neck and then waited, making sure he hadn't disturbed her rest. Once he was certain, he blew her a kiss and then quietly got out of bed. Remembering again that he was in someone else's home, he opted not to raid the fridge in the nude, but grabbed an oversize towel from the bathroom and wrapped it around his waist.

The apartment was unfamiliar in the dark, but there was a night-light at the end of the hall and another in the living room. He managed to make it to the kitchen without tripping on any furniture. When he got there, he turned on a small light over the sink.

He tightened the towel around his waist, then opened the refrigerator door and peered in. There was an interesting assortment of foil packs and plastic bowls, but they were too opaque to see what was inside, which left him with no other option but to snoop. As he began opening lids, it occurred to him that he was about to see another facet of January DeLena's life.

The first two bowls he chose had a total of three items in them. A boiled egg in one bowl and two left-over sausages in another.

Hmm. Maybe a little obsessive. Then he amended that by deciding she just wasn't into wasting things, which was good.

He picked up a foil packet. Before it was completely undone, he could tell it was something that should have gone down the disposal. It smelled faintly of fish, but when he looked in, it appeared to be beef. He didn't want to delve any deeper, and tossed it into the garbage. There was a rather odd oblong, foil-wrapped packet that looked promising. When he dug into it, found four leftover barbecued ribs.

He sniffed them.

They weren't rank.

These were a definite possibility.

He set them on the counter.

Within minutes he'd gone through the rest of the bowls and packets. He'd tossed four into the trash, eaten the complete contents of one and was ready to tackle the ribs when he sensed he was no longer alone.

He turned around, an excuse and an apology both at the ready, when, once again, January took him by surprise. Wearing nothing but an oversize T-shirt, she walked over to the counter, opened a drawer and took out a spoon. Then she moved to the refrigerator, took a pint of Ben and Jerry's Chunky Monkey ice cream from the freezer and moved to a barstool. Without looking up, she took the lid off the carton and dug her spoon into it.

"Umm," she said, closing her eyes as the bite of ice cream melted in her mouth.

"You gonna eat all that by yourself?" Ben asked.

January looked up at him, then down at the ice cream, and nodded.

He grinned. So she was also a little bit selfish. It wasn't something he'd expected, but damn, she was fun.

"I ate all that Chinese stuff," he said.

She frowned as another bite began melting in her mouth. "I didn't have any Chinese leftovers."

"Crap," Ben muttered, as he peered at the empty carton he'd set in the sink.

"Don't have any crap, either. It was Indian curried rice with some vegetables."

He laughed. "My mistake, Ms. DeLena. So . . . I ate all of your Indian curried rice and vegetables."

"Okay."

He pointed to the ribs. "Got any immediate intentions toward these?" he asked.

"Nope. Have at 'em," she said.

"Thanks." Ben picked one up and took a bite. The meat was cold but tender, and all but fell off the bone. "Umm, these are good," he said. "Did you make them?"

She arched an eyebrow and looked at him over the rim of the pint of ice cream.

"What do you think?"

He flashed back to their first dinner together and the Mexican food she'd bought, and grinned.

"Barbecue Bob's ribs to go?"

"Now we're talking," she said. "Did you find the

286

potato salad that went with them?"

"Yeah, but it was fuzzy. I tossed it. Is that okay?"

January waved her spoon at him. "Listen, lover boy, any man who has the guts to clean out my refrigerator is okay with me."

Then she got up, yanked a handful of paper towels from the roll and handed them to him in lieu of napkins.

"Thanks," Ben muttered, around a mouthful of meat.

"Welcome," January said, and took another bite of ice cream.

It wasn't until she had eaten her last spoonful and Ben had polished off the last rib that their conversation resumed.

He was cleaning the counter. January had returned what was left of the ice cream to the freezer and put her spoon into the sink. At that point she turned around, leaned against the edge and just watched him for a few moments.

He was so damn gorgeous it made her ache—all lean body and hard muscles. Making love with this man could become addictive. Without thinking, she slid her arms around his waist and then laid her cheek in the middle of his back.

Ben was stunned by the gesture and the tenderness in her touch.

"Hey, honey," he said softly, as he turned and wrapped his arms around her.

"Hey yourself," she said, and hugged him fiercely.

Ben tunneled his fingers through her hair, then lifted her chin for his kiss.

"Umm . . . Chunky Monkey," he said.

"Umm-hmm . . . Barbecue Bob," she echoed.

He kissed her again, then cupped her face.

His hands were sure and strong, and January knew she hadn't felt this safe since she'd left her parents' house years ago.

"Ben?"

"What, honey?"

"I'm thinking real hard about the *L* word."

"The *L* word? What do you—oh. *That L* word." She sighed. "Am I crazy?"

"I don't know about you, but I sure am. Crazy in love."

She nodded. "Yeah . . . me, too."

The muscles in the back of Ben's throat suddenly tightened. He tried to say something, but the words wouldn't come. He touched her face, then her hair, then traced the shape of her mouth with his thumb.

"January."

"What?"

"Nothing, just saying your name." And it was then he remembered Rodrigo Rivera's dig about her name. "Hey, honey, you never did tell me what your real name is. And don't worry. If it's something like Hortense, I can still handle it."

January tried to smile, but Ben saw past it to the nervousness. Now he was frowning.

"What?" he asked. "And don't tell me 'nothing,'

because I can see 'something' in your eyes."

"Let's go to bed," January said. "It's almost five. We still have a couple of hours before we have to get up."

"I don't work tomorrow, and neither do you."

January frowned. "Please. I'm really tired. We can talk in bed, okay?"

Now he knew something was up. He took her by the hand and all but dragged her out of the kitchen, turning off the lights as he went. When they were back in her bedroom, he waited while she went into the bathroom, and was still standing there when she came out.

"Why aren't you in bed?" she asked.

"I'm waiting," Ben said.

January sighed, then sat down on the side of the bed and turned on the lamp.

Ben sat beside her.

She'd made a ball of her fists and pressed them into her lap to keep them from shaking. She'd never given voice to the niggling fear that had been hers alone for so many months. Still, she wanted Ben to know, if only to hear him blow off her worries as no big deal.

"I don't know why this is such an issue. In fact, I like my name. A producer I once worked with in Arizona is the one who shortened it. He said it was just too big a mouthful for the public to remember."

Ben didn't comment.

January took a breath.

"My given name is January Maria Magdalena. The producer dropped my middle name, tweaked the spelling of my last name to conform to Anglo tongues, and here I am."

Ben frowned. "That's a beautiful name. I don't understand the big secret. January is the unusual part of your name and you're using it. Maria Magdalena is—"

His expression froze.

January could see the pupils in his eyes actually dilating as understanding dawned.

"Mary Magdalene . . . God in heaven, January, and you didn't think this was worth telling me? Who else knows this? Is this common knowledge in the business? Can you—"

"Stop!" she cried, and then put her hands over her ears. "Stop, stop, stop! You're not saying anything I haven't already thought about. It's not common knowledge, in the business or otherwise, so I have no reason to assume I'm in any danger from the Sinner because of it."

"Then why has he fixated on you?"

"I'm the one who went after him, remember? I called attention to myself. It's only natural that he'd be curious about me."

Ben thought about it for a bit, then nodded. "Yeah, okay, I see your point. Still, it's one hell of a coincidence, don't you think?"

January wanted to agree, but her conscience wouldn't let her lie. "I don't think any of this is a coincidence in the way that you mean."

"But—"

"Wait. Let me explain." She took a deep breath, then went on. "I think God works in mysterious ways. I think our paths . . . the Sinner's and mine . . . were meant to cross. I don't yet know how this is all going to play out, but I truly believe that."

Ben looked at her. Twice he started to say something, but each time he was defeated by the certainty on her face. Finally he had no choice but to give in.

"Well, hell."

"I know," she said. "I could make myself nuts with this if I wanted to panic."

"But you're not the panicky type, are you?"

"No."

Ben slid his arms around her and pulled her close. "And that's only part of why I love you."

She buried her nose in the curve of his neck. "Do you really . . . love me, I mean?"

Ben nodded. "Yes. Really. And if you want the rest of the truth, you need to know that scares me to death. You're being stalked by a head case who, if your theory is right, thinks that kidnapping and killing is what it's going to take to get him to heaven. Now, after what you just told me, I'm honest to God sick to my stomach."

January felt his body trembling. His truth was hers, as well. She'd been alone with these fears for months. It felt good to have Ben on her side.

"Thank you for believing in me, and for trusting me," she said.

"Come to bed with me now. I need to hold you. At

least for now I'll know where you are."

January curled up in his arms as he scooted them both onto the mattress.

"It's not my whereabouts that are the problem," she said. "It's his. We need to find him, Ben."

Ben held her close.

"We're trying, honey. God knows we're trying."

Jay slept while his disciples wept and begged and cursed him in every way they knew how. Their condition was worsening. Sores that had come from the filth in which they were living were horribly infected. The wounds on Matthew's head where he'd pulled out his hair were crusted, except for one that was crawling with maggots. They'd tried to escape. They'd begged for their freedom. Now they were praying to die.

But there was one yet to gather, Tom knew.

The disciple most crucial to their captor's quest had yet to be found.

Judas.

The betrayer.

Judith Morris was thirty-three, six feet two inches tall, and ten pounds shy of three hundred pounds. Her hair was worn in a buzz cut, and the earring she wore in her left ear was made out of barbed wire. She had a barbed wire tattoo around her neck and matching designs on her forearms. She could bench-press almost four hundred pounds and was missing an upper eyetooth.

Technically, she'd started life on the streets as a runaway, although she'd long since reached the age of consent. Now her residence in the universe was her business. She ran a little numbers game out of an alley between an Italian restaurant and a Greek deli, and once in a while worked as a bouncer at Club Lesbo. In fact, few people even knew Judith had been born a woman, and those that didn't would have been shocked by the news. Her nose had been broken, and there was a scar on her chin.

She looked like anything but a female.

And she went by the name of Jude.

Jay felt like an impersonator. Even though he believed his transformation had been a direct message from God, he didn't feel comfortable. But he'd done what he'd done and now had to live with it. However, living was becoming a moot point. In addition to the pain that had been Jay's constant companion for the past few months, he believed his body was beginning to break down.

Yesterday he'd eaten some breakfast right after letting out a fare, and within minutes of finishing the meal, had to pull into a gas station to throw up. It had been unnerving to know that his body was betraying him. And now that his hair was cut off, he'd found sore and swollen knots on his neck. After a panicked and thorough check of the rest of his body, he'd found one under his arm, as well.

Lymph glands.

Cancer's freeway to the body.

He had even less time than he'd planned for. Finding Judas had become his primary focus, only the phone-book had yielded nothing in the way of a Judas.

Jude came out of her hole-in-the-wall apartment with a hangover and an attitude. Her bitch had taken a hike in the night after complaining of being knocked around. Jude was somewhat pissed off that she hadn't been the one to make the decision, but she was secretly glad the loser was gone.

Her stride was defiant, her hands almost always curled into fists. Today was no different. She headed for the deli on the corner to get some breakfast before making her rounds. It was past time to confront the losers who owed her money, and she wasn't above breaking an arm or two to collect.

She entered the deli with her usual swagger, shoved a Gucci-suited lawyer type out of line and took his place. One old woman muttered something in what sounded like Russian. Jude laughed in her face and answered her in pig latin, a skill left over from her elementary school days, then yelled out her order.

"You! You wait you turn," the clerk shouted, and waved for her to move back.

"Fuck you," Jude said. She snatched two bagels from a basket on top of the meat case, then threw a five dollar bill on the floor. "Keep the change," she said, and took a bottle of orange juice from a cooler on her way out.

"Hey, Jude! Come back here, damn it! You owe me another dollar," the clerk shouted.

"The bagels are cold, the juice isn't, and you aren't getting shit," she yelled back, and kept walking.

Jay had been standing in line for more than fifteen minutes, but the moment he heard the clerk call the man by name, his hunger was forgotten. He stepped out of the queue and followed the big man out the door. He had absolutely no idea how he would ever get this huge man into his cab, but he'd prayed for his Judas, and God had answered.

Jude was halfway down the block, eating as she walked. Her stride was as forceful as the bites she was taking, but her mind was already on the rest of her day.

When Jay realized his man was on the move, he jumped in his cab and began following, staying at least a block behind. Several times he had to pull over to the curb and wait for Jude to exit different stores. He thought it strange that, even though he'd gone into at least five stores in the last hour, he hadn't made a single purchase in any of them.

It was almost noon when he realized Jude was heading for a street corner. When Jude stopped and looked up and down, obviously waiting to hail a cab, it was all he could do not to shout. But when he glanced into his rearview mirror and saw another cab bearing down on the corner, Jay panicked. He set his jaw and peeled out from the curb as skillfully as if he'd come off the starting line at the Indy 500, and beat the driver to the fare.

The other cab driver honked at Jay and then shouted something foul as he drove past.

Jude stepped off the curb, opened the back door of the cab and slid in.

"Where to, mister?" Jay asked.

A frown slid across Jude's face, and then she snorted beneath her breath.

"Do you know where the Little China Tea House is?" she asked.

Jay had never heard of it, but it hardly mattered.

"Sure do," he said.

"Get me there in ten minutes and I'll make it worth your while," Jude growled.

The voice wasn't as deep as Jay had expected, but he shrugged it off. It didn't matter what Jude sounded like. It was the name that counted.

He put the cab in gear and pulled away from the curb. Jude passed out before they'd gone two blocks.

Jay glanced up in the rearview mirror to make sure the big man was unconscious, then headed for the warehouse. There was no more space in the old blast furnace, but it didn't matter. He had a special place for his Judas.

When Jude came to and found a rat running across her belly, she screamed. It was the first female thing she'd done in years, and even to her, it sounded foreign. As it ran off her chest, she shuddered and tried to sit up. When she realized there were chains around her wrists, she couldn't believe it. All she could think was that she was dreaming and at any time would wake up. It wasn't until she gave the chains a yank and the pain raced up her arms that she realized it was no dream.

With a little maneuvering, she finally managed to sit up. Nothing looked familiar, and she had no memory of how she'd gotten here. The last thing she remembered was . . .

Her mind went blank. She had no memory of anything after coming out of Lee's Chinese Laundry.

Think. Think. Out of the laundry. Up the street.

The cab! There'd been a cab at the corner.

"I took a cab," Jude muttered, and was startled that her voice echoed. "Where the hell am I?" Then she started to shout. "Hey! Help! Help! Is anybody there? Help, someone! I need help!"

No one answered.

A second rat stuck its head out of a hole in the corner of a wall.

"Fuck you!" Jude yelled, and kicked out with her foot. It didn't even move. "Damn it," she muttered, and then groaned as she shifted her position, trying to ease the strain.

She needed to pee. It was inevitable. One of the few reminders she still had of being female. Despite her size, her bladder was small, and the flesh pressing in around it was always an urgent signal that waiting would not be wise.

"Hey!" she yelled. "Someone! I gotta go!"

No one came.

No one cared.

She waited until tears pooled in the corners of her eyes and the pain in her side was too sharp to bear any longer.

"God damn you!" she yelled. "God *damn* you!"

The release of urine was at once an immediate relief and an embarrassment. She hadn't pissed her pants since she was a kid. The shame of it, coupled with a rage so strong it made her shake, overwhelmed her. She didn't know whether to curse or cry, sitting in a puddle of her own pee and caught in a web of someone else's making.

Three days later

Rick had been to the dentist and was coming in late. The front desk was a madhouse, and the sergeant on duty had turned red in the face from frustration and was a breath shy of losing his temper. Rick's jaw was hurting, and he felt about the same way. He waved at the sergeant as he went by and was almost to the stairs when someone grabbed him by the arm.

It was a woman. A very small, thin woman.

"Hey, mister, are you a cop?" she asked.

He nodded.

"I can't get anyone to listen to me, but I got a friend who's disappeared."

"You need to report him to missing persons," Rick mumbled, then winced. "Sorry. Been to the dentist."

She made a sympathetic face but stood her ground.

"That cop at the desk told me to go to missing persons, too. But he didn't tell me where to go. Can you help me?"

"Sure, why not?" Rick said. "Come on. I'll walk you up. What's your name?"

"Mitzi Fontaine."

"Nice to meet you, Miss Fontaine. Now let's see if we can get you some help."

"Thank you," Mitzi said. "I really appreciate this."

Rick shrugged. "No problem. So, what's your friend's name . . . the one who's missing?"

"Jude."

Rick stumbled on a step, but caught himself before he could fall.

"Dang painkillers. Always make me woozy," he said, but it wasn't exactly what he was thinking. Last count he and Ben had, that street preacher still needed a Judas. This was a long shot, but the whole case was so far out that ignoring a lead, no matter how far-fetched, wasn't an option.

"So what does this Jude guy do?"

"Oh, Jude isn't a guy. She's a girl. Only you can't really tell it. She's the bouncer at Club Lesbo, where I dance, only she hasn't been around in three days, and that isn't like her. It isn't like her at all."

Rick's hopes fell. A dyke. That didn't fit.

"A woman, huh?" Then he keyed in on what Mitzi had said. "What do you mean, you can't tell she's a woman?"

"I'm serious," Mitzi said. "I like her a lot. She's

always nice to me, but I'd hate to be her enemy. She's big, you know?"

"How big?" Rick asked.

"Like . . . way over six feet tall. And her body . . . well, it's like a man's body. I think she works out or something. She doesn't have any boobs, or if she does, you can't tell it. She looks like this really big weight lifter. Short hair, spooky barbed wire earring and barbed wire tattoos."

"I don't suppose you have a picture," Rick asked.

Mitzi nodded as she dug in her purse.

"Actually, I do. I came prepared. It isn't like Jude to miss work without calling in. That's why I know something's happened to her."

Mitzi paused on the stairs and handed Rick the picture. It was of four people, sitting at a table in a bar.

"Which one is she?" Rick asked.

"There. The one on the far right."

It was the last one Rick would have guessed to be female.

"You're kidding," he mumbled.

"No. I told you she looks like a guy. That's why I'm worried. You know how people hate queers."

"She looks pretty tough to me," Rick said.

"I guess, but we bleed just like everyone else, you know."

"We?" Rick said.

Her chin rose just a fraction. "Yeah. We."

Rick eyed her curiously. She didn't look queer, but what did he know?

"Come on," he said. "I want you to talk to my partner."

"Why?" she said.

"Just because."

She shrugged. It was a better reason than most people gave her.

"Whatever. I just want someone to help me find my friend."

Seventeen

Rick found Ben coming out of Captain Borger's office and waved him over to the desk. As he went, Ben took note of the tiny woman Rick was escorting. Her hair was streaked with pink and purple. Her clothes were brief, tight and revealing. But nothing was more revealing than her eyes. They were large, blue and shimmering with tears. Her chin was trembling, as was her lower lip. Whatever was going on in her life had obviously knocked her for a loop.

Rick had her by the elbow, guiding her to a chair, when Ben got to the desk.

"Mitzi, this is my partner, Ben North."

Ben nodded cordially, then looked at Rick. "What's up?"

"Not sure," Rick said. "But it might be something to do with our preacher."

Ben arched an eyebrow but remained noncommittal

301

as he sat down beside her. Rick took the chair on the opposite side of the desk. As soon as they were settled, Rick pointed to Mitzi.

"This lady has a friend who's gone missing. Three days now, you said. Isn't that right?"

Mitzi nodded.

Ben knew immediately where Rick was going, and cut to the chase. "What's his name?" Ben asked.

"It's not a he, it's a she," Mitzi said.

Ben frowned, then looked at Rick. "Come on, Rick. You know this doesn't—"

"Maybe . . . maybe not. Hear us out."

Ben leaned back, waiting for them to make their case.

"The missing friend goes by the name of Jude, right, Mitzi?"

She nodded.

Ben's interest sharpened. As far as he knew, the preacher hadn't taken a Judas. Maybe Rick was on to something after all.

"Now tell my partner what you told me about Jude's appearance," Rick said.

Mitzi's eyes pooled and overflowed. "We're always being misjudged," she whispered.

"I don't get it," Ben said.

"Mitzi is a dancer at the Club Lesbo. Jude is one of the bouncers," Rick said; then he turned to Mitzi. "Tell Ben what Jude looks like. If you wanted Ben to find her in a crowd, what would he need to look for?"

"Okay." Then she sighed. "She's really big, you

know? Like way over six feet tall, with a body like a guy who's a bodybuilder. You can't see her boobs or anything for the muscles in her chest. And, uh . . . her hair . . . she wears it buzzed, and she has barbed wire tattoos. One around her neck like a necklace, and one on each arm, up here." She grabbed her own arms at the biceps. "Oh, and, uh . . . she wears a piece of barbed wire in her ear for an earring. She's really good to me, but Jude doesn't look like a woman. Doesn't walk like a woman. Doesn't talk like a woman, and she never misses work. Never does the disappearing act with a new lover like some. Something has happened to her. I just know it, but I can't make anybody listen."

Ben eyed Rick with respect.

"Okay, partner, I get where you're going with this, and it's not a bad guess." He looked back at Mitzi. "I don't suppose you'd have a picture of your friend?"

Mitzi nodded.

"I do. I already showed your partner. It was taken just this past year on New Year's Eve. This is Jude at the far right."

Ben's mouth dropped. He knew he was staring, but he couldn't seem to stop.

"That's a woman?"

Mitzi nodded.

"Now do you see what I mean?" Rick asked.

"Take her in to the captain. I'm going to give January a call. She was going to talk to her friend, the nun who helps run the Sisters of Mercy shelter. Maybe she can verify this, or maybe they've heard of another Jude being snatched, in which case we need to get Mitzi here up to missing persons."

Mitzi looked confused.

"But I thought this *was* the place to report missing persons."

"No, ma'am. This is homicide," Ben said.

Mitzi gasped and then started to cry. "Do you already know something about Jude?"

Ben touched her shoulder in a comforting gesture.

"No, we don't, and I'm sorry I led you to believe that. However, there is a possibility that if your friend Jude has truly gone missing, she might be the victim of a serial kidnapper."

"But why would you think that?" Mitzi asked.

Ben hesitated briefly. "Because she fits the profile. We don't know this, and we have nothing to base our suspicions on other than theory, okay?" Then he held up the picture. "Do you mind if we keep this? I'll make sure you get it back."

"No, it's okay. I have others," Mitzi said. "So what do I do?"

"Give Detective Meeks your address and any phone numbers where you can be reached. We'll be in touch."

"Yes, all right," she said.

"I'll take her in to the captain," Rick said.

"And I'm going to call January."

January was on the scene of a house fire, doing an

interview with a mother who'd gotten herself and her baby out of the house by using her husband's mountain climbing equipment. She'd fastened her infant into her baby carrier, then lowered it and the child into the flower garden below. Then she'd used a second set of ropes, with one end fastened to their king-size bed, to lower herself out the window. A ten-year-old neighbor across the street, who had been home with the flu, was the one who'd called 911, then caught the whole thing on tape.

January had already interviewed the boy, who was the hero of the hour, and she was wrapping up an interview with the mother as she and the baby were being examined by the paramedics. With the tape of the rescue in her purse and the footage with the mother just finished, she had another big scoop for the six-o'clock news.

She pointed to her cameraman.

"Okay, Hank, that's a wrap." Then she turned to the mother. "You know something, Jessica? I'm so thankful you and your baby are okay, and I hope if I'm ever faced with danger, that I'm as brave and cool-headed as you were today."

The woman was teary-eyed but remarkably calm as she cradled her infant in her arms.

"I never used to be," she said, then looked down at her daughter, who'd fallen asleep in her arms. "But when you have someone else you love more than your own life, it's amazing what you can do."

January touched the baby's hair, then brushed a fingertip over her tiny hand.

"I completely understand," she said, then added, "This will air on the six-o'clock and eleven-o'clock news."

"Hey, January," Hank said. "I'm ready when you are."

"Okay," she said, and then waved goodbye. "Take care. We'll be in touch."

She started across the street and was dodging fire hoses and water puddles on her way to the news van when her cell phone rang. She jammed her hand into her purse to grab it, and answered on the move.

"Hello?"

"Hey, honey. Can you talk?"

January broke into a smile. "Hey, yourself, and yes, I can. What's up?"

"I was wondering . . . have you and your little nun friend come up with any more missing men?"

January's smile disappeared.

"No. Why?"

"Well, we just had a missing person complaint come into the precinct that might fit, only there's a twist."

"What's the missing person's name, and what's the twist?"

"Jude . . . but it's a woman."

January sighed. "Not possible," she said.

"Wait a minute," Ben said. "Let me explain."

"Honey, there's no way our preacher can make that work for him," she said.

"What if he didn't know Jude was a woman?"

Now he had January's attention.

"How could he not?" she asked.

"We've got a missing person who's well over six feet tall, built like a bodybuilder, no visible signs of femininity, butch haircut, barbed wire tattoos, barbed wire earring, pretty damn scary-looking character. In fact, I'm staring at her picture right now, and I would never have guessed it was a woman."

"Really?"

"Really," Ben said.

"What does this Jude do?"

"She's a bouncer at Club Lesbo."

"Okay. I'm with you," January said. "How long has she been missing?"

"Three days, and according to her friend who made the report, it's one hundred percent not in her behavior to pull a disappearing act. So do you agree it's a possibility?"

"Given all that, then I have to say yes."

"That's what Rick and I think, too."

"You know what this means, then, don't you?"

"What are you getting at?" Ben asked.

"If he has all his disciples, and if he's experiencing some kind of mental or physical breakdown, he may be moving toward some kind of climax."

"Climax? Like what?" Ben asked. "What the hell comes next . . . crucifixion?"

"I don't know. Maybe."

"Well, crap," Ben muttered.

"And if that follows," January said, "you have to

consider what happened to Judas in the Bible. This preacher has beheaded his own John the Baptist, killed his Bartholomew for being the wrong one, and God knows what else that we don't know about. What we do know is that Judas hanged himself. If the preacher feels the need to recreate that, as well, I can guarantee you that your missing Jude is going to get some help in making that happen."

There was a long silence, followed by a muffled curse.

"You're being careful, aren't you, honey?" Ben asked.

"Yes."

"Will you do something for me?"

"Yes," she said.

"Call your Mother Mary Theresa again and talk to her. See if she's heard anything new."

"Okay."

"And let me know what she says."

"Okay."

"I love you, baby," Ben said.

January exhaled softly. "I love you, too."

"See you tonight?"

"Yes," she said. "But it will be late. I don't get off until after the eleven-o'clock news."

"That works for me. I'll bring supper."

She grinned. "Fabulous."

"Anything in particular you want to eat?"

"Surprise me," she said.

"Okay. See you later," Ben said, and hung up.

January disconnected, then dropped her cell phone back in her purse and hurried toward the van. She slid into the passenger seat and grinned at her cameraman.

"Okay, Hank, let's get this show on the road. I'm going to need at least an hour to edit the tape and do any necessary voice-overs."

"So . . . buckle up," Hank said, and put the van into gear.

Jay was on the way to the Lincoln Memorial with a back seat full of blue-haired women, all over the age of seventy. They'd been arguing with each other for the past fifteen minutes over the merits of water soluble fiber as opposed to getting it naturally through food. He now knew more than he'd ever wanted to know about intestinal gas. As a means of changing the subject, when they stopped at a red light, Jay cleared his throat and then raised his voice so as to be heard above their voices.

"Ladies . . . ladies."

The silence that came was so welcome that for a moment he considered saying nothing, but then he figured they would just resume their conversation, and he viewed this as an opportunity to witness for the Lord.

"Ladies," he repeated. "Do you know the Lord?"

One of the four cupped her ear and said, "Eh? What did he say?"

"He asked if we knew Gerald Ford."

Jay frowned. "No, I said—"

The little lady in the middle held up both her hands. "No, he didn't," she said. "He asked if we were getting bored." Then she leaned forward and patted the back of the front seat. "We're just fine, young man," she said. "How long before we get there?"

Jay frowned. He didn't like being thwarted, but they weren't arguing with him. They just couldn't hear.

"About five minutes . . . maybe ten, depending on the traffic."

"What did he say?" the first one asked.

"He said we were too graphic. I told you it was rude to talk about constipation."

"No, he didn't," the one in the middle said. "He said—"

The light turned green. Jay stomped on the accelerator, which ended the conversation. He took every shortcut he knew to get to the memorial and was nothing but relieved when he let them out.

He kept telling himself that the fares he was earning were worth any kind of hassle if the money kept his people fed and helped him finish his quest. To say he was disappointed with what was happening with his followers would be putting it mildly. They'd been apathetic, even refusing to eat.

And then there was Judas. He'd been the biggest disappointment of all. The man was vicious, and if Jay had known a way, he would have taken him back. His threats and curses were actually frightening. As it was, Jay was stuck with having to feed him to keep him quiet.

It was after three o'clock and he had yet to eat lunch himself. He drove away from the three blue-haired ladies, thinking about food with fiber and trying not to think about the confusion he'd somehow created on his way to heaven.

He drove for twenty minutes, passing up several different fares trying to flag him down, just to get to a café he knew that served chicken-fried steaks like he used to get in Dallas. It was strange how nostalgic he had become. Food used to hold no interest for him at all, other than as a means to feed the engine of his body. Now he caught himself remembering cookies his mother used to make, and the smell of turkey roasting on Thanksgiving. To his horror, he had to struggle against the urge to cry.

He was dying. Food had no purpose where he would be going. Maybe that was why he was trying to get as much as he could of his favorite things before it was too late.

That was why he was going to Joe's Diner.

It was an inconspicuous name for an inconspicuous place. But it was the food that drew the customers, who came back time after time for the Southern-fried specialties.

Jay saw the sign from half a block away. His stomach growled in anticipation of the meal he planned to order. The turn signal was on and he was moving into the center lane to turn left when the pain hit. It was like getting struck in the back of the head with a baseball bat, then having the responsibility of holding his skull together with both hands.

He stomped on the brakes and somehow managed to put the cab into Park before his leg went numb. All the feeling had disappeared from his face and right arm, and he wondered if he was having a stroke.

God . . . no . . . please, not like this.

Tires burned rubber. Horns honked. Brakes screeched. There was one fender bender because someone was following the car in front too close, but it was little more than bouncing bumpers. Both drivers leaned out their windows, cursed each other in languages other than English, and then drove away before someone could suggest calling a cop.

A bicycle messenger pedaled up beside Jay's window and stopped.

"Hey, mister, are you all right?" he asked.

The light was so bright in Jay's eyes that he thought for sure he was dying. It wasn't until the pain began to subside that he realized it wasn't the bright light of heaven he'd been seeing. He'd been staring into the sun.

His lips were still numb as he put the cab into gear and eased back into traffic. Food was forgotten in his need to get to the warehouse and lie down. That was all he wanted. Just a place to lie down.

He been driving for at least half an hour when he realized he was half a block away from the Sisters of Mercy shelter, not the warehouse. He pulled into a place reserved for loading and unloading, put the engine in Park, and then dropped his head down on the steering wheel. He didn't think about why he was there. All he knew was that it was a safe place to be.

Mother Mary Theresa didn't feel well. She hadn't felt well all day, but today was a special day for Joseph Callum, one of her most devoted volunteers. Joseph had been thirty-two when he'd come to the shelter with his aging mother. At that time, they'd been homeless for three years. His mother, worn-out from living on the street and her years of tending to a son born with Down syndrome, died at the shelter on their fifth night there. After her burial, Joseph stayed on, partly because Mother Mary T. knew he had nowhere else to go, and partly because Joseph expected his mother to come back and get him.

Eight years later he was still there, and today was his fortieth birthday. She'd promised him a birthday cake, and she wasn't going back on her promise.

The cake had been baked at the convent kitchen. Mother Mary T. had iced it at the shelter. Now all she had left to do was write Happy Birthday Joseph on the icing, stick in a couple of candles for him to blow out, and it would be done.

She was on the last word when Joseph himself came running into the kitchen.

"Mother Mary, Mother Mary, you need to come. Someone is sick."

She dropped the tube of colored icing, wiped her hands on a dish towel and hurried outside.

"Where, Joseph? Show me," she said.

Joseph pointed to the loading zone. At first she only saw the cab; then she realized someone was slumped over the steering wheel.

When she reached the taxi, she opened the door. The man was a stranger to her. She felt for a pulse at the base of his neck and breathed a sigh of relief when she felt a steady thump. She put a hand on his forehead, then gently pushed him back. His head lolled sideways against the headrest.

Then he moaned.

"Sir. Sir. What's your name? Can you tell me your name?"

"Jay Carpenter."

Mother Mary T. grabbed Joseph by the arm.

"Joseph, I need you to go to the shelter and tell Sister Sarah to call 911."

"Is he dead?" Joseph asked.

"No. Now hurry! Go!"

The man was slow, both in body and mind, but he could follow simple instructions. Confident that he could do what she asked, she turned her attention back to the cab driver, who, to her relief, was beginning to come around.

"Mr. Carpenter. Can you hear me?"

Jay nodded, trying to focus on the sound of her voice. He knew it. He'd been hearing it in his dreams for months.

"Mother . . . Mother Mary . . . is it you?"

Mother Mary T. frowned. She'd never seen him, but he seemed to know her.

"Yes, I'm Mother Mary Theresa. Can you tell me what's wrong? Are you ill? Do you hurt?"

Jay shook his head, trying to clear his mind. He needed to do something, but he couldn't remember what.

"Mr. Carpenter, can you hear me?"

Jay nodded.

"Just rest, and don't worry. There's an ambulance on the way."

"No, no ambulance," he mumbled, and turned toward the sound of her voice.

"It's you," he said, as he opened his eyes.

Mother Mary T. frowned. "Do we know each other?"

Jay grabbed her wrist.

"Mother . . . will you pray with me?"

She tried to pull free, but his grip was surprisingly firm.

"Yes, of course I will," she said. "But you need to let me go first."

Jay nodded, but he didn't let her go. Instead, he managed to slide out of the cab, then open the back door.

"You . . . sit there," he said, and shoved her toward the back seat.

"I don't need to sit," she said. "Just let me—"

"You sit!" he said, this time more forcefully.

Mother Mary Theresa stumbled, then fell headfirst into the seat. As she was trying to get up, she was being pushed farther inside.

315

"Stop! Stop! Let me up! Help!"

The door slammed on her cries for help. The driver climbed behind the wheel. Just as she reached for the handle, she heard a distinct click.

The door wouldn't open, and, to her horror, the driver was shutting and locking a glass panel between the front and back seats.

She began to beat on the window, begging to be let out, but no one seemed to notice her predicament.

She turned to the driver, pounding on the safety window. She saw him look up into the rearview mirror.

Their gazes met.

It was then she realized that she knew him, after all.

He'd cut his hair and shaved off his beard, and he'd given up his style of dress for something more contemporary, but it was the preacher. She would know those cold, soulless eyes anywhere. She'd found the man January was looking for, but feared it wasn't going to matter.

He started the motor.

She heard a soft hissing sound and then nothing at all.

January finished the taped piece only minutes before airtime. Her assistant hand-carried it to the producer, who was in the production booth muttering beneath his breath. He glared, took the tape and shut the door in the assistant's face.

January breathed a sigh of relief and then reached

for her coffee cup, intent on a quick pick-me-up, when her cell phone rang.

It was Ben.

"Hey," she said. "Don't tell me you're going to renege on our date. I'm counting on you for my sustenance, among other things."

She expected him to laugh—at the least chuckle. She got neither.

"January . . . honey . . ."

Her stomach knotted.

"What's wrong?"

"Your friend Mother Mary Theresa was kidnapped about two hours ago. She was last seen with a cab driver who appeared to be ill. She sent someone inside to call 911. By the time the message was delivered, she was gone, and so were the cab and driver."

"Oh God, oh God . . . no. Please, not her."

"I'm so sorry, honey. It appears he's begun taking women now. The captain is leaning toward the theory that he knew Jude was a woman after all."

"No. No. It's not that," January said, and then started to cry. "He has all his disciples, now he's moved on to family. It's obvious, Ben. Her name is Mother Mary, therefore she must be Mary, the mother."

"Well, damn," Ben muttered. "We should have seen that."

"You haven't lived with this theory as long as I have."

"Rick and I are going to the shelter."

"I'll meet you there."

"Yeah, okay, but drive safe."

January dropped her cell phone into her pocket, set her coffee cup back on her desk and grabbed her purse.

"Hey! Where are you going?" her assistant asked.

"I just got a tip on a story I've been working on. I'll let you in on it later."

"The boss isn't going to like this."

"Trust me, when I break this story, it will be worth more to him than pure gold."

Eighteen

January didn't remember a moment of the drive through the streets of D.C. She kept going through a thousand scenarios that the little nun might have experienced, and none of them were good.

They still had no idea what was happening to the victims who were being kidnapped, and the very thought of the tiny old woman coming to harm at the hands of the Sinner made her physically sick. By the time she reached the shelter, she was in tears.

She pulled into the parking lot in a skid. Two uniformed patrolmen turned abruptly. One put his hand on his service revolver as they both started toward her.

Ben heard the screech of tires and knew before he

turned around that it was January. He could only imagine how upset she must be, and stopped the patrolmen before they reached her.

"I've got this one," he said quickly, and started toward her at a jog.

January slammed the car into Park and killed the engine. She was already out of the car and running before she saw Ben, and when she did, she ran straight into his arms.

"Oh, Ben, tell me there's been a mistake. Please tell me that she's been found."

"I'm sorry, honey, but it's no mistake."

"Damn it. Damn it to hell," she said, and pulled out of Ben's embrace. With tears still on her face, she curled her fingers into fists. "Tell me," she demanded. "Tell me what you know."

"Come with me," he said. "We're interviewing the only witness right now."

January followed Ben back to where the police had gathered. She recognized Captain Borger, as well as Rick Meeks. A couple of uniformed officers were standing beside a patrol car. She didn't know either of them.

The witness had his back to her, but when she came closer, she quickly realized it was Joseph.

The officers gave her a "What are you doing here?" look, which she ignored. She eyed the captain and decided that practicing a little decorum would be in order.

"Captain Borger."

He nodded, then gave Ben a glance that was less than pleased.

It set her teeth on edge, and decorum went out the window.

"You might as well save that look for someone you can intimidate," she snapped. "I'm not here for the story. I'm here because of Mother Mary Theresa. I think I involved her in this when I began trying to find this man, and I know why he took her."

"Look, Miss DeLena, we appreciate your position," Borger said. "But we have no definite proof that she was a victim of this preacher of yours. Besides that, this is a police matter and—"

"And you wouldn't know shit if it wasn't for me. So do we continue to trade verbal barbs over who's got the biggest balls, or do we act like the grown-ups we are and find Mother Mary T. before she winds up like Scofield?"

Borger wanted to be mad, but he liked her style.

"Okay, Miss DeLena. You win. Your balls are the biggest. Now what can you tell us that we don't already know?"

She fired back with a question of her own. "What have you learned from Joseph?"

Borger's eyes widened.

"You know this man?" he asked, as he pointed to their witness.

"Of course," she said. "I've done volunteer work here for years. I know all the regulars. Besides, Joseph lives here, don't you, Joey?"

Joseph recognized January and clapped his hands. "Jannie . . . it's Jannie. Did you bring me a surprise?"

January moved past the police and gave Joseph a hug.

"Hi, honey. No, I didn't come with a surprise today. I came to help find Mother Mary T."

Joseph's expression crumpled. His small, almond-shaped eyes filled with tears as he covered his face with his hands.

"Can't find my Mother Mary. Mother Mary reads to me. Who's gonna read me stories?"

January's heart went out to him. Truth was, she was about as scared as Joseph. She just couldn't show it.

"Let's go sit down on the bench, okay? You can tell me what happened."

January led him to a bench. They sat down, still holding hands.

"Now, honey, you know how proud I am of you, and how smart Mother Mary T. says you are. So I need you to tell me what happened."

Tears had puddled in the fat wrinkles at the corners of Joseph's eyes, and there was a little stream of snot at the edge of his upper lip.

January looked up at Ben. "May I have your handkerchief?"

He handed it over.

"Thanks," she said, dabbing at Joseph's eyes, then his nose, then handing him the handkerchief. "You may keep this. Ben won't mind."

Joseph smiled at Ben, then folded it in his hands.

"Now, let's talk about the man, okay, honey?" January said.

Joseph smiled again. If January said things were okay, then it was good enough for him.

"Man was sick. Mother Mary say go tell Sister Sarah to call 911. I didn't find Sister Sarah. I look, and I look, and I didn't find her."

January stifled a groan, wondering how much precious time had been lost that might have been spent in hunting Mother Mary Theresa.

"So then what did you do?" January asked.

"I go to office. I can call 911. I will call 911, but Sister Ruth say no. I say Mother Mary tell me to find Sister Sarah. Sister Ruth tell me not to use the phone. I cry."

At that point, he started to cry again.

January put her arms around him and rocked him where they sat.

"It's okay, honey. It's not your fault."

"I cry now," he said.

"And it's still okay," January said.

"Look, we're not going to get anything from him," Borger said.

"For Pete's sake, you can wait a few minutes, okay?" January said. "You don't have anything else. At least give him a chance." Then she took the handkerchief and dabbed at Joseph's tears again.

Finally his sobs subsided. With his head on January's shoulder, she began questioning him again.

"Okay, honey, where was Mother Mary T. when you saw her last?"

Joseph stood up and pointed to the loading zone.

"What was she doing?"

"Talking to the man."

"What did she say to him?" January asked.

"She say, 'What your name? What your name?'"

"Did he tell her?" January asked.

"Yes."

January's hopes rose. "What did he say his name was?"

Joseph frowned. The longer he sat there, the more confused he became. He started rocking back and forth, hitting his knee with his fist and then crying some more.

"It's all right," January said. "Let's think. Jannie will help you think. Is that okay?"

"Yes. Yes. Jannie will help."

January's thoughts were racing. She needed another way to trigger Joseph's memories. Finally she thought of the sketches.

"Ben, do you have those sketches with you?"

"Yes," he said.

"I'll get them," Rick offered, and ran toward the car, returning quickly. "Here they are."

January smoothed out the three pictures, then laid them down on the ground in front of Joseph.

"Now, Joseph, I need you to look at these pictures for me, okay?"

"Okay," he said, and leaned over.

"Do you see the man who took Mother Mary T.?"

"Yes."

"Show me," January said, expecting him to point to one of the pictures in which the preacher had a beard and long hair. To her surprise, he pointed to the clean-shaven one. "Are you sure?" she asked.

Joseph nodded.

"What color were his clothes?" she asked.

"He had a green shirt. I like green."

"I do, too, honey. Now tell me something else. When Mother Mary T. asked this man his name, what did he say?"

"He is the blue bird. He makes houses for the birds."

"Hell on wheels," Borger muttered. "I'm going back to the precinct. Call me if you have any news."

Ben had been silent, allowing January to do the talking because Joseph knew her. But he was beginning to follow January's line of thought. Coming at the same questions from different angles seemed to help her connect with the man's simple thought processes.

"Which blue bird, Joseph?" Ben asked. "Can you show me?"

Joseph nodded, then took Ben by the hand and led him to the back of the shelter to a bench beneath some trees. He pointed up into the branches.

"That bird. See. His name is the bird."

As Joseph pointed, a large blue jay dropped from a branch down to the ground, pecked at a bug, then took off with it in its beak.

"That's a blue jay," Ben said.

"Yes, yes," Joseph said. "Jay. He say Jay. His name makes houses."

"Who makes houses?" Rick muttered.

Ben began running through words, hoping they'd get a hit. "Builders . . . contractors . . ."

Then January offered a name. "How about carpenter? Joseph . . . did he say carpenter?"

"Yes. He say carpenter. That's what he say."

January was elated. She hugged Joseph warmly, then turned to Borger.

"You've got a face, and now, thanks to Joseph, you've got a name. Do something with it and let me know what you find out."

Rick picked up the sketches.

Borger grimaced, but apologized. "Again, it seems we have to thank you."

"I don't need thanks," January said. "I just need you to find my friend."

"We'll run this name and face through the computer and see if we get a hit," Ben said.

"I'm going to take Joseph inside," January said.

Ben hesitated. He wanted to stay, but he needed to get to work on the new information.

"Call me when you get home, okay?" he asked.

"You call me if you get a hit," she countered.

Ben nodded, then followed Rick to the car.

Within a few minutes, the police were gone. January was inside with Joseph, helping him make peace with Sister Sarah and Sister Ruth, while Jay was trying to make peace with his mother.

Mother Mary Theresa awakened to find herself in

what appeared to be a filthy room in some derelict building. The cot she was lying on was dusty but appeared to be new. Not one thing was familiar, except the man who was sitting at the foot of her cot. She recognized the cab driver.

"Mr. Carpenter, isn't it?"

Jay frowned. Her calmness was unnerving, as was the fact that she'd called him by name. He didn't remember that he'd told her, so her knowledge seemed to confirm his belief that she must be divine.

"Mother . . . how do you know the name by which men call your son?"

She didn't get his meaning.

"I have no son," she said.

Jay reeled as if he'd been slapped. This wasn't right. She was supposed to call him son and help him through his last days. Angry and confused, he stood up, then stumbled as he moved to the head of the cot. His ears were ringing, and there was a sick feeling in the pit of his stomach. He put his hands over his ears to shut out the rejection of her words.

Mother Mary T. swung her legs to the edge of the cot and sat up. The room was spinning. She grabbed hold of the bed to steady the world.

"Please, you need to let me go," she said. "I'm not well."

"Shut up," he said. "You don't talk to me now."

Mother Mary Theresa was afraid. She had no inkling of what he wanted with her, or what he might do. She wanted to panic, but then there would be two of them flying out of control, and that wouldn't do.

She closed her eyes, and as she did, she pictured the Virgin Mary at the altar in her room, and the thought gave her peace. This man had told her not to talk, which suited her fine. She didn't have to talk to him, but she could still talk to God.

She bowed her head, clasped her hands together in her lap, then closed her eyes and began to pray quietly.

Jay saw her, and warmth flowed over him. This was what he needed. This was what she was meant to do. She was in prayer for her son, whose last days on earth were swiftly dwindling.

Relieved, he sat down on the side of the cot and closed his own eyes. He wanted the blessing of her prayers, but to his horror, he realized she wasn't praying for him, she was praying for herself—praying to be delivered from this hell.

He jumped up from the cot, then slapped her hard on the face.

She fell backward, knocking her head against the wall. The solid thunk of her skull against the wall should have concerned him, but he was too out of control to think.

"Damn you, woman! This isn't about you. You're not the one who's facing their mortality. You're not the one who survived hell. You're nothing. Nothing!" he screamed. "Why can't anybody understand? Don't they see the danger I'm in? Doesn't anyone care for my immortal soul?"

He grabbed a bottle of water from a nearby crate and

flung it against a wall. It cracked and splattered as he stomped out the door, slamming it fiercely behind him as he went.

The sound echoed inside the old warehouse, sending pigeons flying and rats scurrying. It also set off a series of howls and shouts from the men down the way. The disappointment of this mass mutiny swept over him again, and he started yelling back, telling them all to shut up and pray. But they never heard him above the sounds of their own wails.

Enraged, he started running toward the old blast furnace, screaming as he went. When he got there, he picked up a piece of pipe and began hammering on the outside of the furnace, beating on it like a drum. The sound within was deafening and painful—so much so that all ten of the men went to the floor with their hands on their ears, begging for mercy.

Jay threw the pipe as far as he could throw it, then staggered toward the room where his Judas was waiting. He lifted the bar he'd put on the door, then opened it wide. Judas was sitting on the floor on the far side of the room. When they saw each other, to Jay's dismay, Judas added to the mutiny by cursing him in combinations of words he'd never heard before.

Jay stared. He couldn't help it. The man was huge— his biceps so enormous that the sleeves of his T-shirt had been ripped to accommodate the size—and his thighs were massive, the circumference of small trees. It was daunting to think of being hated by that much humanity. He wanted to cry, but it would have done no good. He didn't understand it. It should have been beautiful—living as Jesus had lived. Instead, it was becoming a nightmare.

"Let me loose, you crazy bastard! You aren't getting anything from me. If you lay a hand on me, I'll kill you!" Jude shouted.

"You don't understand," Jay mumbled. "You're in no danger from me. You are my disciple . . . my Judas."

"I'm not your anything," Jude snapped, then yanked at the chains that bound her.

The rattle of the links echoed from one side of Jay's skull to the other. He shook his head, trying to clear his thoughts, and as he did, his gaze shifted from Judas's thighs to the dark puddle in which he was sitting. At first he thought it was only urine, but it didn't look right. Frowning, he stepped into the room for a closer look, then frowned as he pointed.

"What's wrong with you?"

Jude laughed. It was the ultimate humiliation for someone who'd been born into the wrong body.

"I got my period, that's what, and I hope you're happy. This is damn humiliating. Is that what you wanted? To humiliate me? Well, it worked."

Jay's lips went slack. He was hearing the words, but they didn't make sense.

"Judas . . . please . . . what's wrong? If you've got health issues, we can deal with it."

"Judas? What the hell planet are you from? That's

not my name. My name is Jude, and I told you what's wrong. I deal with this crap every month, whether I like it or not."

Jay pointed to Jude's hair and face . . . the tattoos, the body, they were all blatantly male.

"Stop it!" he demanded. "Men don't have periods."

Jude snorted rudely, then loudly clapped her hands.

"Well, hell, give the stupid bastard a cigar. No one said they did, and I never said I was a man."

Jay gasped. He covered his ears and turned his back on the sight.

"No, no, no," Jay whispered. "That's not possible."

Jude laughed, and the sound raked through Jay's head like fingernails on a chalkboard.

"It's not only possible, it's a damn fact," she said.

Jay's hands dropped to his sides as he turned slowly, staring intently at every feature on Jude's face and body.

"You're not a man?" he finally asked.

"Fucking hell!" Jude screamed. "Let me go, you stupid creep."

"Answer me!" Jay shouted. "Are you a man?"

Jude began laughing and screaming all at the same time as she pulled her shirt up, then pulled her jeans to her knees, revealing the dark thatch of hair between her legs.

"Do you see a dick down there anywhere? I don't. That don't mean I wouldn't give my right arm to have been born with one. Now I don't know what kind of a pervert you are, but you better kill me now, because if

I ever get free, I will rip your fucking head from your body with my bare hands."

Jay staggered backward, tripped on the threshold and fell flat on his backside.

"Oh, Lord . . . Oh, no . . . I didn't mean . . . I didn't know . . . How was I to—"

Jude was screaming again, cursing and pointing and calling Jay names. He scrambled to his feet and slammed the door shut, then dropped the bar, locking her in.

Jude's voice was still evident, but muted. He heard nothing from the blast furnace but the sound of someone puking. Instead of the grand finale he'd planned on, this day had turned into the beginnings of a nightmare.

And he was sick, so sick.

He started the long walk from one end of the warehouse to the other. Although there were several more hours of daylight left, he couldn't bear the truth of his world any longer. He wanted nothing more than to lie down on his bed, close his eyes and never wake up.

But the fear of the hereafter kept him going. He needed God's approval, only it was getting harder and harder to remember how to make that happen.

By the time he got to his room, his clothes were drenched with sweat. He glanced toward the cab, wondered if he'd locked the door to the outside, then decided it didn't matter, staggered into his room and shut the door.

Memories of the clean sheets and comfort of the

motel room swept over him as he dropped down onto his cot and stretched out. The bedding here was filthy, and the floor was covered with rat droppings. Once in his life he'd known a far better way of living, but he'd given that up to prove he was worthy of heaven.

Why hadn't it worked?

Why had everything changed?

He didn't understand.

He didn't understand any of it.

The basis of his plan had been flawless.

When had the devil interfered?

Mother Mary Theresa's prayers had been answered. Her head was throbbing from the blow that she'd suffered, and she was still the pawn of a madman, but she was no longer afraid. Her strength came from her faith.

But before she'd given her life to God, she'd been a girl from the Bronx. And that girl would not have thrown up her hands and quit. Before this, her age had been nothing to her but a number, but now she needed more than strength of mind to get out of this mess.

So she'd walked the room, checking corners, gauging the height of the single window and looking for something to use as a weapon. She knew God had bade His followers to turn the other cheek, but she was certain He hadn't meant for them to give up life without a fight.

As time wore on, she found nothing that would help

her. Even worse, she was getting shaky and weak, and her fever was up.

She'd already found the portable toilet, as well as some bottled water and crackers. She didn't know what this man's intentions were, but it was obvious he'd been planning this for some time. When her foray turned up nothing but useless garbage and dirt, she stumbled back to the cot and then collapsed.

She thought she heard screaming and shouting in the distance but knew that whatever was happening, it was out of her hands. With a muffled groan, she rolled over onto her side and passed out.

Tom Gerlich wasn't a man who panicked easily, but he was getting there. One of the disciples was dead. He knew it for certain. It had happened sometime after sundown, but he'd chosen not to voice his fears to the others. He'd heard more than one death rattle during his years in Vietnam. Death had its own presence. Tom knew it might seem strange to some people, but he always knew when a soul left the body. To him, there was a sense of emptiness that was impossible to explain.

And there were the rats. They were braver now. With no one to chase them back, they were taking advantage of the large smorgasbord of body that had suddenly become available. He thought about waking the others. If they made enough noise and rattled enough chains, it might keep the rats at bay.

But then he reminded himself that it no longer mattered. Whoever was dead was the lucky one. He had escaped.

Nineteen

Captain Borger had been in the hot seat with the mayor ever since the investigation into Bart Scofield's murder had stalled. No one was more excited about learning the identity of the man they suspected of the crime than Borger, but they still had one big problem. They didn't know where to find him.

January hadn't heard a thing from Ben all night. She'd fallen asleep by the phone and was horrified when she woke to find out the entire night had passed in silence. She rolled out of bed and was reaching for the receiver when it finally rang.

"Hello?"

"It's me," Ben said. "Did I wake you?"

"No. I just woke up. Why didn't you call? Have you found out anything about Carpenter?"

"He has a rap sheet."

"For what?"

Ben sighed. He'd been up all night running down leads that had gone nowhere. He was tired and pissed that they still didn't know where to find him.

"He has a sealed juvenile record. Later, a couple of stints in the pen for armed robbery and assault with a deadly weapon. Arrested for running a prostitution ring. Arrested for arson, but no convictions, and the list goes on. Bottom line, he's capable of anything but maintaining a permanent address."

"Dear Lord," January whispered. "Poor little Mother Mary T."

The images that he'd put in her head made her sick. She would like nothing better than to crawl back into bed and hide until all this was over, but that wasn't going to happen. Instead, she made herself focus on the facts.

"So there's no address for him?"

"Rick and I have been following up on last known addresses and acquaintances all night, and the answer is no. His last known residence was over two years ago. No one who knew him before has seen him since he went into the hospital."

"Then he really was hospitalized?" January asked.

"Yes, for almost a month, and then another three weeks in the psych ward."

Psych ward? That didn't sound good. "Did the records confirm his death and resuscitation?" she asked.

"Yes," Ben said.

"I'll be darned," January muttered. "Then it's true about his near-death experience."

"Maybe, maybe not. That's not something we can prove. What the doctors did note was that he had a complete psychological breakdown after he was revived. That's when they put him in the psych ward.

It took three weeks before he calmed down enough to be dismissed."

"What was making him sick?" January asked.

Ben fumbled through some notes.

"Umm, let me see, I've got it down here somewhere . . . oh yeah, here it is. Uh . . . tumor around the pituitary gland. Spread into the brain. Removed most of it. Prognosis was not a cure, just remission."

January frowned. "Pituitary? Isn't it possible for there to be problems with psychosis when the pituitary is involved?"

"Beats me," Ben said.

"I'll have to do some checking, but I think I'm right," she murmured. "And if I am, it would explain his irrational behavior . . . believing he could control his fate by acting as he's been doing."

"It's the most we've known about this whole mess so far, but it's not enough to tell us anything about his whereabouts now. We're still at a loss. D.C. is too damn big to pinpoint one outlaw taxicab, and unfortunately, the homeless population makes it all but impossible to find where one particular lost soul might be hiding."

January stared down at the sunlight shining on her bare feet, absently noting there was a nick in the nail polish on one of her big toes.

She had hoped they would be able to lay their hands on Jay Carpenter as soon as they'd discovered his identity. But given these new facts, she knew that if they had a chance of getting Mother Mary T. back alive, January was going to have to play her trump card.

"I know how to find him," she said softly.

Ben froze, then shifted the receiver to his other ear.

"What did you say?"

"I said . . . I know how to find him."

"How?"

"Are you going in to the office this morning?" she asked.

"Not until after noon," he said. "I haven't slept in more than thirty-six hours."

"That's just as well," January said. "It will give me time to get the rest of the plan in place."

"What plan? What the hell are you talking about?"

"The plan that will bring Jay Carpenter out of hiding."

"And how do you propose to do that?" Ben asked.

"By using me for bait."

Ben felt as if he'd been punched in the gut. It took him a few moments to catch his breath, and when he did, he began to argue.

"Bait? Damn it, January, not only no, but *hell* no."

"We don't have a choice," she said. "Think of all those men who've disappeared. Think of that little nun. You saw her, Ben. You know how fragile she is. She's in her seventies, for God's sake. And remember at the shelter? They said she was ill. What if she's in need of medical attention? What if she dies in some godforsaken place because I was afraid to take a chance? Mother Mary T.'s life may hinge on how quickly we can get to her and you know it."

"I don't want you to do this," he said.

January heard the panic in his voice but would not admit to the same kind of fear.

"I don't really want to do it, either, but I couldn't live with myself if I didn't try."

"God in heaven," Ben muttered. There were a few moments of silence; then he asked, "So how do we make this happen?"

"I just received a big-deal award, remember? So don't you think it would be nice if the television station I work for did a personal piece on the award and on my life? I think the public deserves to know a little bit about my background. To our knowledge, Carpenter has yet to find himself a Mary Magdalene."

"I won't be sleeping now, that's for damn sure," Ben muttered. "Get your pretty ass down to headquarters ASAP. If you're going to do this, I'm by God going to have you so wired that you won't be able to buy a package of gum without setting off sensors at the White House."

"Are we talking tracking devices?" she asked.

"Yes."

"Okay. I can deal with that."

Ben shuddered. He wished he was with her, not talking on a phone. He needed to hold her.

"You're making me crazy," he said.

"Don't fight me on this," January said.

Ben wanted to argue, but if the situation were reversed and it was his friend, he would be just as determined as January was.

"I'm not," he said. "But you've got to understand. I don't like it one damn bit."

"Neither do I," she said, and then glanced at the clock. "I've got to hurry if we want to get this on the noon news as well as in tomorrow's paper. I'll see you at the precinct about twelve. Try to get some sleep."

"Sleep? Sweetheart, I may never sleep again."

January sighed. "I'm sorry."

"Forget it," Ben muttered. "Just keep yourself breathing and in one piece. That's all I ask. I'll see you later."

The line went dead in January's ear before she could say more. She'd wanted to say, "I love you," but that was something she would rather share when they were face-to-face. She hung up the phone long enough to get a clear line, then dialed the station. There was a whole lot that needed to be done before her plan could be set in place, and precious little time to do it. Lives were riding on making this work.

Jay's morning started off bad and got worse. He woke up in enough pain that it made him ill. He emptied what was left of a bottle of painkillers into his hand, then popped them in his mouth and chewed. The dry, acidic chunks turned to a sour-tasting powder on his tongue as he reached for his clothes.

His nose wrinkled as he began to put them on. There was nothing he would have liked better than a hot bath and clean clothes, maybe some eggs and bacon, with biscuits and gravy. As soon as he saw to the others' food and water, he might just head for his favorite diner and treat himself.

He stumbled to the portable toilet outside his room and held his breath as he relieved himself, thankful he would soon have no more need of these earthly props.

As soon as he was finished, he went back into his room, gathered what was left of the groceries into one sack and started toward the other end of the building.

There was a prayer on his lips and a smile on his face as he entered the blast furnace, but his good feelings swiftly changed.

One of the men had hanged himself. He'd taken one of the chains fastened to his wrist and wrapped it around his neck, then sat down, letting his own body weight do the rest. And it appeared that the rats had been at him all night. In places the flesh on his face had been eaten all the way to the bone.

"Dear God! What happened here?" he cried.

Tom Gerlich looked up but didn't bother to move.

"What the fuck do you think, you crazy bastard? He killed himself, and now he's rotting, and the only question that should be in your head is, who's next?"

Jay was horrified by the sight. Thanks to the rats, he had to count off the names in his head to figure out who had died. When he realized it was Matthew, he dropped the sack of groceries and covered his mouth with his hands to stifle a wail. It was an omen. Matthew had been with him almost from the first, and now he was gone. What did this mean?

340

"I don't understand," Jay cried, and lifted his hands toward the sky. "Lord, how could you let this happen?"

Someone laughed. Jay spun toward the sound. It was Simon Peters, and he was pointing at Jay.

"He doesn't understand," Simon said, speaking to the other captives, who were yelling and cursing and begging to be let free.

But Simon wasn't done. "He doesn't understand. Can you believe that? He doesn't understand."

He pointed at Jay again. "You lie, you crazy bastard, and the Lord doesn't have anything to do with it. It happened because you chained him up and starved him, and you know it. Look at his wrists, you son of a bitch. The wounds have turned to gangrene, and there are maggots in the sores on his head. He's been out of his mind for weeks, and you don't understand how this could happen? Damn you! Damn you to hell!"

"Not that!" Jay screamed, and began staggering backward. "Not that! Not that! Never that!"

He stumbled over the threshold, then turned and started to run. He could hear Judas screaming to be let out and thought of the blood between his—no, not his, her—the blood between *her* legs. Nothing was going right. It didn't make sense. The plan had been flawless.

His heart was pounding so hard and so fast that he couldn't hear the sound of his own footsteps. The walls of the warehouse appeared to be moving in and out like bellows. When he looked toward the roof, the pigeons roosting overhead morphed into demons, staring down at him with smiling faces.

He screamed, then put his hands over his eyes. It wasn't real. It couldn't be real.

He sank to his knees with his arms over his head, expecting to be devoured at any moment. But nothing happened. When he looked again and there was nothing there, he wailed. Not even the pigeons he'd imagined before.

His head hurt. It hurt so much these days. Nearly all the time. He needed quiet. He needed to pray. He needed to figure out what he'd done wrong, but the dull pain at the back of his neck was ballooning. By the time he reached his cab, his legs were refusing to work properly and his right arm had gone numb. He managed to get inside before he collapsed. Just as he rolled over onto his back in the front seat, his body began to convulse. The last thing he remembered was seeing a tear in the head liner and smelling feces.

January walked into the precinct wearing a pair of white slacks, a yellow camisole and a yellow-and-white waist-length jacket. Her hair was loose and her heels were high. Her red lipstick said, "Look at me," and at the same time, the jut to her chin was a warning to the faint of heart to stay back.

Ben looked up when he heard a wolf whistle from the other side of the room. Then he saw January coming toward him and understood. However, it didn't stop him from glaring at the file clerk who'd dared to whistle, which earned a grin from the clerk in return. Before Ben could comment, January was at his side.

"I'm here," she said.

He eyed her appreciatively, then frowned.

"You sure are," he said. "I don't know about this outfit, though, honey. It's a little drab. Don't you think you could have dolled up just a little bit more . . . like, uh, oh . . . I don't know . . . maybe stripping butt-naked and doing a Lady Godiva down Pennsylvania Avenue?"

January smiled. "Thank you. I try."

He stifled a curse and took her by the elbow.

"So, let's go into the captain's office. They're waiting for you there."

"Who's waiting for me?" January asked.

"Borger, Rick and two techies from surveillance."

"Okay," she said. "I'm ready."

Ben looked at her, then looked away. "Just so you know, I'm *never* going to be ready for this."

January slipped her hand into his. "I need to tell you something before we get started," she said.

"What?" Ben asked.

"I'm so in love with you. I want to spend the rest of my life with you . . . but, I won't be horrified if you don't feel the same. Still I wanted to say it anyway . . . just in case."

Ben's vision blurred. He'd been waiting a lifetime to hear those words from the right woman, and the moment she'd said them, he knew she was the one.

Even though he'd been feeling some of the same emotions himself, he hadn't let himself put it into words, and now she'd gone and beaten him to it.

"Ah, honey, you humble me. You know that?"

She shook her head, but he could tell she was lying. She knew he was smitten, and suddenly he didn't give a damn who was watching or where they were. He wrapped his arms around her and pulled her close, then laid his cheek against the crown of her head.

"I would love to spend the rest of our lives together," he whispered softly. "More than I can say, and what you're about to do may just cost me my sanity."

January put her arms around his waist, ignoring the whistles and cheers from the onlookers, and planted a long, slow kiss square in the middle of his mouth.

"I'm going to be fine. You're going to see to that," she said. "Now let's get me wired. I have a news conference to do, and a couple of interviews with some reporters."

"Hey, North!"

Ben looked up. Borger was standing in the doorway of his office.

"If you two are finished with the CPR lesson, bring her in here."

"Yes, sir," Ben said, then eyed her closely, admiring her determination. "Just so you know, I'm really proud of you, and I promise I won't let anything happen to you, okay?"

January nodded. "I'm going to hold you to that."

The interview she'd done at the television station had gone out live. Thanks to an understanding producer, as well as the owner of the station, they'd focused the entire feature section of the noon newscast on her. And even better, they'd found a way to work her full given name into the interview five times, as well as use it three times as taglines beneath pictures illustrating different phases of her life.

By now, the entire city of Washington, D.C., knew that their favorite on-the-spot television journalist had been born January Maria Magdalena in a little village outside of Juarez, Mexico, and raised in Houston.

With one newspaper interview finished and one left to go, January felt she'd covered all the bases. Now it was up to Jay Carpenter. If he was on the up and up about trying to relive the life of Jesus Christ, then he was definitely going to need a Mary Magdalene.

And after her trip to the D.C. police department, she wasn't nearly as nervous about setting herself up as bait. The techies from the D.C. surveillance team had used a total of three tracking devices. One had been fastened to the inside of her bra. One was in a tube of lipstick in her purse, and the last one had been fastened to her car. They had also given her a tiny spray can of Mace for her purse.

They talked about her carrying a gun, but January told them that although she already owned one, if she had one in her purse but didn't use it and Jay Car-

345

penter found it later, it might alert him to the fact that he was being set up.

The whole purpose of the plan was to get herself taken to the place where he'd taken the others, and that wouldn't happen if she pulled a gun. It was going to be up to the police to find her and, hopefully, the rest of the missing people, as well. She'd done all she could do. Now it was simply a matter of going through the motions and seeing if the Sinner took the bait.

Jay was wearing his last change of clothes and an attitude that was difficult to discern. Although there was a wild, angry gleam in his eyes, his manner was quiet, almost subservient.

When he'd come to in the cab only to find he'd shit his pants, it had been the last straw. He wanted this over. He needed it to be over before anything else went wrong. He still had hopes that he'd done enough good to outweigh the bad. After all, no one on earth was supposed to be perfect. People with the best intentions still failed from time to time. Some even faltered in their faith. They just needed to keep asking for forgiveness. That was what he kept telling himself. That was what kept him moving from place to place.

There had to be a reason why everything was unraveling. He just couldn't put his finger on what it was. But he would. He hadn't worked this long and hard only to have it all blow up in his face.

So when he dropped off his last fare and realized it was almost noon, he turned on the Off Duty sign and headed for a diner to get some food. He'd missed breakfast. He needed to eat something to be able to finish out the day, and right now, he couldn't bear to think about facing what was waiting for him at the warehouse.

Jay's choice of restaurant was dictated by the availability of a parking space, so he passed a half-dozen places before he saw one with an empty spot out front. That it happened to be a barbecue joint didn't matter. He just needed to eat. He parked quickly and hurried inside. His plan was to grab a bite, then get back to the warehouse. He needed to get Matthew's body and give it a proper burial. He wouldn't let himself think of the pervasive anger within the group. They just didn't understand how vital they were to God's plan.

He slid onto a barstool at the counter and picked up a menu from between a pair of napkin holders.

"Coffee, mister?"

He glanced up. A waitress was standing in front of him with a coffeepot in one hand and a cup in the other.

He nodded.

She poured.

"Know what you wanna eat?" she asked.

"Chopped brisket sandwich with fries."

"Hot or mild sauce?"

"Hot. On the side."

She set a glass of water beside his coffee. "Comin' right up," she said, and hurried away to turn in his order.

Jay lifted the coffee cup to his lips, wincing when the first sip burned his tongue. He spooned a couple of ice cubes from his glass of water into the coffee, then stirred. The temperature was perfect.

Half a cup of coffee later, the caffeine had begun to kick in. Jay took a deep breath and then exhaled slowly. For a few moments he thought about getting back into the cab and driving it off the nearest bridge into the Potomac, then quickly shook off the thought.

Suicide was forbidden.

He couldn't get to heaven that way.

He had to trust the process.

It would work.

It had to.

"Here you go, mister," the waitress said, as she slid a plate in front of him. "Can I get you anything else?"

Jay scanned the plate, then pointed down the counter.

"Ketchup."

She furnished his request and disappeared.

Jay shook the ketchup bottle, then squirted a good dose onto his fries and dug in. Halfway through his meal, someone yelled, "Hey, Trudy, turn up the volume. That's January DeLena on the tube, and she's hot."

The waitress rolled her eyes, but she did as the customer asked.

The customer wasn't the only one curious as to what January was doing on the noon news. Jay paused in the act of taking another bite as the sound came up. He didn't recognize the interviewer talking to January, but he zeroed in on her and began to listen.

". . . in Juarez, Mexico. So when did your family come to the United States?"

"When I was nine," January said. "My maternal grandmother had been a resident of Houston, Texas, all her life, and when she died, Mother, who was a citizen of the U.S., too, inherited the property. We all moved back here, and the rest, as they say, is history."

"Fascinating," the interviewer said. "So what led you to this job?"

January laughed. "If you can believe it . . . a boyfriend."

The interviewer laughed with her. "You're kidding?"

"No. It was in college. He wanted to be in television and was taking classes to follow his passion. I followed him. The classes were great. He quit. I didn't. End of story."

"So that was the beginning for January Maria Magdalena."

"Yes."

"Since I've mentioned your given name, it might be interesting for our viewers to know when and why you shortened your name from January Maria Magdalena to January DeLena."

"Well, it certainly wasn't my idea," January said. "It was at one of my earlier jobs, and the producer said it was too much of a mouthful. He actually changed it without my okay by introducing me on air one night as January DeLena. As furious as I was, he proved himself right. It stuck. However, I am fiercely proud of my Latino heritage."

The interview went on, highlighting her recent award, but Jay didn't hear it. His mind was in rewind. Now he knew why his plans were going awry. Jesus had had a Mary Magdalene. He needed one, too. Even more, she'd been right under his nose all the time. God had been trying to show him time and time again, and even though he knew he'd been drawn to her, he'd been oblivious to the clues.

But no more.

He dug into his pocket, pulled out some cash and tossed it on the counter before hurrying out into the sunlight. He paused on the sidewalk and inhaled deeply. It was going to be all right.

"Praise the Lord," he muttered, then headed for his cab.

Mother Mary Theresa was lying on the cot in nothing but her shift. Her habit was folded on the only chair in the room, and her shoes and stockings were under it. Sweat had beaded on every inch of her skin, and her breathing was shallow. She ached in every muscle and joint, and was only faintly aware that she was not at the Sisters of Mercy.

Every now and then she thought she could hear someone crying. It sounded like Joseph. She needed to get up and see to him, but her legs didn't seem to want to work. She kept telling herself that she would rest just a little bit longer, then get up. But time passed and the sounds dissipated, and still she didn't move.

The small ray of sunlight coming in through the window near the ceiling began to fade. Shadows lengthened. The room darkened and finally night came to Mother Mary T., marking the end of her second day in captivity.

Twenty

Jay didn't make it back to the warehouse until after dark. He thought about removing Matthew's body, then changed his mind. He needed more light than what a lantern would provide. Besides, one more night could hardly hurt. Matthew was already in a better place. All that was left was a shell.

Now that he'd convinced himself of that, all he needed to do was point that out to the others. He wanted to talk to Mother Mary, but there were no sounds coming from inside her room, and he didn't want to wake her, so he bypassed her door.

The others had been without food and water all day. They had to be tended, and he was ready. He couldn't wait to see their faces when they realized what he'd brought them. Chicken dinners with all the fixings, compliments of the supermarket deli where he usually shopped. He wished he'd come earlier so that Mother Mary could enjoy her meal, too, but he would just save it for tomorrow. She could have it for breakfast.

He set one for her in his ice chest, then took the others, picked up a large fluorescent flashlight and started the long walk down.

He paused in front of the barred door and took out one dinner.

Judas.

No. Jude.

God had led him to this woman, so he had to believe it wasn't a mistake. He removed the bar, took the dinner and the lantern, and opened the door, then flashed the light in her face.

Jude was lying on her side. She'd pulled her pants back up to her waist, but they were still undone, revealing a bulge of fat and muscle. The blood from her menstrual cycle had soaked through her jeans and onto the floor.

Jay looked away.

"If you haven't come to let me go, then get the fuck out of my face," Jude said.

Jay could tell she'd been crying. Her eyes were almost swollen shut, and her nose was red. Her condition was at such odds with her appearance that he couldn't quit staring. Then he remembered why he was there.

"You must be hungry. I brought you some food. It's a chicken dinner."

Jude pushed herself up from the floor and then held

up her hands. In the dark, the palms looked black.

"You see this?" she said. "It's blood. You think I'm going to put food in my mouth with hands that look like this? Get out," she said. "Get the fuck out and don't come back."

The absence of emotion in her voice undid him.

"You can wash your hands with some of your water. I'll get you some water."

"All I can smell is my blood. Get that food out of here before I puke. I mean it. Get the fuck out of the room, wacko!"

Even though Jay was supposed to be the one in charge, he felt helpless in the face of her disgust. He backed out of the room, still carrying the chicken dinner, and then, almost as an afterthought, replaced the bar on the door.

"Fine," he muttered, as he turned toward the blast furnace. "At least the others will be appreciative."

He stepped into the opening and was hit with a smell that nearly gagged him. He swept the room with the flashlight and then gritted his teeth.

"Who's sick?" he asked.

"Four of us," someone said. "We've all got the shits, and Matthew is rotting. Go to hell."

Jay's pulse kicked.

"Don't say that," he said. "I told you never to say that."

"So what are you going to do about it?" another asked. "Kill us?"

A titter of laughter filtered through the space,

shocking Jay by the fury it held.

"I brought all of you chicken dinners."

"Shove them up your ass. Or better yet, bend over and let me."

Jay swept the light across the faces staring back at him. Dirt and whiskers marked every one, as well as numerous weeping sores. Rattled, he set the sack of dinners down and then toed it toward the man closest to the opening.

"You pass them around," he said.

"James is unconscious," Tom said. "Has been for hours. Probably be dead by morning, too, so if you want to get rid of your chicken dinners, take off the lids and leave them on the floor. It'll give the damn rats something to eat besides Matthew."

Jay swung the light toward the voice, then flinched.

Tom Gerlich was wearing filth and standing in filth, but he *was* standing, and the fire in his eyes was startling.

Jay shifted the lantern from one hand to the other, and then felt behind him for the opening, in case he needed to run. Before he'd seen the error of his ways, he'd done bad things and never known fear. But that was then, and this was now, and every breath he'd drawn since he'd been brought back to life had been taken in fear.

His Thomas doubted him. It was to be expected. But they would all see. Everything would change when he corrected his mistake.

"I know there have been complications," Jay said.

"This just got out of hand. But I promise you, by tomorrow, all will be rectified. We've been missing an important member of our group. Once she comes, this will all go away. You will be healed and comforted as only God can do. You'll see. You'll all see."

"You're one sick fucker," Tom said.

"Mister . . . mister . . . please let me go. I got a wife and kids back in Kentucky. They're bound to be worried sick 'cause they haven't heard from me. I call them every week. They'll know somethin' is wrong. Please, mister, please. I just want to go home."

Jay swung the light around the room until it landed on Phillip. The man was down on his knees.

"Get up, Phillip. Begging is beneath you."

Phillip dropped his head, his shoulders shaking as he began to cry.

"Stop that!" Jay demanded. "You must believe. You must all understand. I need you to be with me to get to heaven."

Tom laughed again.

"After what you've done to us, you're damn sure not going to heaven. Besides that, the man can't get up. He's the first one who got the shits. He's dehydrated and dying, so you better get ready to lose another disciple, which means you better start worrying, because you damn sure can't get your ride to heaven on a crippled bus."

Jay turned and walked out.

He would show them. All he had to do was get his Mary Magdalene and the circle would be complete.

· · ·

January hadn't talked to Ben since they'd parted at the precinct. They'd made no plans to be together tonight, and yet she knew he would come.

It was fifteen minutes after midnight when she heard the ding of the elevator on her floor. She got up from the sofa where she'd been waiting, and walked into the foyer. Her hand was on the knob when the doorbell rang; then she heard his voice.

"January, it's me."

She opened the door.

"Hello, me. I knew you would come."

His eyes darkened with emotion as he picked her up and kicked the door shut behind him as he entered. It locked automatically.

"I've waited for this all day," he said.

"Then come to bed," January said.

Ben carried her down the hall, then into the bedroom. The bedding was turned back; the lights were down low. He could tell she'd been waiting for him, too.

He set her down long enough to undo her robe and take it off; then he began to undress, as well.

"I should probably shower," he said.

January crawled onto the bed, then patted the mattress beside her.

"Afterward," she said.

He didn't need a second invitation.

Within moments, they were lying face-to-face and looking into each other's eyes.

"Make love to me, Ben."

He rolled her over onto her back and straddled her legs.

"Close your eyes."

January's heart skipped a beat. She started to say something, but when she saw his expression, her breath caught at the back of her throat. Slowly, slowly, she lowered her eyelids. The last thing she saw before they went shut was Ben's face coming toward her.

His mouth was on her lips. His fingers were in her hair, and when she felt his lips move from the hollow at the base of her throat to her breasts, her muscles quivered.

There was a sudden dampness on her nipples, and she could feel his tongue tracing the areola, then moving in a thin line of sensation all the way to her navel.

She grabbed his hair with both hands, afraid to hold on, afraid to let go. He was talking to her now, whispering sweet promises that only the shadows were a witness to, telling her things that made her blush—then made her hot.

She spoke his name aloud—or so she thought—until he spread her legs and she realized she'd been holding her breath. She felt his fingers, then his lips, then went out of her mind.

The climax came suddenly, leaving her breathless and spent, and he still wasn't through. He rose up, put his hands on either side of her shoulders and slid between her legs, then inside her while her muscles were still quaking.

He left her with no doubts as to his intentions, and rode her hard and fast. When she was only a breath away from a second climax, he let himself go.

A grunt, then a guttural groan, came out of Ben's mouth as his seed spilled into January. She bit her lip—a feeble attempt to keep from screaming. Then, overwhelmed with emotion, she started to cry.

They rode the passion of the free fall back down together, then fell asleep in each other's arms.

It was just after 11:00 a.m. the next day when January was ordered out on a breaking news story. Less than an hour earlier, two teenage girls had saved a trucker from his wrecked vehicle just before it burst into flames.

Hank, her favorite cameraman, was already out of the station on a different job and had been called to proceed to the scene of the new story, while January would go on her own and meet up with him there.

As she left the building, she was glad she'd worn slacks to work. It would be far more convenient, should she wind up in the midst of on-the-scene turmoil. She was going over the brief set of notes she'd been given as she hurried across the parking lot to her car.

She tossed her bag and notes in the other seat as she got in, fumbling with her keys before she got the right one in the ignition. Her mind was on everything but car trouble until the car wouldn't start. Not a rumble. Not even a grinding sound. Just a tiny click, click, every time she turned the key.

"Oh, for Pete's sake!" she said, and got out. She was heading back to the station to borrow another vehicle when a cab pulled into the lot.

She was so startled by the sudden arrival that her senses went on alert. Was this it? Had her plan worked this fast? She had to find out and flagged the taxi down, then ran back to her car to gather her things.

By the time the cab pulled up to where she was waiting, she was nervous and shaking and trying to hide her fear. She blurted out an address, then added, "Hurry, please."

When the cab didn't move, she gritted her teeth and looked up. The driver was staring at her from the rearview mirror. She knew those eyes. She'd seen them before, up close and frighteningly personal. Panic hit—hard and fast. It was him!

Oh shit.

"Good morning, Maria Magdalena, I've been waiting for you."

A muscle at her left eye twitched. This was the moment she'd planned for, expected, yet her first instinct was to flee. She reached for the door handle, only to find it wouldn't work.

"Don't bother, dear," Jay said. "You're coming with me."

January had all the tracking devices that the police had put on her, and still she was afraid to trust the process. Her head was spinning. She didn't know what was coming next, but something told her that she wasn't going to have a say in it. Without breaking eye contact with him, she slipped her hand into her purse, feeling for her cell phone.

Well aware that she had to go through the motions to be believable, January began kicking at the back seat and thumping on the door.

"Let me out! Let me out!" she cried, as her fingers curled around the phone. "You must be out of your mind if you think you're going to get away with this."

Still kicking and yelling, she punched in the code for Ben's cell and hoped she'd hit all the right numbers. Any second now it would connect and he would be able to hear their conversation. She pulled it to the top of her purse, then slipped it into an outer pocket so that the sound of their conversation would not be muted.

"Calm down," Jay said. "In a short while we'll all be together again."

Ben had come to work with a smile on his face, and it was still there. Last night had been magic, and the morning even better. They'd shared a shower, made love, then eaten breakfast together. He'd already told her he loved her, but after last night and this morning, he was convinced that spending the rest of their lives together would be his idea of heaven.

His cell phone rang just as he was finishing up a

360

report. He typed in the last two words, then checked the caller ID and started to grin.

"Hello, honey."

". . . we'll all be together again."

Ben's heart stopped. That wasn't January's voice, but the next one was.

"You don't want to do this," January said. "You have to let me go."

"But that's impossible," Jay said. "You have to be with me. It's the only way to heaven."

"You can't get to heaven with blood on your hands," January said.

"Shut up!" Jay shouted, then slammed the window shut between the seats and hit the button to release the sleeping gas.

January heard a soft hissing sound; then everything began to go blank.

"Help me," she mumbled. "Help . . ."

After that, Ben heard nothing more from January, only the faint sounds of traffic.

He flew out of his seat with the phone still in his hand.

"It's going down!" he yelled.

Everyone's function had already been determined, so when Rick heard Ben's panicked call, he reached for the phone. His first job was to contact the surveillance van that was down in the parking lot, while Ben headed for Borger's office.

Ben barged in without knocking.

"Captain, he's got her."

Borger didn't have to be told twice.

"I've got backup on the way," he said. "The surveillance van is outside. Ride with them." Then he pointed to Ben's phone. "Is she still on the line?"

Ben put the phone to his ear. The silence was sickening.

"No."

"Get going," Borger said.

Ben turned and ran.

Someone was carrying her, but January couldn't move or speak. She didn't know what she'd inhaled, but she knew it was going to make her sick.

A moan slid out from between her lips.

"Poor Mary Magdalene. Life was never easy for you, was it?"

January felt breath against her face and wanted to scream. She didn't know what was going to happen to her, but if it happened soon, she was going to be helpless to fight against it.

"Wha . . ."

"Don't talk," Jay said. "Save your strength for later."

Later? Oh, dear God. Was that an ominous promise or a deadly warning?

Metal banged. Dust motes lifted from the surfaces on which they'd been lying, and thickened the air.

"Put . . . down," January mumbled, and tried to push

362

at Jay's hands, but she was too weak to make an impact.

Jay smiled down at her as he carried her into his room, then laid her on the cot. He'd thought about putting her in the room with Mother Mary, but it didn't seem right. Jay's take on Christ's life had always been skewed, but now, with the tumors sucking the life from him, it was off the wall.

Mary Magdalene's purpose in the Bible was vague. Biblical scholars had their own take on her place in Jesus's life. Jay just knew she was supposed to be there.

And she was so beautiful, his Mary Magdalene. The others were going to be so happy to see her. This was going to make all the difference.

But she was coming to now, and he didn't have much time. She would fight him when she could. That was inevitable. But he couldn't let her get hurt. Her presence was too vital to making everything work.

He wasn't sure what he needed to do next, but she was within the fold where she belonged. Everything else would come in its own time.

Her eyes were open now, glaring at him in mute fury. She tried to make her arms and legs work, but mobility took longer to return than consciousness.

He sat down on the side of the cot, then splayed his hand on the middle of her belly. It was, at the same time, both suggestive and threatening.

January's panic rose. She hadn't counted on this, but then she hadn't counted on a whole lot of what had been happening the last few months.

"Don't touch . . . me," she finally managed to say.

Jay purposefully left his hand on her belly just a little bit longer to prove who was in charge. Then he moved it to her face, tracing the curve of her cheek with his thumb.

"Mary Magdalene. Right under my nose all this time." He stood, then moved to the end of the cot. "They had a very special relationship—Jesus and his Mary Magdalene."

January rolled over and tried to sit up, but when she moved, the bed turned into a carnival ride. It was all she could do not to throw up.

"Oh God . . . oh God . . . please help," January whispered.

Jay smiled.

"See, already you intercede for me."

January wanted to scream, but she could barely breathe without gagging.

"I'll be back shortly," he said. "There are some people I want you to meet. In the meantime, drink this. It'll help you wake up."

Seconds later, he was gone.

January's hopes rose. People he wanted her to meet? Maybe it was Mother Mary and the missing men. Was it possible that they were all still alive?

Please, God . . . please let Mother Mary T. be all right.

January felt her bra, taking comfort in the tracking device still safely in place, and pictured the authorities racing to this location. But just in case, she needed to be able to think.

A little leery of Jay Carpenter's motives, she sniffed the cup he'd set on the floor. It smelled like coffee, and the cup appeared to be clean. Retaining her senses was imperative if she was to come out of this in one piece, so she took off the lid and tasted it. It was luke-warm coffee—strong and black. By the time it was gone, she was able to stand.

She stumbled to the door and tried the knob. As she'd expected, it was locked, but she'd had to try. She circled the room, hammering on the walls, calling out to anyone who might hear.

There was an ice chest in one corner, and an empty grocery sack with equally empty tuna and Vienna sausage cans, as well as some cracker wrappers. Three bottles out of a six-pack of water were on the floor near the sack. She opened one and then splashed some on her face before taking a small drink.

She thought of Hank, waiting for her at the scene of the accident, and knew it was only a matter of time before the cops figured it out.

Frustrated, she beat on the door again, shouting to be freed.

Jay heard her and frowned. He wanted the men to see her, but not like this. Then it occurred to him how he could control her rage. Mother Mary would help.

He hurried to Mother's room, expecting to see her sitting on the side of the cot, or at the least in prayer. What he didn't expect was that she was still in the same position she'd been in earlier that morning.

"Mother? Mother Mary?"

She didn't answer, and her skin was hot to the touch. He ran a hand over her forehead, smoothing back the short wisps of hair that had stuck to the skin, and for the first time saw her as more than the habit in which she'd spent the better part of her life.

She was very thin, with tiny bones. And her skin was so fair that he could see the bluish-purple tint of veins just beneath the surface. Her fingernails were clean and clipped. When he put a hand on her back, he realized he could feel every bone beneath his palm.

Nervously, he felt for her pulse. It was erratic and thready, but it was still there.

A sharp pain hit him right behind an eye.

"No," he muttered. "Not now."

He ran to the table, poured some water onto a handful of paper towels, and when they were thoroughly wetted, he folded them up and carried them back to the cot to put on her forehead.

"Mother Mary, can you hear me?" he asked.

She sighed, then groaned.

A second pain skittered up the back of his neck, then settled behind his right ear.

"No, damn it! Not now, I said."

"Help," she mumbled.

"Yes. Yes. I'll get help," he said, and ran out of the room, leaving the door ajar.

When he burst into his own room, January was

taken aback. He was bathed in sweat and breathing rapidly. He grabbed her arm without explanation or ceremony, and held her fiercely.

"Come with me," he said. "You need to pray for the mother."

January's mind went blank. She wouldn't let herself panic until she saw the truth for herself.

Within seconds, they were out of that room and into the next. Even after they were there and January saw the tiny woman in a cotton shift, lying on a cot, she didn't recognize her as the wiry, independent little nun. Then she saw the familiar black-and-white habit folded and lying on a nearby chair, and she gasped. "Oh, no!"

She ran to Mother Mary T., then went down on her knees. Mother Mary Theresa's skin was hot and dry.

January turned to her captor.

"She's burning up with fever. We have to get her to a doctor."

"No. No. We go nowhere," Jay said. "Pray for her. That's all she needs, just prayers."

January jumped to her feet. Waiting on the police suddenly seemed a dangerous thing to do. She came at Jay, delivering two good blows before he put her on the floor with a strike from his fist.

The impact was hard and painful, and she tasted blood as she crawled to her feet.

"Fine," she said, as she doubled up her fists. "You want to play rough. I can play rough."

She came at him again, and again he hit her.

"Know your place, woman!" he shouted, as she fell to the floor.

January rolled over onto her knees and pushed herself up. There was a cut near her left eye that was beginning to bleed, and another cut on her lower lip, which had started to swell. A tiny drop of blood rolled from her nostril down onto her lip, which she wiped on the back of her sleeve.

"You're not going to get away with this," she said.

Jay pointed to the nun. "You come at me again, and she's the one who's going to suffer."

January stopped, then tilted her head slightly, listening for the sounds of approaching sirens, but she heard nothing.

It frightened her. Why weren't they here? How long could it possibly take to track her down? Then a horrible thought invaded. What if the devices weren't working? What if they had no idea where she was?

She glanced down at Mother Mary T. and then back up at Jay. The man was demented. Of that there was no doubt. So how did one deal with a madman?

"What do you want me to do?" she asked.

Jay shook his head, like a dog shedding water, then grabbed her wrist. This time his grasp was not only firm, it was painful, only January didn't let on. She was too afraid of dying.

"Come with me," Jay said. "You must meet my disciples. They will have many questions of you. You will reassure them that all is well."

She made no comment.

Jay yanked at her arm.

"Do you hear me?" he shouted.

January nodded.

"We're going to the end of the building," he said. "And when we get there, I expect you to be smiling. If you run from me, the Mother will suffer."

She nodded, blinking back tears as he dragged her out of the room and started the long walk. As they went, January could see sky through missing pieces of roof, as well as pigeons roosting in the rafters overhead. All along the floor, there were signs of rat infestation and other inhabitants—street people who'd once been inside long enough to make small fires to stay warm.

She wondered how he'd managed to stay undetected, then realized she had no idea where they were. She'd just assumed this place was within the confines of D.C., but for all she knew, they could be miles away from the city.

"We're almost there," he said, and pointed toward what appeared to be an enormous furnace. "Remember what I said . . . no arguing with me, or the Mother will pay."

"Yes, I remember," she answered.

When they were within a few yards from the opening, January stopped.

"Come on," Jay said. "It's just a little bit more."

But January's inner alarms were going off all over the place.

"What's that smell?" she asked, and then realized

she was whispering.

"Nothing that matters," he stated. "Now come on."

Still she stood her ground.

"I think I'm going to be sick," she said.

He squeezed her wrist tighter.

"I think you're not," he warned. "Now move."

January's stomach knotted as she let herself be led. Every inch of skin on the back of her neck felt like it was crawling with ants, and she had an overwhelming urge to pee. When they were only a few feet from the doorway, she started to pray silently, begging for strength.

"We're here," he announced, then stepped inside, pulling her with him. "My dear disciples, look who's come! It's none other than Mary Magdalene. Now you understand why it was so important for you all to be with me. Now you can see why I need all of you, and Mother. I needed you all to be with me when she came."

January entered with a hand over her nose and breathing through her mouth, but she still would have sworn she could taste the scent. At first she could see nothing but Jay's face. It took a few moments for her eyes to adjust to the lack of light, and when she finally saw what was there, she screamed, and then screamed again.

It echoed within the furnace and into the men's heads, setting off a cacophony of cries and wails that, to January, sounded as if they were coming from the pits of hell.

She swung at Jay with every ounce of her being and caught him unexpectedly on the chin. He went down like a felled ox. Her hand was on fire, but she didn't have time to think of herself as she moved from man to man, asking them their names and promising that help was on the way.

"You've got to run, lady," Tom Gerlich said. "You've got to get away from here as fast as you can before he comes to. Get help. Get us all some help."

January grabbed his hand without care for the filth on his skin and clothes, and then held it to her breast as she would have a child.

"It's okay," she said, then choked on a sob. "Help is on the way . . . help is already on the way."

"He's waking up!" another cried. "Run, lady. Run!"

January turned and looked just as Jay lifted a hand to his face and moaned. As she did, her gaze fell on the body that had been a man named Matthew, and rage swelled within her so fast that it took her breath away.

"You devil! You're not going to get away with this," she screamed, and darted past him and out of the furnace.

Her legs felt weak, and she kept swallowing bile as she ran toward the light at the other end of the building. Sirens were screaming all over the place. She started to cry.

Ben. It was Ben.

And then something hit her from behind. With a cry of dismay, she went down.

Twenty-One

Four police cruisers slid to a halt at one end of the warehouse, as a half-dozen more appeared in the doorway at the opposite end. The surveillance van was right behind them and pulled into place only seconds later.

Ben and Rick jumped out of their car before it stopped rolling. They'd seen the blip that was January through twelve-plus miles of D.C. traffic. Ben had cursed and prayed and begged God in every way he knew how that they would get there in time to save her from harm.

Uniformed officers were standing just outside the open doorways, waiting for orders, and on Ben's word, followed him inside, while a second group entered from the other end.

At first all they could see was a derelict building. Holes in the roof. Doors hanging on broken hinges and debris everywhere.

After they moved past a stack of wooden pallets, they saw a yellow cab parked a few yards down, near a group of doors that must once have led to offices. Suddenly they heard a series of three heart-stopping screams.

"Son of a bitch," Ben said, and started to run toward the sound, scattering rats and pigeons in his wake.

Only moments later, a figure appeared out of nowhere, running in the other direction. It was January. He recognized the clothes she was wearing. His joy that she was still alive was short-lived when he saw a man giving chase.

Too far away to get a clean shot, he just kept running, hoping the second wave of cops could get to her before she got hurt.

Jay couldn't believe that she'd struck him again. Not after he'd sworn harm to the Mother if she didn't obey. By the time he came to himself enough to function, she was already out the door. His head was pounding as he scrambled to his feet. The pain added to his fury as he bolted after her.

He caught her in midstride, and they both went down, her body cushioning his fall. Within seconds, he had her on her back and his fingers were around her throat.

"You've ruined it!" he shrieked. "It's all your fault! You've ruined everything for me!"

January couldn't breathe. She was beating at his arms and clawing at his face, but she couldn't reach anything vital. His fingers were pressing harder and harder on her windpipe, until she knew she was done, and then, just when she thought it was over, he bucked, then froze. After that, everything seemed to happen in slow motion.

January was screaming and crying as she crawled out from under him, and he was holding both hands over his heart as blood spilled through his fingers.

"Damn you!" January cried, as she thought of those poor men. "God damn you to hell!"

"No," he begged, as he staggered to his feet, then turned and looked at the man with the gun.

It was Ben.

"What have you done? What have you done?" he whispered. Then, as he began to topple, he cried softly, "God forgive me," and went facedown onto the floor like a felled tree.

January's throat was on fire, and she was gulping in oxygen as fast as she could take it in. Never had air tasted so sweet. Ben hurried past the fallen man and grabbed her, holding her to him in silent desperation.

"I'm all right. I'm all right," she said, as he tried to check her for wounds. "You have to call for ambulances. There are so many, and they're so hurt. So dreadfully hurt." Then she started to cry.

"Who's hurt, honey?"

January pointed toward the other end of the building.

"Mother Mary Theresa is in the first room on the right. She's burning up with a fever. You've got to get her to a hospital."

Ben sent two officers in that direction, as January led him toward the furnace.

"The rest are in there. I don't know what it will take to set them free."

"Who, honey? Who are you talking about?"

"The missing men . . . they're in there. One's dead,

the others aren't far behind, and oh, Ben . . . their bodies . . . their faces."

He ran toward the doorway, then inside. He wasn't in there more than five seconds before he came staggering out.

"Rick! Radio for ambulances. At least a dozen. And get some firemen in here. We need cutting torches and bolt cutters, ASAP."

Rick could tell by the look on his partner's face that now was not the time to ask questions. He began relaying messages, while more uniformed officers moved into the furnace.

One came out and threw up. A couple of others staggered out wiping away tears, only to run back in with first-aid kits and blankets from the trunks of their cars.

As the rescue began, Ben noticed the barred door across the way.

"Have you been in there?" he asked.

January shook her head.

"Wait here," he said.

"No," January argued. "I'm seeing this through to the end."

He lifted the bar on the door, then walked inside. January was right behind him.

"Sweet Jesus," Ben muttered, and then ran out of the room to get some water and blankets.

January moved closer.

Jude was lying with her face to the door and her eyes closed. She'd heard the chaos outside. Even recognized the gunshots, and assumed that this was going to

375

finally be the end. She was ready to welcome death as she had never welcomed a new day, and was waiting for it all to be over. She'd heard the bar come off her door, then the footsteps, and braced herself for the worst.

"Just get it over with," she said, and wished her voice hadn't cracked. She would have liked to be tough all the way to the end.

Instead, there was a gentle hand on her face, and then on her arm.

"Are you Judith?"

Jude's heart stopped, then started again with a chaotic thump. It took a few breaths before she dared open her eyes and look. When she did, she saw a woman bending over her.

"What did you say?" Jude asked.

January touched Jude's face again, wiping the dried blood from a cut on her forehead while skirting the bruises.

"I said . . . are you Judith?"

It was the first time in more than eighteen years that Jude had heard her true name from someone else's lips. She nodded.

"The police are here. You're going to be okay."

Jude took a deep breath, but it turned into a sob. Horrified that she was crying like a baby, she tried to stay tough, but the harder she tried, the harder she cried.

Ben ran back into the room with a blanket and a bottle of water.

"Is she all right?" he asked.

January had already seen the blood on the woman's clothes.

"I don't know," she said, and then covered Jude's body with the blanket.

"I'm all right," Jude blubbered. "All I need is a hot cup of coffee, a three-hour bath and a box of tampons, and I'll be good to go." Then she looked up at Ben. "Are you really a cop?"

"Yes, ma'am."

Jude nodded as the sound of sirens could be heard.

"I need to go," Ben said. "I'll be back."

"We're fine," January said.

When they were alone, Jude looked away, as if ashamed of what she was about to say.

"I thought I was going to die," she stated, and then tears came anew.

January put her arms around Jude's neck and gave her a brief hug.

"I know, I know. So did I."

"How did you know I was here?" Jude asked.

"Your friend Mitzi, from the Club Lesbo, reported you as a missing person."

Jude struggled to maintain her emotions.

"I didn't think I had any friends," she finally said.

"Well, you have one, and a very good one," January said. "She wouldn't quit until someone listened."

Jude looked up then, staring straight into January's face. She saw the cuts, the blood and the fresh bruising.

"He do that to you?" she asked.

"Yes."

"How come?" Jude said.

"I don't know what you did, but I thoroughly pissed him off," January said.

Jude laughed. It wasn't a big sound, and it didn't last long, but that she could still find joy in something surprised them both.

Jude quickly stifled her smile and looked away. It was a brief acknowledgment of a shared fear, although nothing more was said.

January's wounds were fresh. Jude's were not, and yet they'd both suffered in a similar fashion. The bond was not one they would forget.

"You're that television reporter, aren't you?" Jude asked.

"Yes."

"Is he dead?" Jude asked.

"Yes."

Jude shuddered.

"What was wrong with him? What the hell was he trying to prove?" she asked.

January grimaced at Jude's choice of words. "That's just it," she said. "It was hell that started him down this path, and if I had to venture a guess, I'd say it led him straight back there in the end."

Then she heard Ben calling her name.

"I've got to go," she said. "But I won't be far. Just outside the door. Okay?"

Jude pulled the blanket up beneath her chin, then shrugged.

"Just don't let them forget I'm in here."

"Not a chance," January said, and hurried outside.

Ben was standing over Carpenter's body. He'd turned it over and was staring down into the dead man's face.

"What?" January asked.

"What do you make of that?" Ben asked, as he pointed to the expression on the street preacher's face.

January looked, then shivered.

Carpenter's eyes were wide-open, as was his mouth. His face looked as if it had frozen in the middle of a scream. But what was strange was the texture of his skin. It had what she could only describe as a sunburned appearance, which hadn't been there before. When she squatted down for a closer look, she could see what appeared to be tiny blisters beneath the surface.

She gasped, then stood up and stepped backward, putting as much distance between herself and the body as she could.

Ben slid an arm around her shoulder and pulled her close. "Did you see that?" he asked.

She nodded.

"What happened to his face?" Ben asked. "Was he like that before or—"

"No."

"I've never seen lividity appear so quickly, but he went facedown when he died," Ben said, then squinted as he looked up and around. "The light's not so good in here. Maybe you just didn't notice before."

"I was as close to his face as a person could be," she argued. "It didn't look like that earlier."

Ben shook his head. "That doesn't make sense."

"It does to me," January said.

Ben frowned. "I thought you said—"

"I said it didn't look like that earlier. I didn't say I didn't understand."

"Then what?" Ben asked.

"Remember him claiming that he'd already been to hell?"

"Yeah? So?"

"So his face has been burned. It looks to me as if he just made a return trip."

"Christ Almighty," Ben whispered. "Do you know what you're saying?"

"Yes. And you tell me what else besides the fires of hell would have burned and blistered a dead man's skin."

Ben stared down at the man for a few more seconds, then suddenly took January in his arms and pulled her close.

"After what he did to you, and to the rest of these people . . ."

"Let it go," January said. "It's over. Now can we please go to the hospital? I need to make sure that Mother Mary is going to be all right."

By nightfall the story was on every television station in the nation. Psychiatrists and medical doctors debated the whys and wherefores of tumor growth that

380

might have caused a man to enact such a fantasy. Religious scholars, pastors and priests all had an opinion as to why a man might believe it was possible to earn his way into heaven so literally. Psychics were claiming that his name and initials were clues to what had happened. Jay Carpenter. J. C. Jesus Christ. And then the name "Carpenter," the same trade that Jesus had been trained in.

But January knew that trying to figure out why this man had chosen to sacrifice others to reach his own goals was a moot point. No one was ever going to understand why he'd done it. Jay Carpenter had probably never understood it himself, and now it was over. Wherever his immortal soul had landed, it wasn't coming back.

Bart Scofield's murderer had been brought to justice.

The man responsible for the kidnappings was dead.

The focus was, as it should be, on the survivors.

The appearance of the kidnapped men caused a sensation at the hospital. Removing the filth from their bodies was the first step in treating their wounds, and every staffer who could be spared showed up in E.R.

The men were rank and covered with rat bites and sores. When the first gurney was unloaded from an ambulance and wheeled into the hospital, there was a brief moment of stunned silence, then soft cries of disbelief.

Instead of being disgusted by the men's appearances, the doctors and nurses demonstrated an instant empathy. Jobs that ordinarily fell to nurses and orderlies, such as changing bedpans and cleaning up vomit, were attacked with vigor by doctors and nurses alike. Orderlies ran back and forth filling garbage bag after garbage bag with the clothes that had to be cut off the men, then brought basins of warm water and soap to bathe their emaciated and wounded bodies.

Two pink ladies with degrees in cosmetology heard about what was happening down in E.R. and volunteered to shave the men's hair and beards so their bodies could be treated.

Within hours of the rescue, all the victims' names had been released to the public, including the one who had died. The uproar of shock and dismay was citywide. The good citizens of D.C., who on an ordinary day would have complained about the homeless, came forward with every kind of offer imaginable.

Psychiatrists offered their services free. People with rental properties offered housing. Job offers abounded. Monetary donations were being taken at several downtown banks. The city hadn't pulled together in such a fashion since 9-11, and January wondered why it always took a tragedy for people to remember their fellow man.

Ben wouldn't leave her side, not even when she was being examined. The fact that she'd pulled off the rescue made him so proud of her, but he was still struggling with the fact that things had gotten so out of control that she'd almost died. He was the cop. He was the one who'd taken an oath to serve and protect, and he'd let her get in harm's way, and had nearly lost her. He still had nightmares of seeing Carpenter astraddle January, his hands around her throat. If they'd arrived even a single minute later, she would have died.

If January had been aware of Ben's state of mind, she would have told him to get over it. She'd been in charge of her own fate since the day she left home, and no one, even the love of her life, was ever going to tell her what she could and couldn't do. She'd said it at the beginning and still believed it was true. If she hadn't set herself up as bait, she would never have been able to live with herself.

Mother Mary Theresa was on the road to recovery, but another couple of days without a doctor's care and there might have been a different outcome. As for the others, the ones Carpenter called his disciples, January still couldn't think about them without crying. The extent of their suffering had been mind-boggling. That they hadn't given up was a testament to their courage, and she was making sure the world knew it.

For the first time in her life, January was on the other side of the camera, not as an unbiased reporter, but as one of the victims, and it was even harder than she'd expected.

She had announced to her bosses that the macabre film coverage of the men's concentration-camp appearance had been done and overdone. What she wanted the public to know was how special each victim was—how each one's journey through life had provided the strength of mind to survive. And she intended to speak about the wounded spirit of Matthew Farmer, who had succumbed.

Even as the victims were being treated and healed, Jay Carpenter's body was undergoing an autopsy. It surprised no one that he'd died from a single shot to the heart and that the tumor in his brain was no longer in remission. What the coroner couldn't explain were the odd burns and tiny blisters on his face.

Even as suppositions were being tossed around by cops and coroners alike, January knew why. That she chose to keep it to herself was of no consequence. She didn't have to be believed to be satisfied by the outcome.

Not in this case.

The irony was that when he'd been sick before, he'd signed papers indicating a wish to be cremated. That what was left of him was still going to be consumed by fire seemed oddly fitting.

January had been home for a couple of days, on leave from the job and suffering flashbacks from time to time.

Her cuts were healing, her bruises beginning to fade, although her throat was still terribly sore.

She'd made it her business to find out the fates of the others who'd been rescued, and for the most part was quietly pleased with what she had learned.

Thad Ormin had gone to home to Millie, his devoted and loving wife.

Simon Peters had returned to the shelter, along with both Jameses, who'd settled their differences, and the other Simon, who swore his addiction to alcohol had been cured.

An uncle from another city had seen the story on the news, recognized Andrew as his long-lost brother's boy and arrived to claim the big, simple man.

John Marino, who'd made his living digging through other people's trash for items he could recycle, was given a job with the D.C. Department of Sanitation.

Phillip Benton's wife had appeared on the third day after the story broke, with bus tickets to get both of them home to Kentucky.

Jude left D.C. the same day she was released. She packed her belongings, bought herself and Mitzi one-way tickets to Florida, and went home to the Keys. She'd grown up on a fishing boat working alongside her father, and although he was dead now, she still knew how to bait traps with the best of them, and vowed Mitzi had danced her last dance at a club like the Lesbo.

Once Tom Gerlich was healed and released from the hospital, he'd gone back to the streets and intentionally disappeared.

Mother Mary Theresa had given over the running of the shelter to others in the order and now spent her days at the convent, reading and praying.

Life returned to a semblance of normalcy, except for January. She hadn't told anyone, but she had yet to be rid of the man who had tried to be Jesus.

She kept seeing him on the streets, passing by in a yellow cab, turning a corner in the aisle of a super-market as she was shopping, haunting her in her sleep.

She didn't understand it and had yet to tell Ben, although it was only a matter of time. He seemed to know her better than she knew herself. If she didn't tell him soon, he was going to figure out that some-thing was wrong and press her until she told him anyway.

It was Sunday.

January had been up for hours, reading the Sunday paper and enjoying the quiet of the apartment while Ben still slept. He'd moved in with her over a month ago with, as he put it, an option to buy. He'd proposed marriage, and she'd accepted, but when it came to set-ting a date, she'd been the holdup. She didn't want to go into a new life with this man of her heart without getting rid of old ghosts.

Her problem was telling Ben they were there.

Ben woke up suddenly and reached for his gun before he realized where he was. He flopped back down on the pillow and exhaled in disgust. Whatever he'd been dreaming was gone, but the anxiety still remained.

He looked over at January's pillow, then felt the

slight indentation where her head had been. It was cold. He frowned. He didn't know how long she'd been up this time, but he would lay odds it had been hours. There was something wrong with her. He just didn't know what it was, or how to get her to talk about it.

He lay without moving, listening for sounds to indicate what she was doing, and when he finally heard pages rustling, realized she must be reading the Sunday paper.

He rolled out of bed, grabbing a pair of jeans as he went, and headed for the bathroom. Minutes later he was out, freshly showered and shaved, with a hunger for his woman and his coffee.

She was sitting with her back to the hall when he entered the room.

"Hey, you. How long have you been up?" he asked, as he kissed the side of her neck.

January leaned into the kiss and smiled. He looked good on a daily basis, but just out of a shower with his hair still wet and wearing nothing but jeans was his very best look.

"Long enough. Coffee's in the kitchen. Come sit with me and I'll share the paper."

"Sounds good," he said, and went to get a cup. A few moments later he returned.

He sank onto the cushion at the other end of the sofa from where she was sitting, then turned to face her and put his feet in her lap.

She dropped the paper to the floor and, without

thinking, began absently rubbing at his feet.

"Did you sleep well?" she asked.

"Umm," he mumbled, as he swallowed a big sip. "How about you?"

January started to lie. She'd done it a dozen times before, but something inside her just switched.

"No."

"Tell me," Ben said.

For a few moments she sat with her head bowed, still rubbing the arches of his feet. Just when he thought he was going to have to prompt her again, she started to talk.

"Something's wrong with me."

Ben's heart stopped, and when it started again, the beating was physically painful. He set his coffee aside and reached for her, pulling until she was sitting between his legs with her back resting against his chest, and his arms wrapped tightly around her.

"Are you sick, honey? Have you been to the doctor?"

"No. Not wrong like that," she said.

"Then how?"

"It's in my head. I guess I need to see a shrink. Maybe it's just a little case of PTSD."

"That's like being a little bit pregnant," Ben muttered, then looked at her and grinned. "Which, from my standpoint, would be welcome news."

She managed a smile. "Well, it's good to know you would welcome the event, but you can breathe easy. That isn't the issue."

He shrugged. "Just letting you know. Just in case. So what is it, honey?"

January sighed, then relaxed. Everything seemed so much easier to face from the location of Benjamin North's arms.

"I think maybe I'm being haunted."

He flinched. It was the last damn thing he had expected to hear, and, yet in a way, it shouldn't have surprised him.

"Carpenter?"

"Yes."

"Bad dreams?"

"Yes, but that's not all. I think I see him all the time . . . like in the supermarket or driving down the street in a cab. Once I thought I passed him on the sidewalk, but when I turned to look, there was no one there."

Ben frowned and tightened his hold. He couldn't believe she'd been going through this alone.

"You need to see someone," he said. "Talk this all out and understand that what happened was not your fault."

"It's not that," she said. "I don't feel guilt. I don't know how to explain it, but it's almost as if . . . as if . . ." She slapped her leg and then covered her face with her hands. "God . . . this sounds crazy."

"Say it, honey. After the way you cracked that case, I'm completely convinced you're anything but crazy."

"Okay, then. Here goes, but don't say I didn't warn you. I think I keep seeing him because something has been left undone."

"What do you mean?"

"I don't know," she said. "He had such a big master plan. He was going to save himself from the depths of hell, but everything he did seemed to put him closer, not further away. I understand the doctors' explanations about the tumor making it impossible for him to tell reality from fantasy, or understand right from wrong. And I've been told that, in his mind, all the horrible things he did were completely logical."

"Yeah . . . so?"

"So we condemned a sick man, didn't we?"

Ben frowned. "I never really thought of it like that."

"Maybe he wasn't evil. Maybe it was just the symptoms of a horrible illness being manifested in an evil way. And if that's so, then would God blame the person, or forgive him because of the illness?"

"Lord, honey, you're asking the wrong person. I think you need to talk to a priest."

January thought about it for a few minutes, then came to a different conclusion.

"I'll get help," she said. "But I'm not going to talk to a priest. I'm going to talk to Mother Mary Theresa."

"Want me to come with you when you do?"

"Maybe," she said. "But if you do, would you just sit and listen without offering comments? I don't want to hurt your feelings, but this is something I have to work out for myself."

Ben ached for her confusion, and for her fear that she would somehow hurt him in the process.

"Honey, you can't hurt my feelings, and I'll be more

than happy to keep my mouth shut. Besides, religion isn't something I can discuss with any credibility."

"Okay, then," she said. "I'll give her a call."

Mother Mary Theresa was waiting for them in the garden. She had a tray of tea and cookies on a table beside her chair, and her rosary wrapped loosely through her fingers as her hands lay motionless in her lap.

There was a fragility to her that had never been there before, but her mind was still razor sharp. Ever since Ben and January had called to let her know they were coming to visit, she'd been as anxious as a girl on a first date.

When she saw them coming, she waved but didn't get up.

January immediately noticed the difference in her friend's appearance and felt sad that she'd gone downhill so quickly.

"Good afternoon, you two," Mother Mary T. said, then waved them toward the other side of the table. "Sit, sit. We have tea and goodies."

January paused long enough to give the little nun a quick kiss on the cheek, then sat in the nearest chair.

"Me next," Ben said, and kissed Mother Mary T.'s forehead before sitting down beside January.

"We brought you some chocolates," January said, as Ben handed over a gold-foiled box of Godiva chocolates.

"Oooh, my downfall," Mother Mary T. said, and

gleefully accepted the rare treat, then pointed to the tea tray. "January, dear, would you pour?"

January did so, putting two sugars in Ben's, sugar and cream in Mother Mary T.'s, and leaving hers plain.

"The cookies are oatmeal," Mother Mary T. said. "Nutritious, but begging for some raisins or nuts. Unfortunately, Sister Ruth believes in doing without any earthly pleasures, which means I shall not tempt her by offering her any of my chocolates."

January grinned, while Ben laughed out loud.

They shared their tea and cookies, shifting through the pleasantries that having tea demanded. Finally it was Mother Mary T. who cut to the chase.

"Tell me what's wrong."

January blinked. The question had come out of nowhere, and yet she was glad the issue had been raised.

"Why do you think something is wrong?" she asked.

"I know you," the little nun said. "So talk to me."

January bit her lower lip, then leaned forward, resting her elbows on her knees as she moved closer.

"He haunts me."

Mother Mary Theresa flinched. She didn't have to ask who "he" was.

"In your sleep?"

"Everywhere. Awake. Asleep. On the street. In stores. I see him. Why? Why won't he be dead?"

"That's difficult to say."

January shifted to a different line of thought.

"I have a question. It has to do with theology."

"I'll answer if I can," the nun said.

"God says that we only have to ask forgiveness and it is ours, isn't that correct?"

"Yes, if your request is sincere."

"Okay . . . say someone is a terrible sinner. Does terrible things, but if, at the end, this someone then asks the Lord for forgiveness, is it granted?"

Mother Mary Theresa sighed. She knew the confusion. She'd suffered through some of the same in her own lifetime.

"So the Bible says."

"But that doesn't seem fair."

The nun shrugged. "God isn't about fair. God is about love and forgiveness."

There were a few long moments of silence. Mother Mary knew where January was going with this conversation, but waited for the questions just the same.

Finally January asked, "So, if someone does something bad . . . even a lot of bad things . . . but isn't in his right mind, is it his fault? Does God judge him on what he did, or on his true intent?"

"What do you think?" Mother Mary Theresa asked.

January struggled through tears. She hated Jay Carpenter for the horrors he'd done in the name of God and love, but she couldn't find it in her soul to blame him for the illness that had caused the horrors.

"I think . . ." She took a slow breath. "I think that he's forgiven, just like anyone else."

"So you've answered your own question, haven't you?"

"But am I right?"

"You know you are."

"Dear God," January said, and covered her face with her hands. "I wished the man to hell, and he was so afraid of that very thing. Is that a bad sin for me?"

The nun sighed. "Sweetheart, God loves us enough to forgive even the worst. It's only we mortals who struggle with such things as forgiveness."

"Then what is it Carpenter wants from me?" January said. "Why won't he let me be? I didn't do anything to him."

Ben hurt for her, but he'd promised to stay quiet. However, touching did not require speech, so he reached for January's hand and held it.

"If you do, in fact, see this man's spirit, maybe you're reading the wrong thing into that."

"But what else could it be other than that he blames me?"

"Maybe he doesn't need anything from you but for-giveness."

January blinked as if she'd just been slapped. She leaned back abruptly, then stared off into space.

Could the answer be that simple?

She wasn't sure, but she was willing to give it a try.

Twenty-Two

Just as they were sitting down to dinner that same night, Ben was called out to a homicide, leaving January home alone. Her hunger had gone out the door with Ben, so she got up from the table and began putting away the food.

When she was done, the silence in the apartment was uncomfortable. She heard an approaching siren and, out of habit, looked out the window. The cop car came and went, but she never saw it. What she did see, however, was the man beneath the streetlight.

Her heart sank, then began beating so rapidly that she broke out in a sweat.

It was him.

"Stop this!" she cried out. "Please leave me alone!"

She blinked, and he was gone.

It was, for her, the final straw. She didn't know whether Mother Mary Theresa was right or not, but she was tired of living in a constant state of anxiety.

She grabbed her car keys and purse, and ran for the door. Minutes later, she was on her way to an all-night chapel that she'd visited many times before.

When she pulled into the church parking lot a short while later, her hands were shaking and she wanted to throw up, but this had to be done. The parking lot was well-lit, and to her relief, she saw other cars parked there, as well.

She grabbed her purse and got out, then made a run for the door. Inside, soft candlelight bathed the old Gothic edifice in a welcoming glow. She dipped her fingers in the holy water just inside the doorway, then genuflected as she made the sign of the cross.

So far, so good.

She was in God's house.

Nothing bad could happen to her here.

She moved past a half-dozen other worshipers scattered throughout the pews to the altar at the front of the church. A statue of Christ crucified hung high upon the wall, his features contorted in eternal suffering.

She took a taper, then lit a candle before kneeling before the altar. As soon as her knees touched the floor, she closed her eyes and inhaled, and as she did, she knew she was not alone.

It wasn't a presence she could pinpoint, but she felt no threat, so she didn't try to look. It was enough that it was there.

She prayed, and then she listened, and then she prayed some more. And when there was nothing else to say and no other way to say it, she found herself speaking the words the old nun had left in her heart.

"Lord . . . I know you've already forgiven him. I can do no less. Forgive me for my weakness in harboring hate. Forgive me for wanting Jay Carpenter's soul in hell. I pray that he's found his peace."

She felt what could only be described as a breath

against her cheek, but when she opened her eyes, there was no one there.

She stood up, and as she turned around, she thought she saw a man standing in the shadows near the door at the end of the aisle.

She started toward him, needing to know that she'd done the right thing, praying that if it was indeed Jay Carpenter's ghost, that it had been put to rest.

But when she got there, the vestibule was empty. Shrugging off the vision as the result of nothing more than a guilty conscience and an overactive imagination, she stepped out of the church, then paused at the top of the steps.

The sky was clear and full of stars, deceptive beauty in a world that was no longer safe. She scanned the parking lot for lurkers before quickly moving toward her car.

As she started down the steps, something blew across her line of vision.

A bit of paper on the ground.

Probably nothing but trash.

Still, she paused, watching until it caught in some shrubs. Curious, she ran down and picked it up before it could blow away, then stuck it in her pocket as she dashed to her car.

By the time she drove home, she felt as if a weight had been lifted from her heart. It didn't matter now if she saw Jay Carpenter's ghost around every corner. She'd released her hold on the hatred she'd felt.

When she got inside, she realized she was hungry.

She made herself a sandwich, poured a glass of soda and then settled down to eat at the bar in the kitchen. She was almost finished before she remembered the piece of paper.

She felt silly as she went to get it, telling herself it was probably part of a candy wrapper, and that the inside of her pocket would most likely be sticky, which she deserved for being so melodramatic.

She got her jacket and took out the paper, then carried it back to the kitchen, to the light. As she laid it down on the counter, she could tell there was writing on the other side. Definitely no candy wrapper.

Then she turned it over.

Part of the paper had been torn away, but she read what was there and began to cry.

Through whatever power that had been with her, her prayer had been answered.

Awed by the power of God, she stared down at the words, written in a faint, shaky script: *". . . as we forgive those who trespass against us."*

Her heart was pounding, her hands trembling, as she heard the front door open.

It was Ben.

She heard him calling her name, and tried to find the breath to answer.

"Honey . . . it's me! Did you save me some dinner?" he yelled.

January's fingers curled around the paper.

Then she wadded it up and stuffed it into her pocket as she turned toward the sound of his voice.

Center Point Publishing

600 Brooks Road ● PO Box 1
Thorndike ME 04986-0001 USA

(207) 568-3717

US & Canada:
1 800 929-9108